BOOK 1 IN THE SC

THE THING THAT HAPPENED WHEN WE WERE LITTLE

CAROLINE KELLY FRANKLIN

CASTLE BRIDGE MEDIA
DENVER, COLORADO, USA

CASTLE BRIDGE MEDIA
Denver, Colorado

Cover photo by Yohan Marion/Unsplash.
This image has been modified.

This book is a work of fiction. Names, characters, business, events, and incidents are the products of the author's imaginations. Any resemblance to actual persons, living or dead or actual events is purely coincidental.

THE THING THAT HAPPENED WHEN WE WERE LITTLE
©2024 Caroline Kelly Franklin
All rights reserved.

ISBN: 979-8-9917855-1-8

TK

A THING THAT HASN'T HAPPENED YET

Taste is so emotional. The nose remembers.
But the tongue, the tongue feels.

October 30, 2022, 2:00 AM

The Guy in the Chair

THE GUY IN THE CHAIR just couldn't make sense of what he was feeling. Sure, the sticky side of masking tape wasn't his favorite flavor, and waking up blindfolded and tied to a chair was always jarring but not unfamiliar. He was forced into similar predicaments plenty of times when pledging his frat. Now that he was a junior, he was usually the one doing the tying.

But guys from rival houses still pranked upperclassmen. It had to be one of them. There was no stench of piss or beer. They definitely hadn't taken him to one of the frat houses. Yet there was something in the air he recognized.

Fresh linens, the lingering notes of scented candles, this was a girl's room. He had been here before. Probably not for sex. Maybe a day event. There was a faint hint of chlorine. A pool party? He must have wandered into this room to use the bathroom before heading to a rowdier after-party. Whenever it was, it was insignificant but not *bad*. Nothing that *bad* ever really happens in Moss Groves. So no, what he was feeling wasn't right. The guy tied to the chair had no reason to be scared.

5

He could hear someone coming. His mouth went dry, the way it used to when he was eight and the babysitter let him watch *Nightmare on Elm Street*. The footsteps were quick and light. Definitely girls. It was a prank. It had to be a prank. Yeah, okay, it was an aggressive prank for girls. Ashley was pissed at him, but she was a shit-talker, not a kidnapper. Thalia had kind of a wild streak. Maybe it was her. Blood rushed to his cock at the thought.

"Jesus Christ." The voice came through a modulator, deep and drone, but even so, he could hear the annoyance. He felt disappointed eyes on his crotch and all hope this was a sexy surprise left. The erection stayed.

Soft fingers ripped the tape from his mouth. The guy in the chair meant to say something like *Ha-ha, very cute ladies. If you wanted to get me alone, all you had to do was ask.* But despite the dozens of relatively harmless scenarios he'd imagined, his voice went high the instant his lips could move, and he yelled, "Okay! Okay! Look, I don't know who you are but—"

"We are vengeance. We are the night," said the modulated voice.

A second voice also modulated but more annoyed, said, "Wait, is that... it is. That's *Batman*. Don't do *Batman* for this. It's anti-feminist."

"I'm a feminist!" the feminist guy in the chair yelled.

"Oh, *good*. Then you can tell us. Is Batman anti-feminist? Answer right, and we'll let you go," said one voice.

He went silent for a half second before screaming, "HELP! HELP! HELP!" Rapid thumping erupted outside the door. The pounds were so frantic and heavy it sounded more like tennis shoes in the washing machine than knocking. Sudden dampness spread down his inner thigh, filling the room with the first unpretty smell. He had never wet himself in fear before. "Please, I haven't seen your faces. I don't know who you are!"

"Then we'll tell you." The voice was slow and calm. They leaned close enough so he could feel the heat of their skin.

"No, please don't," The urine-soaked guy in the chair begged.

"We were the voice in its head," said one modulated voice.

"We were the voice that said stop," said the other.

"But you made us quiet," said one.

"Please. You don't have to do this." The terrified guy begged.

He felt the heat of their bodies leave him as they stepped back. One said, "That's just it. We're not going to do anything. *At all.*"

In quick succession, a bolt turned, metal scrapped metal releasing a latch, and a knob lock clicked free. The pounding stopped. They walked away as quickly as they'd entered. One door shut, and one slowly opened. He had no certainty about what made the next sounds. Not even the ones coming from him. He'd never made sounds like that before. He didn't have to wonder long, pain like that doesn't allow for much thought.

Through the first few punctures, he still managed some begging. He had a sudden yearning to cry out his own name. As though whatever was happening to him wasn't the sort of thing that would happen to a guy with a name like—

But when his skin started to rip, all words pretty much left him. Only images after that. His mom, his bed, and for a second, Lucy's eyes. Even through the blood loss, he clocked how strange that was. Why her? She was one night. Insignificant but not bad. He didn't recognize the thing in her eyes then. So, he ignored it and kept going. He had this feeling that if he could see himself in a mirror, he had that same look in his eyes now.

Outside the door, the two pulled off their voice modulators. They knew something had gone wrong as panicked screams transitioned to sharp screeches. It wasn't supposed to go this far. The voices in their heads chanted, "Get up. Stop it. Get up. Stop it." But they ignored them and let it keep going.

PART ONE

The Thing That Happened to Susan-Eva

ONE

Two and a half months earlier - August 18, 2022, 6:45 AM

Ella

THERE'S THIS WAY THAT SOMEONE touches you when they know whatever they're about to do will change who you are to each other. It starts as a warning that turns into a dare. A brush of bare skin followed by eye contact that lasts longer than any casual connection allows. A hand venturing into uncharted territory, just above the knee or the pulse point on either side of the neck. Even the inside of the wrist can be a game changer if it's a person who's never touched you there before. After three years on and off again, Ella and Malcolm didn't have uncharted territory in the form of body parts. His firm grip holding her wrists above her head felt as familiar as it did erotic. But something was different that morning.

What was different or how it would change them, Ella didn't know. Maybe it would be fun. Maybe he'd give her new information. Maybe they were about to have another fight. Whatever it was, she knew one thing for certain: it would distract her for the rest of the day if she let it. So she was *not* going to let it. Because Ella had things to do.

She needed to check on her best friend Susan-Eva and make sure the one-night stand she had upstairs wasn't a creep. She had a promotion she

10

was after. She had curls to condition. She had a smudge on her off-white wall that needed removing. She had a crooked painting that needed straightening. She had to not think about her mom. She had bad breath. She had to stop cursing. She had chipped nails. She had Ida.

Most of all, she had Ida. She could not let anything cloud her head for whatever Ida might do today. For whatever Ida might do on any day.

So Ella was not going to let the thing happening with Malcom get to her. Good or bad, whatever happened for the next forty-five minutes, Ella wasn't going to focus on it. The visceral details wouldn't seep in and form a vivid memory as long as she thought about something else. Something annoying. Instead of thinking about *what* was happening, Ella would think about *why* it was happening. She would think about the flag thing.

On the first day of the fall semester, every home in the Moss Groves city limits flew the same purple Florence University flag. It didn't matter if no one in the home attended Florence. It didn't matter if the front porch was hidden from public view. It didn't matter if you forgot to purchase that year's flag. At 6:30 AM on the third Thursday in August, low-level beautification committee members drove to every residence. They generously hung a flag for any home that forgot— and for the founding families. The founders were never to buy their own flags.

Ida was a member of the most prominent of the founding families, the Montgomerys. All the founders were considered local royalty, but for reasons no one could quite explain, the Montgomerys were its longest-reigning monarchs.

Ella and Susan-Eva were not royalty. Outsiders saw them more like ladies in waiting, but they lived with Ida in Parlay House. Parlay House was a Moss Groves historic landmark, and it received the first flag that morning. No surprise there. Parlay House had always received the first flag. It had always received the first everything when it came to signifiers of distinction. Pecking order aside, though, there was already a notable change in the way the flag thing was going this year. They were louder than usual.

That had to be what did it, Ella thought. That must have been what woke Malcolm up, he never woke up before Ella. Usually, flag week was the sort of thing Ella didn't realize had happened until she opened the door and saw it hanging there, but this year was different.

The tradition was always a superstitious one. Not flying the flag the first week of classes was said to be bad luck. Bad luck for what, exactly, was unclear. Florence didn't even have a Division One football team. A very old magnolia tree on campus did die one year after Mrs. Krasinski went to Hawaii and wasn't there to hang hers. Moss Groves had a real thing for trees, so that was the year the committee started driving around checking.

It was the sort of anecdote that should've been embarrassing, but they printed it in brochures. The university publicist found it charming that a dead tree would be taken so seriously. They felt it would serve as further evidence Moss Groves was a safe place to go to school no matter what any Google searches or true crime documentaries might say about Ed Bins and that unfortunate event sixteen years ago. The problem this semester was you didn't need to look back sixteen years to find an alarming story.

For the first time *since that unfortunate event*, Moss Groves made national headlines for something that meant they needed luck for more than the trees. In May, a would-be Florence sophomore went missing and not just any sophomore but Scott Ryan, the son of Florence University's president.

Florence U loved taking their traditions to a ten for anything tragedy-adjacent. So, they decided to make the flag bigger, with heavier material, this year. A bigger flag would symbolize that the community was carrying the weight of Scott's disappearance together. *Or maybe someone put in the wrong dimensions when they placed the order.* Why cop to a mistake when you can just turn it into a metaphor instead? Whatever the real reason, citizens were told to prep for big-flag energy. A newsletter went out warning homeowners to reinforce their bolsters to support the extra weight. It made sense they were louder than usual.

It was the only explanation Ella bought. No other variable was different than any normal morning. No packages would come that early. Every other bedroom in the house was too far for even the most vigorous movement's music to carry through the thick walls. There were squirrels playing outside the sliding glass doors in her bedroom that led to the pool, but Ella couldn't hear them.

Somehow, though, noises from the front porch tended to get through. As though a natural alarm was triggered, warning the girls to stand alert, an outsider was near. No friends or family would stop in before nine, so it had to be the flag. It pulled her out of one of her favorite dreams. When Ella got pulled out of a dream before she was ready, it always brought back the memory of waking up in a tiny room surrounded by a shape that looked like butterflies.

When Ella woke with that memory, she had to do something really stupid and embarrassing. She had to smell her pillow to assure herself she was not in that little room. The earthy scent of feathers meant she was here, now. In a big sunny bedroom with a mahogany bed set, she'd never have picked out for herself but was nice all the same. The rosemary scent in her night cream lingering on the light blue Egyptian cotton threads would prove she was not a little girl anymore. She was a twenty-five-year-old woman who sometimes used the expensive lotions that the Montgomerys provided in her bathroom, even though she claimed they were unnecessary. She claimed that if she needed something like that, she'd just go to CVS and buy it for herself, knowing very well you couldn't buy that cream in any store Ella could afford.

Lastly, she'd inhale the notes of pine left from Malcolm's cologne and remembered she was not alone. She was in bed with her boyfriend, who was not a boy. He was a grown-ass thirty-three-year-old man who wore ties, reading glasses, and button-up shirts with rolled-up sleeves to show off the forearm muscles he used to hold her up with while they had sex against the tree outside the very first time she brought him to Parlay House.

Feathers, rosemary, and pine. Here-now, grown-up, not-alone. If she could just smell the pillow, she'd have all she needed to know that it was silly to let that memory bother her. One good whiff, and she could bury it back where it belonged, along with all the other things that happened on October 31, 2006. But the way Malcolm had Ella's arms pinned above her head meant she couldn't turn far enough to smell the pillow. It was fine. She could push it down some other way.

What was really the worst part of all this was that they were taking new ID pictures at the office today. That was what Ella decided was really bothering her, so now she'd focus on that. A picture wasn't the sort of thing she'd obsess over. Her aims weren't too high. All she wanted was a little extra time to condition her long brown waves so they didn't frizz like crazy in the God-awful hundred-degree day ahead. Maybe spend seven minutes on make-up instead of two. Pop a little smokey liner around her grey eyes. She just wanted to look not sick, not tired, not like she'd stuck her head in a beehive and then got run over by a semi-truck. Reasonable goals. Well, reasonable forty-five minutes ago. Now, all hope was lost. Her eyes would be puffy.

It was her fault. Imagining a day would go how Ella expected, even when she expected the worst, always resulted in surprises. Ella really couldn't remember a single time Malcolm woke up before her. She had every reason to believe those forty-five minutes were hers. Until the sound of someone clunking around outside, hanging the—huge, heavy we care so much, definitely not just a mistake—flag came and ruined everything.

In Ella's dreams, she was trapped in a tiny space until a tsunami came. The power of the wave crushed the walls around her and demolished everything in its path. Everything but Ella. It let her float like a lazy river, offering her a prime view of the destruction it left, asking only that she admire it. It was a dream she'd had many times before. This time, she saw the hand of someone drowning, reaching for her. The longing to save them ignited something primal in her, even though she could not see their face. Just before she reached the hand, her eyes bolted open and flooded with glaring, unwelcome light. Malcolm's eyes were already bright. He'd clearly been awake for a while.

The dream was probably some stupid save-your-inner-child crap that would go away if she did more cardio or yoga or something. She was bummed not to finish it, though. Bummed enough that if she and Malcolm were on better terms, she'd have asked him to let her go back to sleep. Earlier that week, Malcolm asked her to move in with him and she said no. So, they'd been fighting. A lot.

Malcolm always got nervous before the start of classes, and this semester, he'd be directing the fall musical *1776* in addition to teaching. He'd be leaving rehearsals late and wanted to go home to his girlfriend afterward. It was sweet, she thought.

But moving was out of the question. The Montgomerys would never allow it, not for at least a year—at which point Ida would be married. Of course, Ella couldn't tell Malcolm the real reason why. He thought it was a trauma bond she needed to get over.

Sure, maybe they all had a couple of things they'd never fully worked through from the thing that happened when they were little. But if that were all it was, she would have moved away years ago. If that were all it was, she would never have moved in. No one could ever know about those reasons, so her excuses sounded half-hearted. Some version of *it's not the right time.* Malcolm would push, Ella would get defensive, and they'd get loud.

Parlay House didn't mind loud. It was the sort of property a whole family could spend a day in without ever hearing evidence that anyone in a different room existed. Ella and Malcolm really tested that the night before.

He couldn't understand her resistance. Sure, Ella lived in the house off and on since she was nine years old but, obviously, she didn't feel at home there. When she fully moved in as an adult, she didn't change anything to make the guest room feel like hers. That would have made her more comfortable, and when she was comfortable, she was less alert. Less useful. So, she kept the neutral tones and mahogany bed set.

The gold leafing on the throw pillows and wall decor was too flashy for her, even though it was very subtle. Otherwise, when she was totally honest with herself, she liked the room as is. Being without bright colors meant it didn't distract from the view of the woods. Almost like the room itself was a simple frame, perfectly highlighting the superior beauty of nature. She wished she could roll over to look through the glass doors right now and gaze into the sprawling acres of ever-green chaos, but when the thing with Malcolm was done, he started spooning her too tight for that.

In one of their fights, Malcolm said it looked like a high-end gynecologist's waiting room. She'd laughed, and he thought she was conceding. Things got much worse when he realized she wasn't. So, despite being robbed of her crucial last hour of sleep, in some ways, it was a relief that morning when Malcolm's hand went beneath the spandex band of her sleep shorts. She wasn't in the mood, but after so much fighting, she could

15

rally for a little peace.

What happened wasn't what Ella expected, but it *was* something that had happened before. It was fine. She was fine. Something salty was on her lips. Her eyes must have watered during. She felt crusted tears on her cheeks and tried to get up to wash her face, but Malcolm squeezed her tighter and whispered, "You don't get to run away. Not yet. You know you're so much better than all this image-obsessed bullshit. You're so beautiful to me right now." She blinked a fresh tear.

Malcolm was always so gentle after Ella conceded in a fight. If she'd cried in anger during, the softness after always made her cry a little more. Which made her angry all over again. Tears were so freaking annoying.

If it weren't for that freaking flag and all Moss Groves' gosh darn traditions, her eyes would be perfectly mascara-ed by now. And if it weren't for her annoying HR job at the university, she wouldn't be thought-policing her inner dialogue, using lame words like *freaking* and *gosh darn*.

But she wanted that promotion. At work she never let an unprofessional word slip. Outside of work, she had a mild profanity hobby that she was now determined to kick. It's not like she was mimicking the Sopranos or anything, she just deployed well-earned four-letter satisfaction when it was warranted.

Like when she dropped a carton of eggs in the Piggly Wiggly parking lot and yelled, "Gosh-mother-freaking-darn-it! Mother-freaking-yoke! Fudge!" But not stupid like that. The real version. The one she wouldn't even let herself think about now because thinking it meant she might say it out loud, and she was never going to curse out loud again. Because her boss, Colleen Smith, was in the parking lot that day. When she heard Ella, Colleen shook her head like she'd murdered a kitten.

It shouldn't matter. She wasn't at work. They were both adults. It was called *adult language* after all. Colleen Smith saw it differently. To her, they both held a far more sacred title than adult: *ladies*. Colleen was third runner-up for Jr. Miss Louisiana 1995, and she'd endeared herself to judges by claiming never to have seen an R-rated movie. So, it did matter.

Everything you did in public mattered in Moss Groves. That's why the most coveted properties were the ones that offered the utmost privacy.

Properties like Parlay House. It was still hard to believe that Ella actually lived there. Parlay House was a bit much for anyone, but for three unrelated women in their twenties, it was obscene.

Malcolm said that the first time he came over. A slight gasp was usual. Something along the lines of *Wow* was expected from Moss Groves' newbies. Compliments on the ever-changing but always perfect landscaping were customary from competitive locals.

Malcolm wouldn't even allow an impressed smile. He just shook his head and said, "This is obscene." That made Ella smile, and she wasn't generous with smiles.

Controlled smirks were her expression of choice. But when something provoked genuine, unexpected delight, it coursed through her like a small spasm. Whatever muscle the feeling could contort danced like it knew if it didn't escape right then, she'd scare it back inside. Someone daring to insult Parlay House, to her face, warranted a full crescent. Malcolm even got to see teeth.

No one else would risk anything outside a compliment for the luxury of "the living situation." Typically, someone like Ella Kyle would be fair game. She had no relation to the Montgomerys. Or any other founding family. She wasn't even born below the Mason Dixon. But being one of Ida Montgomery's two best friends granted an albeit passive-aggressive social immunity.

All well-raised Southerners knew a compliment could be nearly anything it needed to be anyway. Anyone who didn't was endeared as "touched," "special," or "vegetarian." There were plenty of complimentary ways to judge the fact that, Ella and Susan-Eva, lived in a historic mansion rent-free.

After guests exhausted awed-pleasantries, there was *a moment* they needed to have with one of the non-Montgomerys. At best, it was a thoughtless, "You're so lucky." At worst, it was a pity-filled hand squeeze and, "You girls deserve this after everything you went through when you were little." Then, a pause, in case, in the middle of the house tour, Ella wanted to unveil a juicy traumatic detail of *what they went through.*

Ella was certain on that first visit at least one of Parlay House's features would charm Malcolm. The Greek Revival architecture. The way its pristine white paint took on the color of each day's light. The wrap-around porch and balcony. The arch of Spanish moss hanging from magnolia trees canopying over the long driveway and, good God, the pool. Even as a child, Ella never let herself enjoy the house too much, except for when it came to the pool. In the beginning, if Ella and Susan-Eva were invited for play dates, it usually meant there was some crisis they were being summoned to handle.

But whenever Moss Groves broke a hundred degrees, the play dates really were just play dates. They'd cannonball, stain their lips bright red with icy rocket pops, and take afternoon naps without being asked. Almost like they were normal little girls. Even now, at twenty-five years old, if Ella jumped in on a hot enough day, no matter how hard she fought it, she'd burst up from the water with a grin so big it had to make noise. But in the three years since Malcolm and Ella started dating, he'd never once taken a dip.

At first, Malcolm's distaste for the house felt like an acceptance of Ella. A level of being seen she'd always wanted. That was before he asked her to move into his one-bedroom apartment. Now, the insults felt personal. It was like he was judging her for being associated with it. He didn't even really understand what he was asking her to give up. He *wanted* her to live with him, but Susan-Eva and Ida *needed* her to live with them. It was okay that he couldn't see that. She was used to people not noticing the part she played.

Love, beauty, and joy get the spotlight as life's most savored ingredients. So, it was lucky that Ella hated the spotlight because she was certain she wasn't good at any of those things. All she cared about was being essential. Most essential things happen in the shadows, unnoticed until they're gone.

Nothing made Ella feel more essential than knowing how to be the eye of any hurricane. Even if it meant she disappeared behind the chaos. But there were moments, like this morning, when she wished someone could see how much she'd learned to endure while remaining invisible. Not so they could save her or anything. She didn't need saving. What just happened with Malcolm wasn't even a fight, really. It was a quieter sort of conflict. Nothing much to hear. She never let her tears make noise. But for some reason, Ella couldn't stop staring at an air vent in the ceiling.

When they were little, sometimes they could hear bits of secret conversations if they pressed an ear to the vent upstairs. You could listen to what was going on upstairs in this room too, if you really wanted. It was harder, though. You had to push a chair to the dresser and climb on top to get your ear to the vent. Not something Ella would ever do now, of course. But maybe, she thought, for no reason at all, someone upstairs pressed an ear that morning. Maybe someone heard some of what happened and would ask about the quiet, annoying little conflict before it disappeared and faded into all the others.

A knock rapped the door with a rhythm so familiar Ella could have hummed it. Non-Montgomery resident number two of Parlay house, Susan-Eva was up. The knock was her 'I have a guy in the kitchen' knock. Not her 'Are you okay?' knock. She hadn't pressed her ear to the vent. She hadn't heard.

7:30 AM

"Rise and shine, fellow sinners. Pancakes are up, and while I'm sure whatever you're doing is delicious, it can't be as yummy as my midnight snack, currently finishing his shower. Boyfriend or not, Ella, it is your privilege as my best friend to feast your eyes on the spoils of my victory. Ella?" Susan-Eva said. Then she waited. No response, so she yelled, "ELLA!"

Ella swung open the door glaring, wrapped in Malcolm's wrinkled dark green button-up.

Susan-Eva was already dressed for the day and looked infuriatingly fantastic. She was getting her PhD in social work but she didn't have classes that day so she could wear whatever she wanted. What she wanted on a day this hot was the same thing everyone did: something that breathes. It was only Levi's she'd cut to shorts and a blush pink tee-shirt that hung off one shoulder, but on her, it was inspiring.

Looking at Susan-Eva made you feel like you should do something a little reckless and fun, like drink a full sugar cherry coke before bed or bring up planned parenthood at church. With a mocking curtsy, Susan-Eva presented a coffee mug garnished with fresh mint leaves as a peace offering for her intrusion. Garnish was a secret language amongst the Parlay House trio. Mint leaves could mean three things:

19

1. freshen up
2. stand alert
3. we need to get rid of some mint

Despite Susan-Eva's usual perkiness, Ella correctly guessed it was two; stand alert. Something was up. An outsider would never guess it looking at Susan-Eva, though. It really was obnoxious how effortlessly lovely she always looked in the mornings. Her black hair had a natural bounce that followed her love of movement like a loyal dance partner. Her skin had a dewy glow that only left her with one or two true break-outs in her teen years.

In college, girls loved telling Susan-Eva how jealous they were of her hair and skin. As if their envy was a "Get out of racism free!" card. Then they'd comment how much they loved Mexican culture, ignoring that Susan-Eva was born and raised in Moss Groves.

But rather than point this out Susan-Eva would grin and contribute, "I love German culture! Do you know about Krampus? It's like Santa but scary?" or "I love Japanese culture! Do you know the term Wabi-Sabi? It means an imperfection that leads to a more elegant whole. Isn't that beautiful?" Or "I love Post-Gregorian Pre-Victorian English culture. That midpoint between gluttony and prudishness was a hotbox for inventive erotic literature, right?" Watching people try to figure out Susan-Eva was a phenomenon Ella followed like a favorite sport. Peers never stopped trying to label her, and Susan-Eva never stopped effortlessly contradicting each and every attempt.

The first time Ella ever saw Susan-Eva, she was wearing a glittery tutu and a Batman mask. A fully encompassing classification escaped Ella just like it did everyone else, but whatever it was, she instantly liked it.

"Morning Suz." Malcolm groaned, pulling on boxers from under the sheets. Susan-Eva hated being called "Suz," which Malcolm knew and started as retaliation for her calling him-

"Prof," Susan-Eva retorted with a head nod.

"My first lecture is in an hour. I'm popping in the shower." He kissed the back of Ella's head and disappeared to the bathroom.

The instant the door shut, Susan-Eva dropped the grin. Already knowing the answer, Ella leaned close and asked, "Is this really about your flavor of the week or is it about—"

Susan-Eva shook her head and whispered, "Ida."

Tension shot into Ella's shoulders. The name "Ida" was spoken to them more times than any other name they'd heard in their lives, even their own. Each time, it still provoked an involuntary physical response. Overeating ice cream doesn't build a tolerance for brain freeze.

"She just sent me this text: Shopping inspo *#SOS*. Meet me at the vintage *#store*. The Auction theme is Masquerade! Have to kick it up. *#I'm dying*! *#Tradition.*" Ella grabbed the phone, reading it for herself.

Her eyes went wide with a mix of anxiety and annoyance, "Mask, scull, heart, eggplant, menorah? I've never seen her use emojis or a hashtag. *What's the menorah for?*" Said Ella.

"Yeah!? She knows she's not supposed to use colloquialisms or ideograms. She can't handle it. So, no bailing, I'm not dealing with her alone. Noon?" Susan-Eva said. Ella nodded. "And… is there any way you could feed Alpha? I have a doctor's appointment."

Ella narrowed her gaze and asked, "What kind of doctor's appointment?"

Susan-Eva shrugged with a guilty smirk, "What?! If we're right and Ida's up to something, we could use an objective psychiatric opinion."

"Nothing objective happens when you walk into that office," Said Ella.

"You don't get it," Said Susan-Eva.

"No one does. I'm not feeding Alpha. It's your week." Ella started to close the door, but Susan-Eva yanked it back.

"What are you doing? I was serious. Come and have breakfast. I want you to meet Calvin from last night."

"I really don't need to meet Calvin from last night."

"You really do." Susan-Eva bit her lip with pride. Ella rolled her eyes. Luckily, her dark grey pencil skirt was clean. She could pair it with a light grey silk tank Ida had bought her, pop up a messy top knot, and call it a day. In two minutes, she was dressed and let Susan-Eva pull her down the hall.

There once was a wall that separated the kitchen and living room.

Keeping 'the help' out of sight and mind. In the seventies, Ida's grandmother knocked it down. Now, the kitchen looked onto the living room, where floor-to-ceiling windows revealed the pool and wooded acres behind the house. Beautiful, but the light hitting the water through the summer months made for an air conditioning nightmare. Susan-Eva was a house plant junkie and took full advantage of the light.

With a mix of tropical greens and pastels, she'd transformed the once stuffy space into a whimsical wonderland full of eclectic trinkets and playful local art. When people told her she was lucky to live in Parlay House, she'd say, "I know! I have four Jade plants alive twelve feet from the window! Can you imagine?"

Maple, vanilla, and bacon grease assaulted Ella's nose as Susan-Eva yanked her into the kitchen. It was deceptive. Those were fun smells. Ella knew Ida's text meant this would not be a fun day. She salivated anyway. Then she saw Calvin.

Before this year, Susan-Eva had only been with two sexual partners and was a serial monogamist. To really enjoy sex, she needed to feel what she called "the potential for love." It wasn't that she had judgment for more casual encounters. One of Susan-Eva's favorite hobbies was pestering Ella for details when Ella was in her self-proclaimed "Freudian fuck-phase." But Susan-Eva was a romantic. "What can I say? Being in love turns me on."

Ella knew Susan-Eva was only ever really in love once. But in the past year, something changed. Nearly every weekend, she brought a new guy home. Usually someone from out of town or much older or impractical for some other reason. The only real correlation was that none of them had the potential for love, and most of them didn't seem to know about the thing that happened when they were little. *Or about the thing that happened to Susan-Eva last January*. Most people didn't know about that.

Randos in the kitchen was something Ella had come to expect on Saturday and Sunday mornings. A Thursday was weird, but otherwise, no shock. The sight of Calvin, however, was not the sort of thing you could ever be used to. This was how Malcolm must have felt seeing the house for the first time, Ella thought. Calvin's body was obscene. No one who eats pancakes should be able to look like that.

He sat in a towel, which would seem overconfident, but there was something pure about his comfort—like a turtle on an electric scooter if a turtle could also be ridiculously ripped.

"Calvin drove down all the way from Atlanta to help his brother move into his dorm." Susan-Eva smiled at Calvin before whispering to Ella, "Nom, nom, nom, am I right?" Ella pursed her lips, unable to object. He wasn't her type, or Susan-Eva's, really. But you don't say you're more into expressionism while you're looking at the Sistine Chapel. When in the presence of a masterpiece, taste is of no relevance. You'd have to be a real asshole not to shut up, stand back and appreciate it.

"Mm. Pancakes. So good," said Calvin, almost humming.

"So good," repeated Susan-Eva and Ella in tandem. They both cocked their heads, unapologetically staring as Calvin's shoulder flexed, squeezing maple syrup onto his short stack.

"You both graduated from Florence?" Calvin asked.

"Pretty much everyone who grows up here goes to Florence. Moss Groves is a cradle-to-grave town," Ella said as she grabbed herself a pancake and tore off a bite. No syrup or butter.

"It's a great school. Insane continued education rate. Your brother should pledge. All the Greeks have amazing alumni outreach programs. We're still super involved," said Susan-Eva.

Calvin hooked his arm around Susan-Eva's waist as she walked past him and she sat on his lap. Ella watched the way Calvin looked around, taking in the sheer size of the space. Then she saw him look at the fridge and spot a photo. *The photo.* Don't do it, Ella thought; just keep being a nice, obscenely ripped, slightly goofy dude. It was too late. Calvin was reaching over Susan-Eva's shoulder to pull the photo from under the magnet. *Shit. Shoot! Not Shit!* Ella thought. *Shoot.*

Before Ella could finish letting her thought police put on the handcuffs, Calvin was holding the photo. It was a Polaroid of three little girls wearing witch costumes. Ella and Susan-Eva exchanged a look as Calvin smiled, taking it in. "Is this you guys?" Calvin asked. Susan-Eva nodded. "So cute! Whose number three?"

"That's Ida. You just missed her. She left while you were in the shower,"

23

said Susan-Eva.

"Okay! I have this fun question I always ask roommates. If you guys were all in a sitcom, which ones would you be? Like, what are your archetypes?" Calvin said before whispering in Susan-Eva's ear, "Other than you being the hot one, obviously."

"Hm... Ella is the type-A protective one with a little bit of a sexy dark side. Like Robin from *How I Met Your Mother* meets Faith from *Buffy the Vampire Slayer*." Susan-Eva turned to Ella and said, "Now you do me."

"I don't know," Ella shrugged.

"Wow. I gave you Buffy and you gave me nothing? Noted," Susan-Eva pouted.

"You're the heart. What comparison could possibly do?" Ella said it as casually as she could manage but reveled at the accuracy. Heart. Reduced to cliches until it needs surgery.

"Fine. I love you again." Said Susan-Eva, taking a bite from Calvin's plate.

"And Ida? Which one is she? The shy underdog? The quirky comic relief? The cynic/secret romantic?" Calvin asked. Susan-Eva and Ella exchanged another quick look.

"Ida is hard to describe," said Ella, taking the picture from Calvin and hanging it back on the fridge.

Almost no first-time visitor ever left without a pilgrimage to that photo. If Parlay House was a museum that photo would be its Mona Lisa. Without context, the larger works in the Louvre would grab more attention than its most famous attraction. Plenty of tourists walk right past the room of royal diamonds and jewels, ignore the Greek sculptures, and never take one look up at the gold-lined ceilings. Almost no one misses the Mona Lisa, though. That small portrait of a woman almost smiling draws so many people they have to put up ropes for the lines around it like it's a roller coaster. Because they know what it is. What it represents. Or even if they don't, at the very least, they know it's famous.

Being from out of state meant it was possible Calvin really didn't know the witch costumes photo was such a revered Moss Groves artifact. But Ella thought it was more likely he was playing dumb. It didn't matter.

Innocent curiosity or attempted manipulation would yield the exact same response. In the sixteen years since that photo was taken, the trio's account of what happened later that night and how they managed to survive never changed once.

Even at nine years old, they never let an unrehearsed word slip. Year after year, Moss Groves cooed over how well the girls adjusted. How seemingly untouched three children were by something so scary. Still, everyone wondered... no matter how "untouched" they seemed... one of them must have been. The one thing the police, the podcasters, the papers, and the public all agreed on when it came to what happened the night of October 31, 2006, was that no one knew the whole story.

There were ways Ella, Susan-Eva, and Ida could have stopped the rumors. They could have done interviews. Written a book. Obviously, they didn't mind calling some attention to it. The three made a choice to keep the photo on the fridge. They knew it would invite questions. They knew it would distract. Best of all, they knew it would keep people from looking at all the other masterpieces they were hiding in that house. The padded closet. The drawer with *those* drawings. The hidden keys. Because the biggest secret surrounding the night of October 31, 2006, is that it wasn't their biggest secret.

TWO
August 18, 2022

The girl who had to speak before Ida

"CLASS OF 2022, THIS IS it! Our senior year." The Girl Who Had To Speak Before Ida held the attention of all twenty-six sorority sisters in her graduating class with ease as she recited the short speech she'd prepared. No one would have guessed how close her voice came to trembling.

Speaking never made her nervous, and this was only a fun tradition, a little breakfast to kick off the semester. So why did The Girl Who Had To Speak Before Ida feel at any second, her knees might buckle? For a moment, she forgot her own name. She found an odd grounding comfort in occasionally glancing to the place card at her empty seat. The distant but familiar shape that the letters formed settled her rumbling stomach. Mary. The Girl Who Had To Speak Before Ida's name was Mary. Mary scanned the yard. Everything looked right.

All the graduating sisters were supposed to wear the same white dress they wore on their bid day. Some thought this was a cruel way to call attention to any weight gained in the last three years, but no one dared say it.

Lots of "out of vogue" cultural and ethical ideologies found fertile ground within the city limits. Descending popularity of certain beliefs, in many ways, increased their value to true legacy residents. Body shaming, corporal punishment, and homophobia weren't as commonplace as they once were. But when they made public appearances, they were debuted like mint condition designer vintage. Begging for awe at how well they'd been maintained.

Mary's dress still fit perfectly. The backyard garden was manicured to standard the day before. The sweet scent of a local specialty, pistachio croissants, mingled with notes of fresh-cut grass lofting through the air. It was a lovely morning. Mary simply hoped it was *lovely enough* for their guest of honor, whose presence often made normally lovely things quite dull by comparison.

Swallowing in hopes of smoothing away any shakiness in her voice, Mary continued to the most important part of her speech. "The President of our Alumni chapter is a sister who needs no introduction, but I can't resist giving her one anyway. She was Jr. Miss Moss Groves 2016, and during her tenure as our president, she led our house to wins in every costume and dance competition, renovated the kitchen in our house, and raised more for charity than any of her predecessors. We feel so lucky every time she comes back to visit us and just, pray that she never stops. We'd be lost. So! Without further ado, leading us in our fall semester prayer, Ida Montgomery."

Just as Mary stepped aside, Ida grabbed her hand and mouthed, "Thank you." Mary exhaled. Everyone exhaled. Whenever Ida stepped into the center of attention, a sense of balance was restored. Looking at her felt like nature. When Ida was in a crowd or anywhere where staring was deemed inappropriate, the effort it took to look away was vertigo-inducing. Luckily, it was very rare that Ida was in public without also being the attraction.

She was gorgeous and, of course, very wealthy, but there were lots of beautiful, wealthy women in Moss Groves. In high school, she'd show up on a regular day in full costume. Every other member of the student body, wearing normal uniforms, would assume they'd messed up and forgotten a holiday. There was such confidence in her oddities. Behavior that would make an outcast of anyone else made a trendsetter of Ida. Whimsy couldn't fully explain the unanimous attention Ida's presence demanded, though. It was her mystery.

Even Ida's fiancée, Parker, only needed his fingers to count the one-on-one moments they'd ever had. The only two people who spent real time alone with Ida were Ella and Susan-Eva. Mary thought the same thing everyone else did. It made sense for those three to be close after what they went through as kids. All that was so awful, of course. It would be crazy to be jealous of a trauma bond. Maybe she was a little jealous, though. Mary couldn't help but wish *she* could get into Ida's head and learn how she could have endured something so horrible and still turned out so perfect.

Ida

Ida took in all twenty-six faces. What she saw in each of them was irrelevant *-for now-* but it was an important step. The taking in. Making listeners feel seen. Then came the deep breath. Not a dramatic one, the way someone nervous or anxious might take a deep breath, but a humble deep breath. A breath that says you are breathing in the honor of being there. The next part Ida liked. A slow wet of her lips. This step was not required, but it was permitted as the need for lubrication before speaking was common. Providing lubrication is rarely boring, so she never skipped that one. Next came the long part. The words.

Ida smiled a big, shiny, contagious movie star smile and began, "Sisters, as I look at your beautiful faces, I can't help but reflect on all the masks we wear to cover them up. Moss Groves is known for its legendary theme parties. We keep the costume stores in business year-round. We're proud of our heritage, so I know some of you feel a twinge of disappointment that, due to our changing world, some of our oldest traditions have changed. We've reimagined some of the themes. I encourage you not to see these changes as an abandonment of who we are but as a chance to embrace the most sacred of all our traditions. Being able to take off the masks and, as scary as it may sound, our makeup and show our truest selves. That's what sisterhood is really about: taking off the mask, unleashing your scary and …" Ida paused. This was the important part. The part Ella told her not to attempt because she doubted Ida could pull it off, but Ida practiced. For a very long time. She was patient and felt certain she had mastered the mechanics.

She puffed her lips into a circle, taking a slow, controlled exhalation as though desperately trying to suppress emotion. Then it happened. Like magic, right on cue, her voice cracked as she said, "…through the eyes of your sisters, seeing what you thought was terrifying was beauty all along. Let us pray." Then she blinked one delicate, gracefully rolling sparkle of a tear.

Several sisters grabbed each other's hands and dabbed tears, already overflowing with senior-year sentimentality. Ida gently batted her eyes shut and bowed her head. All twenty-six heads followed.

Ida prayed, "Our Father who art in heaven." Ida's eyes shot open as she continued, "Hallowed be thy name." She scanned each sister, confirming all eyes were closed. They were. Ida was alone. Her shoulders slowly rolled back. "Thy kingdom come thy will be done on Earth as it is in heaven."

Her voice remained warm and reverent, but all the allusiveness left her face as Ida's jaw clenched with annoyance. She couldn't believe how well she'd done under near-impossible circumstances. The floral and fake fruity perfumes. The lilies. The sugar. More than anything, the sugar. There was far, far too much sugar in the air. She was certain the take-a-humble-deep-breath step added enough glucose to her saliva to make simple syrup. If there were a pewter cup with bourbon and mint in sight, she could spit in it and declare she made Juleps.

Of course, there wasn't anything as untamed as booze present. Menus for these sorts of things never featured fire. Honing in on a palatable scent took so much focus that Ida was shocked, and so, so impressed with herself that she remembered the sleepy words part. Knowing she'd proved Ella wrong about tears bought her a little extra motivation, but it was dwindling.

At 8 AM, it was already ninety-five degrees. Ida watched the sun beat down on the bare skin of that girl who spoke before her. A deep breath pushed the girl's breasts to a fleeting moment of cleavage.

There were two things Ida was never, ever, supposed to endure if she was to maintain control. Hunger and boredom. She felt both rumbling within, threatening her composure with every unsated second. At least she had the prayer. Ida loved prayer and thought fondly of God as she continued, "Give us this day our daily bread." Just as she said it, the Lord did as he always did for Ida. He provided.

A girl with freckles dusted across her nose shifted in her seat, uncomfortable with public prayer. She was new, a transfer from Vermont. Unable to take it a second longer, she opened her eyes. Ida met them instantly. The girl smiled, relieved someone else wasn't taking the awkward group prayer part so seriously. She waited for Ida to smile back, having no idea the rare privilege of this experience—to be alone with Ida Montgomery.

Ida held her gaze and let a half smile creep onto her lips. Something about it unsettled the girl with freckles, and she closed her eyes again. Ida kept staring as she said, "Forgive us our trespasses as we forgive those who'd trespass against us."

The girl with freckles fidgeted with her eyes shut, tucking hair behind her ears. It was obvious a worry was getting to the girl. A feeling of something off, a sense she was being watched. Unable to resist, the girl's eyes opened again. She was correct. Ida's eyes were still on her and didn't blink when the girl met her gaze. The girl with freckles swallowed.

Ida kept staring and praying, "And lead us not into temptation but deliver us from evil." The girl with freckles closed her eyes as Ida said, "For thine is the kingdom and the power," The girl with freckles shook her head, trying to resist looking again, but quickly lost her private battle and opened her eyes. Ida's eyes dug deeper. Her smile inched wider. The girl with freckles desperately looked around, hoping someone else could see what was happening, knowing no words could explain it. Her face grew hot and red as Ida said, "And the glory." The girl shook her head and closed her eyes as Ida stared harder and said, "Forever..."

All Ida had to do was wait long enough, and the air would fill with what she needed. As long as she knew it was coming, she could wait for hours, feeding on the ability of her patience to transform the atmosphere.

The girl with freckles fought, squeezing her eyes shut, begging a God she didn't believe in for Ida to say amen, begging that whatever this was would be over. Ida savored her own comfort in the silence like a snake bathing in the sun. None of the other girls would dare sneak a peek before Ida finished the prayer. Every sister's chest rose and fell faster as the silence extended, drawing them into uncertainty. Blood flushed their cheeks. The girl with freckles' lids burst open one final time. The whites of her eyes tinted to the absolute loveliest shade of chastised pink. Three tears fell in quick succession as she blinked, and a sweat bead formed on her chest.

Just like that, something breathable was in the air. Ida felt so close to God, for she had created. All was polite and sweet moments ago. Now, she inhaled something visceral. Something savory. Salt. Hormones. Skin. The girl with freckles watched Ida slowly close her eyes and bow her head as she softly said, "Amen."

Everyone but the girl with freckles repeated, "Amen." They all opened their eyes to Ida's reverent, bowed head. Sunlight hit her flowing red hair and custom-made tulle dress, giving her an other-worldly glow. The girl with freckles glanced around, watching all the other women admire Ida. Ida opened her eyes, flashed a huge, warm grin, and said, "Let's eat!"

The girl got up as discreetly as possible and rushed out of sight. She wasn't missing much. Apparently, one of the underclassmen started a vegetarian initiative—pastries paired with sweet tea. So much sugar and no bacon in sight; it was obscene.

THREE

August 18, 2022

Susan-Eva

"YOU EVER NOTICE HOW SOMETIMES when you're three sheets, time speeds up, but other times it slows down? Like, I had no idea we walked this far back last night. It was pretty, though." Susan-Eva bit her lip with delight as Calvin whispered in her ear, "Not as pretty as the girl behind the bar, but… Anyway! Thanks for the ride back to our cars, man. We were in no condition to drive last night." Calvin said, grabbing Malcolm's shoulder from the backseat of his navy blue Subaru.

Malcolm smirked in the rearview and said, "Didn't really have a choice since you both just got in the back of my car, but no problem."

"Yeah, thanks, Prof!" Susan-Eva said, popping her head between Ella and Malcolm.

Susan-Eva watched Malcolm's grip tighten on the steering wheel; she insisted they take the scenic route. Leaning back to her seat, Susan-Eva saw Calvin grin as they rolled past the historic Creole architecture of Main Street. Watching someone really appreciate the charm of her hometown for the first time always felt like jumping into another life for a few seconds.

They'd peer at the intricate ironwork with swirling designs that lined the second and third-floor balconies of downtown buildings. Ivy and moss-covered statues rising out of courtyard fountains brought a romantic hue to the faces of couples as they held hands and took pictures. It was the kind of feeling Susan-Eva thought she herself might have if she ever got to travel and see gardens in France or ruins in Greece. Forcing herself to see the town through the eyes of a visitor was like going on a five-second vacation. If she saw it like someone without a history here, it couldn't hurt her; it could just be beautiful. Susan-Eva used to find Moss Groves to be so, so beautiful.

"Hey! You okay?" Asked Calvin, taking Susan-Eva's hand. Damn it. She must have accidentally done the sad staring off into space thing. Ella looked back worried, and Susan-Eva scrunched her nose to make a silly face, shooing Ella's concern back to the front seat. Ella didn't get to turn the worry on Susan-Eva. Not after the bullshit 'My Eyes are red from allergies' lie Ella kept feeding Susan-Eva all week.

Susan-Eva grinned at Calvin and said, "Nope! Not *okay*. My pancakes were way too good for just *okay*. I'm a solid *fantastic*." Ella smirked at Susan-Eva through the rearview.

Obviously, the five-second vacation trick didn't work as well as it used to. *Fine, you caught me, I was sad for a second,* Susan-Eva thought as she rolled her eyes at Ella. Calvin put his arm around her. He sure seemed to be enjoying himself. Even if Malcolm was driving a little too fast for them to really appreciate the view. Chauffeuring the whole peanut gallery to their collective destinations was not on his first-day to-do list.

It wasn't Susan-Eva's intention to pick a one-night stand that could have been manufactured in a things-to-torture-pretentious-assholes-like-Malcolm-Dubois factory, but God, was it a benefit.

There was no surprise in Susan-Eva's lack of love for Malcolm. In their sixteen years of friendship, she never liked a single one of Ella's boyfriends. Not Adam Givens, who threw sand in Ella's eyes and who she "kindergarten married" by the monkey bars while her pupils still burned pink. Not Sam Lupin, who she dated in tenth grade until she got a higher score on her pre-SATs, and he accused her of giving the SAT prep instructor a blowjob. And not the SAT prep instructor to whom, to get back at Sam, Ella actually did give a blow job, then dated in secret off and on junior year.

Parker Porter, whom Ella dated her freshman year at Florence, was actually alright. Parker was Joseph Porter's half-brother, and Joseph was Susan-Eva's... well, he was her...

It didn't matter! She would think about that at her appointment later. Right now, she was focused on Ella's life choices, not hers.

So anyway, Parker wasn't perfect, but he was beautiful, kind, and fun. So naturally, Ella dumped him and eventually set him up with Ida. Now Parker and Ida were engaged. The unworthy string of Ella's boys, kindergarten through college, all had one hopeful thing in common: Ella didn't seem to like them that much either.

Malcolm Dubois was different. Ella not only loved him - she loved his disapproval of her. Her muscles would relax with every critique Malcolm offered as though it were confirmation of something she'd always known about herself. For a friend like Susan-Eva, a friend who'd spent years combating Ella's unforgiving self-image, guys like Malcolm were her worst nightmare. Ella never trusted compliments, so it wasn't a shock she devoted to someone who didn't fawn, but with the others, Ella bantered and teased. When they threw dirt, Ella threw mud. With Malcolm, it wasn't only that she didn't swing back, it was that sometimes she said thank you.

So, Susan-Eva started swinging for her. Malcolm seemed to interpret the insults more as an annoying attempt at witty banter than true disdain. He was wrong. Despite the scrolling list of injustices Susan-Eva suffered at the hands of Moss Groves' residents, Malcolm was the only one she allowed herself to hate.

He bothered Ida, too. Susan-Eva knew that was a dangerous problem, but it was under control for now.

A sudden breeze pulled Susan-Eva's attention back to Calvin as he rolled down the window. He stuck his head out, grinning like a golden retriever while they drove past a street of pastel houses with Greek letters hanging on banners. They'd turned onto Sorority Row. Susan-Eva pointed at one of the houses and said, "That was ours, but we never lived there. Only the Frats are allowed to have parties. Ida wanted to stay in Parlay House, so we didn't have to go to the boys to throw down."

Malcolm groaned and turned up local news on the radio. A low voice, desperately trying to repress a southern accent and not quite succeeding, droned through the speaker. "In observation of Florence University President Martin Ryan's missing son, Scott Ryan, his fraternity announces they will be holding a candle-lit prayer before the Moss Groves annual silent auction and charity event."

Ella turned back and asked, "Any chance we can bail on that?"

"After Ida's text? No way," said Susan-Eva, "She already bought us all the tickets."

Malcolm turned the radio further up, "Human remains found near a house undergoing renovations in Shreveport have been identified as belonging to nine-year-old Sally Marks, who was reported missing four months earlier. Police have declared her death a homicide but have not released the names of any suspects. Parallels to the deceased and victims of serial killer Ed Bins have stirred up suspicions of a copycat murderer, as well as fears that Ed's partner, often referred to as "The Second Killer," is still at large. Nov. 1 of this year will mark the sixteen-year anniversary of Ed's death—" Ella turned the radio off.

"That's so scary," said Calvin. "Dylan, my brother, was considering NYU. I was so relieved when he chose Florence instead. He had some issues with the school he was at before. He's a transfer. I figured he'd get into less trouble in a small town. But when I googled it, all this stuff about a child murderer came up."

He knew, Susan-Eva thought. Of course, he knew. How stupid to fantasize about a world where he didn't. A world where a guy with the body of a Greek statue and a Winnie-the-Pooh heart could be a simple night of fun. Well, not fun exactly. None of the one-night stands had been fun yet. Calvin was kind of close. And Susan-Eva had been doing a Meryl Streep-level job of acting like it was the time of her Goddamn life all morning. Now, all of her perfectly good dissociating would be ruined by the Ed thing.

Which wasn't even the thing she was dissociating about! Just because she was dealing with what happened in the park last January by boning as many people as she could didn't mean that every bad thing that ever happened to her was invited to the party. But here she was again. About to have to answer questions about Ed. Like all of her traumas were trying to merge together in a big trauma orgy. Which is kind of the premise of the most successful porn. Maybe she should write an essay about this, maybe Dr. Lorkin could…

"I was getting pretty creeped out, so I didn't dig too deep," Calvin said, jolting Susan-Eva's mind back on topic. He's probably a reporter, Susan-Eva thought. Or maybe a true crime podcaster? A good old-fashioned tragedy tourist?

Susan-Eva could feel Ella's suspicions radiating out of the back of her head. Play along, Susan-Eva thought. He'd be gone in ten minutes. It is possible to google Ed Bins without seeing their names. It is possible for someone not to know. Not every article featured the picture in the witch costumes. So, for ten minutes, couldn't they all pretend to be normal murder-obsessed Americans? Casually talking about serial killers along with *'Real House Wives'* gossip and the weather.

"They never found the second killer?" asked Calvin.

Ella and Susan-Eva breathed in tandem, readying themselves for answers and speeches they'd given a thousand times. But before they had to say anything, Malcolm piped in and said, "They don't have evidence the so-called second killer ever killed anyone but Ed. He could have been a friend who walked in, saw what Ed was doing, killed him in self-defense, and then fled the scene. But that's not as marketable as some unknown bogeyman forever in the shadows. Fear makes money."

"So no one saw him?" asked Calvin. Malcolm glanced to Ella, checking in. She nodded for him to keep going. In the side mirror, Susan-Eva watched the corner of Ella's mouth tilt up to a half smile as she closed her eyes and furrowed her brow. An expression Susan-Eva knew well, it meant Ella was chastising herself for something. It was a look that said, *'See. He's taking care me. He was right. I was wrong. See?'*

Malcolm kept his eyes on the road and explained, "The witnesses weren't reliable. They were just kids. They shouldn't have had to talk about it so much." Ella took his hand and squeezed. Ughhhhhh, fine! That was nice, Susan-Eva thought. Malcolm was a prick, but that was a nice thing for the prick to say.

Calvin said, "Got it. I was only freaked out for Dylan, but Moss Groves is safe, right?"

Malcolm said. "Very. It's a small southern town, so be more scared of the backward thinking than anything else. Don't get me wrong, Ed Bins was a monster, but he's been dead for almost two decades. Bad news gets higher ratings. I bet you anything Scott Ryan's actually just off on a European bender. He'll come back with some bullshit heroic story to make everyone forget all his DUIs until he runs for office one day." Susan-Eva felt a genuine twinge of gratitude for Malcolm's unsolicited interference. Then he tacked on, "Nothing that bad ever really happens in Moss Groves," and Susan-Eva stopped feeling grateful.

In fact, she stopped feeling anything at all. Hearing those eight words caused the kind of pain that send you into a brief numbing shock. The last thing she wanted was for Malcolm to know how much it got to her. But before she could stop herself she was repeating his words. Challenging him. Daring him to double down.

"Nothing that bad?" her voice shook as she said it.

Susan-Eva sounded so unlike herself that Malcolm looked back, unsure it was her who said it even though she was the only woman in his back seat. Her voice usually sounded like an invitation. To play, to fight, to understand, to anything. But she repeated those words like she was repeating a terminal diagnosis.

Susan-Eva saw Malcolm glance at Ella; Ella wasn't breathing.

"I meant people don't get murdered." He quickly responded, but it was too casual an overcorrection. He reached for Ella's hand, and she pulled away. Ella never pulled away. If it weren't for how numb Susan-Eva felt, seeing Ella reject Malcolm for her sake, would have been almost moving. It wouldn't take him that long to argue his way back to her good graces. He'd reassure Ella he wasn't commenting on what happened to Susan-Eva in the park last January. He was on their side! Steering this random idiot away from—and he hated this word—their triggers.

In the rearview, Susan-Eva could see Malcolm glance between Ella and Susan-Eva, as if he was waiting for them to start the argument. That probably would be more comfortable for him than this, Susan-Eva thought. If they'd get angry, he could say they were overreacting. But neither Malcolm's former head of the debate team girlfriend nor her bodyguard of a bestie so much as gave him a side-eye. Instead, Ella stared out the window and Susan-Eva fought to look fine as she tried not to touch the scar on her knee.

The town had a handful of unofficial slogans:

Cradle to Grave, Pre-K to PhD, Moss Groves has everything you'll ever need.

Our holiday hangovers have their own holiday.

What happens in Moss Groves stays in Moss Groves unless it's on the cover of Garden and Gun

But *Nothing that bad ever happens in Moss Groves,* though never carved onto a sign or printed on a brochure, was its most uttered description.

It was said to Florence University Freshman moving in from out of town, almost like a complaint. It was chanted at PTA meetings after a parent shared a story about a middle school bathroom blowjob epidemic a few towns over. "Not here." They'd say, "Thank God nothing like that happens here where we raise our girls right! Nothing *that* bad…"

It was a compliment, an insult, a reassurance, but whenever it was said in earshot of Ella, Susan-Eva, or very rarely even Ida, it was a question. "Nothing that bad happens here, right?" Because by all accounts, the worst thing that ever happened there happened to them, and they survived. So, how bad could it be? How very, unspeakably, unsavory, undeniably deliciously horrific was what happened in that basement with Ed and the other man. The one the media loved, reminding everyone could still be out there.

Ed's house was technically outside the city limits. It didn't really happen in Moss Groves. It was often noted in hushed voices that Ella and Susan-Eva weren't really Moss Grove's daughters. Beloved, to be sure! But the child of a never-married woman from up north and a… most of them weren't sure what to call Susan-Eva, but they knew her mom wasn't born here. Ida, there was no denying.

Ida could not be a sad story. She could be a tragedy. Had she died of childhood cancer or (God willing) been murdered at the peak of her beauty, Moss Groves could digest just fine. The murder of a beautiful daughter pulsing with potential they would've known how to relish, brand, and monetize. But someone touching a girl that prominent when she was *that* young—that wasn't as palatable.

If something like that happened to Ida now, it would cause a stir, a welcome reason to kill. Not as good as if she'd been raped and murdered. But if it were the right kind of violent, from the right kind of wrong outsider, there would be plenty of ways to skew it not only on-brand but toward a welcome bump in publicity.

Harm to outsiders from a 'legacy resident' didn't have the same impact. It was an annoyance. The questions Ella and Susan-Eva were being asked with, "Nothing that bad ever really happens in Moss Groves?" was, "You're not going to make any trouble, are you? You know how lucky you are, don't you? Even if something bad happened, it wasn't *that* bad, was it?" To share a horrific detail would be generous. To share a sad detail would be selfish.

Malcolm found the town's simultaneous obsession with appearance and tragedy hypocritical and small-minded. At least Susan-Eva had heard him say he did a million times. Yet somehow, he still couldn't resist those eight words. Not ironically. Not as a joke. Malcolm, with a note of irritation, told Calvin Moss Groves was a place where *nothing that bad happens.*

Even though Malcolm was one of only a handful of people who knew that this past January, a man battered and raped three women in Marshland Park within a four-hour period. Police told the victims that they had a lead, but due to details they couldn't discuss yet, speaking publicly about it could harm the investigation. Keeping it out of the press and the university crime stats took little effort. Two of the women were from out of town visiting for a women's basketball game. The third was Susan-Eva.

FOUR
August 18, 2022

Susan-Eva

"SO, HE'S A PROFESSOR? AND how long have they been dating?" Calvin asked, walking Susan-Eva through the nearly deserted Craw-Ma's Bar parking lot, where she worked.

"Adjunct Instructor, and on again, off again for years. They claim it started after she graduated and I claim not to know what she looks like when she's lying. We all have secrets," Susan-Eva said. Being back at the bar only a few hours before her next shift was almost unbearable. She took in all the empty spots that would soon be full of the same cars it was most nights and zeroed in on the spot near the back corner of the lot next to a dumpster.

The spot was the furthest walk from the entrance, and it always wreaked. Throughout her shift Susan-Eva would stare through the window at the nearly always empty space like it was a focus-point for balance in the dizzying dance of her night. Only one car ever pulled into that spot, a dark green 2012 dinged-up Range Rover. Susan-Eva half smiled, picturing it.

"Well, safe travels," she said, reaching her own car and barely looking at Calvin. He pulled out his phone.

He said, "What's your number? Next time I'm in town, I'd love to—"

"You're sweet, but I'm not really available for anything... extended."

40

"*Oh.* I didn't realize this was goodbye. Want to go for a walk first? Give me a town tour?"

"I would, but I have an appointment." Susan-Eva yanked her door shut before he could get out another word.

Ella

Florence University's quad was deliberately small, but the ancient Magnolia's around its permitter provided plenty of hiding places when necessary. Hordes of students buzzed around each other, full of first-day nerves. A quick kiss would have been a more than adequate pre-work goodbye for Malcolm most days. Before their lips even parted, Ella's body pulled away, hoping for a quick escape, but he pulled her back in by the hip. "Meet me for lunch."

"I can't, I have an Ida thing." She gave him another quick kiss. He gripped her hip tighter, almost groping, but you'd have to be staring to notice.

"Bail. You'll see her at the house later. My first lecture of the year always pisses someone off. I'll be in a fight with the dean by ten and need you to talk me out of quitting and moving back to Seattle by noon."

"I know you think it shouldn't be such a big deal, but when Ed's name pops up in the news it can be hard on them. We need to check in with each other," Ella said, pleading to the universe he couldn't tell she was lying. Not that what Ella said wasn't true in some contexts. Thinking about Ed was never fun, but they didn't have time to dwell on it. Getting to the bottom of Ida using emojis was number one on the worry list today. Childhood trauma would have to wait.

"Hey. Just because I think you have some co-dependency issues doesn't mean I'm brushing it off. Honestly, some of the case details this time around do match a copycat profile. I still think it's unlikely, but if what happened to Suz was connected, it worries me. Stay at my place for a few weeks. We could think of it like a test run for you moving in."

Ella said, "Let's try next week."

Malcolm tucked hair behind her ear and said, "You're not being weird about what we did this morning, are you? You know I'd never give you more than you could handle."

"I'm not being weird. I just have so much work. Four consults this week. How stupid do you have to be to send a dick pic to a co-worker in this climate," Ella said, knowing shifting the focus to someone else's bad behavior was a surefire way to get him to a new topic.

"These good ole boys. Disgusting. Your patience is saintly," he said, doing his best to sound engaged and supportive.

"And they're shocked to get suspended. Not even fired, but they're genuinely surprised that there are any repercussions." Malcolm shook his head. Then she tacked on a sarcastic, "It's a scary time to be a man in America," and his energy shifted.

He met her eyes and grinned. "I'm not scared." The hint he might be worried about being called out for anything was a call to prove he wasn't. Malcolm kissed Ella sliding his hand below her hip, a test. She passed by, rolling her eyes with a half-smile as he gave her one more look before finally going inside.

Ella looked around to see if any of her colleagues had witnessed the a-bit-too-much-for-their-workplace kiss and drop. No one was looking. Instead, Ella's attention went to a group of girls in white dresses: Phi Kappa's graduating class. They'd been freshmen when Ella was a senior. Her grand little, Lucy, spotted Ella. She squealed and ran over, ringing her arms around Ella's neck. Ella hated how good it made her feel.

She'd never have been a sorority girl if not for Ida. She couldn't stand most of them. Lucy was a great big acceptation. Those Machiavellian mother fuckers knew how to find the few girls she'd kill for and make them Greek family. As Ella squeezed Lucy back, she noticed a girl she hadn't met. A transfer with freckles. There was something about the expression on her face.

She looked scared.

FIVE
August 18, 2022

Joseph

AT TWENTY-EIGHT, JOSEPH PORTER was by far the youngest of the three therapists renting office space at 378 Cherry Lane. It made sense his office would be the smallest. An armchair would've better suited the space, but forgoing the cliché of a sofa was unbearable. He knew the exact one he wanted.

Chair breakthroughs were *probably* not any less meaningful than sofa ones. But when Joseph first sat on the navy blue four-seater at Macy's, he knew nothing else would do. The thing was so cushy that no matter how much anxiety a patient entered with, no matter how insurmountable their issues, when they sat down, their first thought would have to be, "Damn, that's comfortable. This guy clearly knows what he's doing." So, Joseph defied physics by wedging it between the office walls.

Most of the time, Joseph *did* know what he was doing. Not today. Today, his body betrayed him. After months of building trust, his patient, Aaron, finally talked about the things his uncle did before he died. Joseph knew the bullet points from day one, it was all in his file.

Most of his patients were court-mandated from juvenile detention centers in surrounding counties. Most of them had horrific stories. Joseph's dissertation was on therapy for incarcerated sexual predators. He'd centered his life around tragic, unthinkable, disturbing stories.

As an overly empathetic kid, the mere thought of anyone he knew in pain sent him into a panic. Now, he could digest nearly anything with no more reaction than a kind smile and nod of the head. But this boy, this kid, got to him.

The boy delivered the facts of the molestation with little emotion. Obviously, he'd been forced to talk about it before and suffered an array of damaging reactions. Joseph was ready to counter all of them. To be the first grown-up that let him experience anything and everything he needed to feel about it. Anger, tears, shame, Joseph was ready for, but the boy just stared out the window for the longest time. So long, Joseph turned to see if something was happening beyond the glass. Only his battered-up Range Rover was in view.

Finally, the boy said, "I wish—like, I wish he wasn't so cool, outside of that you know? Like he was so… he got it. Everyone keeps trying to make me say shit about how he hurt me. He did. But like that part is…" he gestured disgust. "Like, why do they all want to hear it? The hard part is he was nice. The hard part is that's like one percent of who he was and they make me say it was the whole thing. But for me, it's like, he's dead, and I'm glad the guy who did that gross shit is dead. But no one else in my family can sing. Not like we could. I wish I got to be sad. I wish I got to miss him."

Joseph said all the right things, but his voice cracked. Exactly when, he didn't remember but he knew the boy heard, there was a shift. Joseph had fucked up. At the most unforgivable moment, that kid who panicked at people's pain crept into Joseph's throat to say hello. It was the kind of failure that would keep him up all night. Worse, it was the kind of failure that shook his confidence for whoever was next.

"Carol! When is the next appointment?" He shouted toward the door. All three therapists shared Carol, the never-busy, always-overwhelmed receptionist.

After a long sigh and lots of shuffling, Carol said, "Ah… Let me see here. You got barely over thirty minutes." Joseph looked up, thanking the heavens, and went straight to his mini fridge. He needed to regroup. This was perfect, he'd be able to—

"30 minutes! Perfect! Plenty of time to squeeze me in!" Susan-Eva's voice pierced through his peace with such ease Joseph felt embarrassed for not expecting it. He hung his head and glared at the door.

"Wait! Miss Lorenzo, you don't have a—" said Carol as Susan-Eva burst through Joseph's door. Susan-Eva's eyes met Joseph's, and his gaze narrowed.

"No. Out," said Joseph, pointing at the door.

Susan-Eva put a hand to her head and collapsed on the couch, saying, "But Doctor, my hysteria is acting up again and only your magical vibrating machine will cure it." Joseph fought any hint of a smile so hard that he looked a little like he was seizing.

"I tried to stop her. Should I call the sheriff?" huffed Carol with too much enthusiasm.

"I'll take it from here, Carol," said Joseph, never relenting his glare. Carol trudged out but left the door open. Joseph shut it.

It shouldn't have made such a difference. The two had been in every sort of room together in every sort of public and every sort of private way. But it *did* make a difference. Still. With the click of the close, he gulped an exasperated inhale, and he couldn't help but notice the air in the room tasted familiar. It tasted like theirs.

Joseph crossed his arms and stared down at Susan-Eva.

"Dr. Joseph, you look so stern. Have you been practicing that?" Said Susan-Eva, exaggerating an intimidated tone.

"I can't do this today. I had a brutal session this morning and—"

"With who?" Susan-Eva met his eyes and bit her lip.

He glared harder and shook his head "*No*. And I'm visiting the prison tonight. This is supposed to be my 'me' time, to breathe, meditate, have a little breakfast."

"You can do all that with me here." Susan-Eva situated a pillow under her head and folded her hands on her stomach. "I had another one-night stand. Why do I keep doing that?"

"I'm happy to discuss that with you as a friend. On the phone, or at the bar or anywhere but here, where—"

45

"But I want your professional—"

"I'm not your therapist! I cannot be your therapist. For the millionth time I can refer—"

"I only want you Dr. Joseph."

"Stop calling me Dr. Joseph!"

"I can't!"

"You've called me Joey my whole life why can't you—"

"Because I'm too proud!" Susan-Eva met his eyes with such sudden earnestness he had to swallow to soothe the ache of it. "No one thought you would make it here and *look at you.*" Joseph gave up the glare and plopped next to her on the couch. Susan-Eva put her feet on his lap, and before his brain got any say in the matter, his muscle memory took over and he ran a hand down her calf.

"You can give me one session." She said it so casually like she'd suggested they could go to a movie, that Joseph had to force himself not to nod.

"There is no one who supports you talking to someone more than me. I think everyone should. Especially when they've been through the things you have. Let me refer—"

She shook her head. "The things I'd say are too crazy for anyone but you."

"You're not crazy, Evie." Joseph's confidence in the statement seemed to break her heart a little. Then again, nearly everything Joseph Porter said to Susan-Eva broke both their hearts a little.

"Don't *Yellow Wallpaper* me," she finally replied.

"*Yellow Wallpaper* you?" he asked. She sat up grateful for the ammunition.

"You don't know 'The Yellow Wallpaper?'" He shook his head. "You didn't have to read it in English? Or for any of your psych courses?" Again, he shook his head. "It's written by a woman, so I guess I shouldn't be surprised. Sexist." She nudged his thigh with her foot.

"Hey! I didn't write the curriculum." He grabbed her ankle. His grip sent a wave of goosebumps up her skin. "So, what is 'Yellow Wallpapering?'"

"It's sort of the opposite of gaslighting but also kind of the same thing.

It was this short story written in the early 1900s about a woman who's just had a baby and is depressed, but post-partum wasn't really acknowledged yet. So, everyone tells her she's fine and only needs rest. Her husband locks her in this room with yellow wallpaper. To make sure all she does is rest, he takes away the books and pens so she can't read or write. All she can do is stare at the pattern in the wallpaper. At first, it bothers her. Then she starts seeing things in it, a woman trapped inside. Then, lots of women trapped inside and she's one of them. Eventually, her husband finds her scratching all the paper off the wall with her nails and teeth."

"Jesus," said Joseph.

"We get accused of being crazy when we're not. Then, when we really are having a crisis, you think all we need to do is to rest and be quiet until it's too late. That's Yellow Wallpapering."

"Are you in crisis, Evie?"

"Maybe." She propped herself up and grinned. "But I can only tell you if we have doctor-patient confidentiality. Come on, it's not like we ever really, *really* dated so…"

Susan-Eva

It was true. At first, it was the age distance. Three years was nothing now, but when Joseph started dating at fifteen, she was twelve. He saw her as a little kid. She was devastated. When Joseph broke up with his high school girlfriend, Susan-Eva was sixteen and not only not a little kid but one of the most asked-out girls in town, including the college. She turned nearly everyone down, but at homecoming, the quarterback, Kyle Fisher, asked her out, and they were saying 'I love you' two weeks later. Joseph was devastated.

They didn't miss every window, nor did they always completely wait for one. The thing was, in the pockets of time when Susan-Eva wasn't living at Parlay house, she was living next door to Joseph's mom, Michelle Roberts. If you cut through the woods at Parlay House, you could get to Joseph's dad's house in ten minutes. In one way or another, they were always neighbors.

The real bond started with the night terrors. The screams carried right through the thin walls between their moms' houses. Even the first time, it didn't scare Susan-Eva, despite that she was only seven years old. She hopped out of bed, grabbed her Batman mask and tutu, and ran across the yard. Michelle was already at Joseph's bedside, calming him down, so Susan-Eva hid outside. When his mom was gone, Joseph began to whimper.

"Don't be afraid," Susan-Eva whispered. He wasn't. He knew her whisper. "The monster was real, but I was out patrolling, and I got him! If you let me in, I'll keep guard and protect you so you can sleep." Joseph pushed open his window and helped her in.

"It's important to me that you know, I know, you're not really Batman, Evie. I'm ten. I don't believe in little kid stuff," Joseph said, pulling a pillow and blanket from his bed for her.

"That's okay. I can protect you from big kid stuff, too." She curled up in his window seat, and they both fell asleep. Metaphorical dating windows don't matter so much when you've spent your life climbing in and out of each other's real ones. Even when Susan-Eva's parents were still around, Michelle was her second mom. Most people would have assumed Ida's mother, Trisha Montgomery, held that place in her heart, *funny.*

Michelle got off work first, so she'd watch Susan-Eva after school. Then Mrs. Lorenzo would repay the favor while Michelle took night classes. They spent so much time in and out of each other's houses that it felt more like the driveway between them was a hallway, creating one, still not that big, home. No matter who they dated or how old they got, when big bad monsters came for one of them, they slept over.

They never denied the attraction. They never even really denied being in love with each other. But they knew there was no real point to dating. If they decided to be together, it would become their forever in an instant. Then, one day, they did decide, on Susan-Eva's twenty-fourth birthday. Forever felt even better than they imagined.

Then Ida. Always, relentlessly, Ida. The situation with Joseph's father left him with a lot of trust issues, and he caught Susan-Eva in a lie about Ida. When he asked for the truth, she couldn't give it. He asked if she'd lied to him before. The look on her face gutted him. It was over. He said they couldn't even be friends; it would hurt too much. That lasted a week. They resumed talking on the phone nearly every night -as friends- and let it hurt.

But they didn't see each other much.

Susan-Eva took up jogging. Lush green trees and the smell of marsh felt like freedom. With each jog, her mind expanded with new visions of the future, of everything possible in this big, wonderful world.

Then, one beautiful January morning, alone on the trail, without any real reason, she decided she could tell Joseph about Ida. That maybe she could tell him things about Ida she'd never really been able to tell anyone, even Ella. She texted him to meet her for lunch. He immediately agreed.

For a few moments, she stood in the middle of the trail, staring at her phone, smiling. The idea of Joseph knowing the whole truth had terrified her her whole life. It would change everything. She could lose him, lose the way he looked at her. The thought was unbearable. But… it was possible he'd understand. It was possible telling him meant she could finally really have him.

Hope brought a lightness. She took a deep breath ready to sprint the rest of the trail. At that exact moment, when Susan-Eva felt she could fly, was when someone pushed her from behind. Her knee hit the ground so hard she swore she felt the pavement scrape her bone.

She'd return to that instant of pain over and over. Concrete grinding her bone to dust. Skin stinging and burning as it ripped and mangled rocks into flesh like a mosaic. Most of all, the confusion. Despite all of its agony, the sensations of that moment were all bearable because it was the last moment before she knew what was going to happen to her.

Everything she felt after that she tried to forget. Every time she fought thinking about it, the details grew more vivid. The colors of the dirt, the bugs, his breath, his smell, his everything. Everything but what he looked like. Whoever it was, made sure she didn't see him.

Later, Joseph would torture himself with all the ways he could have gotten there and stopped it. But in the fourteen minutes and twenty-three seconds the event took place, Joseph never crossed Susan-Eva's mind once. She wouldn't let him near anything this ugly. On the trail where her imagination had once been unlimited, it now conjured only one thought:

Ida.

She wished Ida would show up. No other thought in her life had ever made her feel more unlike herself. Thinking of Ida always conjured an array of emotions: trepidation, fear, annoyance, excitement, but never comfort. Until that day. Just knowing Ida existed was suddenly, horrifyingly, illogically, comforting.

Joseph's was the first face she saw in the hospital. Through a foggy haze of sedatives, she opened her eyes to him sitting in the window, keeping watch for monsters. From the hall, she could hear Ella fighting with Trisha Montgomery, trying to keep her from coming in. Someone had brought flowers. White lilies. Probably Trisha. Susan-Eva imagined Trisha carefully considering the most appropriate flowers to buy for someone during a rape kit, as though any physical thing could make her feel better.

But then she spotted something that somehow did make her feel a little better. A cute stuffed squirrel with a bow at the edge of the bed. Something about its placement reminded her of how a cat brings a mouse it's killed to your doorstep. No card. Susan-Eva didn't need one. She knew it was from Ida.

At that moment, she knew she'd never be able to tell Joseph the whole truth, so they were never going to get to be together. The secrets she could explain, but how she felt about them... How could she explain something she didn't even understand?

Almost a year later, as Susan-Eva sat in Joseph's office playfully batting her eyes, he couldn't help but look at the scar on her knee. She still didn't want to tell him everything, but she really did want him to give her a session. Mostly to see what he was like as a therapist so she could revel in pride. "Come on. One time. Since we never really dated, it wouldn't be that unethical."

Joseph sighed and said, "When you were five, you proposed to me under the monkey bars, and I said yes. Technically, we've been engaged for twenty years. Unethical doesn't begin to cover it." Carol swung open the door and huffed at the sight of the two on the couch.

"The prison's calling asking which inmates you're seeing today," said Carol. Joseph nodded and got up.

"What was the reading this week?" asked Susan-Eva as Carol shook her head and walked away. Joseph grabbed a book from his shelf and handed it to her.

"It's about impulse control," he said as she looked it over.

"Do you think it helped?"

Joseph gave a pensive shrug, "I don't know yet. Maybe." Susan-Eva watched him clench and release his fist like he was squeezing a stress ball. He always did that when he was debating whether or not to bring something up.

Finally, he said, "I heard they identified that little girl's remains. Of course, people are running wild with copycat theories and bringing up Ed. I even heard people wondering if Scott Ryan's disappearance might be linked, which is crazy. Anyway, I'm sorry. I know it's always really hard when Ed comes up in the press. I hate that for you."

"It's fine. It happens anytime a kid turns up dead in the state. I'm used to it."

"I know. But it's the first time you've had to hear rumors like that after what happened in the park. I never bought the theory that, that day had anything to do with what happened when we were kids, but if you felt freaked out—"

"I don't," Susan-Eva said, not looking at him.

"Okay. I was going to say you don't have to have a one-night stand to avoid sleeping alone. Not that that's the reason or that you need a reason. I'm just saying if you ever…"

Susan-Eva knew better than to worry about a copycat killer. So, taking Joseph up on the offer would be a lie. She'd lied to him enough for one lifetime. Desperate to leave on a different note, she looked at the book in his hand and asked, "Can I borrow it?"

"Always," He said, handing her the book. "You know, for me, the answer is always, always. If you could tell me why—" Before Joseph could finish, Susan-Eva's phone binged with a text. It was Ida.

"I have to go."

SIX
Easter Sunday sixteen years ago - April 16, 2006

Ella

COLORING AN EASTER EGG WAS something Ella had done before. Coloring a picture of the crucifixion was not. Yet there it was, right in the middle of the Sunday school coloring book. It felt like a test. Kids who grew up going to Sunday school, which Ella hadn't, would know if this was a crayons or markers situation.

She went with markers, thinking it would show confidence. Then she made a mistake. At home, Ella would immediately throw away an imperfect drawing. Like most things, her mother taught her how to draw through math. Perspective wasn't just a neat idea, it was a calculation. Ella loved that. She loved that drawing was both a normal thing she could do with other kids and something she could get right.

Crinkling up a picture of Jesus felt wrong. But so did the enormous accidental pink blotch over his head that made him look like he had a neon halo. Actually, it looked sort of cool, but Ella got the feeling that wasn't the goal. Maybe she could hide it? Mostly, she wished she could go home, but being there was important to her mom.

While Ella's mom disagreed with many cultural aspects of their new home, she knew how important socializing was for Ella's future in the community. Ms. Kyle wanted her daughter to have a reputation outside of her own so that she would have support if things ever got dark again. Getting dark was what they called the times Ella's mom couldn't quite remember. When they were both invited to Easter Sunday at the same church many of her colleagues attended, it felt like a small token of acceptance. So, she didn't mention they weren't religious.

"Act like all the other kids. Fitting in matters, Ella. For both of us." Her mom said. Ella was trying, but the big pink halo over Jesus's head was like a bullseye. Just as she decided to crumple it, the girl next to her saw. It wasn't such a big deal at first. The girl asked why she gave Jesus a pink hat. Then another kid thought it was a joke and told the Sunday School teacher. Ella tried to explain that it was an accident, but the teacher didn't believe her. As she answered questions, things escalated.

So, Ella did one of her favorite things. She disappeared. Slipping out the door when no one was looking. The halls were quiet. She wandered around until she was close enough to the chapel to hear the congregation singing a song:

"Have you been to Jesus for the cleansing power? Are you washed in the blood of the Lamb?"

So much blood talk. Thanking the blood and, drinking the blood and washing in the blood. Ella had never been publicly executed for the sins of all humanity and then resurrected. She was pretty sure, though, that if she had, she still wouldn't want people bathing in her blood, even metaphorically.

When she informed a fellow Sunday school student of this, they informed her she was going to hell. For blasphemy and because her mom was never married to her dad and because she was too tall for her age. At nine years old, this was not the first time Ella had been told she'd eventually spend all eternity tormented in a pit of fire. But today, she had to hear it while wearing tights. Itchy white tights that never stayed pulled up enough.

"Are you fully trusting in His grace this hour?
Are you washed in the blood of the Lamb?"

Could she really be the only one who thought there was something odd about dressing up in pastel flower dresses and eating chocolate bunnies while singing about washing in blood? If this was really what God wanted, Ella was fine with it; she just wondered if it was.

Like the Birthday song! Lots of people hated it. Ella hated it. What if Jesus didn't like everyone singing about his blood but tolerated it because smiting someone over gospel music might send mixed messages? So, Ella did what she thought everyone was there to do. She prayed. "Jesus, really, what do you think of this song?" Right then, someone burst, no, exploded through the chapel doors.

It was the hair Ella saw first. Red. Everywhere. Lashing and jerking through space as though every molecule it contacted was trying to cage it. Ella had never seen anything so resistant. She didn't know resistance at that level was possible. She'd seen tantrums, but this was something more. Whoever this was, she didn't look like a bad little girl. She looked like weather.

And the weather had a mother.

Every woman Ella saw at Calvary Southern Baptist that morning looked ripped out of a catalog. Whoever *this* woman was, she looked ripped out of time. Like she was actually a fifties movie star flung into 2006 by mistake. The hymn grew louder as though it was taunting the mother. One wave of her perfect hair fell out of place while she tried to subdue the girl.

"Are you washed in the blood? In the soul cleansing blood of the Lamb? Are your garments spotless, are they white as snow? Are you washed in the blood of the Lamb?"

Spit projected through the spastic frenzy of hair and onto the mother's blush pink dress. The mother slapped what must have been the girl's face, but Ella still hadn't seen it. This moment was not supposed to be witnessed by anyone. Ella knew that, yet she couldn't look away.

It wasn't the drama. It was the movement. Ella wanted to know exactly what it felt like to move like that. If the flailing girl really had been a tornado, Ella would have let it suck her away and rip her to shreds just for a few seconds of knowing what it felt like to exist in space without caution.

Finally, the mother opened a closet and shoved the weather inside. For a heartbeat, Ella's eyes flooded with emotion, worried she'd never see it again. Then pounding and screaming erupted. The mother leaned to the closet and spoke through her teeth, "If you keep acting like this, this is exactly what will happen. They will lock you up forever. If anyone ever sees what you've done

54

to the animals or those drawings—"

"Ella! Where did you go?" Susan-Eva shouted as she rounded the corner. Ella froze. The mother whipped her head towards her as Susan-Eva ran to her side.

"What are you girls doing here? You should be in Sunday school with the other children." The mother asked. Her beauty was unsettling.

Susan-Eva stood tall and said, "They were being mean. They told Ella she was going to hell because of her mom. Those kids are stupid. You're Mrs. Trisha! Aren't you? My mom cleans your house. You're under-utilizing the natural light in your living room." Trisha squinted, trying to make sense of Susan-Eva, then gave up and focused on Ella.

"I'm sorry. I needed a minute so I wouldn't look upset," Ella said. Trisha studied both girls with diligence. Something in her eyes made them both feel Trisha was allowed to punish them, even if their own mothers said she wasn't. Trisha's shoulders relaxed so far down her back that it made her look like she was allowed to punish everyone.

Nervous fidgeting made Ella feel childish, something she strived never to be as soon as she learned what the word meant. Later, Ella's mother would tell her she was right, and Trisha was allowed to do whatever she wanted. The girls attempted to escape; they barely made it a step.

"Wait, girls. Come here." They hesitated, wondering if they could run. Trisha gave them a soft smile, too soft like it was advertising a thread count. "It's okay. You're not in trouble. I only want to look at you." Trisha motioned them toward her, curling her finger. They slowly obeyed.

Trisha kneeled down and swept a hair from Ella's face as she carefully studied her calm expression. The composure was even more impressive, given how nervous Trisha's presence made Ella. Trisha sweetly grabbed Ella's tiny trembling hand and met her steady eyes. Trisha said, "This is what you look like when someone tells you you're going to hell? That must have been so scary. Didn't you want to scream or cry?"

"People say mean things to us all the time. We're not supposed to let it bother us," said Ella. Trisha salivated.

"You and your mama are new to town?" Ella nodded. "What about your Daddy? Where is he?" Ella looked down and swallowed, unsure what

55

she was supposed to say. Trisha's smile turned to silk. "Moss Groves can be a wonderful place. It has everything you'll ever need if you know the right people. But you girls know how hard it is to make friends when you're a little different. My little girl, Ida, is a little different too. I wonder if you could teach her to act calmly like you. If you do, I know I could make this town so friendly for you."

Ella and Susan-Eva looked at each other. Pounds and screams permeated from the closet, Ella shrugged and stepped toward it.

SEVEN
August 18, 2022

Ella

IDA WAS ALREADY INSIDE. THE Cheshire Cat Antiques and Vintage parking lot was empty except for five cars. Ida's auburn convertible wasn't one of them, but Ella could feel her. In the sixteen years since Ella first met Ida, she'd never failed to predict her presence despite Ida nearly always hiding from view when they first arrived.

The HR office was slower than she expected that morning. The dick pic senders both took jobs elsewhere, hoping to start over at a place where no one had seen their dicks yet and could appreciate their photographic skills with fresh eyes. No longer having to do a one-on-one critique of Tod from Admission's Scrotum or Peter from Advertising's Peter meant Ella could work remotely after lunch. After Ida's text, she decided she might need some privacy to deal with whatever went down.

The rhythmic clicks of Susan-Eva's sandals on the pavement announced her arrival just before her hand slipped into Ella's and squeezed it. They both took a deep breath. A flyer with prayer hands, a photo of Scott Ryan in his lacrosse uniform, and the date and time of the vigil were taped to the widow. They both pretended not to notice it as Ella shoved open the door. A bell dinged.

"I'll be out round back. Holler if y'all need anything, ya' hear?" Mr. Carter, the shop owner, told Ella and Susan-Eva as he helped two old ladies carry a small coffee table out the back door. They couldn't see anyone else in the store.

"Maybe she's late," said Susan-Eva, as an almost joke.

"She's never late." Ella searched every piece of furniture large enough to hide a body. Every rack of clothing. She even scanned the ceiling. It was best never to rule out feats of physics when it came to Ida. The ceiling was clear.

All that was left were three makeshift dressing rooms with curtains for walls in the back corner. Freaking curtains. Always hiding something. Behind the first curtain was a red tutu hung on the mirror. "She's messing with us," said Ella.

"You always do this," Susan-Eva said, putting on a tiara and posing for herself.

"Do what?" asked Ella. The second dressing room had a schoolgirl uniform piled on the floor.

"You get pissed at her before she's done anything," said Susan-Eva. Then she started shopping from the wall of masks hanging from racks in the back. They ranged from comical animal heads to vintage Madi Gras masks with triple-digit price tags.

Ella ripped open the last dressing room curtain, revealing nothing but a single fur coat. An elaborate mask with hand-sewn beading called to Susan-Eva, but she wanted to lighten the mood, so she reached for a giant rubber lizard head instead. It stuck to the rack like it was hooked on something. Susan-Eva tugged harder, and then something released it. Susan-Eva stumbled back, screaming.

They saw it in flashes. Pupil-less black eyes. Blood drizzling from the mouth like water in a decorative fountain. Shrieking so loud, the sting of it hit before the sound. Ella's body jerked and tensed with annoyance as she yelled, "GODDAMN IT!" *So much for not cursing.* Fuck. New rule. Ella could curse while she was having the shit scared out of her.

The rack of masks had wheels. Rookie mistake, Ella thought. Wheels! Always search for wheels. The fucking curtains distracted her. Ida pushed the rack of masks she hid behind aside, laughing hysterically as she wiped fake blood from her mouth. She tried to hug Ella. Ella shoved her off, but not before Ida grazed her nose to Ella's cheek and paused by the pulse point at the neck to inhale her. Their eyes met for a half-second as Ella glared, seething, and pulled away.

"Not funny, Ida!" said Susan-Eva, holding her heart and catching her breath.

"Oh, come on! Hashtag tradition. I had to. It's the last year," said Ida as she pulled out her black contacts.

"Why are you using hashtags?" asked Ella, exasperated.

"What do you mean 'the last year?'" Asked Susan-Eva, still catching her breath.

Ida squinted, confused, then asked, "Didn't you guys get my text?" She cocked her head at Ella, then leaned in and sniffed her hair. "You smell weird. Did you have sex this morning?"

Ella pulled back and said, "Ida cut the shit! We know you're up to something. We all decided getting trendy with communication isn't ideal for you. Colloquialisms and ideograms have cultural and emotional nuances that you struggle to—"

Ida scrunched her face, mimicking Ella, *"Colloquialisms have cultural and emotional nuances,* UGHHH! Does Malcolm's dick instantly…" Ida stuck her finger up and curled it down "… when you start talking? Hashtag." Ella and Susan-Eva waited for her to finish, but Ida just blinked at them.

"Hashtag what? It's not punctuation. This is what I'm saying!" Ella groaned.

"Hey, let's all calm down," Susan-Eva said, stepping between them.

Ida's mouth curved to that high-thread-count smile she inherited from her mother. She grabbed Susan-Eva's hand and swung it, looking her up and down. Ida said, "You look so pretty, babe."

"Aw. You look so pretty, babe!" replied Susan-Eva, matching Ida's voice exactly. Then she wiped fake blood from Ida's chin. Most of Ida's language choices came from the TV characters she studied when they were kids, but her Ida-isms were never completely gone.

Ida turned to Ella and said, "Why can't you be nice like Susie Evie?

You're so much prettier when you're not being an ugly cunt."

"WHY THE FUCK ARE YOU USING HASHTAGS AND EMJOIS?" As Ella started to yell, Mr. Carter returned through the back door.

Pointing his finger at Ella he said, "Hey! Now I love a good old-fashioned 'gotcha' as much as the next fellow, and I am happy to help y'all with your little pranks. You girls deserve to have fun, but I won't tolerate that sort of language in here." A week straight of polite G-rated language, and this was the moment he walked in. At least it was just Mr. Carter. Fuck Mr. Carter. Ella wondered if they'd ever outgrow being 'you girls.' Maybe in five years when they were all 30, but probably not.

"I'm so sorry for her. That Yankee boyfriend is ruining her mouth. You should call her Mamma." Ida never missed a chance to amp up the south in her accent once she learned its effect on older locals.

"Sorry, Mr. Carter, strange morning," said Ella, but Mr. Carter's eyes never left Ida.

"Tell your Daddy I said hello now." The trio nodded and smiled, waiting for Mr. Carter to walk back out of earshot.

Ida whispered to Ella, "What if he really does call your mom? Do you think she'll wash your mouth out like she used to?" Ella glared.

Susan-Eva said, "Ida, what's going on? Please, we know something is up."

"Oh my god! Pay attention, dummies! I already told you in the text," answered Ida.

"All the text said was to meet you here and:" Ella pulled out her phone to read, "Kick it up. I'm dying! #tradition- Then random emojis."

Ida held up her phone and said, "Um, no. Not random. Skull for I'm dying, heart for I love you, food-related penis for obvi, and funeral candles."

"It's a menorah," said Ella. Ida stared blankly, not getting her point. "Like for Hanukkah."

Ida said, "Yeah, special candles. Hanukkah is special, and funerals are special, so…"

"No," Ella said.

"Ida, why are you talking about funerals?" asked Susan-Eva, centering them again. Ida rolled her eyes and went to the leather purse she'd had custom-designed for her twenty-first birthday; *they even let her pick the cow*.

A fake snake, Ella thought, or vodka, or a real snake. No matter what Ida was about to show them, Ella was ready. Nothing else would get to her today. But all Ida pulled from her purse was a folder. She handed it to Susan-Eva with the same annoyed energy as she would gum or water, anything boring. So, the thing inside didn't make any sense. A brain scan with a large tumor circled. A patient diagnoses report with lots of words Ella didn't understand, but two she did. Malignant. Terminal.

Unwelcome water came to Susan-Eva's eyes. No emotion other than confusion moved Ella. It was a prank. It had to be a prank. Except Ida hated paperwork. An elaborate, conspiratorial, overly official prank that in no way fit Ida's MO. Ella wouldn't buy it. It was impossible.

The whole promise of the girl in the closet was that she couldn't get hurt. It was okay that she was bad. It was okay that she was maybe a monster, even. No pain she inflicted took away the one thing that made her worth it. She was invincible. The girl in the closet was supposed to be invincible. That's the only reason Ella opened the door.

EIGHT

Easter Sunday sixteen years ago - April 16, 2006

Susan-Eva and Ella

"IDA, THERE ARE TWO LITTLE girls out here who want to be friends with you, but you have to stop screaming before they come in," Trisha said. Ida unleashed her loudest shriek yet. Ella and Susan-Eva both jumped back. Trisha ran a hand over her face, then waved a hand at the girls, permitting them to run, but they stayed.

Okay! Both girls knew whatever was in that closet was not normal. *Maybe* even unnatural. Now -that- was intriguing to Susan-Eva because maybe it meant it was *supernatural*. Two weeks ago, Joseph's mom let Susan-Eva rent all seven seasons of BUFFY THE VAMPIRE SLAYER from Netflix in the mail. Buffy was cooler than Batman. Even Joseph agreed (when no other boys were around). Buffy dealt with all sorts of things way worse than a little girl's tantrum. So, Susan-Eva was determined not to chicken out.

The slaps against the door turned to heavy thuds. Whatever it was in the closet must have found something to throw. No amount of determination kept the sounds from being scary, but Susan-Eva's mom said, "Brave isn't about not being afraid, it's about not being frozen. Brave is in your heat, Evie. Never let anyone freeze you."

Screaming made Susan-Eva's throat hot, and tears made her face hot.

Roller Coasters, graveyards, and punishments for sneaking into graveyards were all things that made her cry and yell, but they were worth it. Susan-Eva knew how to do all sorts of things she was scared of, even if she screamed and cried the whole time.

Ella's mom said, "Fear is about weakness. Whether or not you feel it is irrelevant, you just have to make sure you never show it." So, Ella knew how to be scared and not let anyone see. Throughout the hour with her grandfather's corpse, after the beep of the heart monitor finally stopped, she was quiet. The week Ella's mom wouldn't get out of bed, and the electricity went out, she was quiet.

They didn't have a flashlight. Ella had to go to the basement alone and find the breaker switch, dragging her hand around the permitter of the damp wall. She heard something down there with her. A mouse? A squirrel? A cat? A person… no. It couldn't have been a person, but it was alive, moving. Each noise it made sounded bigger and closer, but she never screamed. No matter how hard her mother scrubbed her tongue with soap whenever a hint of accent colored her speech (She was supposed to learn how to fit in, not become them), Ella took it without a peep. Sometimes, she cried, but never with noise.

Today, Ella wasn't hiding fear; she simply didn't have it. The noises from the closet sounded so much more animal than human and so much bigger than the small body she watched Mrs. Montgomery shove inside. What sort of other things could a mouth that made sounds like that do? Could it smile? Could it sing? Could it whisper?

That was it! Ella thought. Whisper. When her mom was in the dark place, whispers sometimes brought her out. Ella knelt down and peered under the crack in the closet. She lowered her voice, but not all the way yet, "I have a *really bad* secret. I'll tell you, but it's so bad I can only whisper it. You won't be able to hear unless you quit screaming, so your mom lets us open the door."

One eye popped into the dark gap under the door. It blinked, making out as much of Ella as it could. "I bet it's not *really* bad." The voice was suddenly so much smaller that it seemed impossible it could have produced

63

such enormous sounds only seconds before.

Ella said, "I bet you're scared because you don't have any secrets to tell us, so we won't want to play with you." The eye stared at Ella. Ella stared back, not letting a hint of need show until the eye disappeared. Her heart fell. Then, after a few seconds...

Ida said, "I'll be quiet, mommy." The voice was even smaller than before. An audible sigh of relief escaped Trisha. Ella turned to Trisha, waiting for permission. Trisha nodded. There was a tremble in Ella's hand as she reached for the knob. Later, she'd tell herself over and over it was fear. But the truth of what sent the vibrations scared her more than Ida ever could. Pure, unrelenting excitement.

If Ida had the face of a wolf or some otherworldly creature, Ella would have been disappointed. So when she opened the door and saw it really was just a little girl inside, she had to fight to hide her awe.

Ida was small for her age. Her tiny knuckles were bloody from pounding. Though even the blood you could dismiss as the result of a particularly violent tantrum. Her behavior was extreme but not necessarily curious. She wasn't so different from any other errant child except for the eyes. The chaos of every other aspect of her appearance swarmed around the startling blank pierce of her eyes.

Trisha

Trisha held her breath, half expecting Ida to lunge at the little girl standing in the closet doorway. But Ida, didn't move, she peered up and said to Ella, "Well, are you going to tell me your stupid secrets or what? Because if they're not actually that bad, then I don't—" Before Ida could finish, Ella smiled, knelt to her ear, and whispered something that twitched Ida's mouth into a reluctant grin. Susan-Eva followed. Her whispers produced a sound Trisha had never heard her daughter make before: giggles.

Every ugly problem in Trisha's life prior to Ida's birth had a purchasable disguise that was so efficient and discreet that to the outside world, it appeared all her problems were pretty. For the deer eating her garden, she had her husband's silent sniper rifle and excellent aim. For her husband's mistresses, she had gag orders and blackmail. For Ida, she'd tried Ritalin, she'd tried spanking, she'd tried Xanax, she'd tried God. Two whispering girls were the only thing she'd ever seen work. There was finally a cure she could own.

NINE

August 18, 2022

Ella

"WHAT ABOUT CHEMO?" SUSAN-EVA asked, crying into a coffee mug.

"Yeah, they said that could buy me a few months. But my hair looks so good right now, and the best part about dying young is still being hot, so... I'm thinking just pain management, which they have a lot of options for now. I could feel fine for months." Ida shoved a slice of bacon into her mouth and ripped it in half with her teeth.

Typically, they wouldn't eat in public when Ida was this hungry, but Ella didn't want to go back to the house. Talking in private was something they'd do if this was a real tumor, not a prank tumor like Ella knew it was. So, they went to Butcher's Café near campus.

Every dish on the menu incorporated bacon in some way, even the ice cream. Before two every table got a free plate of greasy thick cut slices. It was very popular on weekends. Lines for breakfast stretched around the corner, but by noon they were slow. Ella read over the diagnosis for the seventh time. It looked so official.

"Does Parker know?" Ella asked.

"Oh God, Parker..." Susan-Eva said, crying harder.

"Oh shit. I forgot I have to tell Parker. Can you tell him?" Ida swirled

66

bacon around her finger like gum and bit it off.

"Can I tell your fiancée you're dying?" Ella squinted at Ida, certain this part of the story would falter and she'd finally confess.

"Yeah, 'cause he's going to cry, and like with Susie, I can do the face because she's so pretty." Ida forced an over-exaggerated sympathetic face and understanding nod at Susan-Eva, then completely dropped it, turning back to Ella. "But with ugly criers, it's so hard, and Parker is *the ugliest crier*. It's hilarious. Not laughing at his mom's funeral was brutal." Ida chuckled and licked the grease off her finger, then suddenly grabbed Ella's hand before she bothered to wipe off the saliva. "Oh! I meant to tell you I pulled off a sentimental well-up at brunch. You'd be so proud. I looked just like her." Ida nodded to Susan-Eva's teary eyes.

"So, you're fine with this?" Ella said, more as an accusation than a question.

Ida squinted like she was thinking, then said, "Not exactly, but I know I'm favored by God, so my afterlife situation is all set. He probably just didn't want me to have to age. You know?"

"Right," Susan-Eva said, still processing shock. They'd heard that explanation for many things over the years. It all sounded insane, but not for Ida. Ella couldn't poke one emotional or psychological hole in her reaction.

A careful small smile formed on Ida's lips as she looked down at her hands. They knew this face. Ida wanted to break a rule. "The doctor said I should use this time to travel or do things I've always wanted. So, don't freak out, *but I was thinking...*"

"No. Absolutely not," said Ella. There it was, she knew it.

"Oh my god! It's like you don't even care that I'm dying," said Ida.

Susan-Eva calmly said, "Ida, you know that's not true."

"Then why are you denying me my dying wish? And I have done SO, so many nice things for you two. Ella! I took you to Beyonce for your birthday and I don't even like her."

"We've talked about that being one of those things you don't say out loud. It gives you away," said Ella.

Susan-Eva shot a look at Ella. "Now's maybe not the time—"

"AND! And! For Christmas, Susan-Eva, I sat through *Star Wars* with you even though you know I hate space. And all I have ever wanted, AT ALL, is to eat a couple of people while they're still alive. And you've never let me do it. Even once. Not on my birthday. Not on Christmas. Not even on Hanukkah."

"YOU'RE NOT JEWISH!" Ella yelled. The few other patrons turned from their tables, hearing the yelling. Ella shrugged, and they went back to their coffee and greasy bacon plates.

Susan-Eva took Ida's hands. "What she means is: Ida, we love you, and we are so sorry that this is happening to you, but you asked us to always help you make decisions about things where your... *lack of emotional capacity* might make people..."

"Realize you're a psychopath!" said Ella.

"Yeah. So, I wouldn't get locked up and ruin my life, but now I'm dying. So, math." Ida squinted at Ella not seeing how she could possibly dispute this flawless logic.

Ella blinked at Ida, then almost petulantly said, "We're not letting you eat someone!"

Ida shrugged, annoyed, and put the scan back into her purse. "Look, I have church group in two hours, and I'm on the decorating committee for the auction. Which will be *amazing* by the way. All I'm asking is that you think about it and realize now that I'm dying, I might do what I want anyway. I mean, *I really want your support,* but life's too short. YOLO. Right?"

Ella's annoyance shifted to panic, "Wait, what? That's not the deal."

All gentility left Susan-Eva's voice; she dropped to a lower register. "Yeah, Ida, you promised you'd always let us choose if something was right or wrong, and this is very, very wrong."

Ida shook her head and stood swinging her purse over her shoulder. "Facing death has brought me a lot of clarity. I realize nobody knows what's right and wrong in every situation. But I do know two things for certain: I am showered in God's light and love, and I want to eat a person alive. Figure out if you're on board." Ida blew kisses and with her signature sign-off: "Nom-nom. Yum-yum. So fun. Bye!" twirled out the door and out of sight.

The waitress came to the table and refilled their water. Ella and Susan-

Eva stared at the swinging door, trying to close their mouths. The waitress reached between them and grabbed the bacon plate, but she paused, hovering it in front of them. There was half a slice left. "Y'all want that last bite?"

TEN
Sixteen years ago - October 27, 2006

Susan-Eva

IT WAS PROBABLY JUST THE excitement, Susan-Eva thought as she lay in her twin bed trying so hard to fall asleep. Tomorrow for the first time ever, Ida and Ella were staying at HER house. All week long. Tuesday was Halloween, and they all would be witches. And not lame generic store-bought costume witches but specially designed, made from scratch costume witches.

Her mom had been working on the skirts for weeks, collecting and sewing on different beads and trinkets from all over the place. Susan-Eva would be shocked, SHOCKED, if they didn't get real-life magic powers when they finally got to dress up. Yeah, she was really very excited, and that's probably why she had this weird, heart-pounding feeling like someone was outside her window.

Any other night, she'd open it up and check. That's what a brave superhero would do. But her mom already caught her three times reading and playing when she wasn't supposed to, and said that if she had to open the door one more time, the sleepover was canceled. No way she was risking that. So, Susan-Eva told herself the sound of something moving outside was Joey's cat.

Ugh! But she was not thinking about Joey because she hated him now. He was not her friend anymore, and she wasn't even going to think about why. Who cares? How many more other friends did she have? Practically millions! It didn't bother her one bit. She barely even noticed that his bedroom light was off all day, which meant he was staying at his dad's house. Before, when they were friends, she'd worry about him when he visited his dad because his dad didn't know how to be nice about the night terrors. Now, she didn't have to think about him at all.

Nope. Not at all. Too bad Ella and Ida weren't there tonight; that would make not thinking about her non-friend much easier. It would make ignoring the noise outside easier, too. Joey's cat usually stayed inside at night. Not always, though. It could be the cat. It sounded like a footstep, not a paw step, but sometimes imagination takes something small and makes it bigger.

There was a creak, too, like something leaning against the wood. But it had been a busy day, so her eyelids got heavy anyway. She had been to cheer practice and tap. Then she had to do WAY too much homework. Her mom made her get the whole weekend's worth done before she could plan activities for the sleepover. After homework, they went grocery shopping, where she got to pick out trick-or-treat candy and she got to see her cool friend, Ed.

Maybe this weekend would be when Susan-Eva finally told Ella about Ed. She wasn't sure why she hadn't. They both had to keep practically a million secrets about Ida from everyone else. So, Susan-Eva and Ella agreed they would never keep secrets from each other. Mrs. Montgomery told them if she ever found out they said Ida acted badly, then both of their moms would get fired.

Ida always acted badly, but she was getting better. Like the vampire Spike in BUFFY! When Ida was good, Mrs. Montgomery gave them all kinds of presents. She didn't have to, though. They would be friends with Ida anyway because she needed their help.

It felt special to be the only people, including grown-ups, who could show Ida how to act. Usually, they eventually had a pretty fun time with each other. It was only when Ida wanted to talk about stuff that made Susan-Eva's stomach flip upside down that she didn't like playing with Ida. Like when she'd described how they cleaned dead animal carcasses at her family's hunting lodge. It was also not so fun when Ida would hide and jump out screaming. The last time Ida did that, Susan-Eva fell and skinned her knee, so Ella made Ida promise never again.

Once or twice in the beginning, they wondered if they should tell their own moms the whole truth about Ida. They decided against it. The whole truth was pretty hard to explain. It didn't happen all at the same time. It wasn't like when you are learning a backflip and you try and try, then suddenly BAM! Your body knows what to do from here on out. They had to learn Ida in pieces. Each piece helped solve a puzzle. When you looked at the pieces individually, though, it was like they all had a whole other puzzle inside them.

The first piece was easy enough. When Ida got bored, she had tantrums. So, don't let Ida get bored. It seemed simple enough. They knew way better now. Nearly everything was boring to Ida, so keeping her entertained was very complicated. The most important thing was thrill. Susan-Eva loved that about Ida because she loved thrill too. Ida was the best buddy for roller coasters, the highest high big kid diving boards, and even watching movies they weren't supposed to. Ella would do all that, too, but she didn't love it like Ida.

It was Ida's reactions to those movies they weren't supposed to watch when Susan-Eva started to feel just how different Ida was. It wasn't the blood. Plenty of boys she knew liked scenes in war movies where heads got blown off. She had babysitters who loved slasher movies, and even if they screamed, they seemed to be smiling, too. The way violent scenes made Ida calm and focused was a little weird, but that she liked them was only weird because she was a little girl. So Susan-Eva was having none of that! If boys were allowed to like bloody gross stuff, so was Ida.

It was the sad scenes and some of the funny ones that gave her away. If they were in a movie theater and people started crying, Ida would stare at their faces like she was confused. She laughed when someone got tricked in a movie or was scared, but she never laughed at jokes, at least not until she heard everyone else laughing. Susan-Eva felt bad for Ida because she got so confused, and maybe that made her feel stupid even though she wasn't.

The longer she spent around her the more Susan-Eva wondered if different people get different amounts of feeling in different places. Sometimes, Susan-Eva's mom said that Susan-Eva was special because her emotions were so big that she could understand what everyone was feeling. It was tough because it meant when she was down, she was way, way down. But it meant that a lot of the time, she was extra happy, too. If Susan-Eva couldn't help that she had too many feelings, then Ida couldn't help that she didn't have enough. It made them good puzzle pieces, she thought. No matter what, Ida was always an adventure, and it was nice to have an adventure to focus on when you're feeling sad.

The heavier Susan-Eva's eyes got, the easier it was to admit that what Joey said made her really sad. Talking to Ed at the grocery store made her feel so much better. He was so funny, and he didn't think she was too young to be friends with, even though he was way older than Joey. That's why she had to keep some of their talks secret.

Because he treated her like an older kid, maybe even like a teenager. So, it was a good idea not to tell her mom or a teacher everything they talked about. Not because they were doing anything wrong but because they may not understand. Ella would probably understand, though. Of anyone, she would get it. More than any kid Susan-Eva had ever met, Ella hated being treated like she was little. Ed would make perfect sense to her. Wouldn't he?

But for some reason every time Susan-Eva started to tell Ella about Ed, she stopped herself. Maybe it was just nice to have her very own secret. Now, her eyes were heavy enough to stay closed, and her thoughts got fuzzier. Whoa. It turned out she was right; the costumes her mom made were magic, and now she was flying around the whole town on her broom. For a second, she could tell she was dreaming, but it was the coolest dream, so she didn't let herself wake up. It was weird, though. Nothing in the dream would make a sound like a camera flash. But she kept hearing it. Click, flash, click, flash, footsteps.

August 18, 2022

Susan-Eva

Ella and Susan-Eva walked through the Butcher's Café parking lot in a dazed shock. "We have to call her mom," said Susan-Eva.

"Yeah, because Trisha's always such a big help," Ella said with as much sarcasm as she could muster. She noticed a streak of mascara on Susan-Eva's cheek. "Why did you cry?"

"Look, I know she's Ida, but she's still our..."

"No. She's not. And I don't believe her. She's not really sick. It's another trick," Ella said, pulling out her keys.

"We can snap her out of this. We always have."

"I don't know. This felt different. She had *that* look."

"What look?"

"I don't know. Feral." Ella's voice sounded more defeated than Susan-Eva had ever heard it. She motioned Ella away from her car and toward her truck.

"Come feed Alpha with me." Ella nodded and got into Susan-Eva's pickup. Trisha gave it to her on her seventeenth birthday, right after Mrs. Lorenzo disappeared. From the first day she drove it, Susan-Eva had always kept a tiny vase with a single pink carnation in the cupholder. Since last January, Susan-Eva added one more constant to the décor, the stuffed squirrel Ida gave her in the hospital.

ELEVEN
Sixteen years ago – October 30, 2006

Ella

"THIS HAS BEEN THE BEST week ever! I wish my mom would never come back, and we could play forever, and I'd never have to go to that stupid church again!" Ida said, beaming at her friends, hugging a trick-or-treat plastic pumpkin to her chest. All three girls claimed a different corner of their favorite play spot, an abandoned treehouse near the Yellow Wood hiking trail.

"I wish you could stay too! Then you could stay with me forever, and we could be sisters for real and put on my mom's lipstick for secrets every night," said Susan-Eva. Since the day they met, Ida, Susan-Eva, and Ella spent nearly every weekend sleeping over at Parlay House per Trisha's request. This weekend was special. Ida's parents had an out-of-town event and finally trusted the girls enough to let Ida out. Pride was a dangerous feeling that Ella tried never to let in. But Trisha agreeing to this gave Ella a feeling bigger than any gold star she'd ever received.

"I love secret lipstick, and guess what! I have more secrets! I'll show you!" Ida said, motioning them to her. Susan-Eva started scooching forward, but Ella flung her hand out, stopping her. Something was off. There was a little too much twinkle in Ida's eyes.

"Wait, Ida... Is this scary? Remember, you can't do scary stuff if we don't like it, and we won't be friends anymore if you do." Ella warned.

Ida rolled her eyes. "I know. I know. Just look in here, it's a really cool secret," Ida said, putting her pumpkin bucket on the ground. Ella and Susan-Eva crept closer and closer, as Ida's smile got bigger and bigger.

Ella knew what was in the bucket *before*. Before she saw the frozen eyes. Before she saw the tiny once curved ribcage cracked into right angles. Before she smelt that smell, the one expired life exudes before the blood cools, but after the pulse has stopped. Before Ella could see or smell it, she knew something dead was in the bucket.

It was the thud as it hit the wood planks they sat on. A jangle could have meant something naughty but fun, like stolen jewelry. A slosh, something disgusting but harmless. But a thud, the heavy and final landing of something soft, rigid, and wet, was the sound something dead makes. Susan-Eva screamed and sobbed.

God, Ida must be fast. That was the first thing Ella thought. Because the dead squirrel in the bucket was small but not a baby. No BB pellet or rock punctured its fur. No bash to the skull. A single bite wound to its ribcage was the animal's only visible injury. There was no sign of tricking, or trapping, or the use of weapons. It seemed the thing had met its fate by person alone. So, Ida must be very, very fast, Ella thought.

Blood stained the fur around each tooth mark. It wasn't the sort of immature, rash violence of a child's fight. It was decisive and lingering, the way a dog holds a stuffed animal in its mouth, savoring the feel of cushion to teeth. How did she catch it? How long did she keep it alive? When? The "When?" was what bothered Ella most.

This was the first time Ella saw it in person, but Ida had shown her drawings. Drawings of Ida attacking… everything. Animals, flowers, houses, people. A world bursting with blood. Even things that didn't bleed, bled in Ida's drawings. She ran all her red crayons down to crumbs just to show herself she could make the sun bleed if she really wanted to.

Coloring was playtime. At playtime you're allowed to make up things that aren't real, Ida justified. When Ella asked why she only showed the drawings to Ella and not Susan-Eva, Ida got quiet, almost shy. Eventually, she looked Ella in the eye and said, "Doesn't it look like so much fun?" So, Ella knew Ida wanted to do those things. Ella thought she could stop her. If she explained the consequences well enough and watched her closely enough, it would only be drawings, but Ella failed.

She was so disappointed in herself. Every second since Trisha Montgomery dropped Ida off, Ella was by her side, like she promised Trisha she would be. So when could it have happened? It must have been while Ella was sleeping.

Ida burst into laughter and said, "Trick or treat? Get it?" Ella shot her eyes up and shook her head at Ida, furious.

"You promised!" said Susan-Eva through her tears.

Ella's fists clenched, fighting the urge to slap Ida. She stood up, towered over Ida, and yelled, "I knew it! I'm telling your mom and—"

"No, NO! Why are you mad?" Ida asked. Her eyes darted around, frantic with genuine panic and confusion. "It's trick or treat! Sometimes it's candy, and sometimes it's scary!" Ida snapped and pointed at Ella, remembering, "Like the werewolf statue at the costume store! It howled when we passed it, and we all screamed, and then we laughed, and it was fun! Remember? You said I'm supposed to act like everyone else, and everyone else is doing scary tricks. Even the stupid teacher. Scary is normal at Halloween." Ida's chest started rising too fast. "I'm being normal! Don't tell my mom. Please, please, please—" Her hands grasped at her own hair and started yanking it.

Ella took a deep breath and crouched down to Ida. "Stop. Ida, breath like me." Ella gently took Ida's hand and put it on her own chest. She demonstrated slow, calm breaths until Ida copied. Ella looked back at the squirrel. "This is different. If someone gets hurt, it's not just a trick. Animals are like people; you can't hurt them."

"I didn't hurt it! I found it like that! I swear. It must have been Joey's cat or—"

"Joey's cat doesn't have claws, and it's mostly inside! Friends don't lie, Ida!" yelled Susan-Eva, wiping tears. So much worry flooded Ida's eyes Ella thought she might actually cry.

"Please don't call my mom," Ida begged. "She'll come home and lock me in the—"

"Okay, but you have to listen to us. Promise?" Ella said. Ida huffed, still confused, but nodded, agreeing.

The truth was if they'd called Trisha she probably wouldn't even have answered. This was the first real break she'd had from Ida since she was born. In the beginning, Trisha hovered over the play dates, bribing and threatening the girls until they got Ida to act as she wanted. But she quickly found they made more progress in private. Just an hour alone with her new friends got Ida to sit calmly through dinner and willingly go to church. But Trisha's greatest pleasure was in the sudden interest Ida took in her appearance.

Once Trisha found the always locked door to her husband's study wide open. She was ready to fire a maid, certain one must have sticky fingers, but the security footage revealed only Ida entered the room. There was an antique box made of mirrors on the desk. Trisha fast-forwarded the security footage and watched her nine-year-old daughter sit perfectly still, staring at her reflection in the small box for three straight hours, riveted by how it altered in the day's fading light. It was unsettling but peaceful. So, Trisha let out a longer leash, often leaving the girls entirely alone at Parlay House.

Some found the trio's sudden friendship a little odd, given how different their backgrounds were. But they were kids. If anything, it added to Trisha's reputation for being the most charitable of her line. Besides, there were other things that made the economic differences less of an issue. While Ella's father was so far from the picture that most suspected Ella's mother, Elaina Kyle, wasn't entirely certain who he was; she was at least a professor. Mathematics. She wasn't hired full-time, but still, academically poor held a uniquely fluid social status.

Susan-Eva's father died in a car crash when she was two, but her mother was beloved by the wealthiest of Moss Groves. She wasn't only employed by them but competed over. Mia Lorenzo cleaned houses but was also the seamstress you went to when the seamstress on the main square told you the only solution was prayer. She was often cited as a family when one of the founding families was accused of racism. "It has nothing to do with color. We just think they should come over here right, but we love them. God, do we love them!"

Even as a child Susan-Eva had a reputation of her own. She was odd, but it was a star-quality odd. Every teacher, preacher, and coach made a point to call her a favorite. They all wanted to say they "knew her when." There was much debate on how, but no one disputed Susan-Eva was supposed to rock the world.

Ella was forgettable. Very smart but at that age, who cared? In many circumstances for a girl like Ella, who cared? She was well-behaved. If she hadn't been, she'd never have survived. One quality distinguished her: she was useful. Always. Not in a know-it-all way, she never raised her hand the highest. Instead, Ella sought out the kid that the teacher made feel like shit the day before and whispered the answer to him. She would hand the teacher a new marker before they even realized theirs had gone dry.

And there was the dance thing. Ella was a cold but extraordinary dancer. Her mother once told her skilled dance turns your body's feelings into arithmetic. Ella loved that. It made her an essential member of the tap and cheer teams. She never overshadowed the stage mom's child but could always do the thing the team needed to win.

So, while unexpected, Ida's bond with the star and the essential from the other side of town had a certain music to it. Susan-Eva the unforgettable melody, Ella the precise rhythm, and Ida the volume, dictating when they got the most attention. Though, at that point, most people hadn't seen much of Ida. Prior to the third grade, Ida was home-schooled. Trisha claimed this was due to her gifted daughter's delicate nerves. Ella and Susan-Eva where the only children she ever had playdates with. This sleepover was more than just a new privilege. It was a test of how public and long-term the friendship would be. The test wasn't only for the girls it was for their families. Mrs. Lorenzo knew that, and if she'd really been able to say "No" to Trisha Montgomery, she would have.

Even at nine years old, Ella understood the stakes. If their Halloween together didn't go well, it wouldn't be bad for Ella alone. It would be bad for her best friend's whole family, and it would be Ella's fault. Because she opened the closet door. So, it wasn't going to go badly.

After the squirrel incident, Ella "ran" Ida while Susan-Eva helped her mom with dinner. When Ida acted out, Ella found distraction worked far better than reason. She'd cascade instant gratification, sugar, cardio, sparkles, blood. Just one picture from a forbidden Google search could sustain Ida for hours.

Susan-Eva would have been horrified, but Ella didn't look at the pictures; she looked at Ida's face. There was hunger; Ida obviously liked the blood and the violence, but there was also relief. Her face looked the way any other kid did when they found out their friend also wet the bed. Or liked Cheez Wiz on Oreos. Or was afraid of SpongeBob. A look that said, "Oh! It's normal. It's okay. This thing I thought was so weird no one else does it is something people do." When Ida looked at pictures of decapitated or mangled bodies, her muscles eased with the relief of "Oh, this is something people do."

Later that night long after Mrs. Lorenzo made them turn off the TV and get in their sleeping bags, Ella lay awake, staring at Ida. Waiting. With her eyes closed and her body still, Ida looked so innocent. It had been hours since everyone else fell asleep. Ella's lids were getting so heavy she could feel herself starting to slip in and out of dreams. Dreams of the sparkly orange and black witch costumes that they'd finally get to wear tomorrow. Dreams of counting and trading candy on the playground. Dreams of squirrels playing, running up trees, and then something getting them. Something bad. Something sharp and painful and—

Ella gasped, jolting herself awake. Ida's eyes were open. She lay facing Ella. Ella expected her to smile and start trying to talk Ella into breaking the rules. But Ida just stared, quiet, almost sad. Ella stared back. Something about choosing the silence made them both feel very grown up.

They didn't know how to say it, but they both knew things little girls weren't supposed to know. Ida wasn't just staring at Ella. She was letting Ella see her. Ida wanted Ella to see her. Little creaks in the walls, the hum of the fan, Susan-Eva's gentle snore, all the noise they could hear in the silence felt like a small secret of the world becoming theirs to share. Bonding them through some visceral code. Finally, Ida whispered, "It wasn't Joey's cat. It was me."

"I know," Ella whispered back.

"It's really bad. Isn't it?" Ella nodded. Ida blinked. "Why do you like

80

playing with me?"

Ella thought for a moment, then made her face very calm and said, "Because you have a swimming pool." Ida reached over and pulled Ella's hair. Ella reached over and pulled Ida's hair, harder. Neither of them whined or even grimaced. All they did was keep staring, studying each other.

"You think you're bad too," Ida said so quietly Ella could barely hear her. "I wish it was true." Ida closed her eyes, curling back up. "If you get in my slumber bag, you can stop watching me and go to sleep. If I get hungry and try to sneak out, you'll feel me moving and wake up and stop me." Ella hesitated. "But if you're too scared of me, then—" Ella unzipped Ida's bag and crawled in. They both were asleep within seconds and slept soundly through the rest of the night.

TWELVE
August 18, 2022

Ella

MARIGOLDS AND QUEEN ANNE'S LACE swayed in clouds of dirt as Susan-Eva's pickup truck whirled down a barely drivable road. High-schoolers nicknamed the street Magic Alley. Not because it was scenic, though it was. There were plenty of hidden ponds and wildflower-spattered clearings along the way, but the magic was in its sound. It was muddy and rocky enough only certain vehicles could drive it. Those types of vehicles all made noise. Anyone coming down that road had entrance music for at least two minutes. Plenty of warning time for teens getting drunk to hide evidence. For lovers to throw on clothes. For screams to be muffled.

The musical road also left little evidence of any mischief seeker's destination as it no longer led to a distinct place. It didn't even truly come to a dead-end. It just faded into the woods. Cracked cement eventually turned to crumbles, then disintegrated to gravel, until street and earth were indistinguishable. Driving further was only an option for those who could handle an off-road adventure.

Lot 355 was one of the woods' most challenging pursuits. It was far from the remains of the street or any other clear markings if you didn't know exactly where you were going. It was also surrounded by a tall barbed wire fence with poison oak growing around the entirety of the permitter. The few who stumbled on the fence and weren't deterred by the threat of rash were stopped by a gate secured with four rusted locks. It was assumed all the keys were long lost.

Ella and Susan-Eva both had copies of a master that opened all four.

There was a vacant Victorian-style home on the lot but it was a storm cellar a few yards away from the house that the girls made use of. It's where they kept "Alpha." Usually, when Ella or Susan-Eva got there, they locked the gate behind them, got right out, went down, fed Alpha, and left. On days when Ida was being particularly Ida-y, however, they took refuge in the one spot she'd never look for them.

The day Ida declared she had a tumor and therefore felt they should be cool with her eating a few people alive was a very Ida-y day.

Susan-Eva pulled lawn chairs from the bed of her truck. Ella found the bottle of apple pie moonshine they kept in the hallow of a lightning-split oak. For a few moments, they enjoyed the silence. Clouds morphed from dinosaurs to wolves to battleships as they floated across the sky, and the girls traded turns taking swigs from the bottle. The sting of homemade hundred-fifty--proof whiskey felt like it could disinfect the day. A particularly monstrous-looking cumulous formed a tip, mimicking a funnel cloud. Ella found herself aching for the tip to spin and touch down, sucking her into the sky, but it dissolved into another shape, dashing all hope of a violent, quick end to the problem.

"What if Ida is right?" Susan-Eva asked.

"About what? Dying or being favored by God?" Ella asked in return.

"No. As a Christian and former religious studies minor, I feel extremely confident in saying Ida is not favored by the Father, the Son, the Holy Ghost, Buddha, Allah, Zeus, Aphrodite, Batman, or Yoda." Ella snorted and offered Susan-Eva the bottle. Susan-Eva shook her head, turning it down, and said, "The sip was enough. I just meant about us not always knowing what's right or wrong for her. Maybe no person should be responsible for the conscience of another person."

Ella asked, "What's the alternative? Let her do whatever she wants. Or have her locked up?" Tension filled Ella's throat as she said the words 'locked up' starting to know something she always had but never wanted to.

"I mean… Sometimes I worry, instead of making her better she made us worse," said Susan-Eva. Then, with sad sarcasm, Susan-Eva smirked at the cellar door, "But that's silly, right? When have we ever done anything ethically questionable?" They both glanced at the padlock. With a deep breath, Susan-Eva picked up a Solo Salads to-go bag she'd bought on the way and pulled out her keys.

"I can go down instead if you want?" Offered Ella. "I'm sorry for what Malcolm said earlier about 'nothing that bad…' He wasn't thinking."

Susan-Eva said, "*Yeah.* It's whatever." She plastered a fake grin and added, "I'm sure he's on edge, nervous the Copycat Killer is going to come and get him."

Fuck, Ella thought. It was obviously still bothering her. Susan-Eva making "jokes" about the Copycat Killer was never a good sign.

Ella said, "You know what's crazy? For all his talk of stranger-danger hysteria driving news ratings, I think he actually is kind of spooked. He brought it up when we were on campus. He wants me to stay at his place, just in case. You know, so he can protect me."

"Sweet. I guess we would be creeped out, too. If we didn't know better. But there's no reason for us to be afraid. Right?"

"I really can go down today, Evie. I know Ed being back in the news is hard for you in a different way."

"Well, yeah. Because it was my fault."

Ella narrowed her gaze, not letting that slide. She said, "Oh! Are we riding that trauma train today?"

"Choo-choo!"

"All aboard the misplaced guilt express."

"It's not misplaced."

"It's the city of Atlantis, Evie. Let me go down for you today."

Susan-Eva shook her head and twisted her key to open the lock. "I'm okay. I'm telling you. Switching his food made a difference."

"Okay, twinkie defense. Be careful."

THIRTEEN
August 18, 2022

Susan-Eva

THE PADLOCK WEIGHED LESS THAN a pound, but it seemed to gain weight in Susan-Eva's small hands. As though each time she turned the key some mass left her body and transferred to the metal in her palm. But it never slowed her down or weakened her resolve. She yanked back the doors with a huff and, within seconds, was out of sight beneath the earth.

It was important to appear somewhat casual in front of Ella when they came to the Cellar together. Susan-Eva didn't want to ignite any additional concern regarding her handling of "The Alpha thing." There was no reason to be concerned. It was fine. Every time Susan-Eva descended the soft rotting wood of the cellar stairs, she got a little finer. That's what she repeated to herself, sometimes even forcing a soft smile.

But in those few moments alone, with earth above and below, Susan-Eva always cried. Big, silent, embarrassing tears. Even the times she smiled. Especially the times she smiled. She tried every technique she knew to stop them from falling. Slow breathing. Mantras. Xanax for the first few visits. None of it worked. With each step, the same thoughts always came.

What if the lock broke? What if it happens again? What if it's empty? What if it's not? What if it's exactly like it always is, and nothing has changed, and nothing will ever change? What if it kills me? This will probably kill me.

Still, she forced herself to come back, day after day, to continue what she started, despite having no idea how she would end it. A box sat at the last step with a mask and voice modulator. She pulled them both on and took a deep breath as she stepped into view and walked toward rusted metal bars that split an underground room in half.

On the left side, there was a large shelf and door leading to a short tunnel that connected to the home. On the right, the caged side, there was a mattress, a small TV, a treadmill, a desk, and a chair where Scott Ryan, the missing son of the Florence University President, sat. Code named Alpha so they could talk about it when Ida was in earshot, without worrying she'd understand and come hunting.

Susan-Eva pushed the Solo Salad bag through the bars and said, "It's an organic quinoa bowl." She pulled the book Joseph let her borrow from the bag. "I brought another book to read to you. This one's about impulse control. Do you have any thoughts about the last one?" He was silent. "That little girl that went missing in Watsonville, they found her body. Near a home that was being renovated. People think it could be connected to Ed. She'd been dead for about four months. Her name was Sally Marks. Is there anything you'd like to say about that?"

Scott sat still in the chair, staring at Susan-Eva, and calmly repeated the only thing he had ever said in the entirety of the three months he'd been locked down there.

"I haven't seen your face. Let me go and my dad will give you whatever you want." Susan-Eva sat down, opened the book, and began reading.

FOURTEEN
August 18, 2022

Ella

ABOVE GROUND, ELLA TRIED TO figure out if the squirrels she was staring at were still fighting for the acorn or fucking. Her bet was fucking. New, new, new rule: On days, Ida made up a crazy lie that she was dying, or days Ella had to come to lot 355, or days that she drank Apple Pie Moonshine she could think and say whatever fucking words she wanted.

A birthmark that sat just above Ida's left hip popped into Ella's mind. Flashes of Ida always came uninvited at the most inconvenient times. The feel of it was more vivid than the image. The impossible silkiness of Ida's skin rose to a tiny mound so perfectly heart-shaped it seemed more like jewelry than a mole. Stupid squirrels, brought up such fucking annoying memories.

A sudden rattling noise jolted Ella back to the present. Panicked, she bolted up, darting her eyes around but saw nothing. Then again, the rattling, or no… a buzzing. She looked down. It was her phone. Malcolm was calling. She rolled her eyes and capped the moonshine. Clearly, that last swig was one swig too many.

A picture of Malcolm hooking his arm around her shoulders with a playful stern look on his face appeared on her screen with his name. Ella thought of their quiet little conflict this morning. Malcolm's hot breath on her ear. Her calf cramping into a Charlie horse. The things he whispered. She swiped her thumb to ignore the call with a boozy dramatic flair like it was a magic trick. POOF! No more Malcolm! TA-DA! No more thoughts of the irritating morning! Soon she'd be over it and she'd find his authoritative tone and disapproving squint sexy again. All she needed was a little space then—

Through the phone Malcolm's voice shouted, "Ella? Babe?" Ella gasped, looking down. She'd swiped to answer instead of ignore. Apparently, it wasn't *one* too many swigs of moonshine. It was three. Okay, five. "ELLA?" Malcolm's voice vibrated in her hand. She brought the phone to her ear about to speak then ended the call instead.

A squirrel ran across the cellar door. Ella remembered Ida tugging her hair. Her phone buzzed again. Malcolm's weight on her hips. Ida. Malcolm. Ida. *Thunder.*

The sky was darkening. Relief spread through her body, relaxing every muscle. Nothing soothed Ella's inner chaos like a storm. Suddenly, a cold, decisive feeling coursed through her like a saline flush chilling the veins fresh from the syringe. She pulled up a contact labeled Elmore Psychiatric Facility and dialed.

"Hi, is Dr. Homer available to talk later? It's Ella Kyle." The receptionist started rattling off session times. "No, not an appointment. Tell him I want to know what the process is for committing someone against their will. I'll explain in person." She heard the receptionist mumble something to Dr. Homer, then confirmed she could come at one tomorrow.

One. Great. On her lunch break tomorrow, she'd go find out how to have Ida committed. Like anything else on a to-do list. Poof! No more Ida. Problem solved. As Ella hung up and tucked her phone into her pocket, her eyes welled. She slapped her cheek, checking the emotion before it could turn to tears. Water rolled down her face anyway. It was not coming from her eyes. It was the sky. Lightening flashed and it started to pour. *Something made the weather cry.*

Ella ran to the truck, but it was locked, and Susan-Eva had the keys. There weren't any trees within the fenced area. They never went into the cellar together so that Scott wouldn't know there were two people involved.

Ella couldn't take shelter there. There was nowhere else to go. Then Ella had the strangest realization. Of course, there was. There was the house on the lot. Why not go into the vacant house?

She could take refuge in there. It was abandoned, not condemned. She'd gone in once, Sixteen years ago. She remembered the bones of the structure seeming quite sound. It was old but built to last. The kind of construction you could ignore for decades and return to find all intact. There was no logical reason it was dangerous to go inside. Just emotion. Ella never let her emotions decide anything else, so why this? She needed shelter. The house was shelter. It was only that it used to be Ed Bin's house. Ed was dead. So, really, it was silly not to go in and wait for the rain to stop.

It was like gravity. Her feet started moving toward it before she even realized she'd decided to go. With each step, she grew faster and more certain, as though she'd always known she'd return one day. As though there were answers to all their problems within those walls. Of course, she was supposed to return; in fact, maybe she was never supposed to leave. Wasn't that the reason for all of this?

Ella always told Susan-Eva she was wrong for thinking it was her fault. She never said the whole truth out loud, though. It was Ella's fault. Because Susan-Eva got tricked. Ella knew better and went inside the house anyway. So she should go in the house now and let it all come flooding back. She was almost to the porch. One more step then—

"ELLA!? What are you doing?" yelled Susan-Eva, climbing out of the cellar.

Ella ran through the rain back toward the car. Soaked and panting, she got in the passenger's seat. Susan-Eva raised her eyebrows, waiting for an answer. "What the hell was that about?" A sharp, loud thud hit the windshield. They both turned and saw an acorn rolling off the hood, then looked up. Another squirrel.

PART TWO

The Thing That Happened to Ida

FIFTEEN
Sixteen years ago – October 31, 2006, 5:14 PM

Susan-Eva

"WAIT! THIS IS SIX BLOCKS now! Mrs. Lorenzo said we're only supposed to go three." Ella shouted at Ida and Susan-Eva as they ran ahead in their witches' costumes.

"Well, MY mom said you're not supposed to let me out of your site, and MY mom is WAY more important than Susie Evie's mom," said Ida as she twirled, making the sparkly golden charms on her orange and black skirt jingle.

"Nuh-uh!" Protested Susan-Eva, coming to a halt. "Your mom just has money. But she can't do anything. My mom can do everything! Once, she let us paint my whole room with finger paint, and we even got to use our toes. My mom is smart and fast and fun. Your mom can't even paint her own nails. Your mom is lazy and BORING AND STUPID, IDA!" Ida froze. Susan-Eva had been poking at Ida ever since the squirrel incident the day before.

It scared her, and when Susan-Eva was scared, she faced it. She decided Ida was a bully, and she'd stand up to her every chance she got. Ida's face looked so serious all of a sudden, like she might be hurt, which Susan-Eva instantly realized she didn't want.

So far, it was the perfect Halloween. They had tons of candy. Even

Tori Lee, who was a sixth grader, said their costumes were cool. No matter how mad Susan-Eva was at Ida, she had to admit witches are best as a trio, which they wouldn't be without Ida. But she was determined not to let her guard down. At some point, Ida would ruin Halloween. It was almost a one-million-percent chance. Susan-Eva was ready for it. She watched Ida, waiting for the tantrum.

But Ida said, "Evie... Your right! My mom is so, so, so, SO BORING!" Ida laughed and grabbed Susan-Eva's hands, twirling her around. "I hate her." Ida cocked her head matter of fact and asked, "But why'd you say she's stupid? She's not stupid. I know because I really, really want her to be."

"I was just being mean," said Susan-Eva, flushing with guilt.

"Oh." Ida nodded, trying to understand. "Stop being mean to me."

Susan-Eva stood straight, trying to mimic *Law & Order: SVU.* She told herself justice would make her feel better for hurting her friend. Who she loved. She said, "You were mean yesterday."

"Well, yeah!" Ida said, smiling. "Because I like it. But when you're mean, it makes you smell sad."

"You mean it makes her look sad, Ida." Ella corrected.

"No dummy! I couldn't see her face." Ida turned back to Susan-Eva and squeezed her into a hug, whispering, "Don't be sad anymore. I hate it. If you stop being sad at me, I'll help you sneak into Joey's."

"I don't need help. I sneak in all the time," said Susan-Eva.

"You sneak into his mom's house. I'll help at his dad's house! He has a stupid little brother there, Parker. He's our age and you can get him to do anything. One time after church I made him show me the hunting shed and the locked-up guns, and there was a dead deer on the table with its guts—"

"*Ida,*" said Ella, stopping her.

Susan-Eva said, "It doesn't matter. Joey says now that he's twelve, he's too old to play Buffy with me."

Ida said, "Kiss him like Buffy kisses Angel!"

"EWWWWW!" Giggled Susan-Eva as Ida made dramatic kissy faces. Ella tried not to smile then all three of them burst into laughter.

"Okay, if not Joey, what?" asked Ida, catching her breath. "I'll do anything you want. I just want everyone to see our costumes. You're right your mom is so cool. I wish she was my mom! Ella does too! Don't you, Ella?" Ella shrugged and looked away. "I mean, come on! Don't we look better than any three ever?"

"There is one more house we could trick or treat at," said Susan-Eva, only looking at Ida. It was the idea she'd had all day, but knew Ella would probably say no. Not Ida, though. "The house at the end of Magic Alley."

Ella shook her head and said, "No way. Too far, and your mom said only houses we know."

Susan-Eva said, "It's okay. I know him. He talks to me every time we go to the store. He helps my mom with groceries, and he has a really big dog named Alpha. Let's go!" Susan-Eva hopped on her broom, pretending to fly. It was exactly like her dream.

Ella

Ella could hear Trisha's voice saying she trusted Ella to think like a grown-up, even if it meant standing up to her daughter. Ida grabbed Ella's hand and said, "Come on! It will make her so happy." Ida was right, Susan-Eva did look really excited. It wasn't such a big deal to go to one more house. Especially if it was someone Mrs. Lorenzo knew.

But something else was bothering Ella. Her face scrunched with a thought she couldn't shake. "Ida…" Ella said. Ida paused, and suddenly, their music was back. Ida was patient in a way she was never patient with anyone. The leaves of the trees rustled in the breeze as the sunset washed the world in golden light. Wheels of a car they could not see spun against pavement nearby. In their silence, they could hear the grown-up world. Ella knew if she asked the question on her mind, she'd get a grown-up answer. Ella knew the answer. She didn't want to hear it. She asked anyway, "Do I smell sad when I'm mean?"

Ida's eyes twinkled and she grinned a grin that was much smaller than her usual, as though she was keeping part of it for herself, then she said. "No, Ella. You only smell sad when I have to leave."

SIXTEEN
August 19, 2022 1:00 PM

Ella

ELLA HAD FANTASIZED ABOUT THIS moment. Every time Ida popped out of nowhere, played a trick, or snuck into her bed, Ella imagined telling the truth. At first, she thought a teacher would be best, then the police, but somewhere in the back of her mind, she always knew it would be a doctor. Ella hated doctors, especially Dr. Homer.

Dr. Homer was in his seventies. Like all good ole boys turned MDs he had a special talent for being both patronizing and folksy at the same time. Alongside his framed degrees hung a hand-painted sign that proclaimed: PH.D. AIN'T GOT NOTHING ON M.O.M. Next to it was a school paddle with the carved words: AN OLD-FASHIONED TALKIN' TO!

After the thing that happened when they were little, Ella, Susan-Eva, and Ida all had to see Dr. Homer. Ida only had to go once. He said she was remarkably fine. Susan-Eva was done in a month. But with Ella's family history, he recommended longer. It was never consistent, they binged and purged each other. The sessions were sort of amusing to Ella. She turned talks with Dr. Homer into little games. Her favorite was "Act crazy, get drugs." She never took them, but being the girl at the party with the fun-pharm grab bag was very useful.

Dr. Homer listened without moving through the entirety of Ella's story, squinting at her through his tiny glasses. She'd imagined the words she now said out loud over and over. But as she looked around the office, remembering all the other times she'd been there and all the things she'd done to manipulate a precise reaction, Ella realized something. She'd only fantasized about saying the words. She never dared let herself imagine what would come next. She never imagined a reaction. Dr. Homer stayed silent when she finished for what felt like a Scorsese movie's worth of time before finally managing, "She wants to eat a person?"

"A live one," Ella confirmed without thinking.

"And this is Ida Montgomery?" Dr. Homer asked as though there were an abundance of other Idas it might be.

"I know it's hard to believe, but I really think she's going to hurt someone."

Doctor Homer's eyes went to the side and slowly said, "But she hasn't yet because in third grade, you and the Lorenzo girl promised to be her conscience, and you told her eating people was... bad?"

Ella dug her nails into her palm to keep the frustration out of her voice. Why hadn't she assumed they'd think she was the crazy one? She'd never let the thoughts go that far. Ella tried to start over, "I know it sounds—"

"It sounds like you're accusing a girl I've known since the day she was born, a girl who sat on my lap when I was playing Santa, a girl whose daddy is a deacon at my church of being a cannibal."

"Not exactly. I'm accusing her of *wanting* to be a cannibal." Ella shifted in her seat and tried to steer him back to logistics, saying, "So how do you go about getting someone into treatment if they don't—"

"You know, when you called, I assumed it was about your mom." Dr. Homer's face softened. He pushed a box of Kleenexes toward Ella.

"Well, it's not." Ella's shoes turned in like a preteen version of herself was taking over.

"I saw on the news they found the body of that little girl who was missing. That must have brought up some tough memories." Dr. Homer said, not so subtly, implying this was a cry for help related to what happened with Ed.

"This has nothing to do with that." She looked at the time and crossed her legs, exasperated.

"And you must have some conflicting feelings about Mr. Bin's old house being added to the auction." Ella rolled her eyes about to argue, then paused.

"Wait, what?" It was a stressful day. She must have misheard him. Did Moss Groves love a charity auction? Yes. Would they relish the chance to bid on nearly anything, including a retainer once worn by an alumnus who became an NFL quarterback? Yes. But there had to be a limit. Lot 355 was the limit.

"You hadn't heard? I guess after sixteen years on the market they conceded a traditional sale would never happen. At least if the money goes to charity some light can come out of so much darkness. The Lord works in mysterious ways. I guess a few people are feeling a little touchy about it."

"Yuh think?"

"It's a lot to swallow for you." Ella looked away. "And on top of that, Ida's engagement. It's common with a shared trauma to have feelings of jealousy when a fellow survivor adjusts better than the others. We haven't had a session since you were in school. Let's get something on the books." Dr. Homer opened his schedule.

Ella made an appointment that she had no intention of keeping and left. So many aspects of this interaction were rip-your-hair-out annoying, but there was one part worse than the rest. A reality that made Ella want to tell Doctor Homer he was right; she was nuts, and he should lock her up for good. Being trapped in a padded room would be better than what would come next.

Whether it was a doctor, a cop, or a teacher, when the societal systems of Moss Groves failed the average duck, there was only one way around it. You had to ask for the help of a founding family. The founding family you knew best.

Before she even got out of Doctor Homer's earshot, Ella had Susan-Eva on the phone. "You were right. We have to tell Trisha."

SEVENTEEN
Sixteen years ago - October 31, 2006, 5:25 PM

Ella

IT ONLY TOOK TEN MINUTES for the girls to run from the edge of the woods to the house on Lot 355. Much of the pavement down Magic Alley was still smooth. Even when it dissolved there was a clear dirt road that led to the property. It was hardly the most treacherous trick-or-treat destination of the evening.

Twenty minutes ago, they'd hit Mrs. Comfrey's house and you had to pass a pond that had two baby alligators in it to get to her front door. She had full-sized candy bars, so it was worth it. Susan-Eva swore this would be double worth it.

The sun was setting, but as long as they just rang the doorbell, got the candy, and left, they'd still have time to get back before dark, and before it was obvious they'd gone further than they were supposed to.

Ella wasn't sure why one last spot felt like such a big deal, but it did. From the moment Susan-Eva suggested it, Ella knew they shouldn't go.

"Ed said he's flipping the house! Just like on TV. He showed me this place he fixed in Florida with a whole jungle gym in the back. It was amaze balls!" said Susan-Eva, still pretending to fly on her broom. Her voice squeaked with excitement. Too much excitement. That's what it was.

Susan-Eva was brave. She snuck into graveyards to play *Buffy* at night. She wasn't bad but she didn't care about breaking rules when she thought it was important or worth it. So why the nervous giddiness? And she called him Ed. Even when cool teachers said kids could use their first names, Mrs. Lorenzo insisted Susan-Eva still say Mr. or Ms. or Coach or whatever.

"So, you only met him at the store once, or—" asked Ella, suddenly stopping. Susan-Eva and Ida ignored her, running to the front door. There was a fresh coat of light-yellow paint on the exterior walls with white trim on the window details. It was lovely. '*Maybe I'm being silly the way Mom says I am about the basement,*' Ella thought. When she reached the front porch, she forced a big grin as Ida twirled to face her.

Ida

Ida wanted to say, 'Ella, you're so slow! If you stay that way, one day, you'll be as fat as Miss Putnam!' A clever insult. Ida was certain. She couldn't wait to say it because Ella was always insulting her insults. But she'd never tried the word "fat." The word her mother once took so much pleasure in using to describe her father's new assistant that it made her salivate. Ida imagined Ella slapping her. Or screaming. Any big reaction would do. But in the seconds it took for Ida to pivot her feet and whip her hair around to face Ella, the world changed.

The air was full of something new. Ella was smiling. Her shoulders were back. She met Ida's eyes with an annoyed, ready dare the way she always did when she knew Ida was about to provoke her. To anyone else, Ella would have appeared fine. The difference was so subtle. But she was stiff. It was like every muscle in her body was calcifying around something she couldn't let out. It almost worked. You couldn't hear it, or see it, but Ida could smell it.

"What's wrong?" Ida asked.

Ella rolled her eyes and smiled bigger. "What do you mean?"

Ida's face was blank, the way it always was when she was absorbing new information. "You smell wrong." Ella let go of the smile as the last glowing bit of sun dipped below the horizon.

Ding-Dong! Susan-Eva rang the doorbell. Ed swung open the door so

99

quickly he must have seen them coming. The man towering over them only added to Ida's confusion. Nothing about him could explain how Ella smelled.

Ed looked like your uncle, not the creepy one, the one that your mom lovingly accuses of getting you too hyper from playing tag even though it's almost bedtime. The one with a perfect big white smile. The one who has really pretty girlfriends who are so nice to you because they're hoping to show off their maternal side and convince him to settle down. The one who has a bike and says he's going to some cool-sounding thing called "Burning Man" that your mom stops him from explaining. Ed looked like your favorite volleyball coach, the one who makes a joke after the head coach yells. Like the youth pastor who sings in a band. He was handsome but in a youthful way. Fit but not bulky or intimidating in height.

Ed looked like the fun. So, the way Ella smelled didn't make any sense. She had no reason to be scared. Ed smiled down at them, amused. "S.E.! What are you doing here?" Ed asked.

Ella

S.E.? So, they didn't just know each other. They nickname knew each other, Ella thought. And it was a nickname no one else called her. *He* must have given it to her. But Susan-Eva never mentioned him before. That was weird. Ed had such a nice smile. His voice was warm. The house looked nice. But Susan-Eva having a friend she never mentioned until now wasn't normal.

Ida whipped her head back to Ella and whispered through her teeth, "Okay! What is going on? Why do you keep smelling like that?" Ella squinted, still not understanding. Why did Ida keep saying smell? You can't smell feelings. She could tell Ida wasn't joking, but she had to be getting a word wrong. Ida did that sometimes. She'd say something was warm when she meant it was funny. She'd say she was soft when she meant she was sleepy. Whatever Ida meant, Ella was certain; she couldn't mean smell.

Ed craned his neck out, looking past them. "Please tell me Mrs. L is here?" Susan-Eva shrugged a little guilty, Ed looked to Ella and Ida. "But one of your moms is here, right? You didn't walk all this way by yourselves, did you?"

100

"We're nine, so we're allowed to trick-or-treat alone. It's fine. I know you showed Joey and Parker the dungeon in the storm Cellar. They said it's so cool! We're the same age as Parker. So, if he's old enough, we're old enough."

"Hey, I know you're not some little kid, but Joey and Parker's Dad was here. I sure as hell don't want Mrs. L mad at me." Explained Ed. Then he forced a cartoonish cringe while he bonked his own head and tacked on, "Sorry, I shouldn't say hell in front of you guys." Ed said.

Ida met his eyes and asked, "Why? Are you unfavored by God?"

Ida

That's when Ed's smell started to change. It was a smell Ida knew well, but she'd only ever smelt it on herself before when she was chasing something. It was the smell that meant run.

EIGHTEEN
August 19, 2022

Ella

"MY GORGEOUS, PERFECT ANGEL GIRL!" Cooed Trisha Montgomery as she hugged Susan-Eva in the doorway of Honey Hill House. Then she glanced to the side at Ella and just said, *"Ella."*

Honey Hill House was smaller than Parlay House, but barely, and it was older, so in some ways more prestigious. Ida's grandparents both died in their sleep in this house. Legend had it that it was haunted long before that. Honey Hill had a ghost story for every single holiday.

Gruesomely murdered ghosts for Halloween. Dead lovers for Valentine's Day. Dead servants for Labor Day. Ella didn't believe in ghosts, but she did believe Trisha could buy whatever she wanted, whether it existed or not. When Ella died, she was certain she'd immediately be thrown onto the Honey Hill haunting rotation, probably for Groundhog's Day. Trisha loved blaming Ella for the weather.

When Trisha finally pulled back from squeezing Susan-Eva, Ella opened her mouth to try and get down to business. Trisha held out a hand without even looking at her, signaling Ella to stay quiet another moment as she admired Susan-Eva. Trisha said, "Lashes that long without mascara, Jesus wept." It wouldn't quite be true to say Susan-Eva was the daughter

Trisha always wanted. But Susan-Eva was willing to play the game in a way Ida and Ella couldn't.

Once, in high school when they were cheerleading at a football game, Trisha thought the bow Susan-Eva was wearing looked cheap and pulled her off the sidelines to change it. By the time they were teens she only ever did things like this to Susan-Eva. Fussing over Ida resulted in biting or dead pets. If she tried with Ella, Ella would have ignored her or told her to fuck off. Which would make Ida laugh, so Trisha would concede to prevent Ida from doing anything Ida-y. Susan-Eva, on the other hand, usually handled Trisha with please and thank you. When Susan-Eva came back with a new bow, Ella asked why she always played nice with Trisha. She expected some nonsense about them all having a bond or the value of love and forgiveness.

Instead, Susan-Eva said, "Social Contracts are not frivolous. They act as buffers and boundaries in all contexts. Whether it's a holiday gathering or the United Nations. I don't play nice with Trisha. I engage in her language of choice as an act of diplomacy, knowing one day we'll put her on trial for war crimes." Then she picked up her pom-poms, went back to the sidelines, did a high kick, and waved at Trisha in the stands.

Now standing on Trisha's porch, Ella wondered what the most diplomatic way was to ask if someone's daughter had fake cancer or real cancer.

Trisha took Susan-Eva's hands and said, "Shame on you for not calling and telling me you were coming! I would have had Antonia whip up a pitcher of Martinis. You didn't give me a chance to fix myself. I'm a mess." Trisha said. She was wearing a full face of make-up, perfectly waved hair, and heels. But accepting unannounced visitors without calling yourself "a mess" was an etiquette sin on par with offering unsweetened tea.

"Oh, hush. You always look fabulous, and I have to go to work soon anyway," said Susan-Eva.

Ella said, "We have something important to—"

Trisha ignored Ella, keeping her eyes on Susan-Eva, "Ohhhh. You know I don't like you working at a bar. Call out sick; I'll write you a check for whatever you usually make." Trisha said, giving Susan-Eva's arms a playful tug. A part of Ella wanted Susan-Eva to say yes. That way, they'd have all night to strategize. But checks personalized with the Montgomery Estate seal never came without expectation of a returned favor. Usually, one worth far more than the number written in perfect cursive on the amount line. They'd both learned that the hard way.

With a gentle shake of the head, Susan-Eva gracefully turned down Trisha's offer and said, "Ella's right. We have something serious to ask you about."

Trisha sighed and shook her head with an "Mmm" noise. She always did this when something annoyed her in Ella's presence. As though no matter what it was it must be Ella's fault. Once, Ella walked into the room while the weatherman predicted a fifty percent chance of rain the weekend of Trisha's annual garden party. She hummed and shook her head with a glance at Ella that said, *'Get it down to a twenty percent chance by tomorrow, or I'll have to call your mother.'*

Even from Trisha, the feeling of disappointing someone made Ella's face go red with shame. So, Trisha was always disappointed with Ella. Knowing it would be unacceptable to strike children who were not her own, Trisha took advantage of any hands-free technique she could to scald their cheeks. But when it came to Ida, Ella always had the power.

From that first day in the closet, it was clear Ella had magic that Trisha did not. It was a power dynamic destined to make them both enemies and life-long partners. No matter how the queen loathes the prophets, mystics, and witch doctors, those who want to survive know better than ever to banish them, and those who reign longest find ways to ensure they can never leave.

It wasn't like they always hated each other. When she was little, Ella found Trisha intimidating, but she loved being talked to like a grown-up the way Trisha always did. All the responsibility felt like an honor at first. Being the confidant of a powerful adult is every mature kid's dream.

The older Ella got, the more complicated it was. Though Susan-Eva once told her, there was a very simple explanation for why Ella and Trisha hated each other so much. She said there were things Trisha *wanted* to feel for Ida but didn't and things Ella *didn't* want to feel for Ida but did. It was an explanation that Ella disagreed with and tried never, ever to think about. Trisha had too much control over their lives. That was all. It wasn't emotional. As Trisha led them all to the sitting room, Ella took a deep breath, reminding herself why she was there. It was an urgent Ida matter. Meaning today, Ella was an unburnable witch.

She refused to let old intimidation methods work as Trisha sat with the elegance of a ballerina in the precise center of her white and magenta floral sofa. The throne she always chose when it was necessary to have 'a talk' with her girls. There was a twinkle in her eye like she had fresh ammunition. Ella sat tall, confident, ready for whatever it was. There was no reason anything Trisha said or did would get under her skin today.

Trisha smiled at Ella and said, "I talked to your mamma yesterday." GOD-DAMN-IT, Ella thought. She felt blood rush to her cheeks. Newest rule: Ella could curse in her head whenever her arch nemesis brought up her mother. The topic not only got under Ella's skin, she was pretty sure it got right through the bone. With that sentence alone, Trisha was sucking out the marrow. It had been almost a year since Ella heard her mother's voice. It was for the best. *But*...

Ella cleared her throat and said, "You did? I mean, um... how is she?" Ella tried to sound casual, but her pitch was a little too high.

Trisha met Ella's eyes and said, "She's doing *so* well. My contact at MIT says she's revered by the students. It's likely they'll promote her this year." Dryness spread through Ella's throat, threatening to bring water to her eyes. She swallowed and told herself: *that's so great.* So, so great. Say it's so great.

"That's great!" Ella said much louder than she meant.

Trisha poured three glasses of lemonade from a pitcher on a tray that was sitting there when they walked in, ready in case guests popped by. She handed Ella a glass and said, "That doctor I found is a real miracle worker. She's been on her meds for two years straight. Apparently, she's even dating someone special. It's been six months. They're talking about moving in."

Again, Ella thought, that's so great. That's so great. So, so, so, so great.

"Did she ask about Ella?" Susan-Eva said. Her tone was as close to curt as she'd dare. It shocked Ella that her skin didn't blister from how quickly her blood boiled with embarrassment. I don't care, Evie, she thought. Don't make her think I care. Even as she thought this, Ella couldn't stop herself from leaning closer, desperate to hear what Trisha would say.

Trisha smiled and said, "Of course. She asked if Ella was well. I said she was well."

"And that she's thriving at her job, right?" Said Susan-Eva, protectively leading Trisha to say what she thought Ella needed to hear. She was wrong. Ella didn't care about any of this. At all. Right? She was a grown-up. Grown-ups have difficult relationships with their mothers and don't go around obsessing about it.

"It didn't come up," said Trisha.

Great. They could change the topic and focus on what they were there to do. Fix Ida. Ida was all that mattered. But before she could stop herself, Ella asked, "Well, if you were talking about dating, did you tell her I'm dating someone from Seattle? Malcolm's father actually went to MIT. He's very active in alumni events. Maybe they've crossed paths." Even as she was saying it, she regretted it. It sounded pathetic. *Mommy, watch me dance.* Shut up, Ella.

Trisha reached over and took Ella's hand, a move she could only get away with while on this particular topic. She said, "Honey," the term of endearment she only used on people she owned (it was Honey Hill, after all). "We don't want to overwhelm her with emotional information that isn't permanent. If someone ever offers you a ring, I'll let her know. Until then, let's take the win. Yes? It's so rare for a schizophrenic to thrive the way she is. If I hadn't gotten her into that new drug trial, who knows what would have become of her? You wouldn't ever want anything to pull her away from the place where she's finally found a home and a purpose, would you?"

Ella's shoulders caved in. She could barely hear herself as she said, "No. Of course not. I just wondered." Grab a marshmallow. We've got a witch roasting.

Susan-Eva said, "Well if Mrs. Kyle is doing *so well.* She can handle knowing what's going on with—"

"Oh!" Trisha said, turning back to Susan-Eva. "My sweet girl, I almost forgot. I talked to a friend who knows someone who got promoted in the missing persons unit. Now, I don't know if they'll have any new info, but would you like the number?"

Susan-Eva got quiet and said, "Yes. Of course. Thank you."

Ella could feel her friend sliding back into the couch like she wished it would swallow her. Shame filled Ella's stomach. How dare she feel so upset about not talking to her mom when Susan-Eva didn't even know if hers was alive?

When they were in high school, Susan-Eva's aunt was diagnosed with stage four breast cancer. Mrs. Lorenzo drove to Texas to be with her for every round of chemo, but she never let 24 hours pass without calling her daughter. So, after exactly 24 hours and five minutes of not hearing from her mother, Susan-Eva reported that she was missing.

Everyone said there had to be a reasonable explanation. A flat tire. A dead phone. They would hear from her any minute, and it would all make sense. But Susan-Eva knew. No small, inconsequential thing could keep her mother from contacting her. Minutes turned to weeks and Susan-Eva's 17th birthday passed with no sign of Mrs. Lorenzo. Aunt Eva died right after their high school graduation, and there was an unspoken sentiment that the funeral was for both sisters.

But suspecting the worst isn't the same as knowing it for sure. Susan-Eva and even Ella couldn't help but cling to a tiny aching hope that Mrs. Lorenzo was still out there somewhere. This was all Ella needed to pull herself out of the corner and back into the fight. It's not like it was Trisha's fault that they didn't know what happened to Mrs. Lorenzo, but the way she dangled being able to help made Ella more nauseous than anything Ida had ever done.

Trisha said, "It brings tears to my eyes thinking of how this world has treated the two of you. I'm so glad to have been in a position to help. We've all been so blessed by each other, haven't we?"

"Ida wants to eat some people alive." Ella blurted out.

"Oh," Trisha said. All sentimentality was gone. It was like someone rubbed the makeup off Trisha's voice. It was still her, but the version that didn't care if it was pretty. She stood and went to the bar cart. Clunking large ice cubes into a glass with tongs she said, "Well, tell her not to."

Ella rolled her eyes and said, "Hot take!" She went bar cart. With the mention of Ida, they became equals. Equals that hated each other, but

107

equals. Trisha shoved Ella a glass, then poured them both Vodka from a local distillery *(Playdates to AA mates, Moss Groves is so, so, so, fucking great!)*

Trisha waved the bottle and raised her eyebrows at Susan-Eva, who shook her head and said, "I have to work."

"Suit yourself." Trisha poured herself another splash and put the bottle down. "So. Ida. How long has this been going on?"

Susan-Eva squinted, doing the math and said, "Um, Eleven years? Right? The first time she openly expressed cannibalistic desires was after we went to that *Silence of the Lambs* and *Jennifer's Body* double feature. We were fifteen, right?"

Ella said, "Well, yeah, but the desire was there long before."

Susan-Eva nodded and said, "Because of what happened with Ed."

Ella shook her head and said, "No, I have never bought that theory. It was there before."

Susan-Eva shook her head and said, "Violent Narcissists are often triggered by a traumatic childhood incident."

"I'm not saying there wasn't an incident. I'm saying whatever it was happened before." Ella turned to Trisha and added, "But someone has refused to talk about any possible events—"

"She was born like that. I assure you. I'm not asking when the desire started. I'm asking when she informed you she might act on it."

Ella said, "Oh. Yesterday," then sipped her vodka.

"Are you sure she's not just confused and trying to be trendy? Content on cabalism is very in right now," said Trisha.

"No, it wasn't like in middle school when the last *Twilight* came out, and she tried to throw a blood-drinking party. She let us veto that. Yesterday, she said if we're not on board, she might do it anyway," said Susan-Eva.

Trisha looked up, thinking, taking a sip, then said, "Well. Have you been feeding her appropriately? Is she getting enough iron?"

Ella glared, "Oh my god! Yes."

Trisha said, "Because you know when Ida's iron gets low—"

"Her murder fantasies get more specific. Yes. I know." Ella took a hefty drink and said, "*I'm* the one who told *you* that."

Trisha rang a bell on the cart and yelled, "Antonia, get Ella a cookie.

She noticed ONE helpful thing ONE time."

"ONE TIME?! You couldn't get her through a trip to the playground before me. I had her sitting quietly through two-hour church services after the first month!" Ella said.

"Oh, as though telling her she was favored by God never backfired," Trisha said.

"I did NOT tell her she was favored by God. You told me to get her to listen to the pastor. Ida only liked listening to things that were about her. So, I told her maybe if she listened to the sermon, she'd find out something about herself. That's all. She got to the favored by God thing all on her own."

Susan-Eva nodded and said, "It's true. And she got there fast. It was only like five minutes into the service."

"That's never made sense to me," said Trisha.

Ella gave Trisha a sarcastic smirk and said, "Yeah, because Ida's the first person in history to interpret that book as a justification for their horrible actions."

"So, you agree. Your suggestion could have been more helpful," said Trisha.

"I have made millions of helpful suggestions. 'Cardio when you see a tantrum coming' was me!" Trisha's corgi, Leviticus, ran into the room. Ella pointed at it, "Violent video games as a reward for every time she went a week without torturing an animal was me! Leviticus would be dead if it wasn't— "

"Antonia! Get Ella a bucket of cookies; she did what SHE GOT PAID to do," Yelled Trisha.

"Antonia, get Trisha a 'Mother of the Year' award; she bribed children to fix her daughter instead of taking her to, oh, I don't know, A FUCKING DOCTOR," Yelled Ella.

Susan-Eva clapped her hands together as she said, "Okay. Let's all take a breath." Ella and Trisha both took a drink.

"It's not as though this is the first time my daughter has expressed unfortunate desires. You've always been able to handle it. So why am I being looped in? Why is this different?" asked Trisha. Ella and Susan-Eva glanced at each other, debating who should say it. Trisha squinted at them. "Unless…

this better not be another conversation about either of you moving. After everything I've done for you."

Ella said, "We're not moving. It's just…" She heard the ice in her glass rattle. She looked down to see her hand was shaking. Why did the idea of saying it make her feel like she was suffocating? *Ida says she's dying. We know she isn't. We know it's a prank. Can you confirm?* A simple question. So why couldn't Ella say it out loud?

Trisha said, "It's just…" mimicking Ella.

Susan-Eva stepped in and said, "Ida told us something that might be difficult to hear."

"What did she say?" asked Trisha.

Susan-Eva took a breath and softened her voice. "We know, despite the challenges, Ida is your daughter. So remember—"

"That your daughter is a compulsive liar, so it's not true," said Ella.

Susan-Eva shook her head and said, *"Ella. It's her child. Let's be—"*

"It doesn't matter because it's not true," said Ella.

"Girls, Hellen Keller found the words faster. Spill the tea!" Trisha demanded.

"Oh my God! You can't say that." Said Ella.

Before Trisha could respond Susan-Eva blurted out, "Ida claims she has terminal cancer. A brain tumor."

"Oh," Trisha said. Trisha brought her glass to her lips, hiding her mouth, but Ella could see it in her eyes. She was smiling, hoping it was true. Maybe that was the appropriate reaction. Maybe when you find out someone like Ida is sick, you're supposed to celebrate. So why did Ella want to lunge for Trisha's throat? "As you said, I'm sure it's not true. Does she have any symptoms?"

"Not that we've noticed, but she had a scan. It looked very real," said Susan-Eva.

Trisha picked up her phone and said, "Well, no reason to wonder. If it's true, the head of oncology would know." Trisha hit a contact and brought her phone to her ear.

Ella said, "Doctor-patient confidentiality. They won't be able to—" Trisha gave Ella a look as though she'd said something adorable, then put her phone on speaker.

A man's voice came through the phone. "Trish! You better be calling to apologize on behalf of your husband for the ass-whooping he gave me on the golf course yesterday."

Trisha said, "Oh, you know better. I didn't hear a word about that. What happens at the club stays at the club. Heaven knows I'll never tell you the mischief Clara and I get into during your tee times. No, I'm calling because—" Trisha made her voice sound like it was cracking with emotion, then continued, "I'm sorry. I'm being silly. I'm certain it was... well, just about the cruelest prank anyone has ever tried to play on me. Someone called the house and said they saw my baby at your office. I panicked with worry that something awful was going on, and she hadn't found a way to break the news yet. Now, I know you're not supposed to tell me anything without her permission, but my heart is racing."

The doctor said, "Trisha," Ella held her breath. "That is terrible. People don't think before they gossip. It doesn't violate anything for me to tell you that your daughter has never had an appointment at my practice. That sweet girl was here, bringing flowers to someone else. Now, who, I can't tell you. But I can absolutely confirm your baby is healthy. She's going to be a beautiful bride come October."

Trisha took another drink of her vodka and said, "Thank you for easing my worries. Have Clara give me a call. Bye now." Trisha hung up and looked at Ella. "My, for someone who was so positive it was a lie, you certainly look relieved."

Ella finished her vodka. Susan-Eva said, "Of course she's relieved. We all are. So now the issue is dealing with why she's trying this new tactic. We both feel her impulses may have progressed beyond the point of control without medical intervention. Ella spoke with Doctor Homer, but given the perception most people have of Ida, he didn't—"

"You spoke outside the family on this matter without my permission. At what point have I ever been unclear about discretion?"

Ella said, "This isn't your husband sleeping with another twenty-year-old, Trisha. It's bigger than your reputation. She could hurt someone. We need professional help. Maybe she could see the same doctor you got for my mom. I mean—"

"If you would like your mother to continue seeing him, you won't bring this up to me or anyone else ever again."

Susan-Eva said, "Mrs. Montgomery, we all just want what's best for Ida and everyone's safety." There was a jostle at the front door they all tensed, startled. Leviticus started yapping and ran to nip at Mr. Montgomery, returning home.

From the entrance, he asked, "Did I see my favorite bartender's truck in the driveway?"

With Bruce Montgomery, it was Susan-Eva that went cold. She looked at her phone and said, "I need to call my manager and let him know I'm running late." Susan-Eva kissed Trisha's cheek, knowing it would be seen as an insult not to. She accepted an awkward hug from Bruce, then quickly got out the door before he hugged Ella.

"Mayor Bruce," said Ella with a warm smile. Awkward would not be the word to describe the way Bruce and Ella hugged. At least not for them. For anyone watching, it was a bit *long*.

"My girl! That boyfriend better be treating you well," said Bruce.

"We're in the middle of something, dear," said Trisha.

Bruce put his hands up and said, "Uh oh. I know that voice. I'm blessed with an abundance of fiery women in my life. Fangs in ladies." He poured himself a scotch and went upstairs. Ella and Trisha stared each other down until they heard the bedroom door close.

"It's cute. The way you think flirting could bother me," said Trisha.

"I don't think *flirting* bothers you," said Ella, maintaining eye contact, thinking about the time she was one of *those* twenty-year-olds. Well, almost. She was eighteen.

Trisha smiled and looked up at Ida's senior picture hanging on the wall and said, "God, Ida really is the spitting image of her father. You do have a type, don't you?"

"I don't know what you're talking about." The ice cracked in one of the glasses but neither Trisha or Ella looked down.

"It does surprise me that you'd stir up trouble at a time when the people you love are doing so well," Trisha said.

Ella said, "I'm not stirring up trouble. Our stuff aside, this is serious. It doesn't matter what you threaten me or my mother with. If we really believe Ida is losing control, we have to get help."

"Oh honey, a little part of you thinks she could be cured, don't you? I know this wedding will be hard on you, but get it together."

"It has nothing to do with—"

"How is Evie doing? Really? If I could kill the person who hurt her with my bare hands, I would. You both must be on edge about the Copycat Killer. It's obvious you don't have any respect for yourself, but I always thought you really loved her."

"I do."

"Then focus on being a good friend. With her mother gone and the rape and all that guilt over Ed, I can't imagine how she'd survive one more hardship. If she were to get kicked out of her PhD program or something were to happen to that sweet boy Joseph Porter, she loves so much... After everything she's been through, I think it would break her. Don't you think it would just break her?"

"What are you implying?"

Trisha looked upstairs and then back at Ida's picture. "Ida really does look just exactly like him. Every bit of her looks came from her father. Kind of makes you wonder what she got from me."

NINETEEN
Sixteen years ago - October 31, 2006, 5:30 PM

Ed

THERE WERE STAGES. IT STARTS by selecting the larva. But there were many steps before the larva was to come to the chrysalis. Ed was past the first stage with Susan-Eva but several steps away from the descent. Yet as Susan-Eva peered past Ed through the threshold into his home, so vulnerable with want of an invitation, Ida's words hummed in his mind again and again. *Unfavored by God.* Up until that moment, he planned on giving the girls candy, calling Mrs. Lorenzo, and sending them off.

Bonding was a delicate matter. Ida and Ella were strangers. Private time was never to be had with strangers. It was sacred. It had to be, or else the "Other" would not accept them. Maintaining the sacrality of his encounters took months of careful labor, and he'd only just started on Susan-Eva.

He'd sold the site of his last five transformations for triple its purchase price. Twelve-fourteen Ocean Road, a crumbling shack turned chic-rentable beach house in Destin, Florida. He'd spent two years there. It was a perfect location sandwiched between one neighborhood with the first hints of gentrification creeping in and one that you didn't walk through without a visible loaded gun. At least that's what people who didn't live there said.

The crime rate was higher than average, but it was mostly drug-related.

114

Families with multiple drug charges waited a little longer before going to the police when someone went missing, knowing a loved one would be the first suspect. Even when they had airtight alibis, every member of the family was questioned before they looked anywhere outside. Why would they ever think to question the handsome man who flipped houses just like on TV.

No one thought anything of extra dirt outside a house under construction, especially if you were putting a pool in. In the few hours before the cement truck came, he buried the remains that Alpha couldn't finish. Only inches of mud hid the bones. He'd meditate and watch from the window as someone else unknowingly completed the transformation. Forever hiding the tainted human leftovers, leaving only the angelic metamorphosed forms to behold and carry with him to the next site.

At first, lot 355 seemed ideal. It sat within the Watsonville city limits, a poor industrial highway town. But he'd failed to realize it was at the edge of woods within Moss Groves. If a child disappeared in Watsonville, it may upset people. But a river with dangerous rapids ran through it. You could target kids that played around it, and if they disappeared without evidence long enough, the river would take the blame. There were also two active meth labs. Police would ruin the lives of half the town without ever considering Ed. But Moss Groves was different.

If a child of Moss Groves went missing, it would be a televised town event. If you weren't out walking arm and arm at every flashlight hunt through the woods, it would be noticed. It was a lazy overlook, not checking the surrounding towns more thoroughly. Ed would have to be very careful only to make special friends in Watsonville, and he would have to watch those special friends very closely before he invited them over.

He considered abandoning Lot 355 when he realized the challenge. There was a farmhouse in Harlin, Kentucky, he had his eye on next. But he'd fallen in love with the Watsonville property. The storm cellar was ideal for a prolonged chrysalis stage, which he preferred, and there was an old Larder he could use to display and honor those already in angel form. It would be an insult to the "Other" not to complete at least one transformation on Lot 355. All he had to do was avoid the Larva of Moss Groves.

A few days after he arrived in town, Ed spotted Susan-Eva playing flashlight tag in a Watsonville cemetery. She was the only kid who didn't clutch the arm of a friend with giddy fear of the night. Susan-Eva jumped into the dark and splashed in it like a puddle. Thus began the watch. Through the watch he learned his Larva unfortunately vacillated between towns. Her school was in Moss Groves, where her mother worked, but they went to the grocery and ran errands in Watsonville. Her neighborhood bordered the city line. But it was too late to change. Once the "Other" has seen the Larva it must be transformed.

So, for six weeks, Ed kept his distance. Usually enough that she was out of earshot, rationing each hint of her voice like the last bites of dried meat on a deserted island. On Tuesdays, she'd cartwheel through the parking lot of Sassy's Dance Studio to her ballet lessons, and Ed watched. On Thursdays, she'd help an old lady who lived next to one of her cousins water a tiny garden.

Susan-Eva loved the roses that grew on Mrs. Milano's fence best. She'd squat and search and tiptoe until she smelled every single one. Through a crack in the fence, Ed would watch. On Fridays, she went to the high school football games like the rest of the town and came home so tired she went straight to bed without arguing and fell right to sleep, and Ed would watch. Sometimes from the roof of the vacant house across the street. Sometimes from inside the shed in Susan-Eva's backyard. Sometimes, he'd lay on the ground outside her window, wait until he heard her snore, then press his nose to the glass and watch.

It was at grocery runs to the Piggly Wiggly in Watsonville where it finally happened. Mrs. Lorenzo was very picky about tomatoes. So at 5:45 PM, every Monday, Ed became very picky about tomatoes. Small talk complaints about the selection with Mrs. Lorenzo, turned to swapping tips for growing their own vines in the summer, to joking, to something of a genuine neighborly fondness.

Desperate to be included in any adult conversation, Susan-Eva piped in, "I love tomatoes so much I could bite one like an apple! But that's sort of gross, I guess!" and Ed ignored her. Which was both devasting and confusing.

By nine-years-old Susan-Eva was used to a great many reactions to her peculiar brand of precocious. Annoyance, chastisement, shock, and, more

116

often than not, delight. But never indifference. She felt invisible. She had no idea that even while he looked straight at her mother, Ed was still watching her. Listening would come later.

At 5:55 PM on Mondays, when Mrs. Lorenzo went to the butcher counter, Susan-Eva was always allowed to go get a sugar cookie with blue frosting all by herself. Ed stood right next to Susan-Eva three Mondays in a row, pretending not to notice her. He'd scrutinized over which donuts to choose, joking with Peggy, the eighteen-year-old who worked behind the counter.

Ed would pretend that in the ten minutes since he was laughing with Mrs. Lorenzo at the tomatoes, he'd completely forgotten Susan-Eva. Denying her even a quick glance of recognition. But on the third Monday, Ed asked Peggy if getting twelve chocolate-rainbow-sprinkled-glazed would make him a toddler. Peggy giggled and shook her head. Susan-Eva couldn't take it anymore. She huffed so loud Ed finally looked down.

Susan-Eva pretended to ignore him now and talked only to Peggy as she said, "My ex-friend Joey has a little brother who lives at his dad's house because it's his half-brother, but anyway, his name is Parker. Parker is my age, and sometimes we go to his church instead of our church because Mrs. Trisha invites my mom because there are rumors she slapped one of her maids, so she thinks inviting my mom shows she's nice to the maids, and when Mrs. Trisha invites you to something you have to go. So sometimes we go to her church, and there are donuts there, but it's always the blueberry cake donuts, and Parker says that's the boring grown-up donut flavor and cries until his mom, who's not the same as Joey's mom, takes him to get chocolate-rainbow-sprinkle-glazed. But Joey and I like the blueberry cake ones, especially if you dip it in the coffee, so I guess we're more mature than some people."

Peggy smirked at Ed, expecting him to find this weird little girl as annoying as she did, but Ed said, "Throw one blueberry cake on top." Susan-Eva smiled and turned to go. This was all the victory she needed. She was surprised when she heard Ed holler. "Hold up!" When she turned back Ed was holding out the donut, smiling. *He'd bought it for her.* "So why is Joey your ex-friend?"

"He says twelve-year-olds can't hang out with nine-year-olds."

"Ouch," said Ed, and thus began *The Listen*. Every Monday, Ed bought Susan-Eva a blueberry cake donut, their first secret. Susan-Eva told Ed she was only allowed the cookie before dinner, so he promised not to tell her mom during their tomato talks. Secrets invite more secrets. So, in exchange for every sweet, innocent donut, Ed would offer something savory. Nothing grotesque yet, just mature little tidbits. A funny joke with a bad word. A story about something someone did drunk. All things every kid over-heard but rarely were told directly unless some grown-up in their life gave them the oh-so-special label "mature for their age."

Ed thought Susan-Eva couldn't have been a more perfect larva. Hungry for adventure. Desire to be seen as older. Jealousy at the idea of Ed's friendship with other children, even more so with teenagers. A propensity for wandering off alone. A comfort, a pride even for her ability to keep secrets. Best of all, the more that little shit Joseph Porter decided he was too old to hang out with her, the more desperate she was for Ed's approval.

She was almost ready for step three, the longest phase, *The Feel*. At this point he'd yet to even give her a high five. But come March, she would be ready, and some outsider would take the blame, exactly like they had for nine larvae in four other states.

When remains were discovered, law enforcement would chase dead leads and wild theories. Crazed meth-heads in Florida. Cults in California. Border crossers in Texas. Satan worshippers in Massachusetts. And later this year when Madi Gras tourists wandered their way out of New Orleans for the more "authentic" experiences promised in surrounding small towns, Ed would call in tips to local media outlets about Voodoo tours that went too far.

The community would do the rest for him, creating a frenzy of new folklore that pointed everywhere but at the nice white man who flipped houses just like on T.V., giving him all the time he needed for step four, *The Descent*. Then finally, most importantly, *The Transformation* and *The Flight*.

But it was too early for all that. He had no way of knowing if Ida and Ella were worthy larvae. He'd had more than one special friend in other states but never three at once. Never spontaneous. What he did wasn't an impulse. It was a ritual. He was in control. *Until Ida*. No child had ever looked at him the way Ida stared up at him as she said those words *'Are you unfavored by God?'*

Ed crouched down, getting on eye level with Ida; he smiled as warmly as he could and said, "Unfavored by God? Honey, God doesn't have favorites, surely your Sunday school teacher taught you that. He loves us all equally."

Ida's face stayed blank as she blinked in silence. Then she started laughing. A deep, steady, savory chuckle, as she held Ed's gaze the whole time. All rules dissipated, dissolving into the vibrations Ida's voice sent through the air. The steps were for little girls. Whatever this 3-foot being was, it wasn't a little girl.

Ed turned to Susan-Eva. "So you think you're brave enough for the storm cellar?" Susan-Eva nodded like her life depended on it. "It's real dark down there."

"I've never been afraid of the dark," said Susan-Eva.

Ed swooped Susan-Eva into his arms. Susan-Eva squealed in thrilled surprise as Ed tossed her into a piggyback ride.

The Feel had begun.

TWENTY
August 19, 2022

Ida

THE SERMON AT FIRST BAPTIST was fire and brimstone like it had something to prove that Friday night. It was a special service for someone sick. Or something to do with a baby? Or a cat? *Sick, Baby*, and *Cat,* were all words that meant Ida could stop listening for at least ten minutes. Her ears didn't come back until someone mentioned Pastor Kyle would be leading the service.

Kyle was the new assistant pastor and had what Ella called 'Masturbates to the Crucible Energy.' He was a theater major before seminary who felt the call after a sinful evening led to a near-death experience. Well, he thought it was a near-death experience. His dick turned green, and he was convinced he had a rare STD. He hyperventilated for a half hour until Ella patted him on the shoulder and told him, "Chill dude, I was sucking on a Green-Apple-Jolly-Rancher, and your dick at the same time. Take a shower."

After Ella told Ida this story, Ida wore green whenever she saw Kyle. Seeing beautiful women wearing that color made Kyle smell so good. It sent him into sweats only soothed by yelling at the congregation and that made some of the congregation smell lovely too. Ida made sure always to sign up to sing on Pastor Kyle's nights.

"The next time you accidentally pick up a hot pan without an oven-mitt, or the sun scalds your tender flesh, before you reach for the ice, embrace the pain. Carry it with you through every temptation, imagining that searing, relentless agony for an eternity," preached Pastor Kyle. While old ladies fanned themselves and deacons exchanged whispers about whether young Kyle was *too much,* Ida savored a deep inhale and joined her Fiancée Parker in front of the pulpit.

Even though Parker was the Youth Pastor and was down the hall getting real about JC with teens for most of the evening, they always had him perform a song with Ida after Kyle's sermons to balance things out. Parker was gorgeous in a Gap-ad sort of way, with quarterback energy people mistook as leadership. The sight of Parker and Ida singing gospel side by side brought hands to hearts with hope for the next generation. Neither of them had much musical talent, but charisma and entitlement autotuned them beautifully.

When it was over the betrothed couple stood with Pastor Kyle on the church stairs as everyone filed out. They followed his stern nods with smiley waves. Ida issued staggered hugs to a select worthy few and one random stranger to keep things interesting. As Dr. Homer and his wife walked over, she flung her hands to her heart and exaggerated a loving hum before letting him pull her to his chest and kiss her forehead.

"Beautiful singing, young lady," said Dr. Homer.

"Now, don't you go giving her a big head just so she has to come to you to shrink it, doctor!" said Parker with way too much confidence in his comedic timing.

Mrs. Homer burst into laughter and took Parker's arm, saying, "You are too much!" Then she lowered her voice and grew serious as she said, "I did want to talk to you though. My husband thinks I'm overreacting, but some of the things we hear our grandson, Nelson, saying into his headphones while he's playing this… Stanton, what is it?"

"Call of Duty," said Dr. Homer.

"Call of Duty. The things these boys are saying to each other—well, I thought with a name like that it was a patriotic game, but we sure didn't talk like that in the America I grew up in. I know they all play it, but I don't want to miss signs that he's straying." Mrs. Homer's eyes welled as her husband's rolled.

Parker nodded with genuine empathy and said, "Listen, Nelson is *such* a good guy. I'm sure he's just blending in so he can spread his light. But let's go pray on it." Mrs. Homer sighed in gratitude as Parker led her a few feet away.

Just as Ida was about to make an excuse to evade the skull-to-concrete fantasies that small talk with Dr. Homer was sure to induce, he cleared his throat and said something interesting: "I got a visit from your friend Ella this afternoon."

TWENTY-ONE
August 19, 2022

Susan-Eva

"WHAT IF WE RAN AWAY? No packing. No explanation. We disappear without a trace." Said Ella to Susan-Eva as they passed the sign for the highway exit.

Susan-Eva laughed. How far would they actually get? Susan-Eva wondered. Could they have made it across the state line before Trisha tried to stop them? Susan-Eva doubted it. There were times it surprised her they ever made it to Lot 355. After all it was technically outside the Moss Groves city limits. Once, sophomore year at Florence, three Phi Alpha boys leaned out of an SUV and told Susan-Eva to hop in, they were going to New Orleans for the weekend.

Why not, she thought. The guys were all locals but not legacies. They'd been nerds in high school, not close friends. But she adored them. They'd flirt for fun, knowing her heart was with someone else, and she'd pridefully play wing-woman for them, then talk comic books if they struck out. A rowdy weekend getaway with them would be perfect for those college memories you make just to forget. So that fifty years later you could clutch your heart when you see a picture and have it come flooding back.

Paused at the stop light, before the wheels would have rolled across the city limits, Susan-Eva's phone rang. Trisha had passed them on the road and called to say not this weekend. Not with those boys. Another time. With Ida and Ella. She'd pay for it; they could stay at the Waldorf or rent a mansion in the Garden District and have dinner at Commander's Palace. Did she really want to walk around with trash, drinking hurricanes from plastic cups, and stay in some tiny room with disgusting boys on Bourbon Street? The smell of urine and vomit would cut right through the walls.

Yes. Susan-Eva did want to do all those things. So, she pretended to lose service and hung up on Trisha, an act of war. The room was awful, but they were too excited and too drunk to notice. It had a balcony where Susan-Eva flashed her boobs for Mardi Gras beads as one of the boys puked.

On the last night, that same boy danced with her in the street and told her he was gay, but only a few people knew. After graduation, he'd move to New York or LA. He said she should come. They could be roommates. Whenever they were alone the rest of the night, they whispered little dreams about it. They'd start a production company or a bakery or maybe they should just stay in New Orleans and run a bed and breakfast. They were twenty-one. They could be anything.

Two paper bags of beignets cured their hangovers so well that no one cared about being sticky and coated with powdered sugar the whole drive home. The boys dropped her back at the parking lot on campus where she'd left her pick-up for the weekend. They drove away before Susan-Eva realized the crack in her windshield. Annoying but only a crack. It was when the car wouldn't start that the worry sunk in. Someone had stolen the engine.

It would cost five-to-ten thousand dollars to replace. Not money Susan-Eva had. Plus, it wasn't like she could take it to any mechanic. It was a raven black Ford '74 with Vinyl stripes Trisha had gotten out-of-state for her.

Trisha was the one who'd have the numbers of who to take it to. It was possible it had nothing to do with Trisha. After all, sometimes bad things just happen. She was really nice about it. All she said was. "Oh, that's awful, beautiful. You can borrow one of mine while we're getting it fixed. You do want it fixed, right? I thought you loved that truck."

"I do. But it's too expensive." Sniffled Susan-Eva because she really did love it.

"Oh, don't you worry about that for a second, my sweetest girl. You're breaking my heart right now. I'll pay for it; of course, don't be silly."

"No. I wouldn't feel right about it. It's my fault for leaving it here. It was so stupid."

"It's always hard. Learning how quickly things we love can be taken away. You know your Mama really wanted you to have it. She helped with every detail to make sure it was like the one in that picture of your Daddy you love so much."

"I know," said Susan-Eva, trying not to sob as she thought of the pride her mother must have swallowed to work with Trisha on the gift.

"Let me fix it."

"Okay. I'm so sorry."

"For what, gorgeous?" asked Trisha. It was possible she had nothing to do with it. It could have just happened. So many bad things just happen, and so many people do bad things, Susan-Eva thought. But it was the last time she ever left town without telling Trisha. Because next time, it wouldn't be a car; it would be Ella or Joseph. First offenses warranted a punishment to the offender; second offenses meant the people they loved got punished. Or got jobs that took them out of state.

So, Susan-Eva swallowed and said, "For leaving without... I should have told you."

"Well, yes. My feelings were hurt."

"I'm sorry."

"Because I worry about my girls so much."

"I'm sorry."

"If anything ever happened to you, you know Ida would be lost. She'd be so heartbroken. Who knows what she'd do? Who knows what I'd have to do about it?"

"I know. I'm sorry."

"We're all so lucky to have each other. Aren't we?"

"Yes. I'm sorry."

"Well, it was a lesson. That's what college is all about. As long as you learned, all is forgiven."

"I learned. I'm sorry."

"Good. I wish your mamma was here to see the good woman you're becoming. She would be so proud of you," said Trisha. Susan-Eva's wanted to tell her to fuck off, to say how dare you bring up my mother. But instead, she started crying. "Oh, my sweet baby. It's okay. It's all going to be okay."

Now, approaching the exit ramp with Ella at her side, Susan-Eva's fingers itched to flick on her blinker and hit the gas. But then she remembered Ida wasn't the only secret that required daily attention, "Who would figure out what to do about Alpha?" Said Susan-Eva. Ella pressed her head to the window. "Besides, a new band is trying out at the Bar tonight. Could be the next Beatles, you never know."

The monotony of opening side work at Craw-Ma's came as a relief to Susan-Eva. Even the sting of bleach in her nostrils as she scrubbed away hardened grenadine from the wooden bar felt comforting in its predictability. Craw-Ma's was a relatively new bar but an instant favorite. It was the sort of rustic chic that got away with claiming a casual come-as-you-are vibe while overcharging for cocktails named after local streets.

Music was the big draw. They had live bands every night of the week, filling a void for the post-college/pre-family crowd that still wanted to hang but wouldn't be caught dead at a frat party. But neither the band nor the happy hour crowd had arrived yet. Other than five grad students sharing a pitcher of beer over their first study group and one early-bird dinner, Ella and Susan-Eva had the bar to themselves.

"Fuck Trisha," said Ella as Susan-Eva reached across the bar with the fountain gun to top off Ella's ginger ale.

Mr. Carter from The Cheshire Cat leaned out from the 'early bird booth' booth, shaking his head at Ella. It wasn't like she screamed it. Mr. Carter had a sixth sense for anything he could give a disapproving head shake to. "I think that's my cue," said Ella as she grabbed her purse.

The first of the happy hour crowd pushed through the entrance and showered the bar with unwelcome sunlight so blinding Susan-Eva couldn't make out any of their faces. But she heard a familiar voice asking Dan the doorman: "Now, be real with me. Is this a true local spot, or is this where y'all rip off outsiders like me?"

Susan-Eva and Ella both cocked their heads. The sunlight relented, and they were instantly met with Calvin's turtle on an electric scooter smile.

"Go on in." Mumbled Dan, glancing at Calvin's id and ignoring the dumb-ass question.

"Um... going back for seconds?" Ella asked Susan-Eva.

"No. He was supposed to leave. And I'm starting to feel we should avoid food-related analogies for people," said Susan-Eva.

Ella nodded, *fair enough*, then leaned back in to whisper, "Hey, not to be a buzzkill, but he's probably a reporter."

Susan-Eva put the back of her hand to her forehead like a swooning silent film actress and gasped before performing, "A reporter? What do you mean? Ella, we made love! I think he might be the one! I think he likes me; I think he really, really—" Ella rolled her eyes, and Susan-Eva smirked. Calvin waved and started chatting up the hostess. Susan-Eva cocked her head taking him in again. He'd changed into jeans. "No shit, he's probably a reporter. *But damn.*"

"Indeed." Agreed Ella. A barback handed Susan-Eva a case of beers, and she disappeared under the bar, loading the fridge. She heard the buzz of someone new coming in, but from under the bar, she couldn't see. "If you want to get rid of him, you could always tell him your fiancée just walked in."

"What?" asked Susan-Eva. As soon as she stood back up her, question was answered. The someone new coming in was Joseph Porter.

TWENTY-TWO
August 19, 2022

Ella

"PORTER!" DAN, THE DOORMAN, SAID, standing from his stool and pulling Joseph into a hug. It was remarkable, Ella thought. Getting to witness Susan-Eva's fake swoon act, followed by the involuntary physical response she had to the sound of Joseph's last name. He showed up for at least one of her shifts every week but never the same one. Now, Susan-Eva would perform a different act. An act filled with casual glances anywhere but at him, pretending she didn't notice he was there, pretending her heart was pounding at its average pace, pretending she couldn't feel him.

Sometimes, he'd meet friends at a table and not even bother to say hello, claiming he didn't want to bother her while she was busy. But that wasn't an option at a slow 5:30. So, they'd do their "friends" thing.

This act was far more convincing than the swoon. But Ella could see the hairs on Susan-Eva's arm raise. She didn't even glance at Calvin as he pulled up the bar stool right in front of her. Every inch of her focus went to cleaning a fake smudge from a glass so she could hide her face until the rush subsided.

"Joseph Washington Porter," said Ella, giving him a quick hug.

"Eleanor Jane Kyle," said Joseph, hugging her back. As two kids who often got accused of ruining the fun by acting too grown-up, Joseph and Ella had a bond. At some point, they decided to lean into it and always greet each other formally with their full names. It was probably while they were refusing to do something stupid like the cha-cha slide or 'enjoy the moment.'

"Look who's showing up without an appointment now, Dr. Porter," said Susan-Eva.

"Someone's got to make sure you get enough tips to pay for that PhD," said Joseph, sitting one stool over from Calvin.

Calvin leaned forward like he'd been invited to join their conversation. "I decided to stay until the auction Saturday. It sounds like such an event; I didn't want to miss it. You're getting your PhD! That's so neat."

"So neat. Who are you?" Said Joseph, making no attempt to hide his sarcasm.

"This is Calvin. *We met last night,*" said Susan-Eva, meeting Joseph's eyes.

"Ah." Nodded Joseph, holding her gaze with something between a glare and a smile. It was so weird that the two of them talked about Susan-Eva's hookups. He'd never discouraged her from telling him, even though that had to be what Susan-Eva wanted him to do. She wanted him to say the idea of her with anyone else was unbearable. Or that he didn't approve of her sudden change in character. Or to snap and call her immature. Or irresponsible. Or scream she was a slut. Anything. But she knew he would never.

He'd let her torture him with details and torture herself in a way not even she understood, and he'd never say more than that; however she needed to move through what happened to her in the park was okay. He'd say even if it had nothing to do with what happened, it was okay. Then he'd ask how she felt about it and if she was okay, and she'd make an excuse to get off the phone.

It was a relief to have someone who shared Ella's concern for Susan-Eva, but Jesus. Yeah, yeah you can be evolved and stay friends with your exes. But this was something else. At first Ella hoped it was a temporary period of insanity before they surrendered to fate and got back together. There was no one further from a romantic than Ella, but if there was one fairytale love she believed in, it was theirs. Of course, fucking dealing with

Ida had to ruin it. If there's one thing fairytales don't have, it's cannibalism. Unless it's Hansel and Gretel (seriously, what was up with that).

The lie that broke them up was a year ago, and as far as Ella could see, neither was budging. But maybe Calvin would be the X factor that rewrote their equation. Hearing about it was one thing. But seeing one of these men who up until now must have been faceless and certainly ab-less in Joseph's mind was another matter entirely. Susan-Eva handed Calvin a beer. People who drink beer aren't supposed to look like that.

"Who are you?" Calvin asked Joseph.

Susan-Eva met Joseph's eyes and smiled as she said, "This is Joseph Porter. He's my—"

"Don't—" Interrupted Joseph.

"Therapist," said Susan-Eva.

"Why do I even bother?" asked Joseph with a smirk.

"I really don't know," Susan-Eva said.

Calvin said, "Must be weird being a therapist in a small town and running into your patients everywhere."

"Yes. That is what is making this weird. Absolutely nothing else," Ella said so deadpan that even Calvin couldn't mistake it as genuine.

Susan-Eva smiled at all three of them and said, "Shots?" Ella shook her head, but Joseph and Calvin shrugged 'why not.' Joseph never did shots, not even in college. But he was the first to down his tequila. Another group settled at the other end of the bar and waved Susan-Eva over. Calvin smiled at Ella and Joseph about to start talking and they both instinctively got up and went to a bar table before he could get a word out.

"Calvin from last night," Joseph said to Ella once they were out of earshot.

"Calvin from last night," repeated Ella. "He pulled the witch costume picture off the fridge this morning and acted like he didn't know what it was. Maybe he didn't. *But.*"

"But maybe he did," said Joseph. Joseph's knowledge of what happened with Ed was as limited as everyone else's, but he was there for every stage of the aftermath, so it wasn't hard for him to share Ella's distrust.

"Maybe he did. Anyway, I'm really sick of all these guys. So, could you do me a quick favor and put a ring on it? You've been engaged for like twenty years this is ridiculous," Said Ella.

"That's not a quick favor. That's a lifelong commitment," Said Joseph.

"Cool. So you'll do it," Ella said, and Joseph rolled his eyes. "You're both so stupid. All because of one lie. Do you really believe you can't love someone and lie to them? Explain Santa then."

"St. Nicholas was a fourth-century Greek bishop—"

"I'm not asking you to mansplain Christmas to me, Joseph."

"You literally just said explain—"

"Santa is proof we're all cool with lying for the sake of happiness. So, get over it."

He glared with a smirk. She grinned. They missed each other. The breakup wasn't the kind that required picking sides. But it wasn't like they really hung out in a group anymore. "Are you and Malcolm still good?" Joseph asked.

Ugh, that was the one thing that made Joseph annoying. Stupid, invested questions he really wanted honest answers to. Ella said, "We're great. We might move in together after Ida gets married."

"Wow. That's huge."

"Yeah," Ella said, politely smiling.

"It's weird. Thinking of the three of you not living together," said Joseph.

"*Yeah.* It is! Isn't it?" Ella responded.

"So weird." He agreed.

"Malcolm doesn't get that. Not that anyone really can. But it's not like I'm saying I won't do it. I just want him to acknowledge it's a big deal. We've been fighting about it, and then yesterday morning he… It doesn't matter. It's not like I said no. It was fine. It just was…" What the fuck was she doing? Ella couldn't talk to Joey Porter about sex. *Especially not that kind of sex.* He would flip out and be all concerned and compassionate. Gross. "Sorry. I don't know why I said all that."

Joseph said, "Don't be sorry. What were you going to say?"

Ella smirked and said, "Don't."

"Don't what?"

131

"Therapist me."

"This is not me therapist-ing you."

"No? What is it then?"

"I'd have to consult a sociologist, but I think the word for it is friendship."

"Ew," Ella said, and they both smirked. "I should go." They looked at the bar.

"Maybe I should too," said Joseph, seeing Susan-Eva talking to Calvin.

"Stay."

"Why?"

"It could be real," said Ella. "He could be some guy who doesn't know about Ed and likes her. After all, everyone likes her. What if she starts to like him back, and this is the moment you lose her, and all you had to do was…"

"Accept that she can never be completely honest with me?"

"No one is ever completely honest with anyone," said Ella. She stepped to leave.

"Do you know? The thing she lies about. Do you know what it is?"

Ella paused, and then she turned back. "You know, sometimes I kind of want to know what you're like as a therapist, too. Not in the insane way she does, but I think everyone who really knows you wants to know."

"Why?"

"Because we all know what it's like to have a problem and have someone not listen. But it's impossible to imagine you not listening. Not because you're a good man. I mean, you are, you know, I think you're— insert genuine friendship comment here— whatever. But that's not why you listen. You listen because you're too interested not to. You really want to know. It's what makes you, you." Ella met his eyes and said, "She lied to protect you."

Joseph said, "I don't want her to protect me. I want her to trust me."

"Joseph. Trust *me*. This is the one thing even you don't want to know."

TWENTY-THREE

Sixteen years ago – October 31, 2006, 5:30 PM

Ida

IDA KNEW HOW DANGEROUS IT was to laugh at Ed. That's why she did it. To test him. And because what Ed said was so stupid, she couldn't help it. *"God loves us all equally."* It wasn't that she thought he believed it. He said it in the pitch of a lie. That slightly high and sing-songy one all grown-ups used when they said things like "Everything will be alright." Or "It won't hurt that bad." Or "Everyone is beautiful in their own way." But those lies were said to comfort.

Ed wanted it to sound comforting but couldn't completely hide his rage. As though he believed he was one of the favored. A sin Ida had to challenge immediately. There was no better challenge to pride than the laugh. That laugh was the only thing that ever made her father lose his temper enough to slap her the way her mother did.

Laughing at men who weren't joking was Ida's favorite spell for a violence trade. She hated physical discomfort but knew whenever she got men like her father, the sort that saw himself as patient and gentle, to hit her, she'd gain hours of free reign.

Once at the Montgomery hunting lodge, Ida's Uncle Lyle lost his wedding ring in the guts of a deer he was cleaning. Pink in his cheeks deepened to a maroon that covered his whole face the longer his hands trailed intestines and could find no sign of the gold band.

Ida was not allowed in the shed where they cleaned the meat. But she snuck in and watched him from the corner. By the time Uncle Lyle noticed her, he was too lost in his task to do anything about it. Until she laughed. As his hands got coated with a thicker layer of chunks that her daddy called "innards," Ida laughed harder and harder.

Uncle Lyle snapped at her to stop. She laughed louder. He threatened to tell her mother. Louder. Her father. Louder. Finally, he spotted a stick on the floor and threatened to switch her himself if she didn't leave that instant, and Ida laughed in her lowest register, erasing any hint of a smile from her face.

He grabbed the stick, yanked her arm, and gave her a hard swat. It stung bad enough to make her scream, so she bit her tongue until it bled, knowing focused determination on self-inflected pain could keep her silent through another two swats. On swat three, she let go.

The shriek was so loud that Ida felt tension shoot through Uncle Lyle's hands at the shock of it. Soft, pitiful little whimpers followed so quickly that he instantly thought he'd imagined all of her nastiness. His own frenzied insanity must have made him think his adorable little niece was a demon cackling in the corner.

Remembering how much worse he'd received as a boy for far less and his conviction that Ida's generation was too soft soothed most of his guilt. He decided he'd still give her a stern talking to, then buy her a present the next day and put the incident behind him. That was before he saw her face.

When Uncle Lyle dropped the switch and turned Ida back to face him, he expected her cheeks to be stained with tears. The sight of her was so shocking that, at first, he couldn't comprehend what the bright red liquid coating her chin was.

He'd been arms-deep in the guts of a deer most of the day. He wasn't squeamish when it came to the gore of hunting. But the sight of this eight-year-old girl covered in blood brought vomit to his throat. It was impossible. He'd lost his temper; maybe he'd struck her harder than he thought, but nothing that would break the skin.

Unexpected red is the most useful of all unexpected colors. Even when people have no idea why it's there, they know it means STOP! So, as soon as Ida felt her tongue start to bleed, she let her mouth fill with saliva, then bit just above the cut to squeeze out as much as possible before letting it drizzle out. Uncle Lyle searched her face for cuts, trying to see where the blood came from, but Ida pretended to run away in fear. After that, whenever Ida snuck into the shed and Uncle Lyle caught her, he pretended not to notice. Even when she played with the knives. *Even when he saw what she was doing to the squirrels.*

Ida doubted Ed would hit her for laughing since he was a stranger, but she knew his reaction would reveal something. He remained smiley. But he started to smell like run. This was intriguing. But not so much so that it was worth it to stay. He hadn't even offered them candy. If she was with anyone else, she would have left right then. But Ella followed Ed inside, and Ida was supposed to act like Ella. That was how she stayed out of the closet.

Ella

Ella thought if Ed put Susan-Eva down from his back, she could whisper they had to go. She just needed to use her serious voice. She'd follow them inside and then get them right out. "Ya'll like dogs?" Ed shouted from the house. "Mine's named Alpha. He's a nut. But he loves kids once he gets to know them. Come on, he's out back."

"I'm allergic to dogs." Lied Ella, looking back at Ida.

"Me too," said Ida, grabbing Ella's hand. Ella exhaled in relief that Ida caught on.

"No, you're not. You've both played with Joey's dog lots of times," said Susan-Eva.

Ed said, "That's all right. I get nervous around dogs I don't know, too. Why don't you two wait here while I show S.E. Then y'all better get going so you get home before dark."

Ella wanted to argue. She racked her brain for an excuse to stop Susan-Eva from going with him. But Susan-Eva knew Ed. They visited pets at grown-ups' houses all the time. Parker and Joey Porter's dad was really protective, and they'd been here, so obviously, he thought Ed was fine. Ella knew it would be rude to argue with an adult who was friends with two of her classmate's parents. Rude was the word that got her into the most trouble. So she kept quiet as Ed carried Susan-Eva through the back door on his back and disappeared.

The screen door rattled, hitting the frame. Swooshing her skirt, jangling all its charms with a dramatic pivot, Ida turned to face Ella and said, "Fess up! Why do you smell scared? Why does Ed smell like—" The door rattled again Ella jumped. Ed walked back in without Susan-Eva.

"Sorry, there's no AC yet. I've got some of Milo's Sweet Tea in the fridge. I'll get you some, so you don't burn in here." Ed poured them two glasses and went back outside. It had been hours since they'd had a drink of water, and Ella was never allowed to have anything with as much sugar as Milo's Sweet tea at her house. She drank half the glass before Ida took a sip.

"Ella, what's going on? I won't be mean, I swear. Just tell me why you smell like that?" asked Ida.

"I don't know. Drink the tea." So, Ida drank the tea. Then two Ida's were drinking tea. Everything in the room became two to Ella. Then everything became one. One big blob of blurry color. And then darkness.

TWENTY-FOUR
August 19, 2022

Ella

THE WHITE PAINT THAT COVERED Parlay House turned Rose Gold at sunset. The driveway was empty when Ella pulled in. It should have been a relief to be alone. But the mass of the house consumed her. She felt a dull ache. An unacceptable yearning to hide under a blanket. Like the house was a monster from a nightmare she'd grow out of one day.

As she passed through the front door, the ache transformed. In rare moments alone within the walls of Parlay House, its grandeur still had an entrancing effect on Ella. She let herself become absorbed by the pink and orange hues reflecting on the pool water like a sheet of jewels. Dropping her bag onto a chair, she rolled her neck and stretched her spine from side to side. Savoring the spectacle. Letting the intensity of the glare bring water to her eyes. It was so quiet.

The translucent reflection of Ella's body in the glass door cast her image atop the sparkles as though she was one with the light and the water. Indulging in the fantasy of dissolving was usually violent. She'd picture a bomb and her body becoming mist in an instant. A return to the nothingness she was always meant to be. Just for this instant the dissolve felt beautiful, a return to everythingness, to light.

In that light, two sparks reflected brighter than all the others. Circles of white with green in the center. There was another reflection in the window with her, sitting on the stairs, lording over the scene like a conductor. Ella closed her eyes and breathed in the weight of Ida's presence.

"I thought you had decorating committee?" Said Ella without turning. From the reflection, she could see Ida standing; she was wearing a catholic schoolgirl uniform. "We're too old to go to the Prep Bros and Catholic hoes party, and even if we weren't, they stopped throwing it three years ago so they wouldn't get canceled."

"I hear you're trying to get me locked up. I guess you think I need good girl/bad girl lessons again. Thought I'd dress for class," said Ida, in a voice she only used on Ella. And only when they were alone. Ida slowly walked down the stairs.

"I don't know what you're talking about," said Ella.

"I saw Dr. Homer at church. We had a little chat. He's such a sweetheart," said Ida.

"Yeah, that's what you want in a doctor, sweet guy who apparently doesn't give a fuck about Doctor-patient confidentiality."

"You weren't seeing him as a patient," said Ida.

"Like you weren't seeing anyone in Oncology as a patient. We know you're lying about the tumor. What did you do, bribe someone to make a fake scan? Good one."

"I didn't go to the doctor here. I went to a better one. I'm not lying," said Ida.

Ella rolled her eyes at Ida and went to the kitchen. Ida followed. "Joseph Porter and Evie's one-night stand are both at the bar right now. Want to go watch?" asked Ella.

"Why? Are you afraid to be alone with me? Since I know you betrayed me," said Ida.

"What did you expect me to do?"

"Exactly what you did. I'm not stupid. I knew you'd tell, and I knew no one would believe you. It doesn't mean it didn't hurt my feelings."

"I've *never* said you were stupid. And hurt your feelings? Is that a fucking joke?"

138

"All that soap really never did any good, did it?" Ida leaned against the wall at the kitchen entrance as Ella filled a glass of water. "You didn't answer me. Are you afraid to be alone with me?"

Ella turned to Ida and took a drink, staying at the opposite end of the kitchen. "You told me you want to kill someone, and there's probably nothing I can do about it. Of course I'm afraid of you."

"You don't smell afraid. You smell annoyed."

"Okay," said Ella, pretending not to believe her. Pretending she didn't know better than anyone how accurate the smell thing turned out to be.

"Why didn't you cry when you found out I was dying?"

"Because I know it's a trick."

"It's not. So, you're saying you would cry if you believed it."

"No. I'd be relieved. We're not friends, Ida. I stay because I'm afraid of what you'd do if I didn't. Because I think you're a monster." Monster was a new word for Ella. In the last sixteen years, Ida and Ella flung insults at each other like they were auditioning for *Heathers the Musical.* But dehumanizing was something that started after Ida's engagement with Parker.

Sliding her hand along the island, Ida crossed the room. "Remember how you taught me to act at dances in middle school? Want to play good touch, bad touch?"

"Stop," said Ella. But she didn't move.

"Why? If you're so scared of what I'll do, I must need a refresher on the rules." Ella knew she should step back, but it had been *such* a long day. So she stood still. Waiting for it. Hoping for it.

The familiar grip of Ida's hands clutched Ella's hips so firmly she could feel her palm press against the bone. The inseam of her jeans tightened as Ida pushed her fingertips into the soft rise of Ella's curves. Push away, Ella told herself, but then Ida started to sway. Ella's body obeyed like it was pulled into a current.

Ida said, "Rule one: friends can dance sexy. But it's a performance for the boys. We have to look at them." Ella's eyes fell to the floor. Ida grabbed her chin, forcing Ella to meet her gaze. "Not each other, not long anyway. We can touch here." The pressure of Ida's fingers relented and slid slowly up and around until the back of her left pointer rested just above the button of Ella's jeans. "But never here." Ida's finger dipped barely under the waistband.

Stiff fabric compressed around Ella's thighs and hips as the seam tightened between her legs. Like a harness sending pulsing warm reminders of support and control. Ella's breath hitched, and Ida leaned closer and said, "But my favorite lesson was about whispering. You said we could whisper and giggle and glance at them. But what kind of whispering are we not allowed to do? Show me."

"I can't," Ella said, unable to stop her voice from shrinking to a whimper. Balmy waves coursed through her body as Ida's hand slid further down until it found lace. Under the lace, something tender and throbbing with life growing evermore slick and inviting as Ida found its opening. She always found it so quickly. Ida was always so, so fast.

"Oh no, Ella," said Ida mimicking Ella's whimper as she pulled out her hand and used Ella's hips to turn her around and hold her from behind. "It seems like you're the one who's forgotten the rules. But I guess that's always been the real secret. You knew how to teach me how to pretend because you're pretending too, aren't you? Because guess what? When people are scared of someone, they suck up. They don't call them a monster. So, you're a liar, aren't you? You want to be scared of me. You've always wanted that. But you're not. Because the truth is, around me is the only time you ever really feel safe. You are right, though. We're not friends." Ida's bottom lip brushed against Ella's ear lobe. "Because what kind of whispering are friends not allowed to do?"

Before her mind could tell them to stop, Ella's lips moved, breathing her answer. "The kind where you linger. The kind where the heat of your breath is there longer than the words," said Ella. She closed her eyes like she was surrendering to execution.

"And then you showed me, didn't you?" whispered Ida. Tightness surrounded Ella's chest and throat as her mouth dried. Inexcusable water glazed her eyes, threatening tears. A surge of rage shot tension through her spine as she finally found movement and twisted back to face Ida, clasping the back of her neck.

"Tell the truth. You're not *really* dying, are you?" demanded Ella, her voice pained and shaking. Ida smiled and stared at her calmly.

140

"Now you smell scared." Ella clutched Ida's hair into a fist. Ida leaned in—

"Babe?" Malcolm's voice cut through from the front door. An exhale with so much frustration it was almost a cry fell from Ella's lips. Ida smirked, and they both stepped back.

The roughness of Malcolm's hand felt jarring as he tilted Ella's chin up and pecked her lips. The clunk of his bag as he dropped it to the ground, like the ring of a phone in the middle of the ballet. In the middle of anything.

"I thought you had work to do?" Said Ella, clearing her throat.

"I finished early. We'll get dinner," said Malcolm.

Ida exaggerated a bend over the island like she was assuming the position. She drank from Ella's water glass. Malcolm took in her plaid skirt and knee socks. "Hey, Ida. *Nice outfit.*"

"It's all for you, Mr. Dubois." Ida brushed past him and went to the stairs. Ella took the glass to get more water but froze, seeing Ida stop halfway up and stare down at her.

"What if I let you choose?" asked Ida.

"Choose what?" asked Malcolm, for some reason assuming the question was for him.

"Dinner," said Ida.

"Um. I meant more of a solo date night," said Malcolm. He shifted, confused.

Ida looked back to Ella and said, "Another time." Ella swallowed as Ida held her gaze and then disappeared upstairs.

"She is so weird," said Malcolm.

Ella grabbed her keys. "Let's go."

TWENTY-FIVE

August 19, 2022

Joseph

BY TEN, CRAW-MA'S WAS winding down. The new band was on its final set. Susan-Eva started closing side-work and Joseph had downed his sixth shot. He wanted to forget Ella's warning. It didn't work. Though his world was…unsteady.

Even through his tequila haze he could feel the sting of Calvin. The worst part was if he wasn't so certain there was an ulterior motive, he didn't hate the guy. If he could endure the idea of anyone other than him with Susan-Eva (which he couldn't), it would be a guy like Calvin. Kind, doting, protective, and more than willing to let her be the star she couldn't help but be.

Most importantly, she clearly enjoyed him. Not that Calvin had much of a reason to think so. She kept turning him down. But when she wasn't facing him, she'd smile whenever he said something to her. So it was a good thing Joseph was absolutely certain Calvin *did* have an ulterior motive. Otherwise, he would, of course, do the right thing and go home, probably. Maybe. Seriously, how could a guy who drinks beer have abs like that?

"One dance. Your manager last night didn't mind," Said Calvin as Susan-Eva filled him a fresh glass of IPA from the draft.

142

A fast bluegrass beat encouraged the final partners on the floor to showcase spins and twists. Joseph watched Susan-Eva bite her lip and glance at the band, clearly wanting to say yes to Calvin. Showing off was an end-of-night tradition for the final songs every night. But she glanced at the half-empty bottle of Tequila, then shook her head and said, "Yeah, well, last night Laura was managing. She'd let me turn this place into an opium den as long as it was clean by morning. But Tyler's a real hard ass, sorry."

"What if something were to happen to Tyler?" Calvin suggested with a playful smirk.

"Something like what?" asked Susan-Eva with a surprised grin.

"Shark attack," Calvin blurted, and Susan-Eva snorted. "Just my first thought. But they say go with your gut. And yes, I realize that would require locating shark-infested waters and getting Tyler to agree to swim in them. Which might be difficult to do before the end of the song. But I think it's still worth a shot." Susan-Eva rolled her eyes and went back to cleaning. But as soon as she was certain her face was out of his view, there was that smile again. Calvin hadn't attempted a joke before. God help her. She loved a goofy sense of humor.

No one knew this better than Joseph. So he ordered his sixth beer. Even at his peak drinking junior year of college, this was a beer too many, and that was without the shots. But tonight, he needed it. Tonight, Joseph was not a therapist, or an evolved twenty-first-century man, or an ally. For one night only, Joseph Porter wanted, *needed* to be a dude. He hadn't just endured knowing about Susan-Eva's hookups. He'd asked questions about them. And yeah, he knew this was unhealthy. Hell, it was outright masochistic.

He knew about the time in the pool, the time in the back of her pick-up truck in the middle of her shift, about the time on top of this very bar. It was torture. Not just the jealousy, but… it was all so unlike her. He wasn't judging her, but he was really worried.

It was possible they were taking the friends thing too far. Boundaries were needed. BUT! *But.* If Joseph listened to enough, maybe one day Susan-Eva would realize she really could tell him anything. After the first one, she called him, sobbing and apologizing, but wouldn't say for what.

"I'm so, so sorry. I don't know what's wrong with me. I can't stop. I'm so sorry." Susan-Eva had begged. They weren't together. She didn't owe him anything, but when he assured her of all of this, she said. "No. Not for doing it. For calling you. I don't know why, I can't—"

"Don't ever apologize for calling me," Joseph interrupted.

Lila, a twenty-two-year-old waitress, bussed an empty peanut basket in front of Calvin. She smiled and leaned much further over the bar than she needed to before inviting him to a house party. Declining politely enough to remain liked while still ending a conversation is a rare skill, but apparently, Calvin had mastered it.

There was no way the good guy act was legit. Dude-Joseph wasn't having it. He puffed up his chest, doing his best Pop-eye impression, and pushed himself back from the bar to face Calvin. "Enough," declared Joseph loud enough for Calvin to squint at him in shock. "Which is it? Podcaster or reporter?"

"I don't know what you're talking about, man; I'm in town to drop off my brother," Calvin replied, with a friendly raise of his beer.

"What's his name?" asked Joseph.

"Dylan," Calvin said.

Sober Joseph would have come up with a gotcha question that required more than making up a name. Sober Joseph probably would've had Calvin confessing his true motives hours ago. By now, they'd have moved on to Calvin's childhood traumas. They'd start to unpack why everything he does is because his dad didn't believe in him. They'd be dipping their toes into the real reason Calvin has a reoccurring erotic dream about a Laker's-themed rubber ducky. But drunk Joseph couldn't do better than shaking his head and saying, "Then why isn't Dylan here? Doesn't track, buddy. Does. Not. Track."

"I can call him right now and—"

"No one gives a shit about your fake brother, Calvin. You're here for the story. So, what is it this time? Podcast, paper, magazine, Lifetime movie, TikTok channel? It doesn't matter. They won't talk to you. And what's more, she knows. Fuck you for using her. But don't kid yourself. She's using you right back."

"What story?" Calvin asked, invested *but not too invested.*

"Shut your mouth and tell me what your angle is," demanded Joseph, unwilling to listen to the little voice in his head, wondering if maybe Calvin really was just some dumb, nice dude with a crush on the woman he still believed was his future wife.

"Your first request is a little at odds with the second there, buddy," replied Calvin, with a smile that managed to be sympathetic without being condescending.

"SEE! You're not -that- stupid," Joseph said, jabbing his finger into the bar and knocking over his empty shot glass.

"Um, thanks," Calvin nodded.

"The whole innocent, abs-for-brains thing is an act to get her to let her guard down. She's been through enough. Leave her the fuck alone." Joseph's voice went a little hoarse.

"What do mean? Did something happen to her?" Calvin asked, putting his beer down.

"Of course. Something happens to almost everyone and they should get to choose when and if they tell the story of it. But vultures like you decide certain stories belong to you. To profit and exploit and—"

"Look at her," Calvin said, watching Susan-Eva sway and hum to herself as she wiped down liquor bottles. "The only reason anyone needs to spend time with a girl like that is her letting you. So, the only story I want to hear is how you lost her so I don't screw it up like you did."

Retorts spun in Joseph's brain like he was searching an old rolodex and found each card too faded to read. So, instead, he turned back to the bar and said, "Hey, Evie." Susan-Eva stopped wiping bottles. "Dance with me."

She didn't even bother responding or looking back at them. She walked straight out onto the dance floor and held her hand out until Joseph took it.

People on their way out the door stopped and turned. The barback pulled glasses off the drying rack, knowing the night was no longer over. Even the band seemed to consult each other, making eye contact and shaking their heads as they debated a song worthy of the occasion. No cradle-to-grave town survives without its daycare-to-dentures romances. Whether you were for it or against it, the Porter-Lorenzo love story was one any true Moss Groves lifer had a stake in.

Everyone but Calvin in Craw-Ma's knew the two hadn't shared a public dance since the breakup. Whatever happened on the floor would be tea to share, spill, and tax by tomorrow. With a nod from the lead guitarist to the drummer, a waltz hidden in a modern country song began, and all eyes glued themselves to Joseph and Susan-Eva. They could both feel it. It felt good. They missed the gravity of each other.

"You two have a nice a nice talk?" asked Susan-Evan as Joseph's hand found the small of her back.

"Yeah. We're going golfing," said Joseph as he spun her out.

"You don't golf," said Susan-Eva, spinning back in.

"Oh yeah. Guess I'll have to think of something else to do."

"You probably shouldn't have asked me to dance. You don't want your new bud to get the wrong idea about us."

"You probably shouldn't have said yes. You don't want your new boyfriend to get offended and leave. Did he leave yet?"

Susan-Eva shook her head. "Come on, you know better than that. He won't leave until he gets the story." Joseph met her eyes with a mix of arousal and relief at their shared suspicions as the song picked up speed, and they started moving faster around the floor.

"Poor guy must have no idea who he's dealing with. You never let a word slip you don't want to."

"What I want has nothing to do with it." She met his eyes. "You know, all you have to do is tell me to kick him out, and he's gone." The song ended. They both had to catch their breath. Joseph glanced to the stool where Calvin sat; he'd turned away reading something on his phone. It should have been an easy thing to say. Joseph wanted nothing more than never to have to see this guy again. But it wasn't easy. He couldn't do it. The look on Susan-Eva's face went from hope to pleading to disappointment. Joseph shook his head, and she nodded and said, "I think you should go."

TWENTY-SIX

Sixteen years ago - October 31, 2006 – 5:51 PM

Susan-Eva

ALONE. SUSAN-EVA SAVORED THE word like a treat. Parker and Joseph had to see the cellar with their Dad, Ed, and each other, like they were on one of those boring tours. But halfway through the yard, Ed stopped and said, "Shoot, I ought to get your friends water or something while they wait. Here—" He said, putting Susan-Eva down and handing her the keys! "You go on down. And don't you worry; Alpha's gonna bark real loud, but I won't let him out until he's calmed down." So Susan-Eva got to explore the dungeon ALONE.

She couldn't believe her luck. To explore a historic sight all by herself! It was better than an overnight at a museum. It was so exciting. Every step down to the cellar made Susan-Eva grin bigger. Signs of adventure were everywhere. It was dark just like Ed said it would be, but not so dark you couldn't see since there was a lightbulb on the stairs. It smelled musty, but not like an old lady's attic—the kind of musty you smell when you open a forbidden chest full of secrets! In fact, it smelled very much like her favorite cave over by Chickasaw Creek.

Alpha's barks were indeed loud and ferocious, which made Susan-Eva jump, but it made the journey feel all the more epic. A destination guarded by

147

a monstrous beast where only the bravest of souls would venture. Susan-Eva couldn't wait to prove she was the only one who'd brave it ALONE!

Whatever mix of breeds Alpha was must have been big, but he looked kind of skinny. Normally, greeting a new dog would have been Susan-Eva's first priority, but she'd heard so much about the dungeon that she couldn't help but run to it. Old, rusted chains still hung from on the wall, just like Parker said. She had to get all the details from Parker because Joseph was barely talking to her at all now. Pressing her face through two bars for a better look, she found every detail told the story of something treacherous, and now she was part of the legend. The gate was locked, but there was more than one key on the chain Ed gave her, and to her pleasure, the third one fit the hole perfectly.

It was important when exploring to be curious but also respectful, so she folded her hands behind her back. Showing reverence for the space. Once she explored the permitter, she stood right in the center and closed her eyes, imagining. A soldier, trapped, dreaming of his beloved far away. A werewolf honorably locked underground to keep his town safe when the full moon came. A damsel waiting for her captor to return so she could outsmart him and escape. That last one made her smile. A damsel who turns out to be the real hero and saves the day was her favorite surprise in a story, though she already knew it was a little cliché. There was a loud creak and footsteps. Susan-Eva jumped.

"It's not an act. You really are that brave, aren't you?" Ed said. He was standing at the bottom of the stairs. He sounded and looked more serious than he ever had before. When she turned she saw he was beaming at her with genuine admiration. It was hard to hide her disappointment at that the solo part of her adventure was over now that Ed joined her. But she tried.

With a clear of her throat, she took on a more studious posture. It felt more appropriate to be academic than playful in a grown-up place. The chains caught her eye again as she scanned the walls. Then she walked over to them and looked back at Ed.

She said, "They kept civil war prisoners down here, right? Or at least that's what they think. Or maybe they have no idea and made it up because people are always trying to claim stuff is connected to the civil war around here. I think it's weird. Because they're proud of it, but it was all so awful. Not that you're like that, I mean." She looked back at the chains, taking in every detail, feeling very much like Indiana Jones. "Even if it had nothing to do with the war, it is obviously quite old. So very impressive, no matter what. Because if a place is around long enough, you know it's full of stories. Don't you think? Ed?"

Ed stared. His usual cool dude smile was back, but something felt different. Susan-Eva shifted back and forth, suddenly self-conscious. "You are very, very special."

So serious again. Ed had always been playful and nice but never serious. Now, he stared into her eyes the way a grown-up did when they wanted you to know how much they meant something. It was the look they had when they were about to tell you something they knew you didn't want to hear, like that you were moving or that your dog went to live in Florida. Maybe if she made a joke, he would lighten up.

"Your mom's special," she said with a smirk. *Your mom* insults were very in with the fourth graders.

Ed ignored the joke and came into the cage. "Want to get locked in the cuffs?"

"That's okay. I should get back to my friends."

"You didn't come this far to chicken out now, did you?" Ed said, taking the keys from her.

"I guess so," said Susan-Eva with a confident shrug. Calling someone chicken was something lazy people did, like bullies and bad coaches, so she never rewarded it with a response. Usually, Ed didn't seem lazy but everything about him seemed a little different, off. The adventure was slipping away. The thrill of Alpha's growls started to turn to anxiety. Standing in the dark felt more stupid than brave. She moved to the gate, but Ed stopped her.

"This was Joseph's favorite part," Ed said, nodding her to the chains.

"I want my friends," she said, pulling away.

"I thought we were friends?" Said Ed.

"Real friends don't lie. Joseph didn't let you put him in the cuffs."

"I thought you said he wouldn't talk to you anymore. Who's the liar now?" He said, bringing back a playful tone, but he knelt down and held her shoulder so he could look her right in the eye. She swallowed but didn't look away.

Susan-Eva said, "He isn't talking to me. But he doesn't like games like that, and he doesn't care when people call him chicken, either. I don't like it down here anymore. I'm going to back up now."

He wouldn't let her move, and she knew. A tiny little voice that was there from the first time he gave her the donut started shouting. Blood flushed her cheeks, and angry, embarrassed tears filled her eyes as she asked, "You were never really my friend, were you?"

"I think you might be the most special friend I've ever had," Ed said, wiping her tears. "Those things up there aren't your friends. I'm going to show you. I have so many special things to show," said Ed.

All of her gymnastics training, comic book studying, and Buffy the Vampire watching prepared her for this moment. The squat and high kick were perfect. The impact of her foot to the center of his chest was so intense it felt like she broke her ankle. But the pain didn't stop her from running as he panted for breath.

The damsel outsmarts her captor and saves the day! Her favorite story. Now, all she had to do was get back to Ella. Then get Ida's mom to call the police because police responded faster when it was Ida's mom calling. Then the police would come and get Ed and—

He didn't even have to get up to grab her. His arms were longer than the distance her short legs could run. Susan-Eva wished Ed had picked her up and thrown her against the wall. It would have been less humiliating. All it took was a good tug back on the collar of her dress. She lost her balance, and he stepped over her and locked her in the cage with no more force than a parent stopping a toddler from running after a bee.

He looked at her through the bars and said, "You're right. Places like this are full of stories. This is the beginning of ours. There are two kinds of people in a story: the ones that it's happening to and the ones that make things happen. All the others before you were the first kind, and I was the second. But because you brought me this gift. You get to be the second kind. You will not endure the metamorphoses. You will order it. You will bear witness. You will become one with the Other."

"The Other?" whimpered Susan-Eva. Ed glanced at a door on the other side she hadn't noticed. "He's down here with you. He's always been with you. Soon, you will get to meet him." Ed walked to a shelf in the corner and pulled down a journal. "Read it. When I come back, you'll help me write the next part. And then something miraculous will happen. Right before your very eyes. The Other will make an angel."

TWENTY-SEVEN

August 20, 2022, 12:01 AM

Susan-Eva

DUST PUFFED INTO CALVIN'S FACE as he pulled the heavy metal security gate down over the entrance of Craw-Ma's. The cocktail of dirt and God knows what else that accumulated each night was an end-of-shift special usually only reserved for Susan-Eva. But Calvin insisted on staying and helping her close, like he had the night before. He must have been one of those reporters who fed on the nitty-gritty details, Susan-Eva thought.

It was odd. Calvin stayed seven hours. Seven hours of drinking just enough beer not to get drunk. Seven hours of asking about her family. Her studies. Whether she liked *Home Alone* or *Home Alone 2* better. Never once did he bring up the photo in the witch costumes.

He asked about Ida. But things like "Is your mom friends with her mom? All the parents in the neighborhood I grew up in were so tight. We never got away with anything. Someone's mom was always watching. Now, all the kids have moved away, but the parents have a party every other week. I think it's nice. Was it like that with your parents?"

"Our parents never lived in the same neighborhood." Susan-Eva had replied.

"So, they aren't friends?"

"My mom cleaned Ida's house."

"Still?"

"No, my mom isn't… *she doesn't live here anymore.*" At that point, Susan-Eva pretended someone at the other end of the bar was waving her over.

When she looked back, she saw Joseph and Calvin talking. Calvin didn't ask any more questions about her childhood or family for the rest of the night. He never even circled back to that oh-so-scary stuff about a child murder. All he did was ask about her life now. How she liked the town. How the town treated her. How amazing she was. Was it okay that he touched her waist? Was it okay if he put his number into her phone? She handed it over as they walked away from the gate.

"Any chance you'll call?" Calvin asked, putting his number in her phone. His voice was lower. The turtle was gone. She was right that the over-the-top sweet guy thing was something of an act. But seeing him drop it now, as he braced himself for rejection, made it feel more like a defense mechanism than an intentional manipulation. She thought he'd been acting dumb to hide smart. Looking at him now, he seemed sad. That profound kind of sad that was hard to imagine someone truly unintelligent feeling.

"I will promise to think about considering it," Susan-Eva said. Calvin shrugged and walked away. Susan-Eva squinted. That was weird, too. No final attempt? Susan-Eva panicked. Not in want of validation but in regret of being cold to someone who may have only acted how he did because he liked her. Before last January she was never a person who'd take the feelings of anyone else lightly. "Hey! It wasn't because I didn't have a nice time. It's just because—"

The sound of jangling metal hitting pavement turned both of their heads. Calvin and Susan-Eva watched Joseph stumble to pick up his keys from the ground and miss them, then reach again, then again.

"It's because of your therapist. Who's obviously not really your therapist?" Calvin said. Okay, definitely not *that* stupid, Susan-Eva thought. "You break his heart or something?"

"Or something. My life is… If it ever eases up, maybe I'll give you a call," said Susan-Eva, watching Joseph stumble again. "I did over-serve him, though, so I'm going to go make sure he's..."

Calvin nodded and looked down, searching for the perfect final words, but she was gone when he looked up again.

After Joseph refused to tell her to send Calvin off, she walked off the dance floor. He left, obviously pissed at her for daring him to cross a line she knew he'd refuse to cross. He said he was going to call someone to pick him up but apparently, he never made it past the bench outside.

"My phone is dead," Joseph said, his voice was still irritated with her while he stumbled despite standing still.

"Keys," said Susan-Eva, holding her hand out to Joseph.

"I'm not driving. I'm going to sleep in my—"

"I'm not letting you sleep in your car, Joseph Porter; you're the only EMDR-certified therapist in town. You have a reputation to protect. Come on." She grabbed his hand and led him to her car.

TWENTY-EIGHT
Sixteen years ago – October 31, 2006, 5:40 PM

Ida

THEY WATCHED ED POUR. HE didn't add anything to the glasses. Whatever drug he used must have already been in the jug, sitting in his fridge, waiting. At first, Ida thought Ella was playing some sort of game she didn't understand, making silly faces. Then Ella said she was sick but was too confused to explain.

How could she explain? Ella had never even had laughing gas at the dentist. She'd never taken a Benadryl. Sedation was a feeling she had no concept of. Ida knew it well. Dusting applesauce with Zanex was the only effective way Trisha found to curb Ida's first tantrums. The older she got, the more immunity Ida built and the harder it got to sneak them in. To Ida, sedation turned her whole body into a locked closet; there was no feeling she hated more. So, when she saw Ella fall to the floor, she knew what was coming.

Ida liked Ella very much, but she liked free more. When the first wave of euphoria washed heat over her face, and she realized something chemical was taking control, she didn't stick around to see if Ella was okay. She ran. It wasn't until Ida got to the patio that heaviness started to slow her legs. By the third wooden step to the yard, her knees buckled.

155

The feeling of forced surrender shot so much rage into her arms that she was able to pull herself forward. Digging her fingers into the grass. Clutching clumps of earth like she was climbing a net at the playground. Dragging her heavy, limp body behind her.

But by the time she reached the driveway, her eyelids grew heavy, too. As they began fluttering, flashing sun to her pupils like the strobe light she loved in the Halloween store, she saw Ed carrying unconscious Ella over his shoulder and putting her in a tiny shed. Ida wondered if Ella was dead. In another flash she watched him open a wooden door in the ground and disappear. In another, she was alone. In another, he was walking back. Another, he was right next to her. Another, his eye hovered just above hers.

Ed's breath felt damp against Ida's ear. Tea whirled in her stomach, fighting to get out as her body warred between the urges to sleep and vomit.

Being trapped was the only torture that spun Ida's thoughts into incoherent madness that replaced words with color. Usually, a bright, blinding red. But this was different. It was a deep maroon now.

Knowing Ed was looking at her while she couldn't move felt somehow familiar. Like a nightmare she had once about a man at the hunting lodge. It was a nightmare her mother told her lots of girls have, but it's never ever real. Usually, she didn't believe anything her mother said. But in the nightmare, she couldn't move, and it made her feel the way she did now, like her skin was the walls of the closet, so the only way out was to slice and rip it all away.

But Ida liked her skin. She liked everything about the way she looked. She didn't want to rip it away. She didn't want the nightmare to be real. So, for once, she quietly believed her mother. When she had the nightmare again, even though she didn't think she went to sleep, her mother told her about reoccurring nightmares; Ida decided to believe that, too. Maybe this was like that. Maybe Ed wasn't even real.

With that thought, her eyes stopped fluttering, and she slipped into the dark with the hope of waking up at her house, or much better Susan-Eva's. Ida's last muscles relaxed into the fantasy of it all being fine. A piercing burst of light shot into one eye like a needle, pushing one final wave of burning consciousness through her. Ed had his thumb pressed hard into her eyebrow, tugging back one of her lids to force her eye open.

TWENTY-NINE

October 31, 2006, 5:45 PM

Ed

'ARE YOU UNFAVORED BY GOD?' It was stuck in Ed's head like a terrible song. Those words and the laugh. A laugh so much lower than a little girl's should be. Her eyes were so much more focused and steady than any child's he'd ever seen.

The thought of this corrupt, disgusting creature befriending his innocent Larva pumped a level of determination through Ed, unlike anything he'd ever experienced. He didn't care if he was caught or his steps were derailed. All that mattered was showing Susan-Eva how unworthy her cohorts were. But Other still wanted them. Other reminded him Lucifer was an Angel too. As long as Susan-Eva chose one to give him, Ed could spare her. At least for a while. Finally, someone else would bear full witness to what Other could do.

How close that would bring Susan-Eva and Other. For her to see the full scope of what he was capable of and how much he'd restrain himself for her. She would have to love him. He would show her wrath and pain so profound and prolonged that it made the things he'd do to her welcome by comparison.

Perhaps Susan-Eva would be the first special friend to ever truly understand how extraordinary Ed was too, not just Other. How he was so much more than man and therefore removed from his petty laws in the same way Other was. Perhaps instead of the one-to-two months he usually kept special friends, he'd keep her years.

Maybe she would change everything, and Moss Groves would become his home. He could get more involved with the church and teach Sunday school. Become a personal trainer at the gym and build a community. Then, he could make special friends in surrounding towns and bring them to Other. Then he could show Susan-Eva over and over the things they *could* do but didn't, only to her. It could all start with Ida.

Even Ida's sedated state found ways to attack and offend Ed. Her skin didn't goose pimple at his touch. Her eye didn't water even when he put his own eye so close to hers that his lashes brushed her pupil when he blinked. Crying was an essential sign Larvae understood the transformation they'd endure together. So, Ed spit into Ida's eye giving her the tears of respect he was owed. Then he whispered in her ear, "I'm your God now, and we'll see how favored you are."

THIRTY
August 20, 2022, 12:20 AM

Susan-Eva

ALL THE WINDOWS OF SUSAN-EVA'S pick-up were rolled down, weaving the night air around her and Joseph, letting the speed of the car transform the stale August heat into a pleasant balmy breeze. Honeysuckle mixed with pine created a perfume so familiar she could have used the scents instead of her eyes to know where she was going. Joseph hung his heavy head out the window like a dog, letting the wind sober him.

In the rearview, she watched exhaustion narrow his once wide eyes. It was the sort of expression that ages you, but all Susan-Eva could think was how young he looked. If only she could remember how to be the girl in the sparkly tutu and the Batman mask again. If she could remember how to crawl through his window. He wouldn't have to be so tired if he'd let her keep watch for monsters so he could sleep.

She thought of it like a thick-knotted rope. That thing that ties us to innocence at the start and breaks either string by string over time or with the swoop of a machete in one event. No matter how weak and taut it was, Susan-Eva knew there was still one string left on Joseph's rope.

To him, it was nothing more than an embarrassment. A character flaw he was certain was gone. But then something would prove it wasn't. Like realizing he still cried at the end of *Big Fish,* even though he'd seen it a million times. Or when his heart raced at the sight of blood. Or when he kept checking his phone on his birthday to see if his dad would text. If there was anything he could do to forever get rid of it all, from the uninvited tears to the uninvited hope, he would. If there was anything she could do to make sure nothing ever severed it, she would. One of many reasons he could never, ever know the whole truth.

"How did the book you gave me go over at the prison yesterday? Did anyone read it?" Susan-Eva asked, hoping to pull him out of his funk.

"It was too heady. A stupid, elitist choice. I should've known better. I'm always doing that. Like, these aren't guys that I grew up with. I'm trying to separate my human—" Joseph put a fist to his mouth as though he might barf, then hiccupped instead and finished, "—my humanity from theirs."

"Have you thought about comic books? Not like the ones for kids but acclaimed ones. *'Watchmen'* or *'The Killing Joke.'* They're kind of the mythology of our time. In a lot of ways, our superheroes and villains are a more accurate reflection of societal mores than politics or religion."

"In a lot of ways, you're a genius."

"In a lot of ways, you're drunk."

"Whose fault is that?" asked Joseph. She smirked and shrugged, trying so hard to look coy and cool. But the goosebumps were back, spreading down her bare thighs the instant his eyes met hers in the rearview. His face got serious, and he said, "It's not okay. You telling me I could have you kick Calvin out. Don't ask me to tell you what to do about other guys. It's not fair."

"Okay," she said, looking away, getting pissed again. She knew it wasn't fair. Nothing that ever happened between them was fair. But hadn't he asked her to dance? Hadn't he decided to stay at the bar? Hadn't they both agreed to 'unfair?' Because at some point, they were supposed to both snap out of it. They would say, *Enough is enough. Anything is better than this. Let's just be together.* Now, it seemed enough finally was enough, and it felt more impossible than ever that they would find their way back.

She said, "Maybe you shouldn't come during my shifts anymore."

"Okay," he said. "And you should stop showing up at my office."

"Okay. And I'll stop calling and telling you every time I—"

He put a hand on her leg, and she stopped talking. "You know that one thing we only say when we're both drunk because we really, really shouldn't say it anymore?" he asked. She nodded, holding her breath. "Will you say it back even though you're sober?" Her eyes watered, and her throat went dry. She nodded and put her hand next to the pink carnation in the cup holder, facing her palm up. He interlaced his fingers with hers without ever looking down and said, "I love you, Susan-Eva Lorenzo."

"I love you, Joseph Porter."

Joseph lived in a simple brick house with a porchlight, courting swing, tomato vines, and roses growing up a trellis. A house Susan-Eva helped him pick out a month before they broke up. Three months before that beautiful January morning when they almost got back together.

Whenever she pulled up next to it, it still felt half hers. Not with a sense of entitlement. But in a way, a certain amount of imagining can make something you've never experienced feel nostalgic. Still holding Susan-Eva's hand, Joseph unbuckled his seatbelt. His eyes went from hers to the scar on her knee. "I know what we're doing isn't healthy. We both deserve a chance to move on. But I don't want you to stop calling."

His eyes were still on the scar. She put her hand over it and said, "Look, I don't need you to keep talking to me out of pity. You're right. It's too much."

"It's not pity. You're my best friend."

"But."

"But. I'm worried. I'm really, really worried about you."

"I'm fine."

"No. You're not. You always say it. But you're not." He shook his head and took a breath. "I get saying it to everyone else. But why me?"

"Everyone else? Most people don't even know about it."

"I don't mean about what happened in January. I mean, what happened with Ed. Why do you act like it wasn't a big deal, even with me? I would never ask you to talk about it if you didn't want to. But why did you feel like you had to say you were okay? Even when we were kids?"

"What happened in the park was terrible. But I'm an adult. It happens to one in four women. I'll get over it. But what happened with Ed wasn't like that. We were all okay because nothing that bad, really—"

"Come on, Evie."

"I got locked in a storm cellar for a few hours. Not one of us sustained a critical injury. And no matter what people think, he didn't touch us. Not like that. I know, for some reason, everyone really needs that to have happened to one of us to make it real, but it didn't. When I say 'nothing that bad happened,' I'm not lying to you. It's a fact. That's why they call us the miracle three. We shouldn't be alive, but we are. So why is it so hard to believe I'm okay?"

Joseph said, "When I got to the hospital, you were sedated, but you would come to every few minutes and say things." Susan-Eva swallowed. She didn't remember that.

"Well, like you said, I was sedated. So, you can't take anything I said…" She ran a hand over her face, unable to resist, and asked, "What did I say?"

"You said it was a long time coming. You said you deserved it for what you did in the cellar. You said he should have killed you."

They were quiet for a long time. Finally, Susan-Eva said, "*Oh.*"

"So, that's why I think you're not okay."

"Okay." She clutched the wheel. "I think you should go inside now. And I think you are right. We both deserve a chance to move on."

"Nothing you've ever done could make you deserve—"

She ignored him and said, "So, I'll stop calling. I should have stopped a long time ago. If I'd known this was about pity."

"It's not—"

"You need to start dating other people."

"I am."

She kept going, not processing it, "I'm fine, and you should be—" then she did process it. Joseph was dating. Who? When? Where? None of her business. *That's so…* "Oh. Good. That's what I want for you."

"Nothing serious. But…"

"That's so wonderful. Joseph. Really. I'll stop calling."

His eyes went back to the scar on her knee. "I wish I could kill him," he said.

Susan-Eva shook her head and said, "No, you don't. That's something you think you're supposed to feel, but it's not you. You don't even know who it was. What if he was sick and had no idea what he was doing? Or just fucked up from all the fucked-up ways we teach men to think. Maybe he got better. Maybe he changed because someone like you helped him."

There had been rage in Joseph's eyes. Now it shifted into something else, grief maybe. Whatever it was, she thought the intensity might bring tears. But instead, his hand found the back of her neck, pulling their foreheads together. For someone so patient and sensitive, the strength of Joseph's grasp always took her by surprise. He never bothered with the pretense of a light caress. He never played rough, either, even to tease. Joseph's touch was rare, full of intention, and unapologetic in its knowledge of what felt good.

"You really can't just tell me why you lie?" he asked.

"No," she confirmed. Her breath hitched.

"So, this is really over? Forever?" His fingers pressed firmly at the nap of her neck.

"Yeah," she whimpered.

"Yeah," he confirmed.

Their mouths were too close. Maybe an inch more distance and they could have escaped the muscle memory. But with their foreheads still touching, they could taste each other's air. Desire they could have resisted. But at this range, it was reflex. It was hopeless. His lips went to hers at the exact instant hers went to his.

All of their studies taught them how easy it was to over-romanticize a lost pleasure. When intrusive fantasies of sex with each other played in their minds, they chanted, "It wasn't *that* good. It couldn't have been that good. Nothing is that good." Like a mantra. But whenever they touched in real life, that damn muscle memory sucked them from logic like a rip tide. Once again, they had to confront the truth. It was that good. Every. Single. Time.

His bottom lip massaged itself into the tender skin beneath hers, sending a wave of warmth from her stomach and into their hips. Susan-Eva writhed in desperation at the ache of it until their tongues found each other for one quick, intuitive hello. As skilled as their hands performing a catch and release on the dance floor.

As it ended, she exhaled with sharp pain. Like a dislocated arm had been snapped back into place. They pressed their foreheads back together as he rubbed his fingers beneath her jaw. It had been one year, three months, and twenty-seven days since their last kiss.

"Tell me why you lie. Whatever it is, it will be okay if you tell me." Joseph begged.

"*Joey,*" Susan-Eva pleaded.

"You can't," he said. She was quiet for so long that it seemed she might give a hint. But she just stared at the toy squirrel next to the carnation. "It's Ida, isn't it? It all has to do with the Montgomerys and Ida." He had never asked so bluntly before.

She forced herself to look away from him, worried she might finally fold. After the eternity of a silent second, the sound of the car door opening turned her head. Within seconds, Joseph was on his porch. She watched, waiting for the moment he'd disappear through his door and he'd really be gone. As he opened it, she held her breath and braced herself.

He looked back and shouted, "Come in anyway."

THIRTY-ONE

Sixteen years ago - October 31, 2006, 9:45 PM

Ella

IT FELT SMALL. THAT WAS the first thing Ella thought about the space she woke up in. Even though she couldn't really see yet. She could feel the proximity of the walls and sensed, for some reason, that she shouldn't touch them. It must have been something to do with the butterflies. Blurred vision really taught you the value of distinct shapes. There must have been other clues in the room but the shape of butterflies was the only thing distinguishable through Ella's haze. They were pinned all over the wall.

At first, she thought she was at a new babysitter's house. Some nerdy teen who liked bugs and Star Wars that Ida would make fun of but that Ella secretly really liked. Even if they made her take a nap after she told them she was too old.

But the more Ella came to, the less that made sense. She was wearing the witch costume. It was Halloween. She was supposed to wake up at Susan-Eva's house. Mrs. Lorenzo would never let them bring even one bug into the house, much less pin dozens to the wall.

Maybe they were moths, not butterflies. They all looked one color, but definitely something with wings. Clinging to certainties in unfamiliar territory was Ella's magic trick for staying calm in almost any situation. A less mature child might panic, but not Ella. She simply followed each clue to its natural conclusion. Her one clue for now was a winged insect of some kind—or perhaps just fun wallpaper. Nothing alarming about that.

If Ella could see the rest of the room, she knew she would remember where she was and why she was there. But for some reason, she couldn't turn her head. Blink after blink her eyes were still blurry. She tried to rub them with her fists, but her limbs were too heavy.

Sense of smell was the first faculty to return in full force. This made not panicking far more difficult. Because the nose remembers. Everything.

Susan-Eva's secret friend. Ed. The too-familiar handshake. The bad feeling. The Dog. The storm cellar. The iced tea. *The iced tea.* Then older memories. Of every grown-up who ever told her not to take candy from strangers. To stay away from vans. To always, always find a woman and ask for help. Then taste returned, and with it, too much feeling. Dry mouth. Metallic. Shame.

She still couldn't move her head, but she could feel she was right about the room. It was very small. Not even a room. A pantry, maybe.

Wherever she was, she was alone.

Sound confirmed that. Creaks of the old house and the soft hum of a fan were audible, but nothing else. No movement. Ida was never still. So, she must have gotten out. Of course she got out. The last thing Ella remembered was Ida standing in front of her. But Ida was the weather. There was no reason to worry about her. As soon as Ida saw Ella get woozy, Ella was certain Ida would abandon her. A sharp breath escaped her lips, relief.

It was very likely that Ida had already found another grown-up and was leading them to the house. Not because she wanted to save them. Obviously. Ella was way too smart to believe Ida would go out of her way to help anyone. But it was stupid to go to this house, and Ida loved making Ella look stupid. So, any minute now, a grown-up would show up, and Ella would be in big trouble. But it would all be okay. But where was Susan-Eva?

Where was Susan-Eva? Ed took her. Alone. Susan-Eva was somewhere alone with him.

No matter what, Ella promised herself, this thing with Ida would never ever hurt Susan-Eva. Enough thinking. She had to get out and find her.

So, Ella pushed herself up, lunged herself out the door, and ran to help her best friend.

Only she didn't. Her brain told her legs to run and her eyes to see. STOP BEING BLURRY! SEE! But the fog wouldn't lift. Her limbs wouldn't budge. For another five minutes Ella grew more and more conscious and focused but couldn't move.

When something scared Ella, she made herself do it over and over until she could bear it with a sarcastic smirk. So whenever she figured out how to escape, she was determined to take enough drugs so that nothing could surprise her like this ever again. Whatever this feeling was coursing through her bloodstream, taking away the control she'd worked so hard for made her more scared than anything in her entire life.

That was until her vision cleared, and she saw the things pinned to the walls weren't butterflies. They weren't moths. They weren't bugs at all.

They were eyelids.

Pinned outside of pinkie fingers.

Each set of lashes centered next to the knuckle, and pierced with needle at each end to fan out like the edges of wings. Each pinkie like the body of an angel.

A tingling sensation returned to Ella's own fingers. Again, her brain cried, "Run!" And this time, her legs could move. But again her body betrayed her. Because running would have meant standing. Standing would have meant seeing. Ella's body decided the only thing that mattered was never seeing what was on the walls again. So, she flung her hands over her eyes and curled into the smallest ball she could.

The noises changed. A door squeaked in another room. Footsteps. Ida? The steps got closer. They were too heavy, but maybe she'd sent someone, police, or—

A voice came from outside the door. Ed's. Every bit as kind and young as it had sounded before as he said, "Be still and know." Ella tucked her face into her knees and covered her head with her arms the way they taught her to for tornados at school. She tried to go back to sleep. To unsee. To stop hearing.

But she couldn't block out the sound of a latch clicking to unlock. The scrap of the door knob turning. The thud of wood pushing free from a tight frame. And the two footsteps it took for him to enter the closet and shut the door.

That's when the size of the space started to change. Even though he didn't touch her, even though it was only words, what she saw and heard would live in every single moment that came after. So, the closet grew. It grew until there was no way to measure where it started or ended. Until there was no way in or out. Until that closet covered in wings that couldn't fly made from eyes that could never shut became the whole entire world.

THIRTY-TWO

August 20, 2022

Susan-Eva

IT WAS 3 AM. TIME TO go home. So, it was odd that instead of taking the left at Chickasaw Avenue toward Parlay House, Susan-Eva took the right toward the Watsonville highway, where she only went when Alpha needed to be fed. Navigating the woods was hard enough on bright, clear days. They never went to Lot 355 at night.

But her truck found its way off the road anyway and seemed to have every subtle detail of the terrain so perfectly memorized that the dark proved an inadequate obstacle. Susan-Eva kept a copy of "The Killing Joke" in her glove compartment because the legitimacy of her geekdom was often called into question. Joseph said the idea was genius. Yes, he was drunk. Yes, he was in love with her. But what if he was right, and it worked? What if it fixed everything? Even what just happened with Joseph.

It wasn't that she thought Scott would read the comic and have some grand epiphany. But any reaction could give her some clue as to why he did what he did. What drove him to be so obsessed with Ed that he'd kill that girl. That he'd go after his intended victim. Was it the way the town talked about Ed so much? Was it the culture of turning serial killers into celebrities? Or did it start with her? Was it something she did?

169

If she knew why, she could study it. If she studied it, she could understand it. If she understood it, she could stop it from ever happening to her again. If she could stop it from happening to her ever again, she could stop it from happening to anyone ever again. She could save the whole entire world. She could be forgiven.

Unfortunately, Susan-Eva didn't need the PhD she was working toward to self-diagnose how delusional this was. None of her desperate rationalizations could cover up the truth anymore. She didn't keep going to the cellar because she thought she could reform Scott. She wasn't even there to punish him. She was there because it hurt. And she *needed* to hurt herself.

Getting through each day, smiling and making jokes, acting like she remembered how to be the girl in the tutu and the mask, made her want to crawl in a hole and die. Luckily, she not only had a hole, she had the very hole she was supposed to die in. There were moments when it felt okay again. When pleasure came back, she savored the sun, adored her friends, and felt hope she'd end up with the love of her life. But then Ida. Always, relentlessly, Ida.

When Scott ground her knee into the pavement like her bone was a mortar and the concrete his pestle, Susan-Eva would never let herself forget she had wished for Ida. Someone should know, she thought. Before what she was about to do.

Sitting in the dirt staring at the cellar door, Susan-Eva was barely conscious of pulling out her phone and calling Calvin's number.

"Please tell me this isn't a butt dial," Calvin said, answering after the second ring.

"Are you a cop? You have to tell me if you are. Are you investigating the Copycat Killer or something?" Susan-Eva's voice was soft and steady, almost trance-like, as she stared at the padlock.

"What? No, why would I—"

"I had sex," said Susan-Eva. It didn't happen right away. Joseph drank water. She made them both food. They made out for hours. But nothing more until he was mostly sober. If it was really the last time, they both wanted to remember every detail.

"Um. Okay. Why are you telling me?" Said Calvin, sounding more confused than offended.

"Because it was good sex. I haven't had good sex since before. It still got ruined by the end. *But the beginning and middle.* It put every cliché to shame. It made me think about our night. It confirmed you're full of shit. So tell me the truth about why you're here, and I'll tell you the truth."

"The truth about what?"

"About what really happened down in the storm cellar. That's the one thing everyone agrees on. There are lots of disagreements on if we lied or if we're too traumatized to remember. But no one thinks the story we told is the whole story, the whole truth. So, what's your angle? Sixteen years later? The Living Angels all grown up? Did you think if we slept together again, maybe I'd let a new detail slip?"

"I'm not a—"

"I almost believe you," said Susan-Eva. "When I left the parking lot, I let myself believe you. I even felt bad for toying with you. I started to like you. But then I had good sex and I thought about ours. Why would you want to see me again after that?"

"Because I had a good time," Calvin said, getting defensive.

"Calvin. I just lie there. Limp with blank, wide eyes. The whole time. Trying not to… No one begs for seconds from a dead fish."

It was true. That's how it was with all the one-night stands. She'd lay there, barely moving, and let them fumble through whatever drunken dance they felt like. Some did try to get her to engage more. After all, they'd met the vibrant, passionate Susan-Eva. Surely, in bed, she was a fire. Her lying back, barely moving, rarely went completely unnoticed. But when they asked what she wanted, she always just said, "Make it fast."

Some pushed harder. They all thought going down on her would fix it. She'd close her legs and say whatever form of flattery she'd assessed would work best.

"No, I want you up here."

"I'm too shy for that."

"Your cock is so big. Don't take it away."

"I'm not like that. I want you to destroy me."

"Dude. Just destroy me."

171

Then they would. One or two left, needing her to be more into it. It was hard to tell with guys like Calvin. She lay still as she did with the others, but he turned looking at her into such an event that she had no trouble buying that was enough for him. It was like her stillness meant they were making love or something. He put his hand to her cheek and gazed into her eyes. For a couple of moments, it was almost nice.

But even with Calvin, Scott was there the whole time. That was the point. She thought if she went through enough, it would be like sorbet. It would cleanse her palette for the main course. She'd get every flash of that day on the trail out of her system, and then when someone she loved touched her, the smell of strange BO and the taste of dirt wouldn't come flooding back.

But it did. She worried that what Scott did to her meant she'd never get to enjoy sex again. But the reality was worse. Sitting there with Calvin on the phone, Susan-Eva could still taste the heat of Joseph's breath on her lips. She could still hear the beautiful music of their hearts beating together. She could feel every muscle in her body relax in the right places to make her dissolve into him. And how it tensed in all the right places to bring her more pleasure at his touch. How they both could sense each other on the cusp, about to tip over and made it there at the same time, sharing it.

But it wasn't enough. Even in the magic and bliss of her soulmate's touch, she still saw her rapist. The loss wasn't that it would never feel good again. It was that it could be at its best again and still be intruded by the worst. That she could forget just long enough so that the flashes hurt like they were new.

That made her wish for Ida again. Which would be bad enough on its own, but there was another part. Confirmation what she said to Joseph in the hospital was the truth. Confirmation Ed should have kept her down there, and every bad thing that happened since was her fault. So, it should hurt being there. It should kill her. It was always supposed to kill her.

Calvin cleared his throat and said, "That's not how it was for me. I thought we were both nervous and—"

Susan-Eva cut him off and said, "I'll tell you something we never told any of the other reporters or the police. If you tell me who you work for."

The pause was so long that Susan-Eva looked at her phone to see if they'd been disconnected. But her screen showed the seconds of their call ticking forward. A deep breath broke the silence. She brought the phone back to her ear and set her jaw, knowing.

"Investigative for the *Atlanta Chronicle.* I'm doing a follow up story that I hope will turn into a book." Calvin conceded. His voice was deeper but the accent was still there. Either he was very committed to the good ole boy act, or it was real; it sounded real. Calvin cleared his throat and added, "But it's not what you think. I really do like you. I didn't know—"

"I don't care," said Susan-Eva. Her voice was deeper now, too. "Here's your scoop. None of us knows the whole story. We said we woke up together in the cellar. But it's a lie. We all woke up alone. In separate rooms. He went back and forth between us. We never told each other what happened during that part. We never asked. He didn't hurt me. Not like that. He just made me choose."

"Choose what?" asked Calvin, calm and patient.

"The journal, the one they use in all the documentaries where he wrote about watching each girl, then what he did to them. He made me read that. Then he told me about what he planned to do to me. But said I would be spared as long as I did one thing. I had to choose which one of my friends he'd do it to first. I always thought if something terrible happened, I would be the brave one, the hero. But I wasn't. I didn't even hesitate. I immediately said, Ida. It told him to kill Ida."

"You were just a kid."

"So was she."

"So, how did you get out? What did he—" Susan-Eva hung up before he could finish the question. Reporters were such a greedy group. Sex *and* the first new detail on the Renovation Child Murderer in sixteen years, and still he asked for more.

Susan-Eva, on the other hand, had gotten everything she needed from Calvin. Now no matter what happened after what she did next, Joseph, Ella, her family, and whoever else cared would know who she really was.

For the very first time, she managed to unlock the storm cellar, make her way down the stairs, pull on the mask, and face Scott Ryan without

173

shedding a single tear. He had never been visited by either of his captors at night, so he knew something was different; she didn't say anything at first. For about ten minutes, she sat in front of the bars, staring at him through the small eyes of her mask. For the first time in months, Scott Ryan looked nervous.

THIRTY-THREE

Sixteen years ago - October 31, 2006, 11:55 PM

Ida

IT SMELT FAMILIAR. WHEN ED dragged Ida into the cellar, that was the first thing she noticed. Not the blood gushing from her own leg. Not that Susan-Eva was locked in a cage. Not that Ella was holding her knees, hiding in the corner. Not the dog growling and convulsing so violently it shook its entire kennel. Her first thought was, what is that? I know that one.

But whatever it was, was too intense to connect with the version Ida had smelled before. Later, she'd figure out that in small amounts, it was a scent so common that it was as hard to distinguish as the aroma of one's own house. It was a smell that came one to five times a day. A scent that meant yearnings for comfort and pleasure was soon to be sated. *In small amounts.*

In large amounts, dire amounts, the feeling behind that scent produced unpredictable results. Desperation, crime, taboo, death, war, chaos, extinction. It was the smell of starving, and it was coming from the dog, Alpha.

After Ida stopped trying to figure out the smell, she exhaled. Because Ed was gone. FINALLY. It had been so close to the perfect weekend, and he had to ruin it. Not only by being gross but also by being boring. Everything in Ida's body hurt. Things had gotten a little violent during her time alone with Ed.

How could he think he was favored? He was a terrible predator. If he wasn't, he'd go after bigger prey, and he wouldn't need help! Yeah, squirrels were small. But they were just practice and they were way faster than people. Ida never needed help catching them. She needed help *not* catching them and *not* going after larger, more interesting prey. But stupid Ed went on and on about some other dumb man that was going to come hurt them. Really? He needs a whole other man to take on three little girls. Whereas Ida was a little girl and needed two more just to stop her!

He kept calling her Larva. It was weird. This whole day was so confusing. Too confusing to know how to act or what to do. The more confused she got, the more the rage color filled her brain. She needed somewhere to put it. Ella said when she had feelings like that, she was supposed to go to her. But Ella and Susan-Eva, were both acting so different than normal. Ida wished it was Easter. Stuff like this never happened on Easter.

Susan-Eva

He knew her mom. He was nice to her mom. Her mom had good instincts. If Ed was really someone who would hurt kids her mom would know. So none of this could be real. This was a strange nightmare. When Susan-Eva woke up she would tell Ella about the man at the grocery store. She would stop taking the donut from the man at the grocery store. She would never let go of her moms hand at the grocery store. She would never keep another secret.

Most of all when she woke up she would know the worst part wasn't real. The part where made her read those things. The part where she said Ida's name. None of those things in the book were going to happen to Ida. There would be no purifying. Because none of this was real. Because—

Ella

"*He knows my mom. He knows my mom. He knows my mom.*" Susan-Eva chanted over and over again, clutching her knees to her chest alone behind the bars. Ella had never seen Susan-Eva panic before. At first, Ella tried to calm her down, reaching her skinny arms through the bars for Susan-Eva's hands. But she wouldn't move. She didn't even seem to fully know

Ella was there.

The sight of her best friend trembling and dirty made her heart race. So, Ella had to stop looking at her, or she'd lose focus. Whatever this was, it was no time for her to get childish and cry like a little girl. But she also had to do whatever she could not to remember what she saw in the small room. The only way to get the images and those things he said to go away was to empty everything out of her head.

Somehow, she ended up in the corner. She couldn't remember why or when. But if she kept rocking back and forth, not letting images come back, then it would be… Butterflies. It was just butterflies. If she thought it enough maybe it would be true.

A cloud of dust puffed into Ella's face. She coughed and looked up to see Ida kicking the ground at her. "Ugh! If he is like that man at the lodge and we miss the rest of trick or treating, I'm going to be so mad! You were scared, so why didn't we run?" Ida huffed.

"He knows my mom. He knows my mom. He knows my mom." Susan-Eva's voice got louder her chest was rising too fast. She was hyperventilating.

"WE KNOW, IDIOT!" Ida screamed through the bars. Susan-Eva finally stopped chanting and fell onto her side, weeping in the fetal position. "This is all your fault!"

"Shut up, Ida!" said Ella. She found her feet and went to pull Ida away from the bars.

"No! You always take her side, but I've never screwed up this bad. My mom knows lots of stupid, annoying grown-ups, and I don't make you play with them!" Through her sobs, Susan-Eva whimpered something they couldn't hear. "WHAT? If you're saying sorry, I don't care! If we get out of here, next time you come to my pool, I'm not letting you have any of the sparkly floats, only the gross, boring old green ones."

"What man, Ida?" Susan-Eva asked loud enough to hear. Ella was so fixated on keeping her brain as empty as she could she didn't pay any attention to that part. Ella knew every reward and threat that worked on Ida. But Susan-Eva studied a different side of their strange third. It was just that the data Susan-Eva understood best was the kind Ida rarely offered.

Susan-Eva

Why would Ida say something like that in a dream. In dreams Ida was a meaner version of her regular self or sweeter one. Sometimes dream Ida tried to kill her. Sometimes dream Ida apologized, but for real. But dream Ida never gave knew information. What if this was real. Susan-Eva sat up, wiping still-falling tears and dirt from her face, and looked at Ida. "You never said anything about a man at the lodge before. That's new. What man, Ida?"

Ida rolled her eyes. "Whatever, I don't think he's real. My Mom says it's a dream lots of little girls have, but it's never real." He was real. Whatever happened to Ida was real. Susan-Eva didn't know how she knew but she did. It wasn't a dream. So that meant… "Why are we talking about that when it's supposed to be my one night for tricks? So, you better have a way to get us out of here, or I'm telling Joey about how you fart in your sleep." This wasn't a dream either. She said Ida's name. He was going to come for her. He was going to—

Ella

"Ida, stop acting like a stupid kid. This is way more serious than not trick or treating. If we don't figure out how to get out of here, Ed might hurt us," said Ella.

Ida said, "He's not going to hurt us."

Ella said, "I know he seemed nice, but he—"

"He's going to kill us. I mean, he's going to try," said Ida. She looked at them both as though they'd all already come to that realization. Susan-Eva had. Ella could tell by the way she buried her head in her knees and wept like she was sad, not shocked. But Ella didn't let herself read that part. She didn't let the logical conclusions come. She was failing. Her brain wasn't working. Butterflies. Butterflies. He said the Other was coming. He said he had an axe. He said one of them would transform into— wait there was something Ella realized she needed. In fact she wasn't supposed to be there at all. That was why this equation stopped making sense. If X equaled Ella then Ella equaled somewhere else but she was here so a factor was off. Something was off.

Ida

Ida squinted at Ella and said, "So, you have a plan to get us out, right? I mean, I know I'm favored by God, so when I die, it will be fine, but who knows what will happen to you?" Ella's eyes darted back and forth in a way Ida had never seen before. "Ella, you're supposed to be in charge! Why would you let us get trapped down here if you didn't have a way to get us out?"

"I didn't know."

"Yes, you did! I could smell it!" Ida whipped her head back to Susan-Eva. "It's her! You would have run but you didn't want to leave her alone. So now he's going to kill all of us, and you both might go to hell, and we won't get to go to Six Flags. UGHHHHH." Ida ran up the cellar stairs and started screaming and pounding on the door.

Susan-Eva

The room was becoming more and more vivid, less and less a dream. But there still had to be hope. There was always hope. People are mostly good. Somewhere inside Ed there was good. Right? "We just need to talk to Ed and figure out why he's doing this," said Susan-Eva, pleading with her eyes for Ella to agree. Ella forced a nod, but they knew each other's lying faces. Susan-Eva swore she heard it. Something inside lashed a machete through a rope and everything she once was or thought she could be fell from her. Then these strange howling noises like someone was screaming while choking for air. She looked around for who it was then realized it was her.

Ella

Something tickled Ella's cheek, and she slapped it away, thinking it was a spider, but then she felt it again on the other cheek, tears. With enough force to knock someone else down Ella slapped her own face to stop the crying. Ida was right. Ella was supposed to be in charge. It was Ella's job to teach Ida how to act normal and stay out of trouble. The three of them getting killed felt like something that might qualify as trouble.

Ella shook herself and said, "It will be okay. We need to find a key or a bat, or um…" Ella spotted a box on the top shelf of a wire rack in the corner. It was too high up. Tapping the bottom corner was as far as her highest jump could get her.

Ella yelled up the stairs, "IDA! Come here." Ida cascaded down to Ella's side eager for any semblance of a plan. "Get on my back like at cheer and tip that box down." Ella got on all fours, and Ida climbed up and punched the bottom of the box. The cardboard tipped so easily that for an instant, she was afraid it was empty. It wasn't. Hundreds of Polaroids rained around them.

Ella had already seen lots of bad things in her nine years of life and she handled them all fine because she was mature. She knew even though grown-ups never bothered calling her mature. They just knew she was and gave her tasks accordingly.

Her grandfather's hospice nurse knew she'd be okay alone with him. Her mom knew she could find the breaker switch all on her own. Trisha knew Ella would understand the word the sociopath. In fact, Ella was the first and only person Trisha used the word sociopath to when describing her daughter. Rather than bribe Ella with treats or future rewards, Trisha knew to offer to help with Ella's mom's career without Ella's mom ever knowing. Ella loved being seen as a grown-up. It was the only trait she allowed herself to be proud of.

So, Ella just couldn't make sense of the words that filled her head as the Polaroids hit the ground. The equation was further and further off. If X equaled Ella, X could not equal little girl. But all she could think as each new image burned into her brain was: *I'm a little girl. I'm not supposed to see things like this. Please, somebody, notice I'm only a little girl.*

Ida started picking up the photos and studying them with clinical fascination.

"Stop looking at them," said Ella. Ida ignored Ella and picked up one after the other as Ella tried to grab them away from her. But Ella's eyes kept blurring with more annoying tears, so it was hard to keep up with Ida. It was getting hard to move because each time she did she saw a different picture it made Ella's thoughts so jumbled.

She tried to force the thought: Get it together, figure it out, it's your job. But it just made the other thoughts louder. I'm a little girl. I'm a little girl. I'M A LITTLE GIRL—

Finally, Ella managed to grab the photos from Ida's hand. "Stop!

180

You're not supposed to see things like this!" Ida picked up more photos.

There was no thrill, no sense of play, no sinister pleasure. Ida's eyes were blank the way they always were when she was receiving new information. She ignored the photos that included Ed with the girls, seeming to have no information to gain from those. But others she picked up like certain sea shells at the beach, carefully spotting the photos with the most unique value. The ones with blood. The ones with chopping. The ones with Alpha eating the limbs.

"STOP LOOKING!" Ella screeched so loud that both Ida and Susan-Eva jumped.

"What are the pictures of?" Susan-Eva whimpered, pressing her face through the bars.

"Um—Just—We just need—Um, I think we need—" Ella looked around, trying to make her brain go.

"There's one of you, Susan-Eva," said Ida, picking up a photo.

"*No.* He never took a picture of me," said Susan-Eva, shaking her head.

"Why would Mrs. Lorenzo let him in your room while you were asleep?" Ida said, taking in the photo. The photo had to have been taken from the window, but there was no glare from the glass, so it was open. Ida handed the picture to Susan-Eva, and Susan-Eva stumbled back and threw up.

Ida turned to Ella and lowered her voice "Seriously, *what do we do?"*

Ella took a deep breath, and suddenly, she had the answer.

Ida

Ida saw Ella relax; she exhaled, ready to do whatever Ella said. "I need…"

"What?" Ida said, looking around, trying to figure it out.

"I need my mom," said Ella. "I need my mom. Can you go get her?"

"What? No, we're all locked down here, idiot, and your mom never—" Then Ida looked Ella up and down, seeing it. Ella's wish was granted. Ida could finally see her keeper really was just a kid who had no idea what to do. "Oh," said Ida. Then she leaned to Ella and whispered, *"I'll try to die first and put in a good word for you with God."*

Ella blinked at Ida, holding her calm, then looked to the ceiling and started screaming, "MOMMY! MOM! MOM! MOMMY PLEASE!"

A key jostled in the door at the side of the room.

Ella

There was another door. Why hadn't Ella noticed the other door? What was behind the other door?

Ida

He said there was someone else. A superior predator. Ida didn't like pain. She didn't want to hurt. She wanted to go home.

Susan-Eva

He said that's where The Other was. The Other was the bad one. The one he had to give her too. The Other was going to kill Ida. Susan-Eva said Ida's name. Susan-Eva killed Ida. Susan-Eva killed Ida. The door was opening.

All Three

Alpha convulsed in his crate so violently it shook from the ground. The Other was there. It was big. It was so much bigger than them. Bigger than Ed. It had to crouch to get through the door frame in slow stomps like hooves. They saw it in flashes. A black cloak. The skull of a goat over it's face like a mask. A chopping block under his arm and an ax in the other.

They all started screaming, even Ida. They shrieked in tandem at the same pitch. Like a call and response at church. With each pound of his foot on the steps, they repeated louder and higher, harmonizing their terror, giving each other permission not to be brave.

"I'm sorry. I'm so sorry, please." Begged Susan-Eva as the man walked toward the bars and knelt down to her level. He set the chopping block and ax in front of her.

The voice was deep and drone, unlike any humans they'd ever heard "For you to understand the gift, you must bear witness to what you are being spared."

"NO! PLEASE! LET THEM GO!" Screamed Susan-Eva, running back

to the bars. Ella and Ida ran, but the corner was the only place to go. The Other grabbed Ida by the hair and dragged her toward the chopping block.

Ella

Ella fell down, trembling. On the ground, she was surrounded by the pictures again; that's when her last string severed. The equation changed again. It started to make sense. It was another picture of Susan-Eva sleeping that did it. She imagined Ed outside Susan-Eva's window. Imagined Ed pretending to be Susan-Eva's friend for months and the things he must have been thinking about her while they talked. Then she looked at Susan-Eva behind the bars.

It wasn't just the terror in her eyes it was the shame. How much more shame was he going to make her feel? In the pictures, the kids behind the bars had hair that started short and got longer. How long was he going to keep her there? The little girl in Ella died, and something focused and cold grew in her place. She looked up and forced herself to watch what was happening to Ida.

Ida's screams were deep and guttural. She flayed with her whole body the same way she had with Trisha the first time Ella saw her at church. All rage. No fear. Even in the hands of a man with an ax, Ida was still the weather. And Ella was the girl who knew how to play with the weather, how to keep it quiet, so that must also mean she knew how to unleash it.

The deep voice of The Other bellowed, "Each of God's creatures begins holy, then is corrupted. The metamorphosis will return you to—"

But Ella was louder. "IDA!" she yelled, meeting her eyes. "BE SCARY!" Every muscle in Ida's face fell blank. She gazed at Ella, and for that instant, the world became theirs again, slow and consumed with knowing each other. Ida's eyes welled and lit up at the same time the way a kid does when they find out they are finally getting that golden retriever.

Ella gave Ida one final nod. Ida turned to the towering man putting her arm to the chopping block and smiled.

She was so fast. So, so fast.

Susan-Eva

Ida lunged for his head and ripped off the skull and horns. Under it

183

was Ed. There was no "other." It was only him. It was always only him. Her sudden strength and speed threw him off, and he stumbled back. He was wearing stilts under the cloak. Ida's hands held fast to his hair. Ed's eyes found Susan-Eva's. He looked so disappointed in her. Like she betrayed him. "CLOSE YOUR EYES!" Ella yelled to Susan-Eva. But she could not stop seeing him, finally.

Ida

It was his left eye that Ed hovered over Ida's when she passed out in the yard, and he held her lid open. So it was his left eye she sunk her teeth into, ripped from the socket, then burst the pupil in her mouth like an overripe cherry.

Ed stopped smelling like run and released a new scent. Something so potent and fresh it must have been the first time it ever exuded from his pores. It was the best thing Ida had ever inhaled and she would never, ever forget it. Each bite contained an event. Hot to warm to cool. Thrashing to throbbing to still. Panic to surrender to exhaust. Sweat, to blood, to blood, to blood, to blood, to blood.

Every swallow elevated her palate. This was the taste of life. How could anything else ever compare? But she didn't get to finish him.

Ella took the keys from Ed while Ida attacked and got Susan-Eva out. But as they tried to run to the stairs, Ed grabbed Susan-Eva's ankle, and she fell to the ground. Having his hands on Susan-Eva gave him renewed energy. He flung Ida off and leaned over Susan-Eva, putting his hands around her neck. That's when Ida got the axe. It was too heavy for her to do much more than drop it. But dropping it into his back was enough.

He was still alive, but the blade sunk deep into his right shoulder, releasing his arm muscles. Ella pulled Susan-Eva from under him. The only move Ed had left was Alpha. The kennel was in reach. With the little movement Ed could manage, he flung his working arm at the kennel latch. At the third hit, the door swung open, and Alpha bolted for them, growling and baring his teeth.

But Ida growled back. Alpha immediately cowered and let them run away. He wasn't born a bad dog. But he had been starved and neglected for too long. Ed trained him to eat limbs chopped with an axe. It didn't matter that Ed was it's human. Anything ignored long enough will eat you alive.

PART THREE

The Thing Happening to Ella

THIRTY-FOUR
August 20, 2022, 9:45 AM

Ella

MALCOLM WAS SNORING. "BABY, YOU'RE snoring," said Ella softly. He snored louder. "Babe. BABE." Nothing. Ella stuck her index finger against his nose, sealing one nostril and containing the snores to one side. It didn't quiet them, but it did make the snores a little more interesting. One side of his nose blew up like a balloon, and the other wheezed. She pressed her thumb to the other side, sealing the whole thing. He woke up with a gasp and rolled on top of her by reflex, pinning down her arms like they'd been wrestling.

"What the fuck?" he asked, catching his breath.

"You were having a nightmare," Ella said with a smile.

"Oh. *Weird.*" He ran a hand over his face and then looked back down at Ella. Exhaling, he reached under the sheets; she expected his hand to slip between her legs. Instead, he pulled out his cock, erect with the blood rush of the morning, and used it to nudge her underwear aside without pulling them down. Tense and unready, she winced, but she grew wet with the shock of it.

A wave of relief at her arousal released a moan from her lips. This was the kind of rough she liked. This was the way he touched her in the beginning. With a rude disregard for anything that resembled pampering. If the things

188

he did to her were being done to anyone else, she would have called it wrong, but because they were happening to her, she called it complicated. It was relaxing, never having to pretend to enjoy sweetness. Writhing her hips with his, she whimpered at the realization she actually might come.

It had been so long since he'd shut up and just fucked her without adding on some test or layer of taboo to prove she was still depraved enough for him. His eyes were closed. Whatever fantasy was taking him there didn't seem to require her involvement. Even better.

With her next moan, he pushed her face aside, covering it with his hand, rendering her more irrelevant. Whether he was truly fantasizing about someone else or getting off on degrading her didn't matter. Either option allowed her to slip into her own fantasy. Staring at the air vent, imagining an ear pressing to it, listening.

Usually, she needed lube to stay this wet, but she grew so slick staring at the vent that Malcolm slipped out by accident. When he shoved himself back, he grabbed her hips, tilting them to press as deeply into her as he could, moving at a slow, steady pace. For the first time in months, Ella was not counting the seconds until it ended but praying it lasted long enough. She was so, so close if only the rhythm stayed just like that and he didn't—

KNOCK. KNOCK. Ella gasped and yelled. "Later, Evie." But it was too late. Malcolm slammed himself into her like a hammer, too hard and fast to allow the release she was on the cusp of, punishing her for the knock on the door. Her arousal dissolved as quickly as it had arrived and by his final two thrusts, the friction left her stinging and raw.

The exit made her wince, he noticed. For a half second, she thought he might apologize, but instead, he smirked and grabbed her jaw, giving her a quick peck before going to the shower. Again, she liked that part. The smart-ass expression on his face said they were both in on some game that they were constantly changing the rules to. But it would've been hotter if she'd actually come. *KNOCK. KNOCK.* Wanting the knocking to stop, Ella skipped looking for sleep shorts and went to the door in her t-shirt and underwear.

Today, she wanted Susan-Eva's morning energy to jolt her back into the present. Even if her determined knocking probably meant Calvin was in the kitchen again. "Oh, Susan-Eva, I've already seen him. But please tell me this means you made breakfast again and—" But as Ella swung open the door it was Ida who leaned in the frame.

"Evie didn't come home," said Ida. Her eyes went straight to Ella's bare hips and tugged the waistband of her underwear. "Cute undies, can I borrow?" Ella smacked Ida's hand away. "After you wash, of course." Ida whiffed in the air and shook her head. "Still no orgasm, huh? Want me to tell him how? HEY MALCOLM—" Ella pushed Ida out of the door and shut it behind her as Ida chuckled.

"Wait, so did Evie call or—"

Ida shook her head and said, "No, and she's not answering. Which sucks because there's the whole #metoo-y thing going on. I guess one of us is going to have to do something. So, do you want me to go to the Sorority house, or do you want to do it? I admit I don't fully 'get' this one. Let's go get in my shower and talk. I can't focus while you smell all... I don't know..." Ida whiffed in the air and scrunched her forehead, exaggerating a contemplative expression. "What is that one?" She sniffed again, "Mediocrity? Settling? Gross?"

"Ida, what are you talking about?"

"How Malcolm can't make you come. Well, he can he just—"

"Not that. Why does one of us need to go to the sorority house?"

"Well, they're going to want some alumni guidance. I'm sure those little sophomore girls will get all emotional because he didn't get in any trouble for what he did to them, so one of the alums should say something. Probably like blah, blah, blah, your feelings are valid, but don't be little bitches about it and ruin the auction party, blah, blah, blah. You or me?"

"Me. But why do you think they want to talk about it now? Did someone call or—"

Ida pulled up something on her phone and said, "You haven't heard? Maybe my dad found out before the press since our families are so close."

"Whose family?"

"Scott Ryan, they found him."

THIRTY-FIVE

January – May 2022

Ella

THERE WAS NO WAY TO defend it. What they did was crazy. And illegal. And not fun crazy and illegal, like rolling on Molly during an Easter Sunday service the way Ida and Ella did senior year. Go to jail for a decade, crazy. If they had money, they'd flee the country crazy.

Ella knew this. They should have just taken Scott to the police. Just go to the police. If you have any new information, come straight to us; that's what they said.

But they'd already tried that.

The first time Susan-Eva talked to the cops about what happened in the park, she was still hooked up to IVs at the hospital. She could barely remember her own name. But Detective Naomi Rydell was like a TV detective. She cared. A comforting tone with an undercurrent of outrage and really excellent eyebrows.

Ella wasn't sure why the eyebrows gave her so much confidence in the detective. But as soon as she walked into the room, Ella exhaled, thinking that any woman who can manage the perfect arch and solve crimes has this.

"It looked like a fleur-de-lis," Susan-Eva had croaked, "I think it was a birthmark or maybe a scar by his hip. I only saw it for a second when he

191

turned me over and…" her voice cracked. She was clutching the stuffed squirrel Ida gave her. Her fingers tightened around it as she swallowed, fighting to maintain control. "Um, sorry, I'm trying to remember, but I think that's it." She swallowed, holding it together. Then Joseph gently took her hand, and she fell apart, dissolving into deep guttural sobs.

Detective Naomi gave Susan-Eva a small journal to jot down any little details that came back. After about a month a few things did. First, the guy was wearing cologne. It was faint, mixed with sweat and BO, but it was expensive. That wasn't very conclusive. It was awful watching Susan-Eva war with wanting to forget while desperately wishing she could remember one detail that would help. Just waiting for the missing piece.

The last place Ella thought she'd find it was at the Phi Alpha's plaid party. The last place she was expecting to find herself was at the Phi Alpha plaid party. The only people who went to undergrad parties, post-diploma, were dudes in their 30s who wanted to fuck nineteen-year-olds. Like mediocre musicians and future senators. If it hadn't been for fucking Pete Goldfein, they never would've known.

Pete and Ella had long-standing beef. Back in high school, he was the guy you went to, to buy weed. Occasionally, he got his hands on Molly or Cocaine, but at seventeen, his hook-ups were limited. So, when Ella started doling out free Xanax, Adderall, and whatever other drug of the week Dr. Homer prescribed her, Pete decided they were competition. But in a hot Mr. and Mrs. Smith way. Ella did not see Pete as competition or hot. She saw him as annoying.

So obviously she dated him for like three months. Then, he started selling opioids. To eighth graders. She liked assholes, not monsters, well… not that kind of monster. Plus, opioids were a bit of a personal problem for Ella back then. They still sort of were. Anyway, it was a whole big thing, and Mrs. Lorenzo ended up having him arrested.

So then Pete hated Ella and Susan-Eva. But for some reason, not Ida, even though she also had him arrested once so that Ella would go to the shooting range with her instead of the movies with him. No one was really allowed to hate Ida.

The night of the Plaid Party, Pete was at Craw-Ma's. When Susan-Eva took out the trash, she overheard him explaining to Scott Ryan that Ketamine worked better than GHB because the euphoric effect made them act hungry for it before it peaked. Scott bought a lot.

Ella wanted to call the cops and send them to the Phi Alpha house. They did, but the cops said they didn't see anything suspicious. So, Susan-Eva insisted they go themselves after her shift.

There were three guys in the room and one girl filming it. Pete was right. Lindsey, the freshman Scott was on top of, did look euphoric, with her half smile and fluttering eyes. She was so euphoric she was drooling. She was so euphoric she barely realized she couldn't breathe because Scott was grinding the side of her face into the pillow so hard.

Susan-Eva was always so quick to act. Ella couldn't understand why she was just standing there transfixed as Ella burst in. Scott laughed and went back to the party with the other guys while Ella yelled at the girl, Casey, who was filming.

"Chill, it's not even the craziest thing I've seen her do. She's fine with it," said Casey.

"So, she told you to film it," demanded Ella.

"She's not a fucking snowflake like apparently you've all become. I mean, seriously, do you want this place to be like Vanderbilt? Girls can't even dress up like Indians anymore. Like, let college be college. Actual Indians, native people, don't even care. Right?" Casey huffed, looking at Susan-Eva, waiting for her to confirm.

"Shut the fuck up and give me your phone, you stupid twat," said Ella. She looked back at Susan-Eva, who was checking on Lindsey, but her face was somewhere else; she didn't seem to hear them at all.

Casey found her vodka and Celsius-filled Yeti mug and said, "You can't say shit like that anymore. You're so lucky I wasn't recording that! Because a woman alumni, especially a woman in power like you, talking to me as a student and calling me a twat is actually way more problematic than me filming a woman being sex-positive."

"DID SHE TELL YOU TO FILM IT?" yelled Ella.

Lindsey moaned from the bed "Mom? I feel… where's mom?"

Ella shook her head at Casey in disgust and said, "Yeah she seems

193

super aware of what's going on."

Casey said, "By morning, she won't care. She had a threesome in high school, so— but whatever, I'll delete it."

"NO!" shouted Susan-Eva, scrambling to her feet and rushing over.

"Right. If she decides to report, it's evidence," said Ella.

Casey backed away and said, "Okay, I don't want to be a part of this. I'm deleting it, and it's done. She's fine." Before Casey could unlock her phone, Susan-Eva smacked it out of her hand and caught it in the air. Ella had to fight, not smile; it was the first time she'd seen the girl in the tutu and mask since what happened in the park.

"What's your password? I need to watch it." Susan-Eva demanded.

"Wow. Now who's the fucked up one?" Casey said, grabbing for her phone as Ella held her back.

Ella glanced over her shoulder at Susan-Eva and lowered her voice. "*Hey*. Send it to me, and I'll take it to the cops if she wants. There's no reason to watch it."

"*I need to see it,*" said Susan-Eva, her voice was shaking.

"You know everyone is only nice to you two because you are Ida's best friends. I have no idea why. She'd be fine with this," said Casey.

"Want to test that theory?" Said Ella, meeting Casey's eyes. "I could call her. Have her come over. She did always love the plaid party." Casey shifted her weight back and forth and swallowed. Ella pulled out her phone. Casey quickly shook her head, pleading: *no, don't call Ida.* Clearly, she had no idea exactly why this threat was so scary. But she wasn't as dumb as she acted. She knew she'd overstepped.

"Whatever. Just hold the screen to me." Casey mumbled, offering her face to unlock the phone.

There it was. It was the motion of his hand that made her certain. There was a methodical back-and-forth rhythm to the way he pressed Lindsey's head to the pillow. He'd done the same thing to Susan-Eva. Rubbing the side of her face back and forth into the ground, so she inhaled dirt every time she gasped for air.

But a lawyer would argue there was nothing conclusive about that. The birthmark was shaped like a fleur de lis; however, the one and only physical detail Susan-Eva remembered, even that night at the hospital, was far more distinguishing. The video was dark. But it was right there on Scott Ryan's hip. Finally, the man in the park wasn't a faceless monster.

To Susan-Eva, it wasn't even a man. After all, she used to babysit him when she was fourteen and Scott was eight. He was a nightmare of a little boy with a scream that could break the glass. It wasn't an out-of-town stranger who could be anywhere. It was a born and bred Moss Groves son who was right downstairs.

When Lindsey's fog started to lift and she saw the video, she started crying. She only remembered taking one shot. She didn't even know Scott. At first, she didn't want to talk to the police because she was afraid she'd be in trouble for drinking underage. But after Susan-Eva told her about what happened in the park, she agreed. Lindsey was still sedated, but she wanted to talk in case she forgot something later.

Even through her K come down, Ella thought Lindsey's statement was clear and believable. Ella only wished it was Detective Rydell with the excellent eyebrows listening, but she'd been transferred to another district so they had to talk to Officer Reynolds. He was usually nice but older. He'd been on the scene at Lot 355 when they were little. Back then, he was still a rookie. When they carried the body out from the cellar, he went to the ambulance. Ella thought he was getting queasy but he actually had gone to get her a shock blanket because she was shaking. It was kind. So even though his eyebrows left something to be desired, she thought he'd handle this with compassion, too.

"We'll both testify. I've never seen a birthmark like that before, and it's in the exact same spot. He's the same size. He even smelled the same. It's Scott Ryan." Susan-Eva said.

Susan-Eva's voice didn't grow emotional. She was clear and concise in her explanation. She said everything she planned to say. It was Ella who had the lump in her throat. She was so proud. They never struggled with what to say to police about the things that happened when they were little. Lies are easier. They chose the words together. Assigned each other parts. It was like telling someone about a movie you saw. It turned out to be much harder to remember everything you wanted to say when you were telling the truth.

Officer Reynolds studied all three of their faces like he was waiting for one of them to crack a smile and yell gotcha. He took a deep breath and said, "You think Scott Ryan is the Marshland Park rapist?"

Susan-Eva cleared her throat and responded, "I know he is. I recognize—"

Officer Reynolds interrupted her by reaching across his desk and squeezing her hand. Then he said, "Honey, I've seen the pictures of what happened to you and the other girl. I get it. I really do. What happened to you that day is every woman's worst nightmare. You want it to be over. It's very common for victims of an unknown attacker to start suspecting everyone they see. It's nothing to be embarrassed about. But I have known Scott Ryan since he was five years old. He didn't do this."

Susan-Eva's face fell with something so much worse than disappointment. Despite having more evidence than anyone that the world was a cruel, unfair place, Susan-Eva had always refused to stop fighting for it. Seeing her with a look that said, "Of course. Of course, this is the way things are. How stupid was I to think any different." It was unbearable.

Ella squinted at Officer Reynolds, livid, but she tried to keep her voice calm as she clarified, "Sorry. I think you misunderstand. We pulled Scott off of Lindsey an hour ago."

Now it was Officer Reynolds who seemed to be fighting to stay calm. He shook his head, taking in Lindsey's Catholic School girl costume. Then he looked back at Ella and said, "Aren't you two a few years past your frat party stage? What were you even doing there?"

"We told you. In the parking lot Susan-Eva heard—" Ella said.

"But you didn't see him spike her drink? Lots of kids are doing K recreationally. It's a problem." He looked at Lindsey. "If I were to ask around, are you telling me you've never used a recreational drug?" Lindsey sank in her seat.

"That has nothing to do with what happened tonight," Ella said. She turned to Susan-Eva, thinking she might join in, but she was staring at an old picture in the corner of the room. Officer Reynolds, with his baby daughter, dressed as a squirrel for her first Halloween.

"It has everything to do with what happened. With what is happening all over this country. I put my life on the line for this town. I got shot busting a meth lab six years ago. And that's okay. That's the job. We're here to protect y'all. And we try to look the other way and let college kids be college kids. No need to ruin anyone's life over a party. But now you've got women coming out of the woodwork using the word assault because someone brushed up against her ass ten years ago. And people are cheering it on. Ruining men's— no, not just men, because what y'all seem to forget is these men have wives, daughters. You're out here destroying entire families." Again, he looked at Lindsey. "We all do things we regret when we're young, and we're drinking; it's okay, honey. This is good. Let this be your wake-up call to take it a little easier on the partying so you make sure something worse doesn't happen, where you really get hurt."

Ella said, "She did really get hurt. He—"

"A one-night stand isn't rape. It just isn't." He looked at Susan-Eva and ran a hand over his face, probably remembering the pictures of injuries again. "I feel pissed as hell for women like you, Susie. Women who had that really happen to them, when I hear that word getting thrown around." Susan-Eva never met his eyes. She just kept staring at the picture on the wall. So he turned to Ella and added, "The man who took you two when you were little, that's who we're here to fight. That's true evil. It's a miracle you survived. I've got more patience for you two than most. So know this is said with love, as a father who knows your own dad's aren't around to say it. But of *anyone*, you should know better. Jogging alone in the woods in a sports bra? If my daughter left the house in... Then you come to me tonight. With her looking like that, trying to throw a good kid—" He inhaled, trying to keep his cool as Ella dug her nails into the palm of her hand. "You should be the ones setting a good example. Jog at the gym. Cover yourself. You want this stuff to stop happening quit putting yourself in danger. Go where it's safe."

Lindsey started crying and said, "Please don't tell my dad."

"Don't worry, honey, these girls are going to get you home. Nobody is going to find out about any of this." Officer Reynolds said, giving Ella a look that made her feel like she was being dismissed from the principal's office.

With her legs still wobbly from the Ketamine, Lindsey tried to push herself up, finally breaking Susan-Eva's trance. Hooking an arm around Lindsey's waist, Susan-Eva led her to the door, carrying most of her weight, never looking back.

Defeated and bewildered, Ella followed, and Officer Reynolds looked back down at a report. There was no point in saying any more. But then he huffed. Out of the corner of her eye, Ella watched the papers on his desk flutter from his annoyed fucking huff. Before her mind knew what was happening, Ella rushed back to the desk, pulled the report from his hands, and slammed it on the floor.

Leaning over him, Ella said with a smile, "I'm sorry. Could you be a little more specific? You said go where it's safe. So, where do you mean exactly? We know you think the woods aren't safe, but actually, statistically, they were the most unlikely place for it to happen. Frat house, sure, I'll give you that one: rape machine. And the gym? Really? You said go to the gym? Didn't you just arrest a trainer for assault last week? I'm an HR consultant, so I can assure you the workplace isn't safe. So where is it exactly? This magic place where it's not our fault. Where is it you want us to go?"

Glaring up at her, Officer Reynolds said, "Home. I want you to go home."

"Seventy-five percent," said Susan-Eva. She was leaning in the doorway, still holding up Lindsey, her face still blank.

"Excuse me?" Said Officer Reynolds, leaning over to look past Ella.

"The percentage of women who get murdered in domestic violence situations. Seventy-five percent get killed while trying to leave home, where it's safe," said Susan-Eva. Lindsey started to slump again and Susan-Eva looked back at Ella. "Can you help me with her?"

...

After that, Susan-Eva pretended none of it happened. She started waking up even earlier, smiling all the time, and being the girl who prided herself on a new hook-up every week. Ella knew she wasn't okay, but she didn't know how to help. Even Joseph was getting the all-perk, all-the-time act. The only person Susan-Eva let her sunshine down around was Ida.

After years of it being an Ella and Ida-only activity, Susan-Eva started joining them at the shooting range. Then Ida and Susan-Eva started hanging out alone. A couple of times, Ella asked Ida what they talked about. But Ida would just grin and tell Ella, jealous smelled so good on her.

So, Ella started spending more nights at Malcolm's. Obviously, she wasn't of any use to either of her survival sisters (That's what Trisha used to call them to the papers). If only she'd known how much of their time went to talking about how much they hated Malcolm and how they were going to get Ella back.

For Ella, being useless was like not existing. Worse than not existing. Existing without earning it. So, she thought about leaving. She even applied to a few jobs out of state. Hating Moss Groves was one of her favorite pastimes, so it didn't make any sense that the thought of living anywhere else made her so sad. Luckily, she never had to figure it out.

Nothing says *I need you, and our friendship means everything to me* like asking someone to commit a felony with you.

THIRTY-SIX
May 14, 2022

Susan-Eva

A NEW LIGHT PURPLE BRA with lace that peeked barely over the cups was the only thing of note. Susan-Eva was genuinely excited to debut it to whoever she ended up with that night, even if she knew what followed would likely be another unsatisfactory failed experiment. For one fleeting moment, she'd stand before someone, feeling she looked romantic and beautiful. Otherwise, it was an irritating but normal bartending shift at Craw-Ma's.

Former frat boys hit on waitresses before stumbling into the girl's bathroom and pissing all over the toilet seat they've left down because they're certain "they've got this" despite no drunk penis in the history of penises ever "having it." The night may even carry a hint of danger. In the two years since she was hired at Craw-Ma's, she'd never seen less than three guns on any given shift. Very little would surprise or unsettle her.

After all, Susan-Eva was fine. More than fine. Super. She was exploring her sexuality. Yay! Lots of victims have to go through therapy before they get intimate again. Not Susan-Eva. She'd skipped the second grade. She saw no reason she couldn't skip PTSD. She'd tested out of most of her gen-ed college requirements. She'd never needed a beginner's level anything. Why start with her reaction to trauma?

Besides, no one could consider her a beginner at trauma. She was the girl who survived Ed Bins even though he'd been grooming her for months and emotionally tortured her. Do you know what she did that same year? Led her dance team to win at state.

So now all she had to do was the grown-up version of winning at state. Apparently, that meant boning a bunch of dudes until it got fun again. Most people didn't even know what happened to her. They just saw that she was in her pastel era, and SHE WAS KILLING IT. Good for her. She deserved fun. So no, nothing at all could get to her.

But she didn't think she'd have to see Scott Ryan. Ever. At least not for more than a few seconds. Her life didn't intersect with undergrads, much less freshman. She could avoid him. Most of the time, she pushed him so far out of her brain it was like he didn't really exist. Just a thing from a nightmare. Officer Reynolds was so certain, at times, it was easier to believe he was right. It wasn't Scott. It couldn't have been. Her mistake.

At Craw-Ma's, she could really relax because you had to be twenty-one to get in, and they were strict about carding. Newbies could get away with a fake ID once or twice but Scott Ryan grew up in Moss Groves. Everyone knew he was underage.

But the security guard was in the bathroom when he came in. When she complained to her manager, he shrugged and pointed to Scott shaking hands with a cop at the bar and said, "If they don't care, why should we?" Then, the cop leaned close to Susan-Eva and ordered Scott a drink.

So, Susan-Eva served him. Like a *fine* person would do. *For hours.* Every time she handed him a beer, he grabbed her hand to take the bottle from her and then slowly caressed her thumb with his index finger. It wasn't as though he was the only patron to use this move. It was a classic.

But most of them didn't do it with that smirk. Like there was something ironic about it. Most of them didn't meet her eyes, showing off how cold and deliberate the choice was, daring her to call attention to it. Most of them didn't smell exactly like the person who made her think she was going to die choking on dirt while he got himself hard again.

So even though she hated Pete Goldfein, Ella's drug dealer ex, that night, Susan-Eva was relieved when he rolled in. Even if he was wearing a new "TOOL 10,000 Faces" shirt he'd ripped holes into so he could claim it was vintage. It meant Scott's attention would be elsewhere. There weren't many women in the bar that night. None alone. Susan-Eva still kept an eye on all their drinks if they went to bathroom or turned away. To her further relief, Scott didn't show any interest in her patrons. Just Pete, the cop, and her.

But then the cop left. Next Pete. So Scott returned to the bar and sat on a stool behind a half-drunk pint-sized margarita with salt turned pink from lipstick. Fifteen minutes earlier its drinker had disappeared into the bathroom with Pete and come back giggling. Five minutes later, she got kicked out for falling asleep at the bar. Susan-Eva hadn't had a chance to bus the glass yet. As soon as Scott sat, she reached for it, but he swooped it out of the way and downed what was left.

"I'm a conservationist. Can't stand the sight of waste," said Scott, again staring into her eyes, cold and deliberate. "Get me a shot of—"

"I already did last call," said Susan-Eva, turning away and pouring a tequila shot for Parker Porter, who was at the other end of the bar.

"Hey! I've got our girl on the phone!" said Parker.

"No shit," said Susan-Eva, forcing a smile and taking the shot with Parker.

"She likes to call me before bed so we can do our nighttime prayers together," Parker said, beaming at his phone.

"Aw. Would you mind if I said hi?" Susan-Eva asked as Scott entered her prefrail on his way over.

"Of course. Hey, you don't have to explain it to me. I get it. I know my Ida, and I know I'm a distant third to my girl's girls," said Parker.

"Uh-huh. Can I have the phone?" Said Susan-Eva, taking the phone from Parker as Scott pulled out the stool.

"Youth Pastor Porter in a bar!" said Scott.

"Hey, Jesus turned water to wine, not the other way around. You, on the other hand, are a few years off from twenty-one by my count." Parker grinned back at Susan-Eva. "He's not given you any trouble, is he?" Susan-Eva walked away with the phone.

"*Ida?*" Breathed Susan-Eva, feeling her heart start to race.

"Come home," said Ida. "Ella is at Malcolm's, and I'm so bored. I've been looking up videos of people torturing cats for two hours on the dark web. But I've already seen all of them. None of these people understand a flattering angle. They start, and the lighting is awful, but you forgive it because there are decent closes on the disembowelment. Then BAM! The camera points up, and it's double-chin-city. It's disgusting like, why would you film that?"

"Yeah, that's super frustrating. Not judging you, but watching those videos is one of those things that I'd put in the evil category," said Susan-Eva, but she felt the tension leaving her shoulders at the sound of Ida's voice.

"Babe," Sighed Ida. "You know, I'm only watching in case one of them fully shows their gross fat face. So I can add them to the list of people for if we ever decide to go the *Dexter* route," said Ida.

"We've made it very, *very* clear we're never ever going to be cool with you going the *Dexter* route," said Susan-Eva. Her eyes floated back at Scott without her permission.

"Are you sure about that?" Ida asked, her voice less playful now. Susan-Eva swallowed. How did Ida always know? Every time Susan-Eva had the thought, it was like Ida could feel it no matter how far away she was.

Of course, they hadn't told Ida that Scott was the man in the park. They had way too much experience with Ida using even the most minor offenses against Ella and Susan-Eva as an excuse to sate her appetite. An -accident-with sizzling bacon grease left Ella's mom with third-degree burns, the one and only time Ida slept over at Ella's. That also happened to be the last time Ms. Kyle would ever wash Ella's mouth out with soap.

It wasn't real affection. They knew that. Avenging them was her excuse and they never, ever condoned it. In fact, they threatened to have her arrested when she did anything illegal. And it worked. Ida never used the same excuse twice. She'd always claim it was something she hadn't understood before, but now she did so it wouldn't happen again.

But if Ida knew about Scott, she'd undoubtedly find a loophole. Some ethics territory they hadn't covered yet and things could get out of hand. It was absolutely out of the question to involve Ida in this in any way. So why had Susan-Eva bothered asking for the phone?

"I should go. I need to start closing," said Susan-Eva.

"Babe… want my help?" asked Ida.

"Help me break down the bar? Yeah, I'll pull out an extra pair of rubber gloves, and you can take out the trash. Hilarious," said Susan-Eva, watching Scott order a shot from the barback.

"You're not laughing," said Ida. Then she waited, but Susan-Eva didn't say anything, her throat was too dry. "Want me to say that stuff you only ask me to say when you're drunk?" asked Ida. Susan-Eva tried to find the word, no, but her head nodded yes. Again, it was like Ida could see her, feel her. "There are twelve points on the human body where a single puncture can be fatal, regardless of strength, age, gender, or health. To strangle the average person it takes…" and so she went.

Susan-Eva listened in silence until Scott stumbled his way out of the bar, suddenly very drunk. "Um. Okay. I have to go," said Susan-Eva, cutting Ida off mid-murder-fact.

"Okay! Nom, nom. Yum, yum. So fun. Night!" Ida made a kissing noise and hung up.

It was over. Susan-Eva had survived yet again, even if it did take hearing Ida recite facts on the quickest paths to fatality in the human body. Just like it would for a completely fine person.

She was so fine that she decided she could do closing side work alone and sent the barback and security home so she could lock up by herself. That way, she could sing as loud as she wanted with music as she cleaned, she told them. But she couldn't find the right song, so she cleaned in silence and told herself the bleach was stinging her eyes and that's what was causing the tears.

Okay, so she wasn't fine, *fine*. She knew that. She knew she needed help, but given how little she'd be able to say about Ida, what was the point? Talking about the park didn't require discussing the Montgomerys, but any good therapist would want to explore the root of her issues. Trisha made sure those roots were buried under NDAs, financial chains, and threats to everything she loved. So, this was life now. She lived in the same town as her rapist, and no one but Ella, Lindsey, and whoever else he got to would believe her. Plenty of women endure far worse. At least he wasn't a friend or family. At least she was all grown up.

Over and over, she was told how lucky she was that Ed didn't really hurt them. Or touch her *like that*. Because that could have really fucked her up. As though the hours in the cellar were more like waiting on the results of cancer screening and then finding out you were clear. Scary. But no reason for lasting damage.

The few who knew about the park agreed it was horrific, but she was a woman now. Horrific was part of the job. Thank god she wasn't a virgin. That might have really fucked her up. Thank God he hadn't scarred her face. That could have really fucked her up. Thank God it wasn't the second killer out to finally finish the job. Dying really would have fucked her up.

Alone in the parking lot, she stared up at the sky, praying to make peace with it. A cool breeze rustled the trees like a sign from God: She'd been heard, and peace was coming. She took a deep breath and stepped into her future, determined that when she got in her pick-up truck and drove back to Parlay House, she would let Scott go.

Until she realized Scott had vomited and passed out in the bed of her truck.

THIRTY-SEVEN

May 15, 4:30 AM

Ella

"I COULDN'T DO IT," SUSAN-EVA said, pacing next to the pool at Parlay House. She was breathing so quickly that Ella could barely understand her. When Ella got the S.O.S. text at 4am and rushed over from Malcolm's, she assumed it was an Ida crisis. But all Ella had really gotten out of Susan-Eva so far was that Ida could never know, so they needed to be careful not to wake her. "In the DC universe, they'd take him to the hospital."

"Who?" asked Ella.

"That's what a big person would do. A person who believes in rehabilitation and redemption would drop him at the hospital if they saw his eyes rolling back like that. It could be an overdose or alcohol poisoning. Or his parent's lawn, at least. But hey, in the Marvel universe, they'd maybe kill him. So— but we both know I have always considered myself a DC girl."

Ella took Susan-Eva's shoulders and said, "Eva. I love you. But you're doing that thing where you panic-speak geek, and I'm only fluent in nerd. Just tell me what happened?"

Susan-Eva's eyes darted back and forth like she was searching for something, then not finding it she shook her head in surrender and repeated, "I couldn't do it."

"You couldn't do what?" asked Ella.

"Why do you keep sleeping at Malcolm's? His apartment sucks!" Susan-Eva said, pulling away from Ella.

"This about is Malcolm?" asked Ella.

"No, but if you'd been here instead of at his place, maybe I would've come home. But I couldn't because it was just Ida here. She's in my head. I'm thinking things and doing things I would never…" Susan-Eva's fanned her shirt, like she was overheating, but it was only fifty-seven degrees. She looked up at the house "You can't leave me here alone with her."

"You kept making plans without me. I thought you wanted to be alone with her," said Ella.

"Exactly!" Susan-Eva whispered like it was a scream. "A clear sign I am losing my mind and I need you. Okay?"

Ella tried not to smile from the relief she felt hearing those words. Susan-Eva ran her hands over her face and said, "You can't abandon me with this. I can't do it alone. We're supposed to be helping her. We're supposed to be protecting people from her. Not… I'm fucking it all up!"

Moving in front of Susan-Eva so Ella could look her in the eye, Ella said, "Hey. I'm sorry. You don't have to do it alone. Ever. I'll never leave you alone with it again." It was astonishing, knowing how much she meant what she'd said. If it took her entire lifetime, Ella didn't care. None of the bad things that happened to her in Moss Groves could eclipse how good it felt to know she was still needed.

"You only say that because you don't know what I did yet. If you knew— FUCK!" Susan-Eva let her weight fall to one of the pool chairs.

"It's okay. You're okay," said Ella, kneeling next to her.

"Why do people think that? Only a psychopath could know the things we know and see the things we saw and be… You date assholes because you think if you see it coming, you won't be scared. It won't hurt the same way because you'll be ready. You're not okay. And I'm…" Susan-Eva stared at the pool. Steam rose from the water and glowed blue in the chlorine-filtered light. "Have you ever gone back?" asked Susan-Eva, her voice turned small.

"Back where?" Ella asked.

"Lot 355." Susan-Eva's eyes didn't leave the pool.

207

It had been years since they talked about it of their own will. For all the rehearsing of what to say, all the micromanaging of the narrative, when it came to discussing the reality of what happened, they were lost. It wasn't taboo or off limits, but it was unpracticed. Intimate.

Outsiders commented how they were lucky to have each other to talk to. To have someone who understood something no one else could. But being in that cellar together only meant they saw the same things. They each experienced what they saw and heard and did differently. That was the main thing they understood. The difference.

Trying to talk about it felt like trying to help someone dismantle a bomb in a language you comprehended but didn't speak well. In low stakes situation a slip of the tongue is comical. In high stakes, a slip could mean you blow everyone up.

"No. I never went back," Ella said, trying to sound gentle but matter-of-fact. She wasn't sure what the right tone of voice was, but she knew there was one. "I went down Magic Alley a couple of times in high school. But the road crumbles halfway through the woods. Um…" Ella told herself she felt calm and fine, but her stupid hands were shaking. She shoved them between her knees and said, "But if it's important to you, we could try to go back one day. I thought I heard once that they tore the house down." She hadn't heard it. She just told herself it was torn down. It felt better to think of it not existing. To her, the house was worse than the cellar. Because that was where she should have stopped it, and it's where she woke up, alone. "I know the city owns the property, but they probably got rid of the house. I really don't think it's there."

"It is. It's all still there," said Susan-Eva, her eyes still on the pool, her hands were shaking too.

"You… When?" Ella gaped, no longer attempting to sound calm.

"I shouldn't tell you. I should leave you out of it."

"I don't care whatever it is. We'll figure it out. Just tell me."

Susan-Eva stared at her, trying to speak, but then she shut her mouth, walked to the pool, pulled off her tee shirt and jeans, and jumped in. Before her brain had any reason for it Ella pulled off the sweats she borrowed from Malcolm and jumped in after her. They treaded water facing each other, watching their breath turn to glowing blue clouds. Mascara streamed down Susan-Eva's face as she shook her head at Ella. "You don't have to follow me every time I do something insane."

Ella said, "You followed me into the church closet. Whatever you did, it's not crazier than the stuff I've done."

"Yes, it is."

"I Dextered Ida."

"No. Dextering her would be telling her it is okay to kill. You did the opposite."

"I used to show her pictures of dead bodies to calm her down."

"This is worse."

"Freshman year at Florence I slept with Ida's dad to get back at her Mom," Ella said.

"Oh, Ella," Susan-Eva said, cringing.

"I sort of thought you knew."

"I sort of did. I just hoped it wasn't true. Bruce is such a piece—"

"It was fine. I initiated."

"We really need to go therapy."

"We really do," said Ella. Susan-Eva stared at her feet under the water. "Whatever you did can't be more messed up than—"

"Scott Ryan passed out in the back of my truck, so I locked him in the storm cellar where we almost got murdered."

Ella blinked a few times. That was not what she was expecting. But there had to be a correct, useful response. When she opened her mouth, all that came out was, "Okay."

"I'm not going to hurt him," said Susan-Eva.

"Okay," Ella repeated. Okay was apparently the only word she knew in the language of this experience. Then, she found a few more to fumble through. "Why? I mean, not that you wouldn't be justified in… but what do you want to…"

"I don't know."

"Okay. Well, it will be fine. We've handled crazier things than this before and it's always turned out completely—"

A shotgun fired.

They screamed then looked up and saw Ida leaning out her bedroom window, with a smoking riffle. She groaned seeing them and said, "It's you! I thought I was going to get to shoot an intruder. UGH. Damn it, Ella."

"You're not supposed to have a fucking gun, Ida!" yelled Ella.

"You're not supposed to be waking me up at five AM, clearly doing 'a thing' without me," said Ida.

Ella glared and said, "Oh my God. We're not doing 'a thing.' We're just talking."

"About what?" asked Ida, eyebrows raised.

Ella and Susan-Eva said, "Nothing." At the same time.

"Oh my God! Yes, you are! You're totally doing a thing. I've never, EVER done 'a thing' in the pool at five AM where Susie Evie is wearing a really, really cute bra and Ella is wearing a really ugly shirt, without you guys," said Ida. She screeched in offense.

"That doesn't even make sense, Ida," said Ella, then she glanced at Susan-Eva's bra and said to her "But that is a cute bra."

"Thank you," said Susan-Eva, looking down at the purple lace.

"Yeah, super cute. Good color on you but—" Ida paused, squinting at something, then pointed the gun at the garden and pulled the trigger. Ella and Susan-Eva both screamed again in shock at the sound. Ida continued, "But the material looks cheap want me to buy you—"

"WHAT THE—" shrieked Ella.

"WHAT? I was just offering to buy her the real version of the bra," said Ida, furious and offended.

Susan-Eva said, "I think she's more wondering why you just fired the gun again, mid-sentence."

"Oh," Ida said shrugging "There was a rabbit eating your mint."

"We've got plenty of mint, babe, no need," said Susan-Eva.

"Heard," said Ida, nodding, chill.

"Why do you have a fucking gun?" yelled Ella.

"It was a gift! I'm pretty sure you both went to really annoying extremes to emphasize the importance of not being rude in public and I think if I turned it down he would have cried. Way to be insensitive, Ella." Yelled Ida.

"Who would have cried?" asked Ella.

"Parker," said Ida.

"Parker gave you a gun. Why?" asked Ella.

"Engagement gift. It's like a family tradition or something. I don't know, I wasn't listening, " said Ida.

"Engagement gift?" asked Susan-Eva.

"Oh. Yeah. Parker proposed. I said yes. Then he cried anyway." Ida snorted. "He looked so ugly. I took a video. Want to see?"

Ella went pale and said, "You said yes. So you…"

"I'm getting married. Which you would've known if you weren't off doing 'a thing' without me. Anyway, I have another headache. I'm going to do a bump of cocaine and masturbate. Nom-nom. Yum-yum. Would have been so fun if you invited me, but you didn't, like mean stupid bitches." Ida leaned back in the house. Ella stared at the water.

"Ella, are you okay?" asked Susan-Eva.

"Of course. Why wouldn't I be?" asked Ella, doing a terrible job hiding how -not okay- she was.

"Ida," said Susan-Eva.

"Yeah, we have to take the gun away," said Ella.

Susan-Eva studied Ella's face and said, "I meant more the, marrying—"

"So you locked Scott Ryan in the cellar storm cellar where we were supposed to die," Ella said, like she was returning to an agenda point at one of her office meetings.

"Yeah," replied Susan-Eva.

"And you want to keep him there?" Susan-Eva nodded. "But you're not sure why and don't have an end game?"

"He looked... He might have O.D.-ed. He might be dead. I should have taken him to the hospital. I couldn't do it. What does that make me?"

"You're my best friend."

THIRTY-EIGHT
August 20, 2022, 9:00 AM

Scott

REFLECTION WAS THE FIRST THING. You don't think about how much control lives in sight and one's own ability to manipulate one's appearance until you lose access to a mirror. Seeing it in the rearview mirror of a stranger's car was not ideal but it would have to do.

She got too close. Finally. In seconds his hand had a fist of her hair. It only took one hard yank of her head to the bars for her to go limp. He did things to make sure she was really out, and she didn't flinch, so she had to be, at the very least, unconscious. He didn't check her breathing. It didn't matter. He was free.

Dawn had just broke. There was a truck sitting there waiting for him to take. But something was strange about the gear shift. He couldn't get it to start. That was fine. Something about the truck felt wrong anyway. Hiking through the woods to the street was more harrowing anyway. It didn't take long to wave down a car. His father was crying and hugging him moments later. Then insisted they go to someone else's home. Whose didn't matter at the moment. All that mattered was that it was a nice home with a full-length mirror. After three months, Scott Ryan finally could see himself. He was not displeased.

His hair had grown from a crew cut to shiny waves, and his skin's natural olive tone was unblemished. With nothing much else to do in the two hundred and fifty square feet behind the metal bars, his muscles were bulkier than the lean boyishness of the physique he had prior to his kidnapping. Reflection was one of many fantasies that carried him through his time in captivity. Now he looked forward to someone else bearing witness to it, someone other than *her.*

Each time the doors opened and sunlight flooded the stairs down to the cellar, he always screamed. Just in case someone new was there. But when he saw it was the same small female figure behind the mask it always was, he went silent and sat in a single chair at the center of his cell. Calmly and with nothing more than resentment, he stared at his captor and noted her sweat. Her tremble. Her shoulders caved toward her chest in fear. Even behind bars, he could feel his control.

Little of his energy was wasted on trying to figure out who she was. Probably one of the women from the park. In which case he was grateful she kept on the mask. The moment he saw her face he'd be robbed of a dream.

For the months Scott was locked in that storm cellar he dreamed of his apartment, his Xbox, his custom mattress, his cocaine, not the kind shared at parties, the expensive bag he saved only for him. He dreamed about visiting his parent's house and swimming and dipping into his dad's scotch collection.

Most of all, he dreamed of the news. Reading. Watching. Listening. A story about him. Not the one where he'd gone missing but the one where he was so much bigger than his name. Bigger than his age. Bigger than his family.

In only two hours Scott Ryan achieved immortality. Losers who shot up schools, put a bullet through their skull with the certainty they'd done the same. How very civilian. How simple. How short-sighted. The name of someone who tweeted that the shooting never happened had more longevity than the name of the shooter. The name of a semi-famous pop star who said something even debatably offensive about the shooting lasted longer than the name of where it happened. Infamy was an aspiration of little men. The pulse of infamy is tied to grief. Grief only lasts a lifetime. At best, after that, its corpse is preserved in museums and tacky ghost tours.

Even legends waxed and waned with the ethos of society. Bending the names of history into opera, film, schoolhouse rock, hip-hop musicals, and physical currency. In and out of vogue, rarely itself and always a reflection. But not a truthful reflection. A deceptively well-lit down-angled mirror. Better yet, a selfie with a meticulously selected filter. The pulse of legends is tied to vanity. Vanity changes with each reigning generation. It's better than infamy; legends are at least recycled. Useful, the way a trophy wife is useful.

Names were the problem. Both the heroes and the villains suffered from what Scott referred to as the disease of the defined. "Disease of the Defined" was a brilliant string of words, Scott was certain.

He used it to title an essay his father refused to let him submit for his college applications. But that only convinced him of their power. So, he used them in a song he wrote for a band he started in high school. They never made it past the garage, but the girls who visited for practice blew them all once. Hidden in his tattoo, the words appeared again, and one day, he was certain "Disease of the Defined" would be the title of his biography. In all its manifestations the words meant that a thing with a name is a thing that can be measured. If you can measure it, you can understand it. Control it.

Long had Scott suffered from the disease of the name Ryan. To be the University president's son meant all he achieved would be dismissed as given to him because of his father. His own intellect dismissed as a given due to his academic upbringing.

Worst of all, Martin Ryan had achieved the impossible task of being a well-liked public figure who was a known southern democrat. Meaning the Ryan family was not only expected to be humbly high achieving and charismatically polite but also comfortingly centrist. The pulse of Ryan was connected, to palatable. To being fucking boring. To being a little bitch. Relevance of the palatable's offspring is shorter lived than reality TV marriage. How many of John McCain's four kids can you name? Meghan? Maybe? Oh wait, he had seven kids. Or five. Or none; Meghan was his stepdaughter. No, it was… who cares?

Scott wanted to attach his pulse to something that would pass from mother to fetus. Something that feeds cancer. Something as alive in the caveman as it is the neuroscientist, the tech giant, the child, and the girls.

Something that's driving action even when you're unaware of its presence. A killer and a savior with no regard for the result it achieved. Scott aspired to fable. Scott wanted to live in cortisol.

Fear was one tool for inducing it, and it was a favorite, to be sure. But stress was far more insidious than fear. Fear was overcome all the time. If it wasn't, there would be no war. But the simple stress of saving a dollar could get people to support child labor, slavery, genocide and the ultimate destruction of the planet. Without stress, there would be no fast fashion.

Legends inspire. Fairytales deceive. Ghost stories scare. *But fables...* fables teach. And there is no more lasting thing to teach than stress.

Marshland Park was where citizens of Moss Groves went to escape their so-called "stresses." In a town like that, there were rarely any real ones. So, while they were jogging away, their petty worries of cellulite in spring break bikinis or taking a nature walk to unwind after the boss raised his voice, it would come for them. After that, no one would step foot on its paths without remembering the fable:

Once, in these woods, someone, something, leveled, debased, and seeded itself into three women in broad daylight. Age, height, race all unknown. All that is known for sure is it could come back at any time to anyone. It could seed and grow in you. As long as Scott's name was never attached to things he did, he could bear witness to his own haunting.

To enjoy it as long as possible, he made sure to choose three he didn't recognize. Each attack started from behind, and then he took whatever measures were necessary to ensure he never saw their faces. One of them choked on so much dirt as he ground her face down he thought he killed her. That would have been inconvenient. When she started gasping, it was a relief. Such a relief he finally got hard again and could finish.

In the weeks that followed he stayed out of public places long enough so that any bruises would have healed. No cheating, no hints. He wanted to walk around high on not knowing. The *she's* could be anyone. The mom pushing the stroller? Probably not. They all felt too tight to be post-kid. But maybe she had c-section. Could be her. Could be the rude pharmacist with the wrist tattoo. It could be the girl sitting three rows down in his sociology class and always staying after to flirt with the TA. It could have been someone who didn't even live here.

As long as he didn't know the faces, every girl in the world could be one of his three. When it became public knowledge, they would probably appear on news stories crying and this special time of not knowing would end. It would be worth it. He couldn't be a fable without anyone knowing what happened, of course. But it was important to savor it while it lasted.

It was alarming how long it lasted, though. Within the first month there were no reports of what happened, or even rumors. But that happened sometimes in Moss Groves. Florence University's PR machine was very adept at incentivizing the press to keep the handling of any on-campus mishaps "in the family," so to speak. Marshland Park was technically owned by the University as of five years ago. They'd repaved the paths, added lamp posts throughout, and touted in brochures it was a safe haven away from the rigors of academia. It was a perfect excuse for another slight tuition increase. It made sense that they'd go out of their way to bury a story like this.

But even in a town that got off on nostalgia as much as Moss Groves, they couldn't ignore the cultural climate entirely. They'd survived "Me too" relatively unscathed, but there was paranoia and stress it could still reach their little bubble. Were there an uptick in rumblings of on-campus sexual misconduct, they'd have to claim they were taking a closer look.

Outside reporters would come in and be astonished to find the story of the Unidentified Marshland Park Predator was swept under the rug. There would be outrage. Terror. Lots of stress. So much cortisol Scott would feel it sucking years of life from all it touched. And eventually, fable.

Three months was plenty of time for all of this to have unfolded. He would make sure the bitch who robbed him the opportunity of watching it unfold was punished. If she wasn't already dead. He hit her head pretty hard the second time, she might be dead. He hoped not. It would unnecessarily complicate things. She was bleeding, though. But if she was it would be fine. Self-defense. It was a huge relief to finally shut her up.

Typing the words "Marshland Park Rapist" into every search rectangle he could was the fantasy he'd lived in every time she read to him in that stupid mask. But no one would give him a phone. Or let him see his mom. Or talk to the fucking cops. Of the things he wanted when he got out, seeing his reflection in a bathroom that wasn't even his was the only goddamn one he'd actually been allowed to do. Now that he had seen it, he had to confront that his return wasn't going as he envisioned.

Yes, his dad cried when he saw Scott alive and said the bullshit "I love you stuff." But other than that he was acting weird. He wouldn't even let him go to his apartment. Instead, Scott was in Peter Fucking Murphy, the family lawyer's, house. After Scott finished in the bathroom, they asked him to talk in Peter's study. He was pacing back and forth with a silver shock blanket around his shoulders, sipping a Red Bull from a straw. "Why aren't we calling the cops? I want that bitch locked up," Scott asked. Again, he kind of wondered if she was dead. Not because he cared, but she deserved worse, and killing wasn't his thing.

"First, we need to get down exactly what you're going to say," said Peter.

"The truth, a crazy bitch drugged me, locked me underground, and forced me to do ethics homework," said Scott, looking to his Dad. But President Ryan's eyes had hardly looked at his son. They were on his lawyer.

"And you have no idea why she would have done that? No relationship to her?" Peter said, squinting at Scott.

"I mean, she's that bartender. And I think maybe she sat for me once," Scott said. He actually remembered sort of liking her as a sitter. It was irrelevant. What if she's dead? She's probably not dead. He probably didn't hit her that hard. She wasn't moving at all when he left but... It didn't matter. Even if he was questioned about it, it was self-defense. It wasn't his fault. "I don't know, she's crazy. She's obviously obsessed with me." Scott finished, shifting his shoulders under the shock blanket.

Martin and Peter looked at each other. Then Peter pulled up a picture of Susan-Eva on his phone and showed it to Scott. Scott said, "Yep, that's her. Susan, something."

"Susan-Eva. Susan-Eva Lorenzo" said Martin, now he was looking at Scott. Glaring actually. Peter went to the arm chair in the corner, out of the way but listening, taking notes as Martin continued. "She's one of the Angel Three. She's participated in every town event you've been to in the last sixteen years. She graduated with honors from MY school. Now she's getting her PhD there, and paying her way by working at the most popular bar in town."

"What's your point?" Said Scott, genuinely not knowing.

"*You know her name.* Everyone in this town knows her name," said Martin.

Yeah, of course, he knew her name. Pretending he didn't was an over-correction. He was off his game. But still, what was his fucking point? Scott shrugged and said, "I guess. But it's not like we were friends. We weren't in school together."

"She didn't just babysit you once. She watched you while your mom was getting chemo every Wednesday. Every Wednesday for six months," said Martin Ryan.

"Okay," said Scott. He sort of remembered that girl. It wasn't a time he let himself think about if he could help it. Memories like that distorted and unfocused his mission. His mom was fine now. There was no point in thinking about it. It was just a thing that happened when he was little. Braces, glitter and a flat chest. He remembered that much about the girl who watched him.

"You hit her once. She said she'd told you three times to stop playing video games and do your homework and you ignored her. Finally, she took the controller out of your hands, and you backhanded her. You were eight."

"Okay." Scott didn't remember that. At all.

"I drove her home that night. I kept apologizing and tried to give her extra money. Do you know what she said? She said 'if I was scared my mom was dying, I'd probably act like a little shit too.' Then she gave me back exactly the extra I paid. She was fourteen, she was a kid."

"So was I." Why were they talking about this? His dad should have still been crying. They should still be in the 'we're so glad you're not dead' part. That was what he'd rehearsed for in his mind driving over once he finally waved down a car at the edge of the woods. He would have driven the bartender's truck but there was something weird about the gears. And the truck gave him a weird feeling. There was something familiar about it. He'd ridden in it before. *Not a relevant memory.* Scott needed to stay focused.

This was a day of triumph. Yes, his father was ruining it. But Martin always ruined Scott's triumphs; they were never palatable enough for Martin to swallow, much less savor. That was why his son's intellect was so misunderstood. Don't let his small mind penetrate yours, Scott told himself.

"I still remember watching the news the day they found her with Ida Montgomery and the other girl. You were a toddler. The image of those three tiny little things covered in blood was more than your mother could take. She kept saying, 'Can you imagine? They will never be okay.' Sixteen years later, she's getting her doctorate in social work, learning how to help other kids who have been through horrible things. Pride of the University, the town, hell, the whole *country* if wasn't so fucked up. I've been to the bar where she works. Seen her deal with everything from bachelorette party catfights to your frat brothers hitting on her all night to meth heads trying to rob the place. Nothing gets under her skin." Martin walked over to Scott and looked him in the eye. "You're sure *that's* the woman who abducted you? Susan-Eva Lorenzo?"

"I told you. Yes. She's still locked down there. Go see for yourself if you don't believe me," said Scott, looking his father in the eye now, trying to hide how much he wondered if she was dead. He didn't see her chest moving. She may not have been breathing.

"I believe you," said Martin, staring back at Scott. "You know what that makes me wonder?"

"How you missed the fact that she's obviously supremely a mess?" said Scott.

"No. It makes me wonder what thing my son did that made that unbreakable girl break. For anyone to go to that extreme... but for someone like her to... you must have...WHAT THE FUCK DID YOU DO, SCOTT?"

"Nothing," Scott replied coolly.

"It was you. I know it was you." Martin said starting to pace. Peter got out of his chair, putting the notepad aside. Scott had almost forgotten the fucking lawyer was there.

"What was me?" Scott said.

"In Marshland Park," Martin said, his eyes darting like he was re-reading the facts.

"You mean what happened to those women?" asked Scott. The hairs on his arm stood. This was it. Finally. All he had to do was convince his apple-cinnamon-oatmeal-basic-ass father he was being paranoid and he'd get away with it. Scott let his eyes well up, certain he was pulling off righteous indignation. "I had nothing to do with that."

"FUCK!" Martin yelled.

Peter walked to Martin's side and said, "Martin. This is manageable. In some ways its ideal."

Okay. Now Scott was getting pissed. They were talking about him like he wasn't there. "What? I didn't do anything to them?"

"To who?" asked Martin. His eyes were narrow and dark like this was the damning question. But it wasn't. How could it be? Scott didn't give anything away.

"To the three women," Scott said, without needing to fake his confusion.

"Oh my God." Martin said under his breath. He shook his head at the ground the way he did when Scott's mom told them about the lump in her breast.

"WHAT?" Yelled Scott.

"No one said anything about three women, son." It was Peter who said this, his dad never called him son. Not like that. Not as term of endearment. Okay, so, apparently revealing the number of women was a slip, but surely even if the names of his victims weren't released, the number of those attacked would have been.

"She mentioned it. While I was down there. She must have read about the other two in the papers." Scott said.

"We kept it out of the papers," said Peter.

"What do you mean you... why would you have anything to do with if it was in the papers." Demanded Scott, but his dad wasn't looking at him anymore. He was sitting on the sofa, burying his head in his hands. Grieving something on a day that should have been nothing but celebrating the fact that his fucking son was alive.

"Your father's running for Senate next year, Scott. He has real shot," said Peter.

"So! It should have been in the papers! That's fucked up, Dad! That's really fucked up. It's a big story. People should know what happened to them." Scott ranted at his dad.

"You should be in jail," said Martin, never looking up.

"I didn't do it," said Scott. He let the anger in but he was steady, a man of conviction. A man being wronged. Even he believed him.

"So, your DNA isn't in her rape kit?" Said Martin.

"Why would they run my DNA?" asked Scott.

"That's not an answer," said Martin.

"Martin. He says he didn't do it. Let's hold on to that for now and focus on the next steps." Peter said.

"The next steps are calling the cops and—"

"If she's on trial for kidnapping you, they'll be looking closer. If you say you didn't do it, I believe you. But if she says you did… regardless, it leaves a bad taste. *So,* what if we go with a different narrative? What if someone *else* kidnapped you?" suggested Peter, casually leaning at the edge of the desk.

Martin looked up at Peter and said, "When Christine Blasey Ford testified, I posted an #ibelieve tweet. I voted for Hillary. I taught him it's never okay to hurt a woman. Who am I if I let this go?"

Scott said, "The same guy who kept it out of the papers." Then, for the first time in his entire life, his father hit him. A fist to the eye. It was the first time Martin had ever hit anyone. It showed in the shocked pain in his eyes as he stared down at his bruised knuckles.

"That's good. He looked too healthy," said Peter as Scott held his eye. Peter pulled Martin aside. "Hey. You are the only Democrat in the state with half a shot. The good you could do for every woman in this country outweighs…" Scott stumbled to the couch as Peter's voice droned on.

The memory in the truck was coming back...

He was ten. The girl driving, Susan-Eva apparently, saw him walking home from baseball and offered to give him a ride. His dad was trying to teach him a lesson about poverty. The field was three blocks from their house, and he said if it wasn't such a wealthy neighborhood, all the kids would walk home; they only didn't because they were spoiled. It was embarrassing. So he got into Susan-Eva's pick-up as fast as he could.

She asked if he recognized her from when she used to babysit him and he said no. He didn't. The braces and the glitter were gone. Plus, he never really looked at her much. Then she lectured him about not getting in the car with strangers, talking to him like he was a little kid. He ignored her and pressed his forehead to the window, counting each of the thirty-four seconds it took to get from Dixie Hot Dog's Baseball Field to his driveway. He opened the door about to leave without looking back, but she said a very dramatic, "Um! You're Welcome!"

So, he had to look back. He had to roll his eyes to make sure she knew he thought she was being lame and he was cooler than that. But when he did, he noticed the pink carnation in the vase she kept in the cup holder and he said, "Do you have that because of the song?"

Her smile. Suddenly Scott remembered her smile way, way too well. She bounced turning to him her eyes wide and lit up. She said, "YES! Thank you. You wouldn't believe how many people don't get it."

Scott lowered his voice to sound as old as possible and said, "Seriously? That's lame. I mean it's old but it's a really famous song. A lot of kids don't have respect for older music. I actually know the whole thing."

"Me too."

"Really?" Scott said, doubting her. "I meant the real one. The long version. Not the short Madonna one."

"Yeah, the Don McLean version. Obviously."

"Obviously," Scott said, trying to hide that he didn't know who Don McClean was. But he did know the whole song.

"Prove it!" She said. He cocked his head, was she serious? He was not going to sing. "The first one to miss a word is the loser." She squinted at him with the glint of a dare in her eye and said, "One. Two. THREE!"

No way. He was definitely not going to sing with her. It would be so embarrassing. But he did sing with her. He couldn't help it. She made it seem impossibly fun. They both started right on cue. By the time they got to the first chorus they both were swaying. By the second they both shouted it as loud as they could. Through all six verses, neither of them missed a single word.

They had to catch their breaths for a second when they finished. Scott realized he was grinning but he didn't mean to. He didn't like smiling too much. It made him feel small. So, he took his baseball bat and opened the truck door. She rolled down her window and said, "Hey! I guess neither of us are losers." He shrugged without looking back and went inside.

That was the girl in the park? It didn't matter. Did he kill her, though? It still didn't matter, right? The whole point was it could be anyone. She was anyone and it happened to be her. Tough. That was the way the world was. You were either someone who did things or someone who let things happen to you. He was bigger than caring about who he did things to. He understood there was no good or evil. There was only nature. Prey and predators. What he was, what he was capable of, was so much more important than one girl.

Only none of the things that were supposed to make what happened in the park matter were happening. There had been no upticks in reports of on-campus sexual assaults. Was that because of his dad, the good guy, the beloved guy, the palatable guy was burying it? Was it because no one reported? Was it because they did report and no one believed them? Was it because there was no noticeable difference? Did Scott think he'd ignited an epidemic when really the things he'd done were so common they got little more attention than allergy season? Was she dead?

Someone needed to go check on her. She was bleeding. There was a cracking sound when he slammed her head back into those metal bars. Her body went limp so quickly. She felt dead. She was probably dead.

It wasn't an act of rage. It was an act of control and power. A moment of evolving beyond feeling. Like all of the most brilliant men, Scott was a high-functioning sociopath. He was certain of it. He was so proud when he realized it. It made him important. Far more important than his family. Capable of things they could never imagine. He couldn't have done what he did in the park if he wasn't a sociopath. If he had any feelings about it.

So, no, this wasn't right. He didn't have any feelings toward Susan-Eva Lorenzo. He'd just prefer the girl from that particular memory not be dead. At his hand. It wasn't emotional it was practical. But he kept hearing that stupid song. *This'll be the day that I die. This will be the day that I—* His thoughts got louder but so did the song like they were shouting at each other.

Is she dead? The verse where the children screamed. Did I kill her? The verse with the Jester. Does this feeling mean I'm not a... The verse with Helter Skelter in the summer swelter. If I'm not a... The verse with Jack be nimble! And I did those things... The verse with a generation lost in space. If I can feel it, what am I? The verse where he can't remember if he cried'

Peter knelt down to face Scott and said, "Listen to us, and you'll be an American hero, son. A legend a—"

Scott threw up his Red Bull all over the shock blanket and Peter's leather sofa. As it turned out, the name Ryan wasn't so palatable. Or even digestible. Peter handed him a tissue and Scott puked again. This time on Peter's shoes.

He hated her for this. It was supposed to be cold. He would never forgive her. Because she was just supposed to be some girl. She wasn't supposed to be the girl with pink the carnation in the pick-up truck. She wasn't supposed to be someone.

THIRTY-NINE
August 20, 2022, 10:15 AM

Ida

THE WHEELS OF ELLA'S CAR screeched as she swerved left, speeding 30 miles over the limit toward Magic Alley. "Never, EVER, even once IN. MY. LIFE. Have I EVER kidnapped and imprisoned someone and not told you about it!" yelled Ida.

"SHUT UP IDA," yelled Ella. The voice that came out of Ella was low. Guttural. Primal. It was a sound Ida could taste. In any other context, Ida would have bathed in it.

She would have grabbed the wheel and forced the car off the road to make Ella yell louder. When she got out to check the damage, Ida would shove Ella over the hood of the car, pull down her jeans, and eat her until she came so hard she cried. Like after prom.

But in this context a rancid heady sent made the air so thick Ida thought she'd choke on it. Normally she loved this sort of smell. On Ella it always smelled wrong. It was worse than a smell you hate. It smelled like your favorite thing but rotting. Thrown up. Sometimes a hint of it would waft through the air vent in the hall upstairs where they used to pass secret messages when they were little. Ida would plug her nose and press her ear to see if Ella was trying to say something but all she could ever hear was

225

Malcolm. Malcolm was not for listening.

Usually, she went back to perfecting her look of the day. But a few mornings ago, she lingered. She heard something she didn't understand. When she didn't understand things, she asked Ella. But somehow, she knew Ella didn't understand it either. If Ida asked Ella would act angry while she smelled sad. It would be irritating. So, Ida didn't ask. But now she was worse than irritated.

Windshield, door, seatback everything was too close to Ida. Too scalding. Being left out was a sensation that itched in an unreachable spot. Ida screamed and slammed her hands on the dashboard.

"I said shut up." Ella repeated, this time through her teeth. God, her voice like that really did feel so pulsing. Ida rolled down the window. Maybe air could cut the smell enough that she could enjoy sound. But Ella turned on the radio. To the news. Ida hated news. It did not sound pulsing. It sounded like oatmeal.

Ella's car was so old and ugly. Trisha had offered to buy her a new one but Ella refused, which was funny because fuck Trisha. But Ida preferred Ella screw over Trisha and take advantage of her money. Like when Ella fucked her dad. That was funny. She tried to explain to Parker once why it was funny. But he kept saying Trauma.

Trauma was a very hard word to understand. It was used often. It was a hand-to-heart and nod word. A word that no matter what Ida was thinking, she was just supposed to put a hand to her heart and nod with a serious look, signaling for Ella and Susan-Eva to come get her out of the conversation. This was also the rule for the words: problematic, dead puppies, and true crime. The last one Ida liked to talk about but Ella said she didn't do it right.

It was apparently okay to say you were "obsessed with murder documentaries," but not okay to say, "I have pictures of chopped-up bodies on my phone. Want to see?" Even though some of the pictures were in the documentaries, so weren't they all getting off on the same thing? Ella said it was not the same because of nuance. Nuance was always what Ella said about things that made no sense.

None of the buttons in the old ugly car made any sense; when Ida started jabbing them to get music instead of the awful oatmeal sound, it went to static. Ella smacked her hand away and turned it back to the news. "Leave it!" Said Ella.

"Why are you yelling at me? You are the one who did something unforgivable!" said Ida.

"Shut up."

"You could go to jail. You could get locked up. That's the worst thing that can happen. It is the worst of all the feelings. Why would you risk that? It's the thing you are never supposed to risk," Ida said as Ella tried to ignore her turning up the oatmeal.

A boring voice blared too loud through the speaker and said, "We can officially report that Scott Ryan is alive. In a few moments, we'll have the Ryan family here making a statement." The sound went back to static.

"We're out of range. Fuck. Fuck. Fuck," Ella said under her breath.

"If you miss the auction over this, I am never forgiving you." Ida asked, raising her voice over the static.

"What the fuck is wrong with you? She could be hurt. She could be in jail right now. Do you get that? She could be—"

"Dead? Yeah. Obviously. So why would you let her do it?" asked Ida. Ella clutched the wheel so hard her knuckles turned white.

It would be sad. If Susan-Eva was dead, it would be sad. Or devastating. Traumatic? Was it that one again? A world without Susan-Eva would be dull. But she knew it was not the word she was supposed to say out loud. Even though it was correct. Ida hated dull. But then, in a few months, Ida would be dead too, and that would be a huge thing that Susan-Eva and she could do together without Ella. Which would be a really good way to get back at Ella for leaving Ida out.

There was more salt in the air. Rain? Ida looked out the window, no clouds. Then she heard a gasping sound. *Oh.* Ella was crying. Crying is salty. And she was sobbing so it started to smell like Long John Silvers. There was snot dripping from her nose. It was gross. Ida felt like she was supposed to do something. She stiffly patted her shoulder and Ella jerked away.

"I HATE YOU. I FUCKING HATE YOU SO MUCH! I wish it was true. I wish you were dying."

Ida calmly said, "It is true."

227

"Fuck you. No, it's not. I wish I'd never met you," Ella said. Sad-Ella was so annoying. But she was lying. Lying Ella meant Ida had control. Fun!

"If you want me gone so bad, why did you make me come with you?" Ida said. Her voice was calm now. So much blood rushed to Ella's face that Ida thought she might be having an aneurysm. Angry heaves made her chest go up and down, up and down. "Huh? Why am I here?"

"I hate you. I hate you. I hate you." Ella chanted almost like a prayer. The car drifted into the wrong lane. A semi-truck blared its horn, inches from collision. Ida grabbed the wheel and steered them off the road. Still heaving for breath, Ella hit the brakes.

"Why am I here?" Ida tucked hair behind Ella's ear. Her sobbing got so heavy it sounded like she was choking.

"Because… what if someone's there—" Ella sounded so little suddenly. Littler than she ever did when they were kids.

Ida worked very hard not to sound excited as she asked, "So if someone else is there and they hurt her. I can—"

Ella shook her head and begged, "Yes! Yes. Please just do whatever you can. You have to save her. Please."

"So I can—"

"Kill them. Mame them. Eat them. Whatever you fucking want. If you can ever stop anything hurting her ever again, just stop it. I don't care. If you really are favored by God, ask fucking God! Just please make it stop. This has to stop. Please make it stop."

The radio came back. His voice sounded different, hoarse, and stiff, clearly reading something, but it was definitely Scott.

"If the men who did this to me are out there listening. I know with the dedicated work of our police, justice will be served. These terrorists did not break me or this nation. I am the same Scott I was the night you abducted me, and to prove it, I will be at the auction showing my continued passion for ending childhood hunger." The indistinguishable shouting of press took over.

Another voice said. "We're not taking any questions at the moment…"

Ida turned it down and asked, "Why would he say it was terrorists?"

"So, they don't run his DNA on her rape kit," Ella said. The panic left

228

her voice. It was replaced with something worse. Something empty. *Empty.*

That was it. That was what Ida heard through the air vent. Something happened to Ella that made her empty. Sometimes Susan-Eva got empty too. Ida didn't like this. But it was proof that she was divine. Because she could always fix it. Ida always found a way to fill people with something.

Ella grabbed the gear to shift back into drive, but before she could, Ida grabbed her hand. Ella tried to pull it away, but Ida's grip was too strong. "Hey," Ida said. Ella tried to pull her hand away again. Ida gripped tighter and yanked her so hard it turned Ella's whole body to face her. With her other hand clutching Ella's chin, Ida said, "If it was you getting hurt, I'd do it even if you told me not to. Even if I'd get locked back in the closet forever. If I ever caught someone hurting you, I'd eat the whole world alive just to make it stop."

Ella swallowed and said, "You're such a fucking liar." Ida shrugged and let go of Ella's hand. In seconds, they were back on the road, speeding toward Magic Alley. Ella kept crying, but she didn't smell empty anymore.

FORTY
August 20, 2022, 10:30 AM

Ella

SUSAN-EVA WAS DEAD. SHE had to be. For the Martins to claim it was terrorists with confidence that Susan-Eva would never refute it, they'd have to kill her, Ella thought. And there was one person and one person alone to blame and she knew exactly who it was, herself.

Ella could have gone to Scott that first morning while his memory was foggy and told him she'd put him down there. That it was a prank and not to be a little bitch about it. He may have let it go. Even if he didn't, at worst, she would have gotten a slap on the wrist. That's what a good person would have done. A sane person. A good person would have worried about their best friend jogging by herself. Just like Officer Reynolds said, jogging alone wasn't safe. Why did Ella never think twice about it? A good person would have insisted on jogging with her. Then Scott never could have gotten to her.

A good person would have said she had a bad feeling about Ed and never let her go inside. Then none of this ever would have happened. Susan-Eva would still be the girl in the tutu and the Batman mask. She'd probably be engaged to Joseph for real by now and making Ella wear a bridesmaid dress she really hated. But Ella was selfish and evil. So instead of marrying the love of her life Susan-Eva was—

"She's alive. I'm not going down there," said Ida, looking at the open cellar door.

"You don't know that. Come on," said Ella.

Ida rolled her eyes and sniffed over the door. "She's down there alone, and she's fine. I mean trauma," Ida said putting a hand to her chest and nodding like it was a reflex. "But no significant blood loss, minimal cortisol—I mean, she could be in a coma, but—" Ida shouted down. "BABE? Are you in a coma? BABE?" Ida shrugged "I don't know. But she'd definitely alone, so you don't need me, so I'm not coming down." Ella watched Ida step away from the cellar. She looked uncomfortable. Almost… "I'm not fucking stupid. You're both being real bitches about my dying wish. How do I know this isn't a trick to lock me down there?"

Any other time Ella would have been transfixed. Whatever this look was, it wasn't one she'd seen Ida make before. But Ida could be wrong. Or she could be lying. So, Ella cascaded down the old rotting stairs so much faster than she knew she could. When she reached the bottom step, the momentum would've brought her to her knees if she didn't clutch the cage bars to keep herself from falling.

The cage was unlocked, the door pushed ajar and Susan-Eva was back down on the treadmill. Her eyes were open. Her chest was moving. She was, at the very least, alive. Something between an exhale and a scream came out of Ella's mouth. It reached a pitch so high in its relief it would've maddened any dog around for miles. But Susan-Eva didn't get up, or turn her head, or even tense at the sound. She lay there, staring up.

Ella ran into the cage and let herself fall to the ground, kneeling at Susan-Eva's side. Susan-Eva didn't take her eyes off the ceiling. She was calm but blank. Some sort of legal form was resting on her chest.

Ella knew how stupid it was to ask if she was okay, but she couldn't help it "Are you—"

"Who are they saying did it?" asked Susan-Eva.

"Are you okay? What did he do?"

"Just tell me who they're blaming?"

"Terrorists."

"Cool," said Susan-Eva. Then she laughed. It was awful. Laughing

with irony at how horrible something was, was an Ella move. Not Susan-Eva. Laughter was sacred to her. She'd never let Ella get away with adulterating a joyful noise with her constant pessimistic surrender to how dark and terrible and doomed everything was.

When Ella laughed like that Susan-Eva would do a ridiculous dance, or fart, or push her in the pool. Anything to wash away her cynical bullshit the way only involuntary genuine giggles could. But all Ella could think to do hearing her own 'I give up' laugh coming from Susan-Eva was ask the stupid question again. "Are you okay?"

Susan-Eva looked up at the monitor on the treadmill and said, "I hate this stupid machine so, so much. Those woods, the yellow trail, that was my infinity. That was my flying. That was where I was invincible. It was the only time that really, truly felt entirely my own. I traded infinity for rubber and a calorie count. And that cop said it like it was nothing. '*Run at the gym.*' Problem solved. Give up flying."

"Evie, we should take you to the hospital."

"Nah. I'm good. Everyone always talks about fight or flight, but there's a third instinctive response to threat: play dead. 'Fight' gets all the credit. That's what heroes do, right? They fight. But it's just branding. In nature, there's no superior response. Each form of defense has equal success rates depending on the threat. I only passed out for second when he slammed my head to the bars".

"You could have a concussion. We should—"

"I'm good. Passed every question on the concussion checklist. His lawyer made sure," said Susan-Eva.

"His lawyer?"

"Yeah, Martin Ryan sent his lawyer to make sure I was okay. Because, you know, no biggie on the whole kidnapping and imprisoning his only son thing. All can be forgiven. After all, I'm such an asset to his university and such an important part of the community. *Well.* Not so important that they want me to stick around, of course. I only get the money if I sign the NDA and transfer out of state." Ella picked up the NDA, reading it over. No signature yet. "He said President Ryan can get me into the University of Houston's Graduate program. It's where Brene Brown got her PhD. With my star quality, I could absolutely be the next Brene Brown. His words, not mine."

"What a fucking prick."

"Yeah."

"You would be a great Brene Brown though."

"Obviously. I'm sure she's locked a few dudes in cellar. Super on brand for her."

"Hey," said Ella with enough of a tone shift that Susan-Eva finally turned to look at her. "I love you." Susan-Eva nodded her face didn't change at all, but tears started rolling down both sides of her face. "Why'd you come here alone in the middle of the night? Were you trying to…What were you trying do?"

Susan-Eva shrugged. For a very long time, they were quiet. The cellar looked so small for such a big thing to have happened there. Eventually, they realized they were both staring at the door in the corner. Where Ed said, "The Other" was waiting. Never once in the times that she'd come to feed Scott did she let herself think about Ed. But staring at the door now she finally did.

Everyone said Ed was a monster. Because dehumanizing him felt better than the truth. He was just a man who felt so small that he learned to walk on stilts and kill little girls just to feel bigger. Nothing worse is ever done than things humans do when they are scared of being small.

"I wished it was a copycat." Susan-Eva finally said. "That's what I thought when I realized what was happening. It finally caught up with me. One way or another it had to be about Ed. *It had to be.* Because there was no way I got groomed by a serial killer when I was eight and then got attacked at twenty-five with no connection. I was ready for that. I swore after Ed I would never be oblivious again. I wouldn't really let my guard down until I truly knew someone. I thought running meant if someone ever came for me, I would be fast enough to…" again, she laughed. Again, it was awful.

"There was nothing you could have—"

"I know. That's the point. That detective, not Reynolds, the first one, the good one with the eyebrows, she thought that he probably stalked me first, like Ed. Ed has all those fan pages. All those documentaries. What better way to honor him than finishing the job he never got to? So, I was surprised when it was Scott. He didn't strike me as a killer, but neither did Ed. Clearly, I was missing something. Something I'd done to spark the obsession. Then, after three months of watching him, I still had no clue. The only thing I hadn't tried was taking off my mask. I stepped too close on purpose. I wanted him to really, really see me. I didn't care. I didn't care what he did to me this time. If it killed me. I just wanted it to make sense. But when I took off the mask he… he…" Susan-Eva paused, exhaling in the search for composure.

Ella held her breath. Certain she knew what was coming. Certain that because she'd gone along with this insane plan, Scott was able to hurt Susan-Eva in the exact same way all over again. But when Susan-Eva found her voice, she said. "He didn't recognize me."

"What?'

"He cocked his head, confused, and said, 'You're that bartender.' He's not the Copycat Killer. I don't think there *is* a Copycat Killer. I think Sally Marks is just another little girl who got murdered for reasons we'll never know. Ella, it didn't have anything to do with the thing that happened when we were little. It didn't have anything to do with me. He didn't look at me in the park. He had no idea who I was. When I took off the mask, he didn't seem to care. I was just a thing on the way to the door. He didn't beat me up. He didn't rape me again. All he did was put a hand up my shirt while I played dead. It didn't really feel sexual. It felt like when someone sees a free cheese sample at Piggly Wiggly, shrugs 'why not' and grabs two without reading the label. It was all for nothing. I put you in danger, and it didn't even work."

"Scott is a broken, messed up, evil kid. You couldn't change him."

"It wasn't supposed to change Scott. It was supposed to change me. It was supposed to be the thing that made me stop—"

"Being scared?"

Susan-Eva shook her head. "To make me stop wishing for Ida. The whole time it was happening all I thought about was her and what she did to Ed. Every time I look at him all I see is her doing it again. And that's so, so fucked up because I'm the whole reason Ed tried to kill her."

"No, you're not. You were a child. You trusted him. You had no way to know—"

"I don't mean it's my fault because I wanted to come here. It's my fault because he made me read about the way he chopped up the ones that came before and told me if I didn't say one of your names, he'd do it to me. I could have offered myself to save you both but I didn't. I told him to kill Ida. I'm the reason she had to do what she did. I'm probably the reason she is the way she is. Then when it came for me I begged God for her. Knowing what she'd do. What would my mom think of me if she knew who I was now?"

"She would be—"

Proud. Your mom would be so proud of you for surviving. She would tell you she would do worse than Ida if she got her hands on the people that hurt you. She would tell you you're magnificent because you are. You are the most magnificent person. But Ella didn't get to say any of that. Because with a guttural, unwavering voice, Susan-Eva cut her off and said, "Don't." Like if anyone ever said anything nice to her again, it would kill her.

So instead, Ella said, "He asked me too. I didn't offer myself up either. He kept telling me to say your name or hers. I should have done whatever I could to save you. I knew what she was even then. But I didn't. I didn't say anything at all. I couldn't even find the word no."

"You played dead," said Susan-Eva. Ella nodded. "That's okay."

"You fought," said Ella. Susan-Eva shook her head. "If the thing I did to survive is okay, the thing you did has to be okay, too. You just said it. Fight, flight, play dead. One doesn't outweigh the other in good or bad."

For a while Susan-Eva stared back up at the ceiling then she smiled to herself and looked back at Ella and said, "You know I babysat him a couple of times. He never listened when I said stop, and he never got in trouble when I told his parents he acted out. But he used to listen when I read to him. I thought maybe he'd listen again, and it would make us both better. Isn't that the stupidest thing you've ever heard?" Ella shook her head.

Susan-Eva looked at the NDA and said, "Come with me. Let's take the money and start over. I'll tell them I'll only sign if there's a job for you, too."

No matter what Susan-Eva thought of herself, she was still the moral compass to Ella. If she thought it was okay to leave, it was okay to leave. Going with her was the right thing. Not even if - for some reason - the idea was breaking her heart. Stupid fucking squirrels popped into her head. She had no idea why. She would not indulge in thoughts of why. "Okay," Ella said.

"Okay?!" said Susan-Eva, a little shocked. "Really. You'll come?"

"Yeah. If you hate it here we should go."

Susan-Eva said, "Okay." They both nodded looking at each other. "I don't hate it. I know I should but I don't."

"I don't hate it either," said Ella.

"Joseph's here. Even if we're not— I still…"

"I know."

"And there's people you love here too."

"Right. I have Malcolm."

Susan-Eva met Ella's eyes and said, "Right. Malcolm. *Just Malcolm.*" Ella pretended not to understand what she meant, even as her eyes involuntarily floated up to where she'd left Ida. Ella took the NDA from Susan-Eva, glancing over. "One hundred thousand dollars. Jesus, he must really love that kid. I mean, I know they have money, but damn."

"I think it came from a backer. He's running for senate."

Ella said. "Oh. Yeah, okay, that makes way more sense." Susan-Eva smirked. Reading over the list of perks Susan-Eva would get if she stayed quiet, Ella shook her head. "It's a shit deal."

"It's a reward for not telling anyone I committed a felony. Six figures so no one knows Scott Ryan got kidnapped by a girl. It's an amazing deal."

Ella glanced down at the form and read out loud, "Or any theoretical grievances with the wronged party that may have motivated the captor." Ella looked up from reading and said, "He never looked scared, did he? The whole time I saw him down here, he looked like it was a prank he knew would end eventually. With you, did he ever—" Susan-Eva shook her head no.

Ella said, "Fuck this deal. Tell him you'll take the money. But we are the goddamn Moss Groves Miracle Three. These founding fucking families inbreed a generation of psychos and ask us to teach them to be people, we almost get murdered, and they claim us as proof the town was blessed, then when what happened to you happened, they just… they asked us to protect them at our most desperate moments and asked us to shut up and go when we made them uncomfortable. If we ever leave, it will be because we want to and probably because we burned the whole thing to the fucking ground."

FORTY-ONE
August 20, 2022

Susan-Eva

IT WAS A SURPRISE TO Susan-Eva that her Ford 74' was still parked by the cellar. She imagined Scott took it. But he probably didn't know how to drive a stick. Both the cars were there, but angel number three was nowhere in sight.

"IDA? Fuck, fuck, fuck. IDA?" Ella yelled. She was panicking. But Susan-Eva was still too dazed for panic. Ella pulled out her phone as she said, "She's hunting. I know it. I told her if someone was hurting you, she could—"

"She's in the house," said Susan-Eva.

"What?" Ella said. Susan-Eva pointed up at the second floor. Ida was sitting in an open window. Breeze swept her long hair against the wood walls. She was straddling the windowsill, hanging her tan bare leg outside, resting her head back, staring up at the clouds. She looked pensive. Ida never looked pensive, never when Susan-Eva had seen. It looked like something off a Pinterest board. Ethereal Sad Princess Aesthetic.

"Why would she go in back there?" asked Ella.

"The same reason I went back down to the cellar. I woke up alone down there. She woke up alone upstairs."

"She told you that?" asked Ella.

Susan-Eva shook her head. "We've never talked about it. Have you two?"

Ella shook her head no, "How did you know what room she was in?"

"Ed told me."

"Oh."

"He said he'd bring her to the nice peaceful bedroom with a corner window upstairs. Then leave her the book so she'd know what was coming. So she could pray and meditate on the purpose she would serve when he gave her to the Other. Where did you wake up? He didn't tell me." Susan-Eva waited, but Ella didn't answer. Looking over her shoulder she could see Ella's hands were shaking and her face was pale.

"It was a closet. Or a pantry or something. It was fine."

"A pantry? You don't mean the one in the… it wasn't the one they showed in the documentary with the—" Ella nodded and shrugged. "Oh my god."

"It wasn't that bad. I didn't really look at it. I mean, he made me when we came in. But then I had to read the journal, so I didn't really have to look anymore. I thought about going back in. To see it without all the… but I don't think I can. I guess it doesn't matter now that they're selling it. They'll probably level the house and build a target. It will be like it never happened. For everyone but us."

"I'm so sorry."

"Hey. At least I didn't get molested. I'm really lucky."

"Reading the journal is still the worst thing that's ever happened to me. Worse than… I think we should stop calling it lucky," Susan-Eva said.

"What do you think it was like for her? No matter how different she is, she must have been… I heard her screaming," Ella said. They both stared up at Ida, wondering.

FORTY-TWO

Sixteen years ago – October 31, 11:40 PM

Ida

"BE STILL AND KNOW," SAID Ed, hovering over Ida with a creepy dumb smile. Then he handed her a book. But not even a real book. She opened it. Handwriting was inside with no pictures.

"This looks like homework. I don't have to do homework today. It's Halloween," said Ida, trying to hand the journal back.

"It is what became of those before you and what will become of you very shortly. Before he takes you, it is important that you understand and tremble for his mercy."

"Whose mercy? God's? I'm God's favorite," said Ida, shoving the journal again.

"Read, and you will know. You will tremble," said Ed.

Ida groaned and said, "I told you! I don't have to do homework on Halloween."

"Read immediately, or death will come now," said Ed. Then it was immediately, and Ida wasn't reading. Then it was now, and Ida wasn't dead. Then Ida got bored and started doing jumping jacks.

"Be still and—"

"I'm not allowed to be still when I'm bored or Ella says I have impulse control issues," said Ida. Ed inhaled deeply through his nose and his face got an ugly purple hue. All of a sudden he charged at her, clutching her shoulders and lifting her into the air. He bared his teeth and growled so loud that spit spewed onto her face, which was gross. But being in the air was fun! Then he threw her on the bed. Loser. He smelled like torture, but the bed was soft. Stupid. He flung the stupid book at her head, but she caught it. Then he yelled, "READ."

He caught his breath and turned to go, "Wait!" said Ida. "Again! Again!" Ed cocked his head confused. "Throw me again." He clutched the doorknob and swallowed. His eyes darted like he was trying to do something impossible in his head, probably a long division. Or spelling Wednesday. Ida thought the first "D" on Wednesday should get canceled. Then he looked like he figured it out and moved to go again.

Ida cleared her throat and asked, "Is this above third-grade reading level? If it is, I can't read it anyway. Even though it says on my report card I passed reading last year, I didn't. All the teachers are scared of my mom. When they put you in the electric chair, she'll come watch. She's like that." Ed opened his mouth to respond but then shut it again and left, locking the door. Whatever. Ida was pretty sure Ella would get her out of this soon. Unless she was dead. Dead Ella would be boring. Thinking about boring things made her hate. An activity was needed.

The journal was not as boring as she thought. The paper was thick, so it made a good sound when you ripped and ripped and ripped it. All the stupid, ugly, boring homework-y handwriting was torn into tiny little pieces. From outside the door, she could hear Ed coming, but this time, he didn't come in. He stood outside the door. HA. *HA*. Ed was too chicken to come back in.

From outside, he said, "If you cannot read, you can still behold. You will tremble at the sight." Then he slid five polaroids under the door. Pictures were less boring than words. These were actually pretty interesting pictures. A good amount of blood. But all the prey was little. Who cares if you can get something smaller than you? Every animal can. Unless they are much faster, like squirrels, then it is impressive. But they don't taste that good, and they die so fast.

Grown-ups are bigger and faster than kids, so why would it be any fun for a grown-up to hunt a kid? It was bothersome that Ida could tell Ed found himself impressive in the way she found herself impressive, even though he was inferior. Still, she didn't like pain for herself. She did not want the things in the pictures to happen to her. But Ella said if she broke the rules, she would get locked away, the worst thing in the world. If she died, it would hurt, but then she'd go to heaven, and that would be fun. So it would be better to die than break the lock-up rules.

Through the door Ed said, "Do you understand what the Other will do to you?"

"Why did you take pictures instead of filming it? Are you poor?"

Ed flung open the door and reached like he was about to grab Ida. But then he froze, his eyes scanning ripped-up paper all over the room and the binding of his journal flung open and empty. He whispered, "What did you do?"

"I made it fun." Ed started threatening her again but Ida stopped listening. A far more important realization dawned on her. Something she'd forgotten, "Wait. Where's my trick-or-treat pumpkin? Where's my candy? Did you take it?" Ed squinted then, shook it off like he was trying to hide that she was making him itchy. He didn't smell like running anymore. He smelled like excuse.

"You are at the valley of the shadow—"

"DID YOU TAKE MY CANDY?" Yelled Ida. He did. She could tell. She worked for that candy. She was looking forward to that candy. It was hers! So Ida started screaming and screaming and screaming the loudest and highest she'd ever shrieked. He dragged her out by the hair. That's when the trembling he promised finally started.

Her legs flailed in resistance but couldn't defy gravity as he put all his weight into pulling her down the stairs using only his grip on her skull. Each part of her clanked against hard, unfinished wood as she tried to twist away. With every step-down, her knees scrapped further open. Splinters stuck into her caves like needles in a push-cushion until every inch of her was covered in sting and throb.

Sting and throb were familiar. No good tantrum was complete without a lasting mark. This was much more painful than usual but not the worst ever. Until Ed's feet hit the ground floor.

Her body was trailing behind him three stairs up. She stopped twisting so she could press both feet to the step and propel herself forward like pushing off the edge of the swimming pool. It worked. The unexpected weightlessness of her body catching air surprised him enough that he lost his grip on her. Hitting the ground would hurt, but it would be her best chance to run. Tension filled her jaw as she braced for impact, ready to ignore the pain and bolt.

The landing was ideal, shoulder first right in the open doorway leading outside. Ed was only a few feet from grabbing her but Ida was fast. She was always so fast. She pressed the ground about to lunge when feeling started to come all the way back. It hadn't hurt. Not at first.

A burning smack of wood to the skin, another round of throbbing from her skull slamming to something hard, even the searing ache of a sprained ankle. For all of that, she was ready. Those were hurts you felt right before you got what you wanted, sometimes for weeks. Adrenaline dulled those pains.

But punctures are different. Especially with something that dull, that thick. Especially when it pushes right past the skin and into the muscle. It wasn't adrenaline that kept her from feeling it. It was a shock.

Her shoulder had slammed straight into a three-inch nail jutting from the door frame. It ruptured skin into muscle and didn't stop until it hit bone. Even though the wave of nausea that came with the first rush of explosive pain, she maintained a few coherent thoughts. But as Ed's fist tightened around her hair again and he yanked her up, he found the nail wouldn't let her shoulder go.

So he yanked much harder, and when her skin started to rip, thoughts pretty much left her until she came to in the cellar a while later. But before she slipped back into the dark, Ida felt a shaking. It had started in his right hand when she refused to read. Then spread to the other when she asked if he was poor. Ed was right. There was trembling. Just not from Ida. But Ed's whole body was trembling like he was in a cheap mall massage chair.

FORTY-THREE
August 20, 2022, 11:00 AM

Ella

SAD COULDN'T BE THE RIGHT word. Ella had long been sure that Ida could not experience sadness. However, Ida often claimed irreparable devastation at small inconveniences. Like rain or finding out most slaughterhouses didn't have air-conditioned viewing areas. But the way she was sitting up in that window at lot 355 could have fooled anyone else.

Those glassy eyes, staring up at the clouds like she was desperately aching for something out of reach, looked so alive with emotion. It could have won her an Oscar. Or at least a role in a sentimental Subaru commercial. If Ella didn't have years of knowing better, she'd call the thing happening in her eyes heartbreak and ask if Ida was okay. But Ella did know better. She knew to call it hungry.

Most of the time, Ella kept several carnivorous snacks in reach, but it was a hectic day. Digging through her purse, the best she could find was a *Slim Jim Beef Stick* from the gas station. It was enough. As soon as the plastic was torn, Ida sniffed the air, and within a few seconds, she was back down in the yard, yanking the Slim Jim out of Ella's hand. Then she looked at Susan-Eva and said, "Glad you're not dead, babe."

Susan-Eva blinked blank-faced and said, "Thanks, babe." Then she shook her head at Ella and said, "I'm going to drive back. I need a minute alone." She looked down at the cellar door, "Somewhere other than in there. I'll see you back at the house."

Ella nodded, and Susan-Eva started to go to her truck. But as her friend walked away, Ella felt a fluttering panic at the idea of her leaving. Ella had really believed Scott killed Susan-Eva. In their trio Susan-Eva was the heart. Ella thought her heart was going to die today. But there she was, still standing, still breathing.

Just as she was about to step out of reach, Ella flung her arms around Susan-Eva. It was so rare for Ella to initiate any form of physical affection, but when she did, she did it with her whole body. Knowing it may never happen again. After a reflexive moment of trying to seem 'okay,' Susan-Eva squeezed back and burrowed her head into Ella's shoulder, and they both let themselves cry.

Ella wasn't ready to let go, but she thought maybe Susan-Eva was and she started to pull away. But Susan-Eva pulled her back in. So, Ella held tighter and said, "So glad you're not dead, babe." Susan-Eva snorted through sobs.

"Hashtag, I said that already," said Ida, shifting her weight from foot to foot, uncomfortable.

"I know. It was kind of a joke," said Ella, still in the hug.

"Then why are you both crying?" Ida asked. Finally, the hug ended so Ella and Susan-Eva could share a look. The relationship between humor and grief was something they knew they could never explain to Ida. They couldn't even explain it to themselves.

Then Susan-Eva's expression changed, remembering something. There was a mix of anxiety and guilt. But she took a deep breath, resigning herself to what she had to do. She said, "Ida, I have to tell you something. Last night, I told a reporter that Ed made me choose who he would go after first. I chose you. I'm sorry."

Ida said, "I don't understand."

Susan-Eva said, "I panicked and—"

"And you said what you had to get out of the cage. Yeah, I get that part. I don't get why you're sorry. When *you* hurt people, it makes you sad, even when they suck. When you're sad, you're really annoying. It doesn't make me sad, though. So I'm much better at it. If one of us was going to get him, it was me. And I did! And I was amazing! Saying my name was smart. Ella, you said my name, too, right?" Ida looked at Ella, and Ella looked away. Ida smiled her smallest smile, then pursed her lips, putting it away. She cleared her throat and made a painful effort to look sympathetic as she said, "Anyway, since you guys have been all off doing your secret 'it's giving trauma' thing—"

"Okay. No! You really can't do 'It's giving.' Trust me, you don't get it enough not to say something really weird in public," said Ella, relieved that the subject changed.

"So, this isn't 'giving trauma'?" asked Ida waving her hand at the house where they got kidnapped and drugged, then the cellar where they almost got murdered, then sixteen years later locked up Susan-Eva's rapist. Ella and Susan-Eva exchanged another look, *it's not, not 'giving trauma'.* Maybe she did get it. "Whatever. What I was trying to say before that devastating interruption was something really nice. I know you're probably too emotional to go to the auction, even though you knew it meant a lot to me, and this day has actually been very horrible and annoying for me. It's giving baby shower." Nope, she didn't get it. Ella squinted about to interject, but Susan-Eva shook her head at Ella with a *not worth it* look. "But since you could have gotten murdered AGAIN, I'll forgive you for not going. Even though it's kind of your fault for not involving me from the beginning. Since, like I just said, I'm way, way better at this stuff than you two."

"That's the really nice thing you have to say?" Said Ella, cocking her head at Ida.

"Yeah." Said Ida, offended.

"Why wouldn't we go to the auction?" Said Susan-Eva, getting into her truck, "You won't let anything happen to us, right?" Ida nodded, and then Susan-Eva got in her truck and drove off.

It occurred to Ella this was the most alone she'd been with Ida in a long time. People were always in and out of Parlay House. There was security in knowing at any moment someone else could walk in. Ella waited for Ida to say something, but she didn't.

There was a soft rustle of breeze against leaves. The hum of the pickup truck getting further and further away. The sound of Ida's four-inch wedge sandals stepping closer. Sounds of a grown-up world. Or maybe not. The older they got, the more it seemed the grown-up world was all about chatter. Ella felt far less certain that she understood it as well as she did when they were little. The space created when she was alone with Ida seemed to be something beyond young or old.

"You didn't tell Ed to kill me," Ida said. Ella waited for more. A question. Or for Ida to tell her she was stupid. Or for her to say the truth. What if Ida knew the truth of how Ella felt about her in a way that even Ella didn't, and she finally said it? But all she did was stare at Ella, savoring her.

Dissociation was a skill Ella practiced like she was up for a promotion at it, and even she struggled to suppress the memories that standing on Lot 355 conjured. Scent always provides recollection without consent. She wondered what Ida was remembering. She could feel an unsated need radiating from Ida. What was to stop her from reenacting what she'd done to Ed on Ella? It would be wise to play nice. But being alone with Ida, choosing the quiet when there was so much to say, was like someone put on their song. And they never danced nice.

Ella narrowed her gaze and shook her head at Ida in disgust, "You're disappointed, aren't you?" Ella asked. Ida stared at Ella and nodded. "You thought someone would be here and you'd get to stop them the way you did back then. You wouldn't have cared if she was dead if it meant you got to do the thing you wanted. Would you?"

Ida's eyes moved, thinking. But not calculating. She looked unsure how to respond. As though Ella had asked her to solve a riddle. Perhaps she had. In whatever version she was capable of, Ella believed Ida held genuine… maybe not affection…maybe preference? Ida had a genuine preference for Susan-Eva's continued existence and even her happiness. But she also badly wanted a kill. Her eyes stilled like she'd settled on an answer.

Ida stepped closer and said, "Do you ever drag your nightstand table to the dresser so you can climb on top and press your ear to the air vent in the corner of your room? Like when we were little?" Ella swallowed and shook her head no. *"Oh."*

246

Ella lowered her voice like someone was standing at the edge of the woods watching them and said, "Do you?"

Ida sat on top of the closed cellar door and said, "Do I ever go to the air vent upstairs, the one right above your room, and lower to my knees? Then bend over as far as I have to and press my ear to the vent? Do I ever lie down next to it? Do I ever listen for hours?" Ella nodded, and Ida nodded back. It was so hard to tell. Was it that Ida didn't understand anything because she could not empathize? Or did she understand better than anyone because she was never distracted by empathy? It always felt like both.

"What do you hear?" Ella asked. "When you listen, do you ever hear anything?" But Ida wouldn't answer. She stared at Ella. "Those things you said in the car. About what you'd do if someone hurt me. You know you can't do that, right? You know I wouldn't want you to ever do anything like that for me. Hurt is complicated. It means really different things to different people." Ida stared at her, blinking. "Ida, I need you to say you wouldn't do that."

Ida looked at the padlock next to her on the door. She said, "You would never lock me up. Would you?"

"Say you would never hurt anyone for me," repeated Ella.

"The only time I ever hurt anyone badly was because you told me to. Because you didn't want them to hurt me. So, the rule is I can stop someone from hurting Susan-Eva. And I can stop someone from hurting me. But I'm not allowed to stop someone from hurting you? *I don't understand.*" She said it deadpan, understanding very well.

"I can take more. Things don't hurt me in the same way. Because some of the things that have happened to you and her never happened to me. Nothing that bad has ever happened to me. So, I don't need anyone to protect me. *Say you'll never hurt anyone for me.*"

"Come help me up," Ida said, holding her arms out. Ella glared, but she obeyed, pulling Ida up to stand. Ida brushed herself off and said, "Now take off your tennis shoes, pull off your jeans, your shirt, and that ugly bra. Then lie back on the cellar door."

Ella meant to say no, but instead, she said, "Why?"

"So, you can show me how much more you can take."

"We said spring break two years ago was the last time."

"Take off your shoes."

"Malcolm. Parker."

"They have nothing to do with this."

"Because you don't understand but—"

"I was ready for a fight. I need…"

"I gave you a snack."

"I need more. I need…"

"What?"

"I need something that moves and changes and dances. That's hot and raw. That I can feel still fighting as I consume it, then feel it relax, so I know the exact moment I've conquered it. I need to taste something alive."

Ella sat on the cellar door and said, "Promise you'll never hurt anyone for me."

Ida lowered to her knees and said, "You know, Parker and I have never even kissed. He wants to wait for the wedding." Ida unzipped Ella's jeans and tugged them down. "The only person I've ever done this with is you."

"Promise you'll never hurt anyone for me."

"Promise you'll never let anyone lock me up."

"I can't." Whimpered Ella. Ida took a strain of Ella's hair and gave it one hard yank. Ella yanked Ida's hair right back. Then Ida pushed Ella down. There was a small hole under the elastic band of her panties. Hooking one finger in the tear, Ida split the cheap cotton cloth open and put her teeth on both sides of Ella's clitoris. But she didn't bite. Not there. Ever. She just let them touch it for the briefest moment, reminding Ella that she could if she wanted to, but she didn't. Then, her tongue pushed through and started tracing a semi-circle on the left side.

Ida always bored so easily. That she could be so patient and diligent here perplexed Ella. No matter how much repetition it required she never stopped before Ella went over the edge, often multiple times. It was shamefully flattering. And God, the way Ida inhaled. It made Ella feel like a high-quality illicit drug, custom made to Ida's taste the way everything else in her life was.

At the first involuntary hitch of breath, when Ella's abs tensed and her shoulder blades found splinters in the wood, Ida detached with a puckering sound. She hovered and inch above Ella's opening, breathing in and sighing, "Mmmm." Then she slipped in her middle finger and started swirling like a tornado. Ella loved tornados. Lips found their way back between the slit cotton. Ida completed the circles with her tongue now and began sucking after each one at a steady building pace.

Vertebra bruised against the wood, as Ella couldn't - as she wouldn't - stop her spine from writhing against the door, overwhelmed by the intensity of heightened sensation. Sun through the leaves made them look lime electric green against a bright, almost cloudless blue sky. The smell of earth and grass unleashed something animal and womanly.

In an attempt to tame it, Ella forced herself to remember where she was. This was a bad place. A violent, tragic place. But she couldn't stop feeling good. She couldn't stop seeing beauty. She couldn't stop remembering other times she inhaled the smell of earth while Ida was between her legs.

Just as pulsing began to tip into eruption, Ida pulled back and said, "Promise you'll never let anyone lock me up.'

"I'll never let anyone lock you up," Ella screamed as Ida grinned and went back down to devour something ever-moving and changing and thrashing with life.

FORTY-FOUR
August 20, 2022, 5:30 PM

Susan-Eva

"GOOD THING SHE DIDN'T PICK something backless for you," said Susan-Eva as she dabbed antiseptic onto cuts on Ella's shoulder blades. Midsummer Night's Dream-role play against a tree with Malcolm yesterday, Ella claimed. A lame fantasy tracked for Malcolm. Ella said he made her speak in iambic pentameter the whole time. A pretentious, lame fantasy tracked even more. Susan-Eva still didn't buy it.

The dude couldn't deal with dirt. Whenever Susan-Eva wanted friend points for inviting him but obviously didn't want him to actually come, she'd suggest a hike or a picnic. He wouldn't even do outdoor seating at restaurants. If he couldn't stand the idea of a fly buzzing around an award-winning food truck sausage, there's no way he could deal with them buzzing near his undoubtedly less impressive one.

But calling Ella out was not something Susan-Eva had the energy for at the moment. To survive the next six hours Susan-Eva needed her whole world to be tasks.

—Keep Ella's back from scaring

—Wash hair

—Get dressed for the Children's Hunger Charity Auction

250

—Refuse hush money from the University President in a way that doesn't kill the vibe

—Endure seeing Scott at charity auction in a way that doesn't kill you

—Keep life-long best friend from cannibalizing dudes at children's hunger charity auction

—See Scott, don't let it kill you

—Pretend not to know other life-long-best friend is maybe in love with an aspiring cannibal (God, Ella really does go for the assholes)

—Don't have a one-night stand. They're not helping

—See Scott

—Know you will have to keep seeing Scott. Don't let it kill you

—Maybe bet on a spa weekend at Auction

—Have a margarita

—Hydrate

—Smile

—Don't cry

—See him

—Don't cry, don't let it kill you

—Don't let it kill you

—Don't let it kill you

—Don't kill him

"I don't think you should go," said Ella. Shit. Susan-Eva thought she was still looking at Ella's back, but at some point, she stared at herself in the mirror; her eyes were watery. She looked all PTSD-y again. Looking PTSD-y was not on the list. Where was her water bottle? Hydrate was on the list. "Even Ida gets it if you don't—"

"One: No, she doesn't. Two: If you let me pretend to be fine for the next few hours, I'll let you keep pretending those cuts aren't so fresh they were clearly made in the last few hours, not yesterday. Three: those dresses are meant to go together. I'm not going to be the one who throws off the aesthetic."

Three complementary but very different vintage Chanel dresses hung side by side on a display rack in Ida's room. There was no need to specify whose was whose. Ida struggled with nuances of emotion, but not the nuances of taste. It wasn't the same as being a good gift-giver. The skill didn't come from a place of connection to a person's joy. She didn't provide them with things they'd secretly hoped to indulge in.

It was a connection to their hunt and gather. To things they wouldn't know they wanted any more than a dog knows it wants to chase the fox a second before it bolts and attacks. To colors that watered the mouth or shot tension through the muscles, intuiting nutrients or poison when picking berries.

Whether activity, food, or fashion, Ida only gave the girls things that spoke to their bodies before their minds. There was no point in lying about how much you liked it, the grin twitching your lips already told her.

For herself, Ida always went custom. She couldn't comprehend the idea of wearing something anyone else had set eyes on before, much less worn. It would be an afront to God's creation. But no matter how different they were, the pieces always looked better next to each other. Together, the triad not only worked, it was beautiful. The way a supermassive black hole swallowing a galaxy can be beautiful.

For Ella, she went timeless and simple. Something that allowed her to fade into the background the way she liked. But nearly always one hundred percent silk-lined, so underneath it felt special, and they were special. Very special.

Most Moss Groves residents wouldn't spot it. Not even the old money legacies or the influencers who pridefully claimed to be fashionistas. But once in a while, an event would garner enough publicity to attract higher profile culture press with trained eyes. Those who'd worked much harder on their look would cock their heads, baffled as to why the vanity fair photographer was ignoring everyone else to beg for a single shot of the girl avoiding the crowd in a black dress. Ella usually didn't know why either, until whoever it was giving her the attention informed her. Susan-Eva and Ida were usually dancing while it happened, but Ida always caught the moment from across the room and pulled Susan-Eva in to let her in on the secret.

"Right now, he's telling Ella that dress was worn by Grace Kelly."

"That necklace was made for Princess Di."

"That was the last he made before he died."

Even with someone like Susan-Eva, who let her mood reinvented her look several times a season, Ida's pick was always perfect. Always a piece you couldn't pin down to one era or trend. Even if Ida purchased from a recognizable designer, she'd pick a piece that was a huge departure from their other work. A contradiction of some kind. Colors and fabrics that had no right to work together spun into a masterpiece. It was rare that Susan-Eva didn't gasp in awe of her selection.

Today wasn't a day for gasps. She was alone when she saw the black dress with gold details Ida hung for her tonight. She'd silently taken it off the hanger, laid down on Ida's bed, and put it over herself like a blanket. She'd told herself by the time she arrived back at Parlay House, she'd decide what to do about the NDA. But her brain was too cut off from feeling to think. She slept, covered in the dress, until she felt Ida jump onto the bed and lay next to her.

When she opened her eyes Ida's head was on the same pillow, staring. Ida ran her fingers over the patterned beads on the dress and said, "You know my favorite book, the one with all the amazing paintings of medieval torture? My favorite used to be the ones where they flayed people alive."

"Uh-huh." Susan-Eva was about to call for Ella. Gore obsession was nothing new from Ida but it was more than she could take today. "Ida, can we talk about something else?"

"I haven't liked looking at it since January. Because that's what you seemed like. Like someone cut you down the center and let everything spill out, but you had to walk around pretending it was okay. I know you think I can't understand. But that's what it felt like, didn't it? What Scott did to you?" For a few seconds Susan-Eva couldn't breathe because, yes. Yes, walking around flayed alive, pretending you're not, is exactly what it had felt like. Ida put her hand on Susan-Eva's cheek "Let me get him for you."

Susan-Eva's lip quivered. She slid her arm under Ida's so she could mirror her, putting a hand to Ida's impossibly silky cheek and said, "No, Babe."

There was nothing that could ever make their origin story pretty. No outcome could undo the fucked-up roots. Those first few months with Ida felt like a noble mission to Susan-Eva. A calling. After what happened with Ed, it felt like atonement. But following her attack in the park, she wasn't sure. Before, it had always been about helping Ida or protecting everyone else from her. Even when Susan-Eva enjoyed it, which she often did, calling Ida a friend didn't bother her the way it did for Ella. It wasn't naivete; it was a boundary given to her by her mother.

Mrs. Lorenzo's greatest fear for her daughter outside of the kidnapping's impacting her physical health was that Susan-Eva would feel shame for her capacity to see the good. The fear was not unfounded. It was clear from the way she reacted to visits from Joey Porter.

When his mom told him about what happened with Ed, he ran next door before she even finished the story. He needed to see in person that the little girl who sat outside his window protecting him from imaginary monsters had survived a real one. But she wouldn't come to the door. Every day, he'd come over and offer their old favorites. Play Buffy or Batman, or just talk. But she kept telling her mom she didn't want to see him. Or anyone. She didn't want to leave her room. Not even to watch TV. She was tired all the time because she could only sleep when she spent the night at Ida's house.

Until one day, Mrs. Lorenzo brought Susan-Eva a letter Joseph mailed her. Even though he lived next door, he put a post stamp on it and gave it to the mailman so it would be more official. A real letter. Like people wrote in historical adventures. Before Ed she would have leapt to her feet and ripped it open before her mom even said who it was from. But she didn't look at it. So, Mrs. Lorenzo read it to her.

"Dear Susan-Eva, I know a few weeks ago I told you I was too old to play with you. It was a mean thing to say and I didn't mean it. My Dad says twelve is the time to start acting like a man. But I don't really like doing the things he says men are supposed to do. He says I shouldn't be friends with girls. He wants to take me hunting and I don't want to go. I signed up for football because he wanted me to. The coach says I have a strong arm and good leadership skills, so I could be a quarterback one day. But I tackled Bobby Kleinberg on Tuesday at practice and he sprained his ankle. He cried. I pretended to have to go to the bathroom, but really, I went to throw up. I hate it. I hate hurting people.

I know I hurt you. I'm so sorry. But that's not why I keep coming over. I keep coming over because I miss you. When I heard something bad happened to you, it was the worst feeling I ever felt. If you're too mad at me to ever be friends again, I get it. But I'm friends with kids three years older than me, so I don't see any irreconcilable (hey, are you still doing word of the week? I am?)reason I can't be friends with someone three years younger, even if it's a girl, no matter what my dad says. Especially if that girl is my best friend. Even when I start dating, which will probably be pretty soon, I'll tell them they have to be nice to you or it's off! Really. Your next-door neighbor, Joey. P.S. In the middle school cafeteria, they have Little Debbie oatmeal cream pies. I know you like them. I can get you one tomorrow if you want. Just have your mom call my mom. But if you hate me too much, that's okay too. But maybe you could stand on the porch for a minute so I could see you're okay. Then I'll leave you alone forever."

When Mrs. Lorenzo looked up from the letter, Susan-Eva was crying. She said, "Please go tell him I don't hate him. But I am not allowed to have Little Debbie treats because I'm in trouble."

Mrs. Lorenzo scooped her up and said, "You're not in trouble. You go tell him! He's home."

Susan-Eva whimpered, "I can't."

"What if we go together? We could all go to Pizza Hut." Susan-Eva shook her head and then buried it in her pillow. "Eva. Just because someone you thought was a friend turned out to be bad doesn't mean your real friends are bad."

"But what if they are? What if bad people like me because I'm like them."

"No. What people do with your love is about them. But nothing can ever make your love bad. Your friendship is always good. Your love is always good."

So, Susan-Eva loved Ida like any other friend because she couldn't help it. Because she didn't need Ida to be able to love her back for the feeling to be good. To result in her doing things that were good. It didn't mean that she thought their situation was ethically right in any quantifiable way. But

255

she was trying very hard to remember that there was nothing wrong with feeling itself.

There was so much guilt over finding the right feelings. Especially when it came to Scott and Ed. Every reaction was too much and too little. Some people would think she was morally weak for not finding pleasure in the punishment of wrongdoers. Some would find her a hypocrite for finding comfort in the idea of a person she loved killing for her. Susan-Eva felt guilt for both. Guilt for believing in forgiveness and rehabilitation no matter the crime, because she didn't think anyone hurting anyone ever did any good. And guilt for feeling safer knowing a killer was holding her hand. Later, as she put on the dress and looked in the mirror, grateful to be alive, she thought both desires, as conflicting as they were, might be evidence somewhere deep inside she still loved herself. Susan-Eva tried to let that be a good thing.

"Do my makeup," Ida demanded of Ella as she swung back into her room with a bottle of champagne. Ella never spent too much time on her own make-up, but knowing how to do it perfectly for everyone else was very useful.

"Fine. But I'm not drinking tonight," said Ella, waving off the flute Ida tried to hand her. "I have early morning plans."

Ida said, "Ella. Susan-Eva and I had a really hard day. It's not the time to tell us about waking up to sniff Malcolm's hashtag dick."

"I'm going jogging in the morning. At Marshland Park," said Ella.

"You hate cardio," said Susan-Eva.

"Yeah. But that's where I'll be. So, no pressure, but if you want—" said Ella.

"Yes," said Susan-Eva.

Ida fidgeted the way she did whenever something sentimental was happening then blurted, "Fine. Whatever, I'll come too. Do my makeup."

Ella rolled her eyes and went to Ida's vanity. An entire drawer was devoted to lip colors. "Gloss, stick, or stain?" Ella asked.

Ida said, "Stain. A long one that won't dull if I eat something wet." Susan-Eva watched Ida catch Ella's eyes in the mirror, her cheeks flushed.

"Color palate?"

FORTY-FIVE

Sixteen years ago – November 1, 2006, 12:30 AM

Ella

RED WAS ALL ELLA COULD see. Her lips must have been there somewhere, but the blood was so thick that all of Ida's delicate features dissolved into each other. Even when she smiled, her teeth were stained maroon. Only the whites of her eyes maintained their color, almost like she was wearing a mask.

That's what it is, Ella told herself. It was a mask, a scary thing from a Halloween store. It's not real. No real little girl could do what Ida did and be dancing right now. On Ed's porch, Ida swooshed her skirt, now heavy and damp, making it jangle as she laughed and twirled.

"Look what I found in his pocket!" Ida said, revealing a flip phone in her hand. "This is the best day ever! Call your mom to come get us, and I bet there's still time to trick-or-treat!" She held the phone out to Susan-Eva. But she wouldn't look at Ida. Her whole body was shaking. Shock. This was how people acted on 'Law and Order SVU' when they were in shock. Ida waved the phone in Susan-Eva's face. "What's the matter with you?"

"We're scared, Ida," said Ella, taking the phone.

"No! Don't you get it? You have me! As long as you keep helping me figure stuff out, I'll always protect you. Did you see his face? It was so

257

funny! I'm so jealous of that dog. If he hadn't come, I would have kept—"
Ida made chomping noises with her teeth and growled in the air like a dog.

Ella grabbed her face and yelled, "HEY! You have to stop. This is it.
This is the thing that could get you locked up. Not just in a closet. Behind
bars like down there. You will never get to go anywhere you want. We won't
ever get to see you again. You will be in a tiny room for the rest of your life."

"NO! You told me to! You told me to be scary! It's your fault. You can't
let them take me. I saved you! I protected you! I—"

Ella said, "I know. I'm so sorry." Then she did something she'd never
done before. She hugged Ida. Tight. As though squeezing her hard enough
could fill the empty parts. If Ida could feel Ella's heart pounding, then maybe
she could feel... *Then maybe she could feel.* When Ella finally pulled back,
her face and hair were sticky. "I won't let them take you. But you have to do
everything I say. Exactly. Okay? But I won't tell. I promise."

Susan-Eva looked up from her knees. She was still shaking, but
she sat on her hands, trying to stop it, and said, "There was another man
down there."

"No, it was the same dumb guy in a cloak. Standing on those weird
wooden things. He was just pretending to be two people," said Ida.

"We'll tell them what he told us. There was someone else down there,"
said Susan-Eva.

Ella understood and added, "Someone who helped him, but we never
saw his face. We'll say we closed our eyes. We didn't see any of it. But
we heard them fight and then we heard Alpha attack and the second killer
run away."

"But there wasn't a second killer. It was me," said Ida.

"Look at me," Said Ella, taking Ida's hands "That's the last time
you can ever say it. You protected us. This is the story we have to tell to
protect you."

"I'm little," said Ida, "And I took down a whole entire grown-up man
mostly by myself, and I didn't even need the dog, and no one will ever even
get to know?"

"We know," said Ella. She started wiping the blood off Ida's face with
her skirt. "But when the police or anyone else asks you, you're going say: I

heard men fighting, and I closed my eyes because I was so, so scared. Say it."

"I heard men fighting, and I closed my eyes because I was so, so scared," Ida repeated. She sounded too calm.

"Eva. Show her how to say it." Ella asked as she watched Susan-Eva try to stop shaking.

Susan-Eva nodded and said, "I heard men fighting and I closed my eyes because," Susan-Eva's voice cracked. Ella could see her eyes reliving what happened; she started sobbing so hard that Ella didn't think she'd be able to say the words. But she got it out. "I was so, so scared"

Ella said, "Look at her face. Make your face like that." Ida studied, then scrunched her face and started breathing fast like Susan-Eva. "Good. Now say it again, but this time, think about getting locked up forever while you say it."

"I heard men fighting, and I closed my eyes because I was so, so scared," Ida said. Her voice trembled, and her eyes were glassy. Ella nodded and kept wiping off Ida's face and rubbing the blood on herself and Susan-Eva so they all looked the same. Ida's eyes stared at the ground, and she was quiet for a few minutes. When she looked up at Ella, she said, "You didn't really close your eyes, did you? You saw it, didn't you?"

Ella looked Ida in the eye and said, "I saw everything." Then she dialed 911 and spent the next sixteen years trying to forget that she saw everything. Because it was true, Ida was what she was before the cellar. But Ella and Susan-Eva were just normal kids before that. What would seeing something like that do to a normal girl's young developing mind? To see that much blood. That much violence. What would it make them capable of? What would it make them suppress? What would it make them believe?

What would it make them?

FORTY-SIX
August 20, 2022, 9:00 PM

Susan-Eva

THEY ARRIVED LATE TO THE Auction and not fashionably so. A full hour after the start time. Time for every other person who would attend to settle in. Time for one specific person to assume their plan had worked. Susan-Eva had left town and would not be a problem. Time for Trisha to have called Ella four times demanding their ETA. The audacity of Martin Ryan thinking he had the power to dismiss one of the Montgomerys' ladies in wait only occurred to Susan-Eva after Ella pointed it out. Was he really so naive as to think his influence outweighed the queens?

Yes, he was. Just like he was naive enough to see the selection of *Midnight in the Garden of Good and Evil* as the Masquerade theme as a nuanced, thoughtful choice. He knew the film had LGBTQ significance and thought the theme selection was a convenient step toward rebranding the town's historically homophobic culture without having to actually make a statement about it. The centrist dream.

It did not occur to him that most of the events committee were born in the 90's, had never read the book, seen the movie, or thought to look up the plot. An influencer most of them followed posted a picture of a party with "Midnight in the Garden of Good and Evil" as the comment. That was the

260

extent of the thought behind the choice.

As always, they nailed the aesthetic. The Moss Grove's town square had a large mossy fountain at the center that lent itself well to parties that thought of Southern Gothic as more of a vibe than a literary movement. Fairy lights wrapped in ivy dripped from the gazebo with the skilled subtlety of a designer's touch. Cater waiters walked around with trays of champagne coups garnished with blackberries. It was enchanting and dark in a way that once would have brought out the adventure-hungry romantic in Susan-Eva. She would have shown up the moment it started and danced until the band left the stage.

But there was no dancing tonight. Scott's harrowing tale made certain committee members feel the band should stick to music that inspired lively but reverent mingling more than the usual jubilation of these types of things. With that in mind, they asked Martin Ryan to say a few words before they opened the bidding tables and announced the items for auction.

It got so quiet when Martin walked to the microphone you could hear the faint sounds of a baseball game a few miles away. He cleared his throat and said, "When I first moved my family to Moss Groves, it was December 2005. Our first town event was the Winter Solstice. My wife and I expected your average small-town winter festival. Food stands and maybe a petting zoo." A soft, knowing chuckle hummed throughout the square. But all eyes stayed on the stage, so no one saw the three come in.

Martin continued, "We showed up in jeans and ugly Christmas sweaters and found you all dressed like... well like you are now. Everyone looks great, by the way. We were mortified and confused. What kind of small town turns a holiday season gathering into a black-tie affair? We were about to turn our car around and drive home before anyone saw us. But Becca and Phil Porter," Martin found Joseph's dad with his wife and Parker in the crowd. He pointed at him; Phil put a hand to his heart and pointed back. Susan-Eva spotted Joseph silently ordering a drink at the square's side. "They spotted us making a run. They weren't having it. They brought us to their house and lent us appropriate attire. We asked them what the deal was. We were told there are events like this all the time, so why the formality? They smiled and said, 'It's about a standard. Stick around long enough, and you'll understand.'

They were right. I've been to university towns with a tradition of academic achievement. We've been to the best food and entertainment cities in the world. We've been to places of exceptional beauty. But what we learned Phil and Becca meant by standard was that Moss Groves believes choosing one distinguishing quality might be good enough for other towns but not here. Here, we treat excellence like its oxygen. At first, it can be daunting. Not everyone is cut out for it. But those who are lucky enough to call this town home know that we apply that excellence to the way we take care of each other. It was in the people who supported us through my wife's cancer. It's probably why she's still sitting here today. And it's what got us through the most terrifying ordeal of our lives: the disappearance of our son. Again, the Ryans are all here today. Stronger than ever." Everyone turned toward Scott sitting next to his mother and clapped. Martin's eyes welled up as they finished and said, "You didn't just support us. You carried us and I promise to continue working every single day to make sure this town carries each and every one of you."

He was about to raise his glass. It shouldn't have been so alarming that someone else got there first. It didn't make sense that he'd turn completely pale when he heard Ida Montgomery say "Here. Here." All eyes turned to her. This was very normal. As was it normal for her to be standing between her two best friends, Ella and Susan-Eva.

Susan-Eva met Martin's eyes and raised her glass. Ida flashed her pageant queen smile and said, "Cradle to Grave," everyone in the crowd joined as reflexively as if she'd started the pledge of allegiance. "Pre-K to PhD, Moss Groves has everything you'll ever need. Those who are lucky never leave." Glasses clinked. Eyes welled. The band started playing again, and Martin went straight to his Lawyer.

"Miss Lorenzo we'd like to speak to you in private," said Peter, the Lawyer, as Susan-Eva stood with Ella and Ida in the auction line. Martin watched from a few yards away.

"Whose we?" Said Susan-Eva, batting her eyes like Bambi.

"You know who. There's no reason to make a scene. If you'll come with me, we can avoid anyone knowing about any of this morning's

262

unpleasantness," said Peter, clearly resisting the urge to grab Susan-Eva by the arm and drag her out.

"Unpleasantness? But she was with us all morning? And that's what we'll tell anyone who asks." Said Ella.

"And it was very pleasant at Parlay house," said Ida.

Peter glanced over at Martin and shook his head. Then he leaned to Susan-Eva's ear so close she could feel the heat of his breath. She wanted to maintain her oblivious act, seeing how much it drove them insane. But aggression at such close proximity still flashed January's memories through her mind. "We offered a chance for you to walk away. If you don't take it, you're not just looking at the end of your academic career. You are looking at jail time."

"Yeah, that's not going to happen," said Susan-Eva. Peter stayed right by her side as the line started to move, and they inched their way along the perimeter, glancing at descriptions of things to bid on. "You already let him say publicly it was terrorists. Admitting to lying about acts of heroism would be political suicide. I don't see him changing his story to say he was kidnapped by a girl. Especially not one that he—"

Peter cut her off, "If you intend to slander—"

Susan-Eva cut him off, "I don't intend to do anything. I have no idea what I'm going to do. Isn't it exciting?"

Peter softened, trying a new tactic. His voice got very low as he said, "Look. He wants this dealt with. I can get him to offer more money. You go anywhere you want. If you stay it will get ugly very quickly. Wouldn't it be nice to start over somewhere where you could feel safe?" Susan-Eva stared blankly at Peter, then turned to the auction table and realized they'd arrived at the item she wanted.

Peter went to find Martin as a woman wearing immaculately applied fake eyelashes offered the girls all pens from a basket. Ella asked her, "Can we bid on something together?" The woman turned to ask another woman who seemed to have slightly more authority but less skill when it came to lash glue.

"Of course." The woman with the drooping lash said, "We've got a couple of groups going in on the speed boat and the Confederate

263

soldier uniform."

Ida grinned and wrote down a bid for the item directly in front of them. Seeing what she bid on, Perfect Lash's eyes went wide, and she glanced at Droopy Lash again, then said, "Um, I think you meant to bid on this one." She held up the clipboard next to the one, Ella was now signing next to Ida's bid. "This is the spa weekend at the Biltmore. That is… well it's…"

"We know what it is. Thanks," said Susan-Eva, putting her name down. Then she turned back to Ella and Ida and said, "Drinks?" They linked arms and walked away, leaving the women behind the table gaping.

Perfect Lash picked up the bid sheet, looking at the list. Her eyes went wide. Droopy Lash leaned over to see, but Droopy Lash's drooping lash was in the way, so she ripped it off. She shook her head as she took in the Miracle Three's bid. "No one else has bid on it?" she asked.

Perfect Lash looked back up and watched the three women crossing the square side by side. "So did they just..."

"Buy the house they almost got murdered in? Yeah." Both women cocked their heads, watching Susan-Eva cheers Ella and Ida.

FORTY-SEVEN
August 20, 2022, 9:30 PM

Susan-Eva

"YOU'RE OKAY?" SAID SOMEONE WHO sounded like, but that Susan-Eva really hoped was not, the reporter formerly known as Calvin. She'd been so focused on how she'd deal with the future senator trying to pay her off, his rapist son, and the whole *my friend says she's dying and wants to eat people* thing. It made her forget that after sixteen years of never saying a single word other than what they rehearsed, she'd called the lying reporter she boned and confessed to picking Ida. It was not a great first week of classes so far.

Gold beading on her black dress brushed the ground as she turned, confirming it was indeed the reporter. Despite being a manipulative piece of shit, he looked great in a suit and that smile. Lying pieces of shit should not be allowed to smile like that. Looking her up and down, he said, "After you called last night, I was worried you were in some sort of trouble. You sounded so different, but you look—"

"Don't," Susan-Eva said. But the words were already coming out of his mouth.

"Amazing. Sorry. I get that you hate me but it had to be said."

"I don't hate you. You have to know who someone is to hate them. I don't even know your real name."

He squinted at her, then looked over his shoulder and motioned to someone. "I want you to meet someone." A younger guy came and stood next to Calvin. "This is Susan-Eva, the woman I told you about."

The guy smiled with recognition and held out his hand "Hey, I'm Dylan Hobbs. My brother said the bar where you work has Gluten-Free jalapeño poppers. I have Celiac so I almost never get bar food, and guys are such dicks about it." Dylan smiled a smile that dashed any speculations he wasn't really Calvin's brother. If he were a couple of years older, they'd look more like twins.

Susan-Eva said, "First week here, and you're already at a town event. Usually, it's only the locals that dish out for tickets to these things."

"All the Phi Alpha's got free admission last minute. I guess that guy they found, Scott, was one of us. When he said he was going, they asked us all to show up in solidarity. It's kind of weird since I've never met him, but brotherhood."

"Brotherhood," said Susan-Eva.

"It was nice to meet you," said Dylan.

Dylan went to the bar, leaving them alone again. Calvin said, "I wasn't lying about him. Nothing I said to you before we slept together was a lie. I didn't realize you were one of The Miracle Three until after. I came home with you because I liked you. That's it."

"You actually expect me to believe you came here to do a story on us and had no idea I—"

"I'm not doing a story on you. I'm doing a follow-up story to a piece I did last year on college campuses that misrepresent their crime statistics."

"Last night you said…"

"I said I was a reporter. I never said the story was about Ed. Yeah, when you offered a new detail, I took it. I wasn't going to turn down a possible scoop on one of the most mysterious serial killer cases of the last thirty years. But I'm not going to write about what you told me."

A tiny gasp of relief escaped her lips. "You're not? Why? You just said it was a huge story."

"First of all, it's not the kind of thing I write about. All that sharing what a kid did in a moment of terror most people can't begin to comprehend would do is create more tragedy porn. When you called, you didn't sound like someone sharing a story they actually wanted to tell. You sounded like someone confessing before they jump off a bridge. Like I drove around looking for you. Are you okay?"

"What is the follow-up story? Will it just be about Florence?"

Calvin shook his head. "I have found some hints about secret societies. All rumors so far. But it tracks. It's not like Northern Ivy leagues are the only ones that do this shit. The Machine at Alabama is arguably more powerful than Skull and Bones. I can't say much. But I've got sources saying it goes back to before the town was founded. Could be more masonic than academic. If you can think of any—"

"You seriously think I'm going to help you with your story after pretending to be a dumbass so you could bone me for details."

"I'm not a good liar. I go overly polite to compensate. But why does nice imply stupid?" Susan-Eva shrugged. Calvin pulled out his phone. "I know there's no second chance after being caught in a lie, and it's not like I'll be able to be completely honest going forward. But it's a bummer. Because I do like you." Susan-Eva looked down, feeling she should reject him in some clever way but finding she didn't want to.

"One question," He went on. "If you don't want to answer it, I'll leave you alone. Have you ever seen this on anyone here?" Then he held up his phone. There was a sketch of a strange shape. The exact same strange shape scarred on Scott's hip. The blood draining from Susan-Eva's face answered for her. Calvin lowered his voice and said, "I get it if you can't say. Both my sources took months to talk. But I already have confirmation of two members of founding families who have the scar."

Susan-Eva was not exactly sure what brought on the feeling. Was it the way his voice was a little deeper now? Was it that the story was so far from what she expected? Was it his curiosity? Was it that she knew she wasn't getting rid of him anytime soon? "Hey, Calvin?"

"Yeah?"

"There's no way for you to be completely honest with me while you're doing this story, is there? You'll protect sources and probably lie again if it will help get you more info. Won't you?"

"Probably. I know it's fucked up. But— "

"Sometimes lying is important," she said, spotting Joseph across the square.

"Yeah."

"I could never be completely honest with you, either." Susan-Eva watched Joseph nod yes to a girl asking him to dance. "I've seen someone with that mark before, a local but not from a founding family. I don't want to talk about it tonight."

Calvin nodded and said, "Okay." He thought for a minute, taking her in. "You didn't seem like a dead fish to me. You seemed like... you were waiting for something, and then you seemed disappointed. I tried asking you out again because I want to know what it's like when you're not disappointed."

"How do you know I wouldn't be disappointed again?"

"What were you waiting for?"

"For it to be fun again."

"Ouch."

She laughed, apologetic and nervous. As though she liked him. Did she like him? Now that she knew he was a liar? Was she turning into Ella? She cleared her throat, refocusing, and said, "Not just with you. It hasn't been since— I had a thing happen. Before it, I used to be... I never had to think about what to do."

"One-night stands aren't really my thing," he said.

"They never used to be mine," she said.

"Well, maybe we should try something we're more comfortable with. Take it slow. We could go out to dinner, gaze into each other's eyes, and lie the entire time."

"I'd like that," she said.

"In the meantime, you should turn around and put your hands on that table."

"Um, why"

"So I can fasten the back of your dress. The top three buttons are undone."

Susan-Eva reached back and felt three buttons free of their clasps, breaking what should have been the smooth line of her dress and flailing it open. "Oh."

"Let me help. Or you can leave it open." She wet her lips but didn't move. Then she reached up and slid her hand to the back of his neck. He held her gaze but didn't move. Even when she stepped closer and let her hips float closer to his, he wouldn't lean his head down. "What? I was serious about taking it slow," he said. The turtle on an electric scooter smile was back. But in this context, it felt different. Still pure, somehow. The smile still implied an awe at how lucky life could be, but nothing about it felt gullible anymore.

"You want me to turn around so you can help fix my dress."

"Yeah, it's undone."

She rolled her eyes and turned around. The firm fabric of her dress tightened around her breasts for an instant, then released with the first button. Once more, faster, as he found the second. His thumb brushed against her bare skin as he reached the final hook. This was ridiculous. He'd been inside of her not seventy-two hours ago. It shouldn't feel like the accidental touch of a crush. Forgettable, undetectable, irrelevant touching was the goal of her sorbet era.

But ending the sorbet experiment was on her to-do list. Maybe that decision alone was responsible for the sudden change. Maybe it was that she saw Joseph smiling, really smiling while he danced with someone else. It hurt but she couldn't help but feel happy for him. Maybe it was that she had just purchased Lot 355, and the world was upside down, so fuck it!

But she suspected it was the lying. Not the lies he told her. She'd suspected those the whole time. But he didn't seem at all bothered that she would lie to him. That he liked her but wasn't here for her. He wasn't in love with her. He wasn't going to let her hurt him. He let go of her dress and said, "All fastened up."

"Calvin. Let's be on a date tonight." He half chuckled about to make a joke but then he glanced at Joseph and peered back her, and nodded. They were on the dance floor in seconds.

FORTY-EIGHT

August 20, 2022, 10:00 PM

Ella

LUXURY PORTA-POTTIES SHOULD HAVE been the Moss Groves Mascot, Ella thought. Always full trailers with exteriors decked out to the theme and interiors that smelled like eucalyptus and lavender, but the thin walls meant you could still hear each other. A perfect metaphor. Moss Groves, you can't see or smell the shit, so just pretend you also can't hear it.

It was the sort of place that always made Ella feel she was being tricked somehow, so she did her best to avoid them. But Malcolm had texted he was on his way. The thing Ella needed the bathroom for was to her mind its most embarrassing use. If she could trade it so the toilet was public, but the mirror was private, she would. If someone walked in, in the middle of a bodily function, and scoffed in disgust, she could roll her eyes and carry on. But if someone walked in and caught her looking in the mirror, smoothing her hair, admiring her dress, hoping that her boyfriend would think she looked pretty, it would kill her. Nothing was more humiliating than hope.

It was rare Malcolm complimented her physical appearance. Especially when she was dressed up for one of these events. They were frivolous and hypocritical. If they really cared about Children's Hunger, they should donate the catering and design budget. Everyone should wear used clothes. He was

270

right. These were all things she ranted about growing up. It was petty of her to wish he'd gaze at her in admiration the way Joseph looked at Susan-Eva.

It was just that she always really fucking liked what Ida picked out. It was so annoying. It was the worst feeling. Looking in the mirror and feeling special. It made her nauseous. Apparently, the beads on this dress came from a sixteenth-century French apothecary store run by a woman who was accused of witchcraft but disappeared before her trial. It sounded like bullshit. So, of course, Ida had these authentication papers proving it was legit. Ella kept touching the beads because, God damn it, she found that cool. How lame. How easily bought she was.

Luckily, the bathroom appeared and sounded empty. No witnesses to her shameful realization that the soft curls Susan-Eva wound into her hair were still falling beautifully. The blue tones in her red lip stain offered a subtle complement to her grey eyes. A thought so much worse than longing for Malcolm's approval popped into her head.

Take a quick selfie and send it to your mom. She'd like this dress. She gave you those eyes. She'd want to see. Wouldn't she? Or maybe someone would take a picture of her with Malcolm she should send. Because the thing that made her most certain of Malcolm was how much she knew her mother would approve.

See mom! I didn't end up with a small-town guy. He's an academic like you. He's from Connecticut. He hates this town just like you did. He holds me to high standards, just like you did. I am not allowing something as silly and fleeting as attraction to control my choices. I am sticking with my smart choice even when it's hard. See! Don't you want to see, would you like a picture?

Of course, she wouldn't actually do it. But the wish was bad enough. Especially as her eyes caught the tiny cut on her shoulder poking out by the sleeve hole, reminding her that a few hours ago she did allow attraction to make her choices.

A rattle came from one of the stalls. Ella jumped, startled. Fantasies this indulgent only survived in solitude. Whoever it was in there, she felt grateful for their noises cutting the air and scaring her embarrassing thought away. Maybe it was Trisha. That would be perfect. Trisha would say something awful to her and insult the dress somehow. Ella would insult her back, and it would all feel so much tougher than this horrible hope.

It seemed she'd been so quiet the person in the stall also thought they were alone. She could hear them mumbling to themselves. Singing, actually. Now Ella was embarrassed for them; she tiptoed toward the exit, hoping to escape so whoever it was would never have to know they were giving her a concert. But the closer she got, the less the singing sounded like someone's lighthearted exorcism of whatever pop was circling their mind and more like the manic, tortured ramblings she'd hear from the people around Doctor Homer's office.

She heard whoever it was singing, *"The jester in the sidelines in a cast. But I knew I was out of luck the day the music—"* Ella clunked her shoes, so they knew someone was there. But now she wanted to wait. She wanted to make sure they were okay. There was a shuffling noise, then a flush. Then Scott came out of the stall.

Why didn't she recognize his voice? She'd seen him once a week for the last three months. But it's not like they really talked. He awkwardly looked her up and down, then went to the sink. There was no recognition in his eyes. He'd never seen her without the mask while he was in the cellar. But he had to know who she was. That she was Susan-Eva's best friend. But it was like Susan-Eva had said. Who they were didn't seem to mean anything to him. Not even enough to try to place her. In the cellar, he always looked so confident and steady. Now, he looked frantic. Not guilty or even afraid of repercussions. Just confused. Confused to the point of panic.

As Scott washed his hands, Ella watched him, directly facing him. He didn't notice. It would make sense after months in captivity to have a psychotic break. But with no signs of mental falter in all his time down there, Ella wondered what about being free had broken him.

The lightweight door swung open, and loud footsteps clunked toward them with tipsy momentum. Some dude Ella didn't know. He looked at her and said, "Oh fuck I thought this was the men's."

"It's unisex," said Ella.

"Un-fucking believable." Just as he was about to go into a rant, his eyes went wide seeing Scott. "Oh my god, I'm going to cry like a little bitch.

You're a goddamn hero! I thought you were dead. I really thought you were dead, man." The dude slammed his drink down on the sink and hugged Scott. Scott went through the motions, even managing a smile, but still looked dazed. "Okay, no camera's here. Was Epstein involved?"

"I didn't see their faces," said Scott. Ella heard her own voice as a child, repeating, '*I closed my eyes because I was so, so scared. I didn't see.*'

"Listen, they're not going to get away with this. I have resources high up in Q—" The door swung open again. It was Martin Ryan.

"I was looking for you," Martin said to Scott. He sounded unsure of his voice like he could tell he was using the wrong one. "You're Mom's getting the car to take you home."

The dude shook his head and put an arm around Scott as he said, "No way! You've got to at least stop by the after-party."

"Son," Martin said to Scott's friend, not Scott, "Scott's been through hell. He needs to rest."

"Right," said the dude, pulling Scott into another hug. "Have one drink with me before you go." Martin looked like he was about to object but they were out the door before he managed to form the words.

Ella watched Martin make eye contact with himself in the mirror. Then turned on the faucet and splashed water on his face. It felt private like she wasn't there. Holding the edge of the sink, he took slow, controlled breaths; Ella stared. Eventually, he felt it and looked over. Unlike Scott, Martin's face flooded with recognition of Ella. Sweat beads formed on his brow as he smiled, expecting her to speak, but she didn't. She watched him adding up the equation of who she was and what she might know. Finally, he broke their silence, grinning as though something common and light had occurred, like bumping into each other.

He said, "I apologize. It's been an emotional day. My mind is working at snail's speed." He reached out his hand, offering it to shake, "Ella Kyle, isn't it? You work in HR at the School but I don't know that we've ever officially met, have we?"

She shook his hand but didn't smile. She said, "Not officially."

"I hear great things. You must be very good at what you do." Ella glanced at the drink Scott's friend left behind. "Actually, I think we did meet.

273

When you were in high school, I attended a Christmas Party at Parlay House. You still live there, don't you? With Ida Montgomery and… the three of you still live there?"

"Yes. Me and Ida and Susan-Eva still there."

"The three of you must be very close. You've been through a lot together." Ella met his eyes. She wanted to shout, Everything you don't want me to know, I know. Everything you don't want me to think, I think. I watched you look in the mirror, hoping to see a good man. I watched you wash your face, like you could wash away what you did. I watched you fantasize none of this was your fault. But giving away any of what she knew, even the most damning, might offer Martin peace. The very thing Susan-Eva was enduring this night was to take from him. So Ella walked past him, leaving the bathroom.

"He was premature," Martin said. Ella stopped in the doorway. "Scott was born two and a half months early. We didn't get to hold him for weeks. They had to intubate him. Sometimes, I still wake up gasping, thinking I'm in a chair in the NICU, watching him fight for every breath. I'd hold his little hand through the plastic and tell him, you get through this, buddy, and I'll get you through everything else. I can't stop seeing him as my child."

Ella smiled and said, "Of course. What else would you see?" As though none of this had made sense. As though she didn't know exactly what it was like to love someone who you knew was a monster. "You should watch him closely, though. Even when someone seems fine after a traumatic event, it always changes them. Sometimes, you don't notice it for years. Then, it creeps up out of nowhere. But you're right. Watching someone fight to survive does bond you to them in ways you'd never expect."

"It's shocking the things we'd do to protect each other," said Martin.

"It's shocking the things we don't," said Ella.

"I'm going to make it right," said Martin.

"No, you're not," said Ella, and she turned away. In the distance, she could see Ida talking to the band. They stood as she told them to go on a break. Then she plugged her phone into the speakers. Ida's dance party playlist blared. She jumped her way through the crowd with her hands in the air. With every twirl, people started dancing in her wake. When she reached the center, she found Ella's eyes as though she'd known exactly where she was the whole time. Susan-Eva was already on the way to her.

Ida pointed at Ella and curled her finger. Martin was speaking again, but Ella wasn't listening anymore. The song was "Tear You Apart." Ida choreographed a dance to it five years ago for a sorority competition. Ella told her it was a fucked up song. It sexualized male violence against women. But it was such an easy song to dance to. The choreography was so simple and repetitive. So they did it. And they won. And while everyone else was at the after party Ida and Ella fucked on the stage while Ida whispered in her ear, "It so dumb that you think only men can tear you apart." And she was right because Ella came so hard she thought it tore the entire world apart.

It barely took any effort to make it to the center of the square. The crowd danced like a current that all pulled toward Ida. The instant Ella was in reach, Ida and Susan-Eva captured her arms and pulled her into the lyrics, *"I want to hold you close."* It came so naturally. What skill was more practiced for any woman than dancing through something monstrous?

At the auction table, Dr. Homer shook his head in disapproval of the lyrics. He hadn't protected them because he thought Ella was crazy. At the bar, Officer Reynolds flirted with the catering waitresses. He hadn't protected them half because he didn't believe Susan-Eva and half because he did and thought she was overreacting. In the distance, Trisha went to the valet. She hadn't protected them because the feeling of safety would have made them harder to control. Then, at the center of the square was Ida, who had always protected them because… who knows? How could Ella ever really know why Ida did anything?

Ida, who was dancing like a diamond, dropped in the water. The people all around copied her subtle shoulder rolls like ripples, fighting to stay near her so they could see themselves reflected in her perfect clarity and cut. In their struggle to stay closer, Ida's force got stronger, repelling them away. Ripples turned into waves, and waves into tsunamis. But whenever the current tried to suck Ella along with it, Ida found her hand and pulled her back in.

Ella felt her anxiety melting away. Because no matter how many times this town had failed them, they had never failed when it came to Ida. Ida

275

pulled Ella in by the waist and waved at Parker and Malcolm walking over. Their whole lives, horrible things happened, and they always found a way to keep dancing through it. They would find a way to bring Scott to justice and keep dancing. Ella and Susan-Eva would desperately miss their mothers and keep dancing. They would figure out something to do with Lot 355 and keep dancing.

Ella would force herself to forget the annoying, quiet little conflicts she kept having with Malcolm, and she'd dance with him. One day, Susan-Eva would tell Joseph everything, and they'd get married, but for tonight, she'd dance with Calvin. Parker pulled in Ida and twirled her around, because Ida was not dying, she couldn't be, so they would keep dancing. Ella would watch Ida get married and keep dancing. Or maybe not. Maybe that's when she'd finally leave. But for tonight, everything was—

An explosion of screams erupted from the parking lot. The music stopped. Everyone but Ida and Ella rushed out of the square and toward the cars to see what happened. Ida grinned to herself, biting her lip.

Ella went pale and leaned in. Her eyes darted, putting it together. Ella said, "Oh my God! Where is Scott? Ida, please tell me you didn't—"

Ida said, "Oh my God. No! He's been avoiding her all night. I think he's losing it. He may go comatose and never hurt anyone ever again."

"Oh, thank god."

"But that Lawyer threatened her and trust me, he smelled like run." Ida smiled like she was saying something obvious, but Ella squinted, not understanding. "You said if anyone was ever trying to hurt her again, I could stop them." Fuck. Ella had said that. She thought it was obvious she meant 'hurt' like rape or kill. "Don't look at me like that. Don't make it a big thing. Come on. There is no way we both would have ended up alone on the roof over there if God didn't want it to happen."

"Ida, what the fuck did you do?"

"Chill out! I didn't kill him." Ella exhaled "I bit out his tongue and swallowed it in front of him while he tried to figure out how to scream. Then I heard someone coming, so I pushed him off the roof, and the concrete killed him!" Ida raised her shoulders, grinning in giddy joy. "It's going to be such a fun year, hashtag!"

THE THING FROM THE BEGINNING
October 30, 2022, 2:20 AM

THE GUY IN THE CHAIR was not supposed to die. He was supposed to be bait. He was supposed to get hurt. On camera. So, they could prove it. So, someone would stop her. The other guys, hiding out of sight in the corner of the room, promised they could stop it before he suffered permanent damage. After all, Parker Porter was a quarterback, Malcolm Dubois could press two-fifty, and Scott Ryan was a serial rapist. Surely, the three of them could take down an unarmed hundred-and-twenty-pound woman.

But Ida's formerly off-white carpet was dyed completely maroon with the guy in the chair's blood. The only explanation they had by the time Ella and Susan-Eva got the door back open was their trembling voices mumbling, "She was so fast. We tried, but she was so, so fast." They all looked to the open window.

Malcolm looked at Ella and said, "I think you need to start preparing yourself for the fact that we're going to have to kill her."

"No shit, Malcolm," said Ella. Her ex was so fucking stupid. Susan-Eva and Ella looked at the guy in a chair and tried to feel the sort of horror and guilt they knew they should. They did not mean for the guy in the chair to die. But they certainly had known it was a possibility. So they made sure to choose someone really fucking bad.

Dylan Hobbs was really fucking bad.

277

CASTLE BRIDGE MEDIA RECOMMENDS...

If you liked this book, you might also enjoy reading the following titles from Castle Bridge Media available on Amazon or by order at your favorite book store:

Animal Charmer
By Rain Nox

Austinites
By In Churl Yo

Bloodsucker City
By Jim Towns

The Burning Gem
By Don Sawyer

*THE CASTLE OF HORROR
ANTHOLOGY SERIES*
Volume 1
Volume 2: *Holiday Horrors*
Volume 3: *Scary Summer
Stories*
Volume 4: *Women Running
From Houses*
Volume 5: *Thinly Veiled:
The 70s*
Volume 6: *Femme Fatales**
Volume 7: *Love Gone Wrong*
Volume 8: *Thinly Veiled:
The 80s*
Volume 9: *Young Adult*
Volume 10: *Thinly Veiled:
Saturday Mournings*
Volume 11: *Revenge*
Edited By Jason Henderson
and In Churl Yo
*Edited By P.J. Hoover

**Castle of Horror Podcast
Book of Great Horror**
Edited By Jason Henderson

Cherry Dark
By R.L. Wilburn

Dream State
By Martin Ott

Dominic
By Lee Guzman

FRENCH DECEPTION
A Forgery in Paris
By Janice Nagourney
A Forgery in Lyon
By Janice Nagourney
A Forgery in Marseille
By Janice Nagourney

FuturePast Sci-Fi Anthology
Edited by In Churl Yo

GLAZIER'S GAP
Ghosts of the Forbidden
By Leanna Renee Hieber

Hellfall
By Jay Gould

Isonation
By In Churl Yo

JAYU CITY CHRONICLES
The Hermes Protocol
By Chris M. Arnone
Necropolis Alpha
By Chris M. Arnone

MID-LIFE CRISIS THRILLERS
18 Miles From Town
By Jason Henderson
Lost Angel
By Sam Knight
Ties That Kill
By Deven Greene

**Junk Film: Why Bad
Movies Matter**
By Katharine Coldiron

**Nightwalkers:
Gothic Horror Movies**
By Bruce Lanier Wright

THE PATH
The Blue-Spangled Blue
By David Bowles
The Deepest Green
By David Bowles

St. Damned
By Ty Drago

SURF MYSTIC
Night of the Book Man
By Peyton Douglas
Dark of the Curl
By Peyton Douglas

The 23rd Hero
By Rebecca Anne Nguyen

**The Thing That Happened
When We Were Little**
By Caroline Kelly Franklin

Vinyl Wonderland
By Mark Rigney

**Yesterday's Tomorrows:
The Golden Age of
Science Fiction Movies**
By Bruce Lanier Wright

Please remember to leave us your reviews on Amazon and Goodreads!

THANK YOU FOR SUPPORTING INDEPENDENT PUBLISHERS AND AUTHORS!
castlebridgemedia.com

www.ingramcontent.com/pod-product-compliance
Lightning Source LLC
Chambersburg PA
CBHW020035170125
20156CB00052B/131